Jack McDevitt is a former naval officer, taxi driver, English teacher, and motivational trainer, and is now a full-time writer. Eleven of his novels have been Nebula finalists. *Seeker* won the award in 2007. McDevitt lives in Georgia with his wife Maureen.

Praise for Jack McDevitt:

'You're going to love it even if you think you don't like science fiction. You might even want to drop me a thank-you note for the tip before racing out to your local bookstore to pick up the Jack McDevitt backlist'
Stephen King

'A real writer has entered our ranks, and his name is Jack McDevitt'
Michael Bishop, Nebula Award winner

'Why read Jack McDevitt? The question should be: Who among us is such a slow pony that s/he isn't reading McDevitt?'
Harlan Ellison, Hugo and Nebula Award winner

'You should definitely read Jack McDevitt'
Gregory Benford, Nebula and Campbell Award winner

'No one does it better than Jack McDevitt'
Robert J. Sawyer, Hugo, Nebula and Campbell Award winner

Jack McDevitt titles published by Headline:

Jack McDevitt

OMEGA

headline

First published in Great Britain in 2013 by
HEADLINE PUBLISHING GROUP

First published in 2003 by Ace Books
A division of Penguin Group (USA) Inc.

1

Cataloguing in Publication Data is available from the British Library

ISBN 978 1 4722 0325 0

Typeset in Sabon by Palimpsest Book Production Limited,
Falkirk, Stirlingshire

Printed and bound in Great Britain by
Clays Ltd, St Ives plc

Headline's policy is to use papers that are natural, renewable and recyclable
products and made from wood grown in sustainable forests. The logging and
manufacturing processes are expected to conform to the environmental
regulations of the country of origin.

HEADLINE PUBLISHING GROUP
An Hachette UK Company
338 Euston Road
London NW1 3BH

www.headline.co.uk
www.hachette.co.uk

For Jean and Scotty Parrish, USN

Acknowledgements

I'm indebted to Sara and Bob Schwager for their work with the manuscript; to Walter Cuirle, physicist and writer, for technical assistance; to Ginjer Buchanan, for editorial guidance; to Ralph Vicinanza, for being there; and to Maureen McDevitt for showing the way.

'Scientists have today confirmed that one of the omega clouds is indeed approaching Earth. First, I want to reassure everyone that it poses no danger to us. It is not expected to arrive in our vicinity for almost a thousand years. So neither we, nor our children, nor our children's children, need be fearful.

'However, we are now aware that these objects have visited the Earth in the past, at intervals of approximately eight thousand years. Apparently, they destroy cities and will attack other kinds of construction. No one knows why. No one knows whether they are natural objects or the results of a perverted science.

'Our generation faces only one danger, that we might say to ourselves this is not our problem, and that we will pass it off to the distant future. That we might shrug and say to ourselves that a thousand years is a long time. That we will become complacent and conclude that this problem will take care of itself.

'But I say to you, we should take no satisfaction in the fact that we ourselves are in no physical danger. This is a hazard to our world, to everything we hope to pass on to future generations. And it is clear that we should act now, while we have the time.

'Therefore, I am directing that the full resources of the Council of Nations be brought to bear. We will learn how this cloud operates, and we will shut it down.'

—MARGARET ISHIRO, GENERAL SECRETARY, WCN
SEPTEMBER 9, 2213

Prologue

On the surface at Brinkmann IV ('Moonlight'), in IC4756,
1300 light-years from Earth.
Autumn 2230.

It was the most majestic series of structures David Collingdale
had ever seen. Steeples and domes and polygons rose out of ice
and snow. Walkways soared among the towers, or their remnants.
Many had collapsed. There were pyramids and open squares that
might once have been parks or courtyards. An obelisk anchored
the center of the city. It was a place out of time, frozen, preserved
for the ages, a landscape that might have been composed by
Montelet. A place of crystal and glass, and, in a kinder age, of
flowering trees and shaped hedges and beckoning forest. Catch
it at the right time, when its giant moon, half as big again as
Luna, was in the sky, and one might have thought that here
was the celestial city, Valhalla, Argolis, El Dorado by night.

It looked too ethereal to have actually served as a home for
a thriving population. Rather, Collingdale could not get away
from the sense that it had been intended by its builders as a
work of art, to remain unused, to stand as a monument rather
than a city. Several of the towers had collapsed, broken fragments
rising out of a thick carpet of snow. Its name was unknown, so

they called it Moonlight, the city and the world and the sense of something lost.

A bleak wind howled down the empty streets, chilling him even in the e-suit, which was apparently not functioning properly. He'd see to getting it adjusted when he got back to the dome. Wouldn't want to have it fail out here at twenty below.

The sun was struggling to get above a flat mountain range. Several thousand years ago, something had gone wrong with it. Abrams had explained it to him, a surfeit of metals or some such thing. Just temporary, he'd insisted. Be back to normal, he expected, in another few thousand years. Not that it would matter.

He was at the equator, where the remnants of the once-global civilization had fled. There were other cities, most in areas that had once been equatorial, some buried in snowfields, still others frozen behind walls of ice.

He and his team knew little yet about the race that had lived here, except that they were a long time dead, and their architecture rivaled anything man had produced. Crystal bridges thrown across mighty rivers, hyperbolic domes, broad walkways in the sky. All frozen now, the bridges as well as the rivers, the crystal as well as the spirit.

It was perhaps a hard irony that Moonlight, which had thrived and died about the time humans were rolling stones out of quarries to build the first pyramids, would probably have remained undiscovered indefinitely had it not been that it was about to receive an unwelcome visitor. A survey ship, the *Harry Coker*, had been watching an omega, one of the monstrous clouds that drifted in waves out of the galactic core, and which seemed bent on destroying any civilization in their path. The *Coker* was anxious to see how the cloud would fare in the complex gravity field of a planetary system, when it spotted evidence of cities on the fourth planet.

Collingdale squinted into the hard gray sky. The cloud was visible from late afternoon until shortly after midnight. It was up there now, partially obscured in the glare of the sunset. In the daytime it looked utterly harmless, a large dark thunderstorm, perhaps, like a million others he had seen in his lifetime. But this one rose and set with the sky beyond the atmosphere. It always described the same path across the heavens and it kept getting bigger.

The omega clouds were old news. They'd been discovered a quarter century earlier. Although no one had ever seen them attack a city, they were tied to massive destruction in ancient times on Quraqua, Beta Pacifica III, and two other worlds. Objects with a wide range of geometric shapes had been floated in front of the omegas, and humans now knew beyond any question that designs not found in nature could expect to draw lightning bolts.

Nobody understood how or why. No one knew where they came from. And few seemed to feel it was likely we would ever find out.

Until now, no one had seen a cloud change course and glide into a planetary system. No one had seen a city under attack.

It was fortunate nobody lived on Moonlight. The inhabitants had obviously been overwhelmed by the ice age brought on by the instability of their sun. Best estimates were that there'd been no one there for about two thousand years.

Collingdale had grown up in Boston with an alcoholic mother and a missing father, who, his mother insisted until the day of her sodden teary death, had gone west on business and would be back any day. He'd spent two years in an orphanage, been adopted by a pair of religious fanatics, run away so many times they'd eventually implanted a tracker, and – despite everything – won a scholarship from the University of Massachusetts. He'd taken a degree in archeology, taken private flying lessons on a whim, and, as he liked to think of it, never again touched ground. Eventually he'd decided that flights between Chicago and Boston were too confining. He'd learned to pilot the superluminals, had taken the command seat for several major corporations and the Academy, had gotten bored hauling people and supplies back and forth through the void, gone back to school, and specialized in a discipline that, at that time, lacked subject matter: xenology.

In the meantime he'd attended the funerals of both his foster parents, who'd died a year apart, the one unable to live without the other. They'd refused longevity treatments on the grounds they were not God's plan. They'd never given up on him, even though they disapproved of the directions his life had taken. He'd stopped going home during the last years of their lives because they kept telling him they forgave him and were sure God would as well.

He didn't know why they intruded on his thoughts while he gazed across the city. He would have liked them to see Moonlight. Surely they would have been caught up in its majesty, and they might have understood what his life was about.

The omegas routinely hurled lightning bolts at perpendiculars. Any object designed with right angles, or sharp departures from nature's natural arcs, could expect to become a target.

It had seemed an old wives' tale when the stories first came back. Collingdale recalled that the scientific community, almost to a person, had scoffed at the reports. The notion that clouds could somehow navigate on their own seemed absurd. That they could bump up to high velocities more absurd still. Most had not accepted the idea until the one approaching Moonlight, the Brinkmann Cloud, had changed course, begun to slow down, and headed insystem. That was four years ago.

The claims had been so outlandish that nobody who cared about his reputation had even tested them. But once the Brinkmann showed its ability to navigate, researchers had come, and an attempt to explain the impossible had begun. It had begun with the discovery of nanos in samples taken from the omega.

Were the clouds natural objects? Or artificial? Did the universe disapprove of intelligent life? Or was there a psychotic force in existence somewhere? Or, as his parents had thought, was God sending a warning?

4

'You coming, Dave?'

They'd cut their way into the base of the northeastern tower, and Jerry Riley was standing aside, leaving for Dave the honor of being first person to enter the structure. He clapped a few shoulders, strode down between banks of dugout snow, paused at the entrance, put his head in, and flashed his lamp around.

The interior was as large as New York's main terminal. The ceiling soared several stories. Benches were scattered throughout the area. Sleek metal columns supported balconies and galleries. Alcoves that might once have been shops were set into the walls. And there was a statue.

He took a few steps inside, scarcely daring to breathe. They knew what the natives looked like because they'd found remains. But they'd never seen any depictions of them. No sculptures, no graphics, no engravings. How odd it had seemed that a species so given to art had given them no copies of its own image.

The others filed in and spread out around him, all enamored of the statue. Jerry raised his lamp slowly, almost reverently, and played the light across it. It was a feline. Claws were replaced by manipulative digits, but the snout and fangs remained. Narrow eyes, in front. A predator. But it wore a hat, rather like an artist's beret, angled down over one eye. It was decked out in trousers, a shirt with long fluffy sleeves, and a jacket that would not have looked out of place in Boston. A bandanna was tied around its neck. And it sported a cane.

One of the women giggled.

Collingdale couldn't suppress a smile himself, and yet despite its comic aspect, the creature displayed a substantial degree of dignity.

There was an inscription on the base, a single line of characters, executed in a style reminiscent of Old English. It was probably a single word. 'Its name?' someone suggested.

Collingdale wondered what the subject had done. A Washington? A Churchill? A Francis Bacon? Perhaps a Mozart.

'The architect,' said Riley, short and generally cynical. 'This is the guy who built the place.' Riley didn't like being out here, but needed this last mission to establish his *bona fides* with the University of Something-or-Other back home. He'd be an inspiration to the students.

It was odd how the intangibles carried over from species to species. Dignity. Majesty. Power. Whether it was seen in an avian or a monkey, or something between, it always had the same look.

His commlink vibrated against his wrist. It was Alexandra, who'd arrived two days before on the *al-Jahani* with a cargo of nukes, which she'd been instructed to use in an effort to blow away the cloud. Nobody believed it could be done, but no other course of action offered itself. The cloud was simply too big, thirty-four thousand kilometers in diameter. A few nukes would have no effect.

'Yes, Alex. What've you got?'

'*It's still slowing down, Dave. And it's still on target.*'

'Okay.'

'*It's coming in on your side of the world. Looks as if it's homed in on your city. We're going to set the bombs off tonight. In about six hours.*'

The omega was slowing down by firing jets of dust and hydrogen forward. Riley thought it might also be twisting gravity, but there was no evidence yet to support that idea. The only thing that mattered was that, however it was managing things, the cloud was going to arrive right on top of Moonlight.

They wandered for hours through the underground. There was a network of smaller chambers connected to the large area. They found an endless number of chairs, bowls, radios, monitors, plumbing fixtures, conference tables. Artifacts they couldn't identify. Much of it was in surprisingly good condition. There were boxes of plastic disks, undoubtedly memory storage units. But electronic records were fragile. Early civilizations carved their history onto clay tablets, which lasted virtually forever. More advanced groups went for paper, which had a reasonable shelf life, provided it was stored in a dry place and not mishandled. But electronic data had no staying power. They had not yet been able to recover a single electronic record.

There were some books, which had *not* been stored properly. Nevertheless, they gathered them into plastic containers. They'd been in the area several weeks, but there was a special urgency about this visit. The cloud was coming. Anything they did not carry off today might not survive.

The walls were covered with engravings. Collingdale assigned one of his people to record as many of them as she could. Some of it was symbolic, much was graphic, usually with bucolic themes, leaves and stems and branches, all of which, when the sun came back, might grow on this world again.

Stairways and shafts rose high into the structure and descended to lower floors, which were encased in ice. 'But that might be a huge piece of good luck,' Collingdale told Ava MacAvoy, who looked unusually attractive in the reflected light. 'It should survive the cloud, whatever happens to the rest of the city.'

They went back outside. It was time to leave, but Collingdale delayed, taking more pictures, recording everything. Ava and Riley and the others had to pull him away.

The cloud was setting by then, and Collingdale wished it was possible to halt the planet on its axis, keep the other side between the omega and the towers. Hide the city.

Damn you.

He stood facing it, as if he would have held it off by sheer will.

Ava took his arm. 'Come on, Dave,' she said. 'It's getting late.'

They retreated to the dome, which had served as their base for the better part of a month. A lander waited beside it. The dome was small, cramped, uncomfortable. They'd brought out too many people, and could in fact have brought several shiploads more. Everyone had wanted to come to Moonlight. The Academy, under time pressure, had tried to accommodate the requests as best it could. It should have said no. That was partly Collingdale's own fault for not demanding they cut things off.

They'd filled the dome with artifacts and shipped them topside to the *al-Jahani*, which now carried a treasure trove of mugs and plates and table lamps and electronic gear, and materials far more esoteric, objects whose function defied analysis. Other pieces were now being loaded. There was more than the lander could handle, but they'd stacked the rest in the dome, hoping that it would be safe there.

Collingdale waited until everybody else was on board – there were seven of them, excluding the pilot – took a last look around, and climbed in. The omega was almost down. Only a black ridge of clouds was visible in the west, and a few streaked plumes soared above the horizon. The pilot started the engines, and the lander rose. Nobody said much.

Jerry commented how scary it was, and Collingdale couldn't restrain a smile. He himself was of the old school. He'd started his archeological career in Iraq, had been shot at, threatened, deported. When archeology went interstellar, as it had a half century ago, it had become, curiously enough, *safer*. There were no deranged local populations defending sacred tombs, no warlords for whom the security payment might be insufficient, no national governments waiting to collapse with dire consequences to the researchers, who might be jailed, beaten, even killed. There were still hazards, but they tended to be less unpredictable, and more within the control of the individual. Don't take foolish chances, and you won't get burned. Don't stay too long in the submerged temple, as had famously happened to Richard Wald twenty-some years earlier, when you know the tidal wave's coming.

So Collingdale was getting his people out in plenty of time. But it didn't prevent them from thinking they were having a narrow escape from something dire. In fact, of course, at no time were they in danger.

He was looking down at the receding city when the pilot informed him he had an incoming transmission from the *al-Jahani*. He opened the channel, turning up the volume so everybody could hear. Alexandra's blond features appeared on-screen. '*We've launched, Dave,*' she said. '*All twelve running true. Detonation in thirty-eight minutes.*'

The missiles were cluster weapons, each carrying sixteen nukes. If the plan worked, the missiles would penetrate two thousand kilometers into the cloud and jettison their weapons, which would explode simultaneously. Or they would explode when their electronics failed. The latter provision arose from the inability of researchers to sink probes more than a few kilometers into the clouds. Once inside, everything tended to shut down. Early on, a few ships had been lost.

'Good luck, Alex,' he said. 'Give it hell.'

The lander, powered by its spike technology, ascended quickly, traveling west. The cloud began to rise also. The flight had been planned to allow the occupants a view of the omega when the missiles reached the target.

Collingdale ached for a success. There was nothing in his life, no award, no intellectual breakthrough, no woman, he had ever wanted as passionately as he wanted to see Alexandra's missiles blow the son of a bitch to hell.

They climbed into orbit and passed into sunlight. Everyone sat quietly, not talking much. Riley and Ava pretended to be examining an electronic device they'd brought up, trying to figure out what it was. Jerry was looking through his notes. Even Collingdale, who prided himself on total honesty, gazed steadfastly at a recently recorded London conference on new Egyptian finds.

The cloud filled the sky again.

'*Three minutes,*' said Alex.

They couldn't see the *al-Jahani* directly. It was too far, and it was lost somewhere in the enormous plumes that fountained off the cloud's surface like so many tendrils reaching toward Moonlight. But its position was known, and Bill, the ship's artificial intelligence, had put a marker on the screen. They could see the cloud, of course, and the positions of the missiles were also marked. Twelve blinking lights closing on the oversize gasbag. Collingdale amused himself by counting the weapons.

'Thirty seconds to impact,' said the pilot.

Collingdale let his head fall back. He wondered whether one could achieve *impact* with a cloud.

Ava watched the time, and her lips were moving, counting down the seconds.

'They're in,' she said. Someone's hand touched his shoulder. Gripped it. Good luck.

Riley adjusted his harness.

Collingdale, knowing his foster parents would have been proud, muttered a prayer.

'*They've gone off.*' Alexandra's voice. '*Too soon.*'

There were a few glimmerings along the surface of the cloud. But he saw no sign of disruption.

'It might take a while before we can really see anything,' said Riley, hopefully.

The hand on his shoulder let go.

'You're right,' said one of the others. 'I mean, the cloud is *so* big.'

'The bombs had to do *some* damage. How could they not?'

'Maybe just screw up the steering mechanism. Hell, that would be enough.'

The glimmering got brighter. Collingdale thought he saw an explosion. Yes, there was no doubt of it. And there. Over there was a second eruption of some kind. They watched several patches grow more incandescent. Watched the cloud pass overhead. Watched it begin to sink toward the rim of the world.

The explosive patches darkened.

On a second orbit, they were still visible, smoldering scars on the otherwise pacific surface of the omega.

'I don't think it's going to work,' said the pilot.

* * *

10

On the third orbit, they rendezvoused with the *Quagmor*, the vessel that had transported them to the system. The mood on the ship was dark, and everybody was making comments about having made a good effort. Just so much we can do.

Alexandra reported that the omega was still on course for Moonlight. '*We didn't get much penetration. There's still a chance we might have done some damage that just doesn't show. I mean, if we blew up the internal skunk works, how would we know? So don't give up, Doc.*'

He didn't. But the view was unsettling. The jets reached out, arcing as if to encircle the planet. The omega was a malignant force, a thing out of religious myth, an agency beyond understanding.

The *al-Jahani* maneuvered around the fringes of the cloud, trying to record as much of the event as it could. Collingdale went to his quarters, slept, got up, slept some more. The cloud closed and, as the city rotated into position, made contact directly above. Winds howled. Lightning ripped through the skies. Tornadoes formed.

It was just after sunset.

Collingdale could hardly bring himself to watch. Electrical discharges had been growing in the cloud, had become more intense as it drew nearer. The storm gathered force, but the towers stood, and the planet rotated, moving the city directly to ground zero and then past. And for a while he hoped it would get clear. But without warning a gigantic bolt tore though the cloud and hammered the city. The chess-piece structures seemed to melt and blacken and sink into the ice. Sprays of pebbles rattled against them, and something blasted into the base of one of the corner towers. The tower shuddered and began to lean precipitously. Other buildings collapsed or were blown away. Once, twice, they lost the picture as satellites were neutralized. Lightning ripped out of the night, scorched the diamond steeples and the crystal polygons. Hurricane-force winds hurled black dust across the snowscape. A few rocks fell from the sky, plowing into glass and crystal. It needed only a few minutes, and when it was over, a ground blizzard buried everything.

Collingdale was hardly a violent or even a confrontational man. He hadn't been in a loud argument as far back as he could remember. But in those moments he would have killed. Rage spilled out of his soul, sheer fury driven to excess by his helplessness.

The cloud wrapped itself around the world, around Moonlight, and it found the other cities. It struck them in a display of sheet lightning, forked lightning, chain lightning, and fireballs. Collingdale couldn't get away from it. He wandered through the ship, downing glasses of rum, extreme behavior for a man who seldom drank. He couldn't stop moving, from the bridge to the mission center to the common room to his cabin to Riley's quarters. ('Hey, Dave, look at what this damned thing is doing in the north.') It fed his rage to watch, and for reasons he would never understand, it gave him a twisted pleasure to hate so fiercely.

When finally the cloud grew dormant, pieces of it broke off and began to drift away, as if there were no gravity near the planet to hold on to them. The skies began to clear.

The cities were charred and wrecked, wreathed in black smoke. Ava was in tears. Most of the others were in a state of shock. The devastation was more complete than anything they had imagined.

Collingdale was drinking black coffee, trying to clear his head, when a couple of the technicians created a commotion. 'Look,' one of them said, pointing at a screen.

At a city. Intact.

Untouched.

Its towers still stood tall. Its hanging walkways still connected rooftops. A monument was down, and, on its southern flank, a minaret had collapsed. Otherwise, it had escaped.

It was halfway around the globe from where the intersection with the cloud had happened. The safest possible place. But that alone wouldn't have been enough. Other cities, equally distant, had been leveled.

They went back and looked at the record.

Collingdale saw it right away: snow. The surviving city had been experiencing a blizzard when the cloud hit.

'It never saw this place,' said Ava.

FIELD REPORT: Moonlight

The only aspects of this civilization that survive are the city that suffered a timely blizzard, and the bases the inhabitants had established on the moon and on the third planet. And in the artifacts that we've managed to haul away.

The loss is incalculable. And I hope that someone, somewhere, will realize that it is time to devise a defense against the omegas. Not to wait until our turn comes, when it might be too late. But to do it now, before the next Moonlight happens.

—David Collingdale
Preliminary Post-omega Report
December 11, 2230

PART ONE
Hedgehogs

1

Arlington.
Tuesday, February 18, 2234.

Harold Tewksbury woke from one of those curious disjointed dreams in which he was wandering down endless corridors while his heart fluttered and he had trouble breathing. Damned thing wouldn't go away anymore.

The doctors wanted to give him a synthetic heart. But he was over a hundred years old, and even if they could fix things so his body wouldn't be tired, *he* was. His wife was long dead, his kids had grown up sixty years ago. Somehow he'd been too busy for his family, and he'd allowed himself to get separated from his grandchildren and great-grandchildren. Now none of them knew him.

The commlink was chiming, and he heard Rhonda's soft voice. *'Harold,'* she was saying. *'The lab.'* Rhonda was the house AI. *'I don't like waking you for these calls, and I think you should let me deal with them.'*

'Can't, Rhonda. Just patch it through.'

'At the very least, you should take your medication first. Are you all right?'

'Yes,' he said, pushing up to a sitting position. 'I'm fine. Just a

17

little short of breath.' He dumped a pill into his hand and swallowed it. And felt better almost immediately.

It was 3:17 A.M.

'Put them on,' he said. And he knew, of course, why they were calling. The only reason they *ever* called at this hour except the time that Josephine had tripped over a rumpled carpet, broken an arm, and had to be taken off to the hospital.

'*Harold.*' Charlie's voice.

'Yes, Charlie? It happened again?'

'*Yes, sir.*'

'Same as the others?'

'*Right. No record there was ever a star there anywhere.*'

'Same signature?'

'*We don't quite have the details down yet, but it looks like it.*'

A nova. But not really. Not the right intensity. Not the right spectroscopic reading. And no evidence of a star having been in the neighborhood. He shook his head. Can't have a nova without a star. 'Where?'

'*Near the Golden Crescent.*'

'On a line with the others?'

'*Yes.*'

And that was what really chilled him. There had been three earlier events. On a line, as if something were marching through the sky.

'Did we catch it at the beginning? Or was it running when the package opened up?'

'At the beginning, Harold.'

'Okay. Pipe it through.'

He rearranged his pillows. A starfield winked on. The Golden Crescent, nursery to a thousand newborn stars, floated over his dresser. To his left, great smoky walls fell away to infinity. The Mogul, a small, dim class-G, was close enough to illuminate the clock. And the long arm of the Milky Way passed through the center of the room.

'*Five seconds,*' said a recorded voice.

He pushed himself higher and watched a dazzling light appear over the dresser. Brilliant and blinding, it overwhelmed everything else in the sky.

It looked like a nova. Behaved like a nova. But it was something else.

He ran it a few more times before closing the record. They had this one from the beginning. If it was like the others, the light would sustain itself for sixty-one days before shutting down.

Through his window the lights of the Washington Monument were a distant blur. The White Eagle Hotel, usually a bright beacon in the night, had been swallowed by an unseasonable fog. He sat quietly, allowing full rein to a rush of sheer pleasure. He was caught up in one of the great mysteries of the age, had no clue what was happening, suspected there would not be a reasonable explanation during his lifetime. And he could not have been happier. The universe, it seemed, was smart enough to keep them all guessing. Which was as it should be.

They'd started trying to sell Weatherman fifteen years ago. The idea was to use their FTL capability to put automated observation packages in strategic locations. They'd presented the program as a means for observing omega clouds, finding out what they were, and possibly learning how to combat them. Fifteen years earlier that had been a very big deal. The clouds had still been relatively new. The news that one was headed toward Earth, even though it wouldn't arrive for roughly nine hundred years, had scared the pants off the general public. But that fear had long since subsided.

The technology had never been right; the program was expensive, and superluminals were needed to make the deliveries. Then there had been a huge piece of luck: the discovery of an alien vehicle at the Twins a few years before provided new technology: a way to build compact self-contained FTL engines and install them as part of the observation package. Push a button, and the Weatherman was on its way.

19

It had been a long time getting there, but it was on the job at last.

A month ago, the first long-range Weatherman package had arrived in the neighborhood of M68, a globular cluster thirty-one thousand light-years away. Since then, several dozen units had unfurled their sails and powered up scopes and sensors and hyperlight transmitters. More units were en route to hundreds of sites.

The first pictures had come in, and they'd popped the champagne. Sylvia Virgil, the director of operations, had come down and gotten wobbly. But that night nobody cared. They'd stood around looking at a sky filled with dusty clouds like great walls, vast star nurseries that rose forever. It was eerie, gothic, ominous, illuminated by occasional smears of light, like the Monument and the White Eagle. The 'walls' were, of course, thousands of light-years across. And they'd watched everything through the eye of the Weatherman. Soon, he'd told himself, they would be everywhere.

Most of Harold's colleagues had been blasé about the kind of results they expected. At the time they thought they understood everything, knew how galaxies formed, had a lock on the life cycles of suns, grasped the general nature of the beasts that haunted the dark reaches between the stars. But right out of the box they'd gotten a surprise.

The first phase of the Weatherman Project consisted of the simultaneous launch of more than six hundred probes. When they all arrived at their stations, the Academy would have coverage of sites ranging from within two thousand light-years of the core all the way out to the rim, from Eta Carina to the Lagoon, from the Ring Nebula to the M15 cluster. They would take the temperature of dust clouds and nebulas, track down gravitational anomalies, and provide pictures of the controlled chaos around the supermassive black hole at the center of the galaxy. With luck, it would all happen during Harold's lifetime.

Actually, there'd been several surprises, from black jets to the galactic wind. But the great anomaly was the quasi nova. Behind his back, his people were already calling them *tewks*. Starlike explosions, eruptions of enormous energy in places where there were no stars. And almost in a line. Not quite, but *almost*. It made his hair stand on end.

There was no use trying to go back to sleep. He disentangled himself from the sheets, wandered into the kitchen, got out two pieces of farm bread, and slugged some strawberry jelly on them. One of his many guilty pleasures.

The explosions, though they were less than nova force, were nevertheless of sufficient intensity to be visible across tens of thousands of light-years. Probably all the way out to Andromeda. They were far away, and for that he felt grateful. Explosions of their magnitude, for which one couldn't account, were disquieting.

Light from the four events would reach Earth toward the end of the millennium. They would be visible in the southern hemisphere, where they'd blaze across the sky, in Libra and Scorpius, not quite lining up. But close.

This was Priscilla Hutchins's second tour in the Academy bureaucracy. She'd served two years as transport chief, gotten bored, returned to piloting, gotten married, and accepted a tempting offer: assistant director of operations. She was at last content to leave the superluminals behind, to get away from the long voyages, to get out of the ships with their virtual beaches and their virtual mountainscapes and their virtual everything-else. The oceans and the breezes and the sand were real now. She had a man who loved her, and a daughter, and a house in the suburbs, and life was good.

But Sylvia Virgil was leaving for a lucrative position in private industry. She was effectively gone, and Hutch had found herself assigned as Acting D.O. With an inside shot at getting a permanent appointment.

21

But the view from the top was turning out to be a bit more complicated than she'd expected. The days in which she made decisions of no consequence to anyone, invested countless hours formulating policy for the record, attended conferences at establishments with convenient golf courses, reviewed reports from the field, and took extraordinarily long lunches abruptly ended.

Hutch was now responsible for coordinating the movements of all Academy vessels, for deciding who piloted those vessels, and for determining passenger transportation. That sounded simple enough. In the old days, when Professor Hoskinson wanted to bump Dr O'Leary from a flight to Pinnacle, Hutch had simply passed the issue along and let Sylvia make the call. Now *she* was in the middle of every food fight, and she had discovered that her clients, for the most part, owned substantial egos and were not above bringing to bear whatever pressure they could manage. Because they were inevitably the top people in their respective fields, the pressure they could bring was considerable.

She had also become responsible, within monetary constraints, for determining which projects the Academy pushed and which it neglected, and for establishing their priority, and the level of resources to be devoted to each. All, of course, controlled by guidelines from the commissioner. She had a staff of scientific advisors, but the decisions tended more often than not to be based on political considerations. Who had clout with Congress? Who had been supportive of the Academy during the previous fiscal year? Whom did Asquith like?

Michael Asquith was the Academy commissioner, her boss, and a man who believed that scientific considerations were necessarily secondary to rewarding the Academy's supporters and punishing its critics. He called it taking the long view. 'We have to give preference to our friends,' he told her in strictest secrecy, as if it weren't a transparent policy. 'If a little science doesn't get done as a consequence, that's a price we're willing to pay. But we have to keep the Academy in business and well funded, and there's only one way to do that.'

The result was that when a program that deserved support on its own merits didn't get it, Hutch took the heat. When a popular initiative went through and provided serious results, the commissioner got the credit. During the three months since she'd accepted the assignment, she'd been bullied, threatened, harassed, and hectored by a substantial representation of the scientific community. Many of them seemed to believe they could take her job. Others promised reprisals, and there'd even been a couple of death threats. Her once benign view of academics, formed over more than two decades of hauling them around the Orion Arm, had gone downhill. Now, when they contacted her, she had to make a conscious effort not to get hostile.

She'd had a modicum of vengeance against Jim Albright, who'd called her to threaten and complain when his turn at one of the Weatherman units had been set back. She'd responded by indiscreetly mentioning the incident to Gregory MacAllister, an editor who'd made a long and happy career of attacking academics, moralists, politicians, and crusaders. MacAllister had gone after Albright with a bludgeon, depicting him as a champion of trivial causes and his program as 'one more example of squandering the taxpayers' money counting stars.' He hadn't mentioned Hutch, but Albright knew.

That didn't matter, because the bottom line was that she didn't hear from Albright again, although she learned later that he'd tried to have her terminated. Asquith understood what had happened, though, and warned her to call off the big dog. 'If it comes out that we're behind any of that, we'll all be out on the street,' he told her. He was right, and Hutch was careful not to use the MacAllister weapon again. But she'd enjoyed watching Albright go to ground.

She was in the middle of trying to decide how to persuade Alan Kimbel, who was currently at Serenity doing research on stellar jets, that he could not stay beyond the original timetable and would have to come home. Kimbel had appealed to her on the ground that there'd been a breakthrough discovery, and he and his team needed a few more weeks. *Please*. The man had been almost in tears.

The problem was that it happened all the time. Space on the outlying stations was scarce, and there were already people en route and more in line. Extensions could be granted under certain conditions, and her advisors had told her that Kimbel was correct in his assessment. But if she granted the extension, she'd have to tell another group already a week into their mission that, when they arrived at Serenity, they wouldn't be able to stay. She couldn't very well do that. And the only alternative was to cut someone else short. She'd looked at the possibilities and, for various reasons, there was no easy pick. In the end, she'd denied the request.

She was recording a response to Kimbel when her link chimed. Harold Tewksbury on the circuit.

Harold was the senior member of the astrophysics staff. He'd been with the Academy when Hutch had toured the place as a high school senior. He was an organization freak, a fussy little man with a penchant for order and procedure. His reputation in the field wasn't good. His colleagues thought him quarrelsome and uncommunicative, but no one seemed to doubt his capabilities. And he was always nice to Hutch.

'Yes, Harold,' she said. 'What are you up to this morning?'

'You busy at the moment?'

She had a hatful of problems. 'It isn't like the old days,' she said. 'But I can make time.'

'Good. When you can, stop by the lab.'

She found him sitting at his desk staring out into the courtyard. He shook his head when he saw her, signaling bewilderment. But he also managed a smile. 'Something odd's going on,' he said.

She thought he was talking about equipment. There *had* been recent problems with spectrometers. Replacing them would have been expensive, so they'd gone with upgrades. Harold didn't like upgrades, didn't like not having the top-of-the-line. 'Spend all this money to send out packages,' he'd grumbled to her just a few days earlier, 'and then skimp on the retrieval-and-analysis gear.'

But he surprised her. 'You know about the quasi novas,' he said.

The tewks. She knew, more or less. It seemed a bit esoteric to her, events a thousand light-years away. Hardly a matter of concern for any but the specialists.

He leaned toward her. His white hair was plumped up and one wing of his collar stuck out sideways. He presented the classic image of a researcher. His blue eyes became unfocused rather easily; he frequently lost his train of thought: and he was inclined often to stop in the middle of a sentence when some new idea occurred to him. In the bright midday sunlight, he looked like an ultimate innocent, a man for whom physical law and mathematics were the only realities. Two cups of coffee arrived.

'They're almost in a line,' he said.

'And the significance of that is—?'

'It shouldn't happen naturally.'

She just didn't know where to go with it. 'What are you telling me, Harold?'

'I don't really know, Hutch. But it scares me.'

'You're sure they're not novas?'

'Positive.' He tried his coffee, examined the cup, sighed. 'Among other things, there's too much energy in the visible spectrum, not enough in the X-ray and gamma.'

'Which means—?'

'You get more visible light for the amount of energy expended. A ton more. It's brighter. By a lot.'

'A lightbulb.'

'You could almost say that.'

'All right,' she said. 'I'll pass it on. You recommend any action?'

He shook his head. 'I'd give quite a lot to have a Weatherman in place the next time one goes off.'

'Can we do that? Can you predict the next one?'

25

Now he was looking at the spoon. 'Unfortunately not. I can take a stab.'

'A stab? What are the odds?'

'Not good.'

'Harold, let's do this: Let's watch for a while. If you reach a point where we know an event is coming, where you can give me a target with a reasonable degree of certainty, we'll take a serious look. Okay?'

It wasn't something she could get excited about. She made a mental note to suggest that Eric Samuels, the public relations director, get in touch with Harold to see whether the Academy couldn't squeeze some publicity out of it. Meantime, she was looking at a busy afternoon.

She had lunch with the president of the SPA, the Superluminal Pilots' Association. They wanted more money, a better retirement system, better career opportunities, you name it. She knew Ben Zalotski well, from her own days on the bridge. Ben was a decent guy, and a hard charger for the pilots. The problem was that he had no compunctions about taking advantage of their long association to get what he wanted. In reality, it wasn't even Hutch's area of responsibility. Jill Watkin in Personnel was supposed to handle all this stuff, but Ben had framed the hour as an opportunity for old friends to get together. She'd known what was coming, but couldn't very easily refuse to see him. She might have simply gotten busy, but she didn't like being devious. In the end she had to tell him she couldn't help, refused even to concede that she sympathized with his objectives, even though she did. But she was part of the management team and her loyalties lay in a different direction. Ben quoted some of her past comments back at her, the pilots are overworked, they can't keep their families together, and nobody gives a damn for them. They're just glorified bus drivers and that's the way they get treated. He allowed himself to look disappointed, and even implied that she'd turned her back on her old comrades.

So she returned to her office in a foul mood, listened to an appeal from Hollis Gunderson, 'speaking for the University of the Netherlands,' to have his pet project put on the docket. The project was a hunt for a white hole, which Hutch's scientific team had advised her didn't exist, couldn't exist, and would be a waste of resources. Gunderson had gotten past the appointments secretary by claiming someone had misunderstood his intentions. Hutch had made time to talk with him, on the assumption it was easier to see him while he was here than to call back and cancel him. Anyhow, there was something to be said for not making enemies unnecessarily. Her now-retiring boss, Sylvia Virgil, had commented on Priscilla's most recent evaluation that she had a tendency to put off confrontations. She'd suggested Hutch was too timid. Hutch had wondered how Virgil would have done on Deepsix, but let it go.

She heard Gunderson out and concluded the 'misunderstanding' to which he'd referred was semantic rather than substantive. Call it by any other name, he still wanted to go looking for a white hole. She told him that, to have the project even considered, he'd have to provide a written statement supporting his views from two of the thirteen physicists certified by the Academy to rule on such matters. 'Until you can satisfy two of them, Professor,' she said, 'I'm afraid we can't help you.'

A young man had a complaint concerning one of the pilots. He'd been gruff, he said, and rude and generally not very talkative. All the way back from Outpost. Did Hutch have any idea what it was like to ride for weeks with a ship's captain who kept to himself? He was talking about Adrian Belmont, whom she'd like to get rid of because there were always complaints, but the SPA would come down hard on the Academy if she terminated him. Better to hire a hit man. Cleaner.

In any case, it wasn't an operational matter. 'I'm terribly sorry,' she told him. 'You should be aware that the pilots frequently make those voyages *alone*. Some of them have simply learned to get along without a social life. We ask the passengers to be understanding. But if you really want to press the matter, I'm afraid you have the wrong department. You'll want Personnel. End of the corridor, turn right, thank you very much.'

She gave an interview to a journalist working on a book about Moonlight, arranged special transportation to Paradise for Abel Kotanik, who'd been requested by the field team, juggled shipping schedules to get a load of medical supplies (which had been mistakenly dropped and left on the pier at Serenity) forwarded to the Twins, and decided to fire the chief engineer at Pinnacle for sins of commission and omission that stretched back three years.

Her final meeting of the day was with Dr Alva K. Emerson. It was another example of granting an interview she would have liked to hand off to someone else. *Anyone* else. Hutch didn't intimidate easily, but she was willing to make an exception on this occasion.

Alva Emerson was an M.D., well into her eighties, and one of the great figures of the age. She had founded and led the Children's Alliance, which had brought modern medical care to hundreds of thousands of kids worldwide during the past forty years. She'd mobilized the wealthy nations, gotten legislation passed by the World Council and in sixty countries around the globe to provide care for the forgotten peoples of the Earth. While we reach for the stars, she'd said in her celebrated remarks twenty years before at the Sudan Memorial, a third of our children cannot reach for a sandwich. The comment was engraved in stone over the entrance to Alliance Headquarters in Lisbon.

The world loved her. Political leaders were terrified of her. Everywhere she went, good things happened. Hospitals rose, doctors poured in, corporate donations swelled the coffers. (No one wanted to be perceived as stingy or mean-spirited when Dr Alva came knocking.) She was credited with saving millions. She'd won the Peace Prize and the Americus, was on first-name terms with the pope and the president of the NAU, and had stopped a civil war in Argentina simply by putting her body in the way.

And there she was to see Hutch. Not the commissioner. Not Asquith. But Priscilla Hutchins. By name.

Asquith had asked her why, but Hutch had no idea.

'Whatever she wants,' Asquith had instructed her, 'don't commit the Academy to *anything*. Tell her we'll take it under advisement.'

He didn't offer to sit in.

Hutch had seen Dr Alva numerous times, of course. Everyone had. Who could forget the blood-soaked images of her kneeling over a dying girl during the aftershocks of the Peruvian earthquake of '21? Or leading the Counselor himself through the wreckage of Bellaconda after the Peacekeepers finally put down the rebels? Or charging out of the flyer in plague-ridden South Africa?

But when she came through the door, Hutch would not have recognized her. She seemed smaller somehow. The windblown hair was under control. There was no sign of the no-nonsense attitude that was such a large part of the legend. She was reserved, polite, almost submissive. A woman, perhaps, headed out shopping.

'Dr Emerson,' said Hutch, rising to greet her, 'it's a privilege to meet you.' Her voice went a few decibels higher than normal.

'Priscilla?' Alva stretched out her hand. 'It's my pleasure.'

Hutch directed her to a wing chair and sat down beside her. 'I hope you didn't have any trouble finding the office.'

Alva wore a pleated navy skirt and a light blue blouse beneath a frayed velomir jacket. Part of the image. Her hair had gone white, 'in the service of the unfortunate,' as Gregory MacAllister had once put it. She was probably the only public figure for whom MacAllister had ever found a kind word.

'None at all, thank you.' She arranged herself, glanced around the office, and smiled approvingly. It was decorated with several of Tor's sketches, images of the Twins and of the Refuge at Vertical, of the illuminated *Memphis* gliding through starlight, of Hutch herself in an antique Phillies uniform. She smiled at that one, and her eyes settled on Hutch. They were dark and penetrating. Sensors, peering *through* the objects in the room. This was not a woman to be jollied along.

'What can I do for you, Doctor?' she asked.

'Priscilla, I need your help.'

Hutch wanted to shift her weight. Move it around a bit. Force herself to relax. But she sat quite still. 'In what way?'

'We need to do something about the omega.'

At first Hutch thought she'd misunderstood. Alva was of course talking about the one headed toward Earth. When people said *the* omega, that was always the one they meant. 'It won't become a problem for almost a thousand years,' she said uneasily. 'Were you suggesting—?'

'I was suggesting we find a way to stop it.'

That was easy to say. 'We've been doing some research.'

'It's been more than twenty years, Priscilla. Or is it *Hutch*?'

'*Hutch* is good.'

'Hutch.' Her tone softened. 'Somehow, in your case, it is a very feminine name.'

'Thank you, Doctor.'

'*Alva.*'

Hutch nodded and tried the name. It was a bit like sitting with Washington and calling him *George*.

Alva leaned forward. 'What have we learned so far?'

Hutch shrugged. 'It's loaded with nanos. Some of our people think it can create gravity fields. To help it navigate.'

'And it doesn't like artificial objects.'

'Yes.'

'Anything else?'

'There's a lot of dust and hydrogen. The clouds vary in size by a factor of about 30 percent. They coast along at a pretty good clip. In the range of 20 million klicks an hour.'

'That's how fast it's coming? *Our* cloud?'

'Yes.' Hutch thought for a minute. 'Oh, and they seem to come

30

in waves. We don't know how wide the waves are because we can't see the end of them. The local waves are 160 light-years apart, give or take, and one of them rolls through the solar system approximately every eight thousand years.'

'But they're not always the same distance apart? The waves?'

'No. It's pretty erratic. At the beginning, we assumed that the local pattern held everywhere, and that there were literally millions of clouds drifting throughout the Orion Arm. But of course that's not true. Fortunately.'

'Anything else?'

'The waves are arcing outward in the general direction that the galaxy is turning. Joining the flow, I suppose.'

'And that's it?'

'Pretty much.'

'It strikes me there's not much we didn't know twenty years ago. As to the questions that come to *my* mind, we don't know where they come from. Or why they behave the way they do. We don't even know if they're natural objects.'

'That's correct.'

'Or how to disable them.'

Hutch got up. She could feel energy radiating out of the woman. 'They're not easy to penetrate,' she said.

Alva smiled. 'Like a virgin.'

Hutch didn't reply.

For a long moment, neither spoke. The commlink blinked a couple of times, then shut off. Incoming traffic. Hyperlight from Broadside, personal for her.

Alva smiled politely and fixed Hutch with those dark eyes. The woman looked simultaneously amused and annoyed. 'Are we making a serious effort?'

'Well,' said Hutch. 'Of course.'

'But we've nothing to show. After twenty years. Thirty years, actually.'

'We're working on it.' She was floundering.

Alva nodded. 'We have to do better.'

'Alva—' She had to struggle to say the word. 'There's no hurry. I mean, the thing's a thousand years away.'

Alva nodded again. But it wasn't a concession, an acknowledgment that she had a point. Rather it was a recognition that Hutch was behaving exactly as expected, saying precisely what Alva had known all along she would say. She straightened her collar. 'Hutch, you've been to Beta Pac.'

Home of the Monument-Makers, the lost race that had left majestic relics of their passing across several thousand light-years. Star-travelers while the Sumerians were learning to bake bricks. Nothing more than savages now, wandering through the ruins of their once-proud cities. 'Yes, I've been there.'

'I have *not*.' Her eyes clouded. 'I've seen quite enough decimation here at home.' Another long silence ensued. Then: 'I understand the Monument-Makers knew about the omegas. Well in advance of their appearance at Beta Pac.'

'That's correct. They even tried to divert the things at Quraqua and at Nok. To save the local inhabitants.'

'With no success.'

Hutch saw where this was going. 'They cut cube moons and inserted them in orbit around Nok hoping the cloud would go for them instead of the cities.' She shrugged.

'In the end,' said Alva, 'they couldn't even save themselves.'

'No. They couldn't. There's evidence they packed up a substantial chunk of the population and cleared out.'

'Yet they had how long to prepare? Two thousand years?'

'A little longer, we think.'

She was on her feet now, moving to the window, drawn by the sunlight, but still not looking at anything. 'How do you think that could have happened? Are the clouds so irresistible that even the Monument-Makers, given two millennia, couldn't do something?'

'It's probably not easy. To stop one of the omegas.'

'Hutch, I would suggest to you that two thousand years was too much time to get ready. That they probably put it off. Somebody else's problem. Get to it next year. Or sometime during the next century. And they continued delaying until it became too late.'

'Maybe it's too late already,' suggested Hutch. But she knew as soon as the words were out of her mouth that it had been the wrong thing to say.

Alva was a diminutive woman, but her presence filled the office. Overwhelmed it and left Hutch feeling like an intruder in her own space. 'Maybe it is,' Alva said. 'But we'd best not make that assumption.'

The office grew briefly darker, then brightened again. A cloud passing over the sun.

'You think,' said Hutch, 'we're going to let the situation get away from us.'

Alva's eyebrows came together. 'I *know* we are. What's going to happen is that people are going to talk and think exactly as you do. And, Hutch, *you've* seen these things in action. You know what they do.' Her gaze turned inward. 'Forgive me. I mean no offense. But the situation calls for honesty. We, too, are looking at the omegas as somebody else's problem. But when it comes, it will be *our* children who are here.'

She was right, of course. Hutch knew that. Anyone who thought about the issue knew it.

Alva reached for a pad, scratched something on it, furrowed her brow. 'Every day,' she said, 'it advances on us by a half billion kilometers.'

It was late. It was past five o'clock and it had been a horribly long day. What did this woman want anyhow? 'You understand,' Hutch said, 'I don't make Academy policy. You should be talking to Dr Asquith.'

'I wasn't trying to influence Academy policy. It's too far down the scale to worry about, Hutch. Any serious effort to do something about the omegas is going to require political will. That doesn't get generated here.'

'Then I don't see—?'

'I didn't come looking to get Academy support for this. It's *your* support I want.'

'Mine?'

'You're the public face of the Academy.'

'No. You've got the wrong person. Eric Samuels is our public affairs chief.'

'*You*, Hutch. You found the first cloud. You and Frank Carson and the others. Incidentally, someone told me you actually did the math. It was *you* who figured it all out. Is that true?'

'Yes,' she said.

'And you're the woman from Deepsix. The woman who rescued her husband from that antique starship, the, what did you call it?'

'The *chindi*. But he wasn't my husband then.'

'No matter. The point is you've been in the public eye for quite some time.' She was back in her seat, leaning toward Hutch, old friends who had been in combat together. 'Hutch, I need you.'

'To—?'

'—become the public persona of the Omega Society.'

Well, it didn't take a mathematician to figure out what the Omega Society was going to be doing. 'Why don't *you* do it, Alva? You're a bit better known than I am.' She managed a weak smile.

'I'm the wrong person.'

'Why?'

'Because I'm associated with charities. With medical care. Nobody's going to take me seriously when I start talking about long-range destruction. *You* aren't taking me seriously and yet you know I'm right and I'm sitting in the same room with you.'

'No, that's not true,' said Hutch. '*I'm* taking you seriously.'

The woman had an infectious smile. She turned it on Hutch, who bathed in its warmth and suddenly realized the secret of her success. The mental agility, the worthiness of her causes, her single-mindedness, none of it would have mattered without that

34

pure living charm. *Nobody ever says no to me. Nobody turns away. This is the moment of decision.*

'I'd stay in the background, of course,' she said. 'Board of directors stuff. But I'd be there if needed. We'd have a couple of major league scientific people out front to direct things, to run the organization. To provide the muscle. But *you* would be its face. Its voice.'

Alva was right. In a moment of startling clarity Hutch saw the centuries slipping away while the cloud drew closer. *Not our problem. There'll be a breakthrough. Don't worry.* How many times had she heard that already? But there probably wouldn't be. Not without a concerted effort. And maybe there was a window that might close. There'd been talk of an all-out program when we'd first learned about the clouds. But when the initial shock wore off, and people began thinking how far away the thirty-second century was . . . Well, it was like worrying about the sun exhausting its fuel.

If she accepted, Hutch would have to give up all claim to being taken seriously ever again. The few who worried about the omegas, even if they were backed by Alva, provided the material for late-night comedians. They were greeted in academic circles with amused smiles and people shaking their heads. And *she'd* be out front.

Alva saw she was reluctant. 'Before you answer,' she said, 'I want to remind you that the public knows you're a hero. You've put yourself at risk on several occasions, and you've saved a few lives. You've gotten credit for your acts.' The Academy's Johanssen Award, which she'd received after Deepsix, hung on one wall. Other plaques commemorated her accomplishments at the Twins and in the rescue of her husband. And, of course, there'd been the sim, in which Hutch had been portrayed by the smoky-voiced, statuesque Ivy Kramer. 'This time,' Alva continued, 'there'll be no credit and no applause. No sim and probably no books. No one will ever really know what you've accomplished, because you'll have saved a world that's quite far away. And we do have short

35

memories. You have a heroic past, Hutch. But *this* time, there isn't just *one* life, or a few lives, in the balance. Unless people like you come forward and act, we're all going the same way as the Monument-Makers.'

The silence between them stretched out. The room seemed unsteady. 'I'm sorry,' said Hutch at last. 'But I can't do this. It would involve a conflict of interest.'

Don't look at me like that. It's true.

'My obligations to the Academy – I can't take up a cause like this and keep my job here. There's no way I can do it.'

'We have adequate funding, Hutch. I'm sure you would find the compensation sufficient.'

'I really can't do it,' said Hutch. 'I have responsibilities here.'

Alva nodded. Sure. Of course you do. How could I not have seen it? Perhaps I misjudged you.

She gave Hutch time to reconsider her decision. Then she rose, and a business card appeared in her hand. 'If you change your mind,' she said, holding it out for her.

'I won't,' said Hutch. 'But I thank you for asking.' And how hollow did *that* sound?

'I appreciate your hearing me out. I know you're a busy woman.' Her gaze dissected Hutch and found her wanting. Not who I thought you were, it appears. Then she was gone, leaving Hutch with a feeling of rejection as overwhelming as any lover could have engendered.

The transmission that had come in during the interview was from Broadside, the newest of the deep-space bases maintained by the Academy. At a distance of more than three thousand light-years, it was three times as far as Serenity, which had for years been the most remote permanent penetration. Its operational chief was Vadim Dolinsk, an easygoing former pilot who was past retirement age but for whom she'd bent the rules because he was the right man for the job.

Vadim was seated at his desk, and his usual blasé expression had lengthened into a frown. '*Hutch*,' he said, '*we're getting a reading on one of the clouds. It's changing course.*'

Hutch was suddenly aware of the room. Of the cone of light projecting down from the desk lamp, of the flow of warm air from the vents, of someone laughing outside in the corridor.

Ironic that this would happen on the day that Alva had asked for help and Hutch had brushed her aside. Even Alva had not seen the real danger, the *immediate* danger. A few years ago, one of the clouds had drifted through the Moonlight system, had spotted the ruins on the fourth world, and had gone after them like a tiger after a buck. What would have happened had they been populated? Millions would have died while the Academy watched, appropriately aghast, unable to help. In the end, they would have shaken their heads, made some philosophical remarks, and gone back to work.

Within the next ten years, clouds would approach seven planetary systems that the Academy knew about. All were presumed empty, because virtually all systems *were* empty. But who could be sure? The systems in question were outside the range of finances rather than technology, so she simply didn't know.

'*Data's attached*,' Vadim continued. '*I've diverted the* Jenkins *to take a look. They were about to start home, so they won't be happy. But I think this is too important to let slide. I'll notify you when I have more.*

'*How's life in Woodbridge these days?*'

Not as good as it was an hour ago.

She looked at the numbers. The cloud in question was another five hundred light-years beyond Broadside. It was approaching a class-G sun known to have three gas giants, but that was all that *was* known about the system. The star was located in the direction of the Dumbbell Nebula.

There were images of the cloud, and she recognized the streamers exploding away from it, trying to continue along the original course while the cloud turned a few degrees onto a new vector.

It had spotted something.

NEWSDESK

MOB CHIEF ASSASSINATED IN PHILLY
Hobson Still Insists There Is No Mob

SALUTEX CEO INDICTED FOR INSIDER TRADING
McBrady Could Face Ten Years

MIRROR STRAIN SPREADING IN CENTRAL AMERICA
Dr Alva Headed for Managua
Outbound Flights Halted

ECONOMY WORSENS
Recession Is Now Official

DEMONSTRATORS OUT IN FORCE AT POSTCOMM SUMMIT
Morrison Has No Sympathy
'They're Against Us, but They Have No Suggestions'

WASHINGTON AREA VOLCANO BECOMING ACTIVE AGAIN?
Disaster Center Issues Warning

ARAB PACT DEMANDS REPARATIONS
Claim Oil Supplies Sold At Fraction of Value
To Keep West Afloat
Al-Kabarah: 'Without Our Sacrifice, the World
Would Still Be in the 18th Century'

IS THERE REALLY A MULTIVERSE?
Gunderson Proposes Hunt for White Hole
'It's Out There Somewhere'

SYRACUSE COPS ARRESTED IN LIGHTBENDER CASE
ACLU Will File Suit To Ban Invisibility

TIME TRAVEL MAY BE POSSIBLE
Technitron Claims to Have Sent Stop Watch
Forward Ten Seconds
Hoax or Error, Say Most Experts

GIANTS FAVORED IN TITLE GAME
Jamieson Says He Is Okay to Play

2

On board the *Peter Quagmor*, near the Bumblebee Nebula.
Sunday, February 23.

The artificial intelligence in all Academy ships had been given
the name *Bill*. His demeanor, and his appearance, tended to
change from vessel to vessel, depending on his relationship with
the captain. Whatever seemed to work with a given personality
type, under whatever local circumstances might prevail. He could
be paternal in the best sense, quarrelsome, sympathetic, persistent,
quiet, even moody. Bill was sometimes a young and energetic
companion, sometimes a gray eminence.

The *Quagmor*'s version reminded Terry Drafts of his garrulous
and mildly ineffectual uncle Clete. The AI took everything very
seriously, and seemed a bit on the frivolous side. Terry had been
asleep when Bill got him up and asked him to come to the bridge.
Jane was waiting.

'What is it?' Terry Drafts was the most senior physicist on the
Academy staff among those who had worked actively at trying
to solve the various problems associated with the omega clouds.
He had been with the Frank Carson group during the initial
encounter, had watched that first cloud attack the decoy shapes

41

that Carson had set out for it on the lifeless world now celebrated as Delta.

Terry had been so entranced by what he'd seen that he had dedicated his life to the omegas. He'd appeared before Congress, had done interviews, had written the definitive account, *Omega*, which had caused a brief stir, all in the hope of rallying public opinion.

But the problem was almost a thousand years away, and he'd never been able to get past that. In the end, he'd given up, and settled for spending his time on monitoring missions. It was Terry who'd discovered that the clouds incorporated nanotechnology, who'd theorized that they manipulated gravity to navigate, that their primary purpose was something other than the destruction of cities. 'Horribly inefficient if that's what they're supposed to do,' he'd argued in *Omega*. 'Ninety-nine point nine percent of the things never *see* a civilization. They're something else—'

But what else, he didn't know.

Terry was tall, quiet, self-effacing. A believer. He was from the Ivory Coast, where they'd named a high school and a science wing at Abidjan University after him. He'd never married because, he'd once told an interviewer, he liked everybody.

At the beginning of his career, he'd formulated a series of ambitions, which awards he hoped to win, what level of prestige he hoped to achieve, what he wanted to accomplish. It had all narrowed down to a single unquenchable desire: to find a way to throttle the clouds.

One of them was currently on the ship's scanners. As was something else.

'I have no idea what it is,' said Jane. It was an object that looked vaguely like an artistically exaggerated thistle, or a hedgehog. It was enormously larger than the *Quagmor*. 'Just spotted it a couple minutes ago.'

Jane Collins was the ship's captain, and the only other person on board. She was one of Terry's favorite people, for reasons he'd have had trouble putting into words. She was in her sixties, with grandchildren out there somewhere. Pictures of them decorated the bridge. She was competent, he could trust her, and she was good company.

'It looks artificial,' he said. But not like any kind of vessel or package he'd ever seen. Spines stuck out all over it. They were rectangular and constructed with geometric precision.

'There's somebody else out here,' said Terry, barely able to contain his excitement. Someone else worrying about the omegas.

'*It has a low-level magnetic field,*' said Bill. '*And it is running on the same course as the cloud.*'

'You're sure, Bill?' asked Jane.

'*No question.*'

'Is it putting out a signal?'

'*Negative,*' said Bill. '*At least, nothing I can detect.*'

'Odd,' said Jane. 'Range to the cloud, Bill?'

'*Sixty thousand kilometers.*' In their rear. '*Something else: It is moving at the same velocity as the cloud. Or if not, it is very close to it.*'

'Pacing it.'

'*Yes. It appears so.*'

'Somebody's keeping an eye on the thing,' said Terry. 'Bill, is the cloud likely to enter any system in the near future?'

'*I have been looking. I cannot see that it could pose a near-term threat to anyone.*'

'How about long-term?'

'*Negative. As far forward as I can track with confidence, I see no intersection with, or close passage past, any star system.*'

'How far forward,' asked Jane, 'can you project? With confidence?'

'*One point two million years.*'

Then what was it doing here? In a half century, no one had yet run into any living creatures with star travel. They'd hardly run into any living creatures, period. 'Bill, what are we getting from the sensors?'

'*The exterior is stony with some nickel,*' said the AI. '*But it's hollow.*' He put a picture of the object on-screen. The projections were blunted triangles. There was a wide range of sizes. They were similar to each other, although of different designs, some narrow, some wide, all flat on top. The overall effect was of a hedgehog covered, not with spines, but with sculpted polygons.

'Can you tell what's inside?'

'*Not clearly. Seems to be two chambers in the base unit. And shafts in the spines. Beyond that I can't make out any details.*'

'The spines?' asked Jane.

'*Some of them measure out to a bit over two kilometers.*' Taller than the world's tallest skyscraper. '*If we consider it as a globe, with the tips of the longest spines marking the limits of the circumference, the diameter is six and a half kilometers. The central section is about two kilometers.*' Bill's image appeared, seated in a chair. Although he could summon whatever likeness he wished, he usually showed up in his middle-aged country lord demeanor. Beige jacket with patched elbows, cool dark eyes, black skin, silver cane, receding silver hair. '*It's a polyhedron,*' he said. '*Specifically, a rhombicosidodecahedron.*'

'A what?'

'*It has 240 sides.*'

'It's an odd coincidence,' he said.

'What is?'

'We know the clouds rain down fire and brimstone on anything that has right angles.'

'Okay.'

Terry pointed an index finger at the image on the screen. 'This thing is loaded with right angles. That's what it is: An oversize complex of right angles.'

They looked at one another. 'Is it designed to be a target?' Jane asked. 'Or are the clouds intended specifically to kill these things?'

'*It is under power,*' said Bill. '*There's only a trace, but we're getting an electronic signature.*' It was rotating. The spines caught and manipulated light from the Bumblebee. '*Once every seven minutes and twelve seconds,*' Bill continued helpfully.

They had drawn within a hundred meters of the object. The spines turned slowly past them. Bill switched on the navigation lights so they could see better. Terry was reminded of the puzzles he used to do as a boy, enter here, find your way through the labyrinth, come out over there.

There were no sharp points anywhere. The tops of all the spines were flat. Ninety degrees.

Jane submitted a report to Serenity. While she talked, Terry studied the object. It had no thrusters, no visible communication devices, no sign of a hatch. It had enough dents and chips to suggest it was old. A couple of the spines had been broken off. Otherwise, the surface was smooth, as if it had come out of a mold. 'Bill,' he said, 'train the lights into the notches. Let's see what it looks like down there.'

It was a long way. No central surface was visible; the spines seemed simply to rise out of each other. Jane took them in almost close enough to touch.

The *Quagmor* was dwarfed.

'Still no reaction of any kind, Bill?'

'*Negative, Terry.*'

They approached the top of one of the spines. It was rectangular, about the dimensions of a basketball court, perfectly smooth save for a couple of chunks gouged out by collisions. The *Quagmor* passed over it, the ship's navigation lights sliding across the surface, over the edge and into a chasm. Then he was looking down the slanted side until the lights lost themselves in the depths, to reappear moments later coming back up another wall, wider and shorter and angled differently.

'Bill,' he asked, 'do you see any more of these things in the neighborhood?'

'*Negative. I haven't been able to do a complete sweep, but I do not see anything else.*'

Jane finished recording and sent her message on to Serenity.

Then she got up and stood beside him, her hand on his shoulder. 'I've always assumed the universe made sense, Terry,' she said. 'I'm beginning to wonder.'

'I've been looking for a hatch.'

'See anything?'

'Nope.'

'Just as well. I don't think I'd want to go calling. Maybe we should try talking to it.'

'You serious? From the looks of it, there hasn't been anything alive in there for the last few million years.'

'That's an interesting estimate. It's derived from—?'

'It looks old.'

'Good. In the end, I can always count on you to fall back on hardheaded logic.' Her eyes sparkled. 'You know, it might be programmed to respond to a signal.'

'It's a thought.' He swung around in his chair and gazed up at the AI's image. 'Bill, we'll use the multichannel. Audio only.'

'*Ready when you are, Terry. The circuit is open.*'

'Okay.' He leaned forward, feeling foolish, and allowed a glib tone to creep into his voice. 'Hello out there. Is anybody home?'

Another spine rotated past.

'Hello. This is us out here talking to you over there.' He looked at Jane. 'Why are you laughing?'

'I was just thinking how you'd react if somebody answered.'

He hadn't even considered the possibility. 'We getting anything, Bill?'

'*There is no response. No reaction of any kind.*'

He stayed with it a few minutes before giving up. The hedgehog sparkled and glowed in the lights of the *Quagmor*. His own interstellar artifact. 'Going to have to break in,' he said.

She shook her head. 'Not a good idea. Serenity will have the information in a few hours, and they'll be sending somebody right out. Let's wait for them.'

There was no way he was going to be sitting on his rear end

46

when they got there, and have to confess he didn't know any more than he and Jane put in the report. 'I want to see what's inside.'

'We don't know what it is.'

'That's why I'd like to see the inside.'

'Let's let the experts do it.'

'You know any experts on interstellar artifacts? Jane, nobody knows anything about this stuff. Nobody's better qualified to open it than you and I.'

She made a face. Don't like the idea. Not a good move. 'You know,' she said, transparently trying to change the subject, 'it's one of the loveliest things I've ever seen.'

'You're kidding.'

'No. I mean it.'

'Jane, it has all the lines of a porcupine.'

'No.' She was looking past him, out the viewport at the bizarre landscape passing by. 'It's a rhombi-whatever. It's magnificent.' She turned a sympathetic smile on him. 'You really don't see it, do you?'

'No.' Terry followed her gaze, watched the shadows from the navigation lights creep up, down, and across the artifact's planes and angles. 'I don't like the clouds. And I don't like these things.' He got out of his chair and headed for the storage locker. 'You want to come along?'

They strapped on e-suits, which would project a Flickinger field around them, protecting them from the void. The field was flexible, molded to the body except for a hard shell that arced over the face, providing breathing space.

They went down to the launch bay, picked up laser cutters and air tanks, and turned on the suits. While the bay depressurized, they did a radio check and strapped on wristlamps.

There was no launch vehicle in the bay, but it didn't matter because it wouldn't have been useful anyhow in the current situation. They pulled go-packs over their shoulders, and Terry hung an imager around his neck. 'Bill,' he said, 'I'll record everything. Transmit live to Serenity.'

'*Do you really think it's that dangerous, Terry? Maybe we should reconsider what we're doing,*' said Bill.

'Just a precaution,' he said.

Bill opened the airlock and admonished them to be careful.

They had left Serenity seven months earlier and had spent the entire time studying the omega. It had a numerical designation, as all the clouds did. But they'd gotten into the habit of referring to this one as George. George was apparently a onetime boyfriend of Jane's, although she refused to provide details. But it amused her to ridicule him. The cloud, she'd said, was inflexible, windy, and took up a lot of space. And it kept coming. No matter what you said or did, it kept coming.

George hung ominously in the background as Terry picked out a spine and directed Bill to match rotation with it, so that it became a stable fixture a few meters from the airlock.

The *Quagmor*, which was affectionately referred to by almost everyone as the *Quagmire*, was the first research vessel designed specifically to operate near the clouds without fear of drawing the lightning. Unlike the polygon object it was inspecting, it had no right angles. The ship's hull, her engine mounts, her antennas, sensing, and navigation equipment, everything, was curved.

They'd even penetrated George's surface mists, gone a few hundred meters into the cloud, taken samples, and tried to listen for the heart of the beast. That was a joke between them, a reaction to the insistence of one school of thought that the clouds were *alive*. It was not a view that Terry took seriously. Yet plunging into it had given him the eerie sensation that there might be some truth to the notion. It was a view easily dismissed when they'd emerged. Like laughing at ghosts when the sun was high.

'Ready?' asked Jane.

'All set.' He was standing at the edge of the airlock trying to decide on a trajectory. This was the first time they'd been outside the ship on this run, except for a brief repair job on the forward sensor pods; Terry nevertheless had long experience working in the void. 'There,' he said, pointing.

One of the higher spines. Nice broad top for them to land on. Easy spot to start. Jane shook her head, signifying that she'd done dumber things but was having trouble remembering when. They exchanged looks that were supposed to register confidence, and he pushed out of the lock, floated across the few meters of space that separated the ship and the spine, and touched down on his target. But the stone surface was slippery, slippery even for the grip shoes, and momentum carried him forward. He slid off the edge, blipped the go-pack, did a 360, and came down smoothly atop the crest.

'Nice maneuver, Flash,' said Jane.

'Be careful,' he said.

She floated over and drifted gently onto the surface, letting him haul her down. 'It's all technique,' she said.

Terry rapped on the stone with the handle of the cutter. 'Feels solid,' he said. 'See any way in?'

She shook her head. No.

He looked into the canyon. Smooth rock all the way down, until the beam faded out. The spine widened as it descended. It looked as if they all did.

'Shall we see what's below?' he asked.

She was wearing a dark green pullover and light gray slacks. A bit dressy for the work. 'Sure,' she said. 'Lead the way.'

He stepped into the chasm and used the go-pack to start down. Jane followed, and they descended slowly, examining the sheer wall as they went.

Plain rock. Smoother than on the roof, because the lower areas took fewer hits. But there was nothing exceptional, all the way to the bottom.

Bill maneuvered the *Quagmire* directly overhead, leaving the spotlights off because they would have been a distraction. But the navigation lights were on.

There was nothing in Terry's experience to which he could compare the place. The spines did indeed grow out of one another. There was no flat or curved surface at the center of the object that could have been described as housing the core. It was dark, surreal, the *Quagmire* no more than a few lights overhead, and the rest of the world walled out.

Terry felt light-headed. Even in the vacuum, he was accustomed to having a flat space underfoot, a moonscape, a ship's hull, *something*. Something to relate to. Here, there was no up or down, and everything was at an angle. 'You okay?' she asked.

'I'm fine,' he said.

He took the cutter out of his harness. 'There's a chance,' he said, 'that this thing is under pressure. I'm going to cut a narrow hole to find out. But stand clear anyhow. Just to be safe.'

She nodded and backed off a few meters. Told him to be careful. Not to stand in front of it.

Terry grinned. How could he make the cut standing over to one side? He pressed the activator and watched the amber lamp come on, felt the unit vibrate as it powered up. 'Big moment,' he said. The lamp turned a bright crimson. He punched the button, and a long red beam of light blinked on. He touched it to the wall.

It cut in. He knew not to lean on it, but simply held it steady while it went deeper.

Jane advanced a few steps. 'How's it going?'

He was about to suggest she try a little patience when it broke through. 'Bingo,' he said.

Somewhere deep in the hedgehog, he sensed movement, as if an engine had started. Then the ground murmured. It trembled. Rose. Shook violently. He told Jane to get out, for God's sake get out, and he stabbed at the go-pack and the thrusters ignited and began to take him up.

And the world went dark.

ARCHIVE

Sky, we lost contact with the *Quagmire* moments ago. Divert. Find out what happened. Render assistance. Report as soon as you have something.

—Audrey D'Allesandro
Hyperlight transmission to the *Patrick Heffernan*

3

Arlington.
Monday, February 24.

The *chindi* had finally begun giving up its secrets. The gigantic alien starship, apparently fully automated, continued its serene slower-than-light voyage toward a class-F star whose catalog number Hutch could never remember. It had taken a major effort, because of its velocity, to get researchers on board. But the Academy had begun to get a good look at its contents, artifacts from hundreds of cultures. And live visual recordings over a span of tens of thousands of years. The ship itself was thought to be more than a quarter million years old.

Its pictures of lost civilizations were opening up whole new areas of knowledge. The vast distances that separated sentient species tended to create the illusion that civilizations were extremely rare. It now appeared they were simply scattered, in time and in space. And, disconcertingly, they did not seem to last long.

They were sometimes suicidal. They were often destroyed by economic, political, or religious fanaticisms; by the selfishness and corruption of leaders; by an inability to stop evermore-deadly wars. They sometimes simply behaved in stupid ways. Some that had avoided the more obvious pitfalls were swept away by something that should not have been there: the clouds.

Hutch had always felt a special kinship with the Monument-Makers, who'd roamed this section of the galaxy for thousands of years, who'd tried to save others from the omegas. She had been to their home world, and had seen the remnants of a race reduced to savagery, unaware of their proud history. They'd been on her mind recently because the *chindi* had, a week ago, provided a record of another demolished culture. She'd sat during the course of a bleak wintry day looking at pictures of smashed buildings and ruined cities. And she'd recognized some of the images. It was the home of the Hawks, the race that had come to the rescue centuries ago on Deepsix when the inhabitants of that unlucky world had faced a brutal ice age.

The images haunted her, the broken columns, the brave symbols scrolled across monuments and public buildings, the overgrown roads, the shattered towers, the cities given over to forest. And perhaps most compelling, the starship found adrift in a solar orbit.

The Hawks and the Monument-Makers. And the human race. It was hard not to dwell on what might have been, had they been allowed to sit down together, to pool their knowledge and their speculations. To cooperate for the general good. To become allies in the great adventure.

As has happened with the Monument-Makers, a few individual Hawks had survived. But their civilization was gone. Their racial memory consisted only of a cycle of myths.

Kellie Collier had been there, had been first to board the Hawk starship, and had complained later to Hutch about the cost imposed by the existence of the clouds. There had been tears in her eyes when she described what she'd seen.

Kellie and the broken cities and the clouds were never far from Hutch's mind. The chilling possibility that they were about to experience another wipeout had kept her awake these last two nights. It would be the most painful of ironies if they had finally found a living civilization, someone other than the Noks, that they could actually talk to, just in time to say goodbye.

The cloud in question was at a substantial distance, more than thirty-one hundred light-years. Nine months away. The *Bill Jenkins* was enroute, diverted from its survey mission by the station at Broadside. But they'd need a month to get there. Add another week for the report to reach her. It would be April before she knew whether she had a problem.

Prudence, and experience, suggested she expect the worst.

She arrived at the Academy bleary-eyed and in a foul mood. She'd talked it over at home with Tor, but all he could think of was to suggest she ease the pressure on herself by quitting. We can live comfortably on my income, he'd suggested. He was a commercial artist, and the money was decent, although they weren't going to wind up with a chalet in the Rockies and a beach home on Sea Island.

She needed to talk to somebody. The commissioner wasn't the right person either, so she put in a call to Harold as soon as she arrived at her desk. He wasn't in yet, his watch officer explained, but they would contact him. Five minutes later he was on the circuit. Just leaving home.

'Harold,' she asked, 'have you had breakfast yet?'

'No,' he said. '*I usually eat in the Canteen.*'

'How about eating with me this morning? My treat.'

'*Is there a problem?*' he asked cautiously.

'I need your advice.'

'*Okay. What did you have in mind?*'

'Meet me at Cleary's,' she said. 'Twenty minutes okay?'

Cleary's was the small, posh coffee shop overlooking the Refuge, the alien habitat that had been hauled in from the Twins and reconstructed on a platform at the edge of the Potomac in Pentagon Park. The sun was warm and bright, and the sky full of lazy clouds. When Harold walked in, Hutch was sitting in a corner booth, stirring coffee and staring out the window, her mind gone for a gallop. She didn't see him until he slid in across from her.

'This is a pleasant surprise, Priscilla.' He smiled shyly.

She knew that she intimidated him, but didn't know why. She'd noticed it years before when she'd provided transportation for him on a couple of occasions. It didn't seem to be all women, just her. 'It's always good to get away for a bit,' she said. She asked him a few questions about Weatherman, and the tewks, to put him at ease.

Cleary's used human waiters. A young woman brought more coffee, and some orange juice.

'So what did you actually want to talk to me about?' he asked.

She told him about the report from Broadside that a cloud was changing course. Heading insystem.

His eyes dropped to the table. 'That's unsettling.' He picked up his spoon, fiddled with it, put it back down, gazed out at the Potomac. 'Well,' he said finally, 'with any kind of luck, it'll be a false alarm.'

She looked at him.

'Priscilla,' he said, 'it doesn't matter. Whatever it turns out to be, there'll be nothing you can do.'

'There might be somebody out there.'

'—In its path. I understand that.' He tasted his coffee, patted his lips with a napkin, shrugged. 'If there is someone there, they'll have to look out for themselves.'

He was trying to be detached, but she heard the resignation in his voice. 'To be honest, Hutch,' he continued, 'it's not worth worrying about. Not if we can't intervene. Anyway, at most it will probably turn out to be more ruins. That's all they ever find out there anyhow.' The waitress was back. 'Bacon and eggs,' he said. 'Home fries and toast.'

She'd heard that he was supposed to be on a diet, egg whites and bran flakes, that sort of thing. But she said nothing, and ordered French toast. What the hell.

When the waitress was gone, he sat back and made himself

comfortable. She liked Harold. He got the job done, never complained, and on Family Day had made a big fuss over Maureen. 'Is that why you asked me here?' he said. 'The omega?'

Hutch nodded. 'Assume the worst happens. Somebody's in the way. Is there really nothing we can do to disable this thing? Blow it up? Scatter it? Something?'

It was a lovely morning, crisp and clear. The Potomac, which had risen considerably during the last century, and was still rising, was not unlike a small inland sea. The Capitol, the White House, most of the monuments, were islands now. Hutch had been around long enough to remember when Rock Creek Park could be reached on foot, when you didn't need a boat to get to the Washington Monument. You could stand out there now on one of the piers, and watch the river, and look out toward Sagitta, which was where the local cloud was, the one with Arlington's number on it, and you got a sense that despite everything, despite the extended life spans and the superluminals and the virtual disappearance of organized violence on the planet, civilization was still losing ground.

'If it had a physical core of some sort,' Harold was saying, 'a vital part, then *yes*. We could go after it. Take a hammer to it. But it seems to be holistic. Throw as many nukes at it as we like and it simply seems to pull itself back together.'

'We don't know how it does that?'

His jaws worked. 'It's not my field. But no, as far as I'm aware, we have no idea. The technology is well beyond anything *we* know about. It uses nanos, but we haven't been able to figure out how they work, what they do, even how they guide the cloud.' He took a long sip of orange juice. 'I look at what those things can do, and I look at the fact they seem to be only dust and hydrogen, and I feel as if I should be sitting off somewhere beating a drum. It's a whole new level of technology.'

Their food came. Harold dumped a substantial amount of catsup on his potatoes.

'Of course,' he continued, 'the real problem is that we can't

57

seem to penetrate the cloud. Ships don't come back. Probes disappear. Even scans and sensors don't give us much.' He sampled the eggs, smiled with satisfaction, covered his toast with strawberry jam, and bit off a piece. 'Good stuff,' he said. 'This where you normally eat?'

'Usually at home,' she said.

'Yes.' He studied her. 'You survived one of those things, Hutch,' he continued. 'You were actually inside it, weren't you? When it came down on Delta?'

Hutch had been with Frank Carson that day. Thirty years ago – my God, had it really been that long? – when they'd deliberately baited a cloud, had structured some plateaus to look artificial, and had watched with horror as the monster came after them. 'Yes,' she said. 'I was there.'

'You survived it.'

'Heaviest weather I've ever seen. Lightning. Tornado winds. Meteors. Not the way you'd want to spend a weekend.'

He used his toast and a fork to finish off the eggs. 'Well, I can understand you might be worried. Where did you say this thing is?'

'Out near the Dumbbell.'

'My God. It's really over in the next county, isn't it? Well, look, your role, it seems to me, is simple. These things attack cities. If it turns out there are actually inhabitants, you just sail in, tell them what's coming, and they can head for the hills. Or maybe they could build themselves some underground shelters.'

Out along the pier a gaggle of kids were trying to get a kite in the air and not having much luck. Beyond, a few sails drifted on the river.

The kite was red, and it had a dragon on it.

She needed a dragon.

When she got back to her office, she called the Lunar Weapons Lab, which had been founded twenty years earlier for the express purpose of developing something that could be used against the omega clouds. The weapons lab was under the control of the Science Advisory Commission, which was a quasi-independent group overseen by the World Council. Like the Academy, it was underfunded.

Arky Chan, the assistant director, was an old friend. He greeted her with a cheery good morning. *'We hear,'* he said, *'you're taking over permanently up there.'*

'They don't tell me anything, Arky.' Thirty-three years ago, on her first flight beyond the solar system, Arky had been one of her passengers. His black hair had grayed only slightly since then, and his smile was as infectious as ever.

'What can I do for you, Hutch?' he asked.

'Find me the key.' It was code for a way to neutralize the clouds.

He nodded. *'Anything else while I'm at it? Maybe produce the universal solvent? Or a time machine?'*

'I'm serious. What's on the table?'

'Why? What's happening?'

'One of the damned things changed course.'

'I heard. You have anything yet on what's in its path?'

'A G-class sun. Presumably a planetary system to go with it. We're still waiting. I'm hoping it just picked up some natural formations and got confused.' That had happened once. A group of remarkably straight stress fractures on a satellite had been attacked. Whatever else the damned things were, they were *not* bright.

'I hope so too. But no, Hutch, I'm sorry to say we haven't really made any progress.'

'Nothing at all?'

'They don't give us any money, love. And the Academy doesn't give us any ships.' That was pointed at her.

'You have *one*.'

'The Rajah *spends more time in the garage than it does in the field.'*

'That'll change,' said Hutch. She'd been trying to free up some money for more than a year.

'Well, I'm glad to hear it, but to tell you the truth, I'll believe it when I see it. What we need is for the cloud to be sitting up over the Capitol. Put a couple of bolts down the pants of the Congress. Then they'd damn soon get serious.'

'You have anything at all we can use, if it becomes necessary?'

'Not really.'

'How about nukes?'

'We tried that at Moonlight.'

'How about something bigger? A supernuke? Or maybe we shovel a load of antimatter into it?'

'The problem we keep having is that the thing seems always able to reconstitute itself. Somewhere it has a heart, a control pod, an AI, probably. But we don't know where it is, we can't probe it, we're blind—' He held out his hands. 'If you have an idea, I'd love to hear it.'

'Arky, if that thing's bearing down on somebody, I don't want to be in the position of having to just sit here and watch.'

'I understand completely.'

'Find me something. Just in case.'

'Look.' His voice got cold. 'It's easy enough for you to demand a miracle. But you people are the ones who keep saying there's plenty of time, don't worry about it, we have other priorities right now.'

She had lunch with Tom Callan, her number two guy. Tom was assistant director of operations for special projects. He'd been, in her opinion, the most capable of the applicants for the D.O.'s job, except herself, of course. Tom was young, ambitious, energetic, and if he hung around long enough, would undoubtedly succeed her. That would be as high as he could go in the Academy, however. The commissioner was a political appointment, and the position never went to anybody in-house.

Tom held a license to pilot superluminals, he could work under pressure, and he didn't mind making decisions. He was about average size, with clean-cut good looks, but without the intensity one usually found in able young people who'd already climbed pretty high. Probably because he knew he was good. 'I was thinking maybe,' he said, 'if we had to, we could decoy the damned thing.'

'How would you go about it? A projection?'

'That's what I had in mind.'

'Throw a big cube out there for it to chase.'

'Yes.' He bit into a turkey sandwich. 'It might work. We've never experimented with it, so we don't really know. It would help if we knew what kind of sensory system it uses.'

If it were strictly visual, then a big picture of a box might be enough. 'Let's look into it,' she said. 'Check the literature. See if you can find anything that either supports the idea or negates it.'

'Okay.'

'And, Tom. Priority. If there's a problem, we won't have much time.'

'Consider it done.' He took a long pull at his iced tea and went after the sandwich again. The kid had an appetite. 'There *is* a good chance it wouldn't be fooled by a holocast.'

'I know.'

'We might try a backup.'

'What did you have in mind?'

'Be ready to put a *real* box out there.'

That brought her back to the kite with the dragon. Her first afternoon call went to Rheal Fabrics. Rheal specialized in producing a range of plastics, films, and textiles for industry. (They also had a division that operated a chain of ice-cream outlets.) Hutch had, on a number of occasions, taken their executives out to Serenity, and she had kept in contact with several over the years.

One of them was Shannon McKay, who had something to do with R&D. Shannon was tall, redheaded, and very much in charge.

They did a couple of minutes' small talk, during which Hutch got congratulated on her forthcoming promotion. She was

61

surprised that Shannon knew. 'We keep track of the important stuff,' Shannon said. The Academy was a major customer for Rheal, so it made sense that they would.

'I need a feasibility study,' Hutch said. She explained what was happening, emphasized that it would probably amount to nothing, but that if a difficult situation arose, she wanted to be ready to deal with it. 'I might need a kite,' she said. 'A big one.'

Shannon nodded. 'Give me the dimensions.'

Who knew? Who had the slightest idea? She tried some numbers and Shannon said okay. They could do it.

'How long will it take?' A blue lamp blinked on. And Harold's name. He was on the line, waiting to talk to her.

'*How long do we have?*'

'From the time you get the go-ahead, not much more than a week. At best.'

'*You're kidding.*'

'Can you manage it?'

'*Let me look into it. I'll get back to you.*'

'Yes, Harold.'

'*Thought you'd like to know. We've got another one.*'

'Another *what*?'

'*Another tewk.*' A quasi nova. It was the first time she'd heard him use the term his people had coined. Short for Tewksbury Object. The pride in his voice was evident.

'Okay.'

'*Different spectrogram. Different color. But the same essentials.*'

'Same area?'

'*Other side of the sky. Different Weatherman.*'

'Okay. You're sure it's a tewk and not a nova?'

'*We're sure.*'

'All right, Harold. Keep me posted.'

'*It's very strange.*'

'When you want to make an announcement, let me know.'

* * *

She directed the AI to get Marge Conway for her at the International Bureau of the Climate in London. Twenty minutes later Marge was on the circuit. *'Been a long time,'* she said. *'What can I do for you, Hutch?'*

Marge and Hutch had been friends at Princeton a long time back, had once competed for a boyfriend, now best forgotten, and had kept in touch over the years. Marge had been thin and quiet in those days. Later she'd become a bodybuilder. She'd gone through several husbands. Wore them out, people said behind her back.

'Is there a way to generate a cloud cover?' Hutch asked. 'For maybe a few days. Hide some stuff.'

'Cloud cover?'

'Yes. I'm talking about a terrestrial atmosphere—'

'Not Earth.'

'No.'

'Okay. How big would the coverage be?'

'Planetary.'

She shook her head. *'No. A few thousand square klicks, maybe, yes. But that's about the limit.'*

'What would it take?'

'You'll need some landers.'

'Okay. That's no problem.'

'Four of them. Plus a hauler. An AV3 would probably be best.'

'All right. What else?'

'How much time do we have?'

'To put it together? Ten days. Maybe a week. No more than that.'

'That's a bit of a rush.'

'I know.'

'And we'd need a helicopter.'

'A helicopter? What's that?'

'Antique aircraft. Propellers on top.'

'Marge, where am I supposed to get a helicopter?'

'Work it out. Keep it small, by the way. The helicopter.'

'I'll see what I can do.'

'*Okay. Let me take a look at things on this end. I'll get back to you.*'

Marge broke the connection and Hutch called Barbara, the Academy AI. 'Find out where there's an air show. Antique aircraft. I'll want to talk to whoever's in charge.'

She disposed of her routine work, handing most of it over to assistants. Eric called to remind her that she'd be expected to make a few remarks at Sylvia Virgil's retirement.

That was tonight! She'd forgotten. '*And you'll be handing out one of the awards,*' he added.

'Okay.'

She had started making notes on what she would say when the commlink blipped again. This time it was the commissioner's three short bursts. She answered, was asked to wait, the commissioner would be with her momentarily, then Asquith's plump, smiling features filled the screen.

'*Hutch,*' he said, '*do you have a minute?*'

'Yes, Michael. What can I do for you?'

'*Why don't you come over to the office? I need to talk to you.*'

When she got there, the blinds were drawn. Asquith waved her in, got up, and came around to the front of his desk. It was a substantial walk because the thing was the size of a soccer field. The office was ringed with leather chairs and walnut side tables. The walls were decorated with pictures of the Andromeda Galaxy and the Twins and the North American Nebula and the Refuge sitting out on the Potomac. Several lamps glowed softly.

'Hutch.' He angled one of the chairs for her. 'How are you doing today?'

'Fine, Michael,' she said, warily.

He waited until she'd sat down. 'Well, last day for Sylvia, I guess.' He managed to look wistful while adjusting the blinds, brightening the room somewhat. Then he went back behind his desk. 'The Academy's going to miss her.'

'Yes, we will.'

'Pity about—' He stopped midsentence, shrugged, and she knew exactly what he was implying. Virgil was retiring under pressure after a couple of major embarrassments. Three people had died a year ago when the *Yves Vignon* had collided with Wayout Station. The problem had been traced to equipment maintenance, and ultimately to a negligent supervisor, but some of it had inevitably washed off on the director of operations at the Academy. And then, just a few months later, a breakdown in scheduling had left the Berkeley mission temporarily stranded at Clendennon III. Not Sylvia's fault, but she'd taken the hit anyhow, just as she had six years ago when Renaissance Station had been destroyed by a massive flare. Renaissance had remained operational for political reasons, and against her continued protests. But none of it had mattered. 'Should have kept an eye on things myself,' Asquith had told a group of Academy researchers. 'Sylvia tried to get it right. Not really her fault. Bad luck.'

Truth be told, Hutch's opinion of Sylvia hadn't been all that high, but that didn't change the reality that she'd been left hanging in the wind. And that Hutch herself now worked for a guy who would go missing at the first sign of trouble.

'Hutch,' he said, 'I know you're busy, so I won't take your time.'

'It's okay, Michael. What can I do for you?'

He opened a drawer and brought out a cream-colored folder, which he opened and placed on his desk. She couldn't see what it was. 'You've done a good job here over the last couple of years.' He extracted a document from the folder and gazed fondly at it. It crackled in his hands. 'Congratulations,' he said, holding it out for her.

She looked down at it. Saw the Academy's coat of arms. And her name. *Priscilla Maureen Hutchins. Promoted to grade fifteen. Director of Operations. Effective Tuesday, March 4, 2234.*

In eight days.

He extended a hand across the desk and beamed at her. 'I wish you a long and happy career, Priscilla.'

'Thank you.' It felt good.

'There'll be a formal presentation early next week. But I wanted you to know.' He took the document back and returned it to its drawer. 'We'll give it to you then.'

'I appreciate your confidence, Michael.' While there had been a selection panel, she knew she would not have been chosen without the commissioner's approval.

He broke out a bottle. 'Vintage pavlais,' he said. And, reading the label, 'Twenty-one ninety.'

Expensive enough to pay the mortgage for a month.

He produced an opener, wrestled the cork out of the bottle, and filled two glasses. She was tempted to embrace him. But the formality of the occasion overwhelmed the impulse. 'To you, Hutch,' he said. 'Never let go.'

It was an echo of the now-celebrated comment by Randall Nightingale, when, with bleeding and broken hands, he'd pulled her out of the clouds over Deepsix. *I'd never have dropped you, Hutch.* It had become a kind of informal Academy watchword.

Their eyes met over the rims of the glasses. Then the moment passed, and it was back to work. He handed her a disk and a sheaf of documents. 'You'll want to look at these,' he said. 'It's all administrative stuff, position description, personnel considerations, and so on. And there are a few operational issues in there you'll need to do something with.'

Hutch was no connoisseur, but she knew good wine when she tasted it. He held out the bottle for her. Did she want more?

Yes! But she was too well bred to drink up the man's expensive store. As a compromise, she accepted a half glass. 'Michael,' she said, 'did you know one of the clouds has changed course?'

'Yes,' he said. 'I heard.'

'I'm concerned there might be somebody out there.'

He beamed. Not to worry. 'Let's wait and see,' he said.

'If there is, would the Academy support intervention?'

His face wrinkled and he made growling noises in his throat. 'That could get a little uncomfortable, couldn't it?'

'We'd probably have to violate the Protocol.'

He waved the problem away. 'No,' he said. 'Don't worry about it. There's no one there.'

'How can you be sure?'

'There's *never* anybody there.' He smiled paternally at her and studied his glass. 'I've been in this office, or otherwise associated with the Academy, for more than twenty years. Do you know how many times we've gotten reports that somebody thought they'd found someone? And you know how many times it actually happened?'

'Twice,' she said. That would be the Angels. And the Hawks.

'That's right. And you were there for one of those. Now if we go back another twenty-five years, there are two more. That makes *four*. In all that time. Out of thousands of systems visited. *Four*. I suggest we put it aside and find more important things to worry about.'

The door opened behind her, as if by magic, and he was ushering her out of the room.

'If it happens,' she persisted, 'we're going to be pressed for time.'

'We'll worry about it when it does, Priscilla.' His smile disappeared as if someone had thrown a switch.

Hutch called up the archive files on the *Pasquarella*, the first vehicle lost researching the clouds. That had been twenty years before. It was a voice-only, the voice belonging to Meg Campbell, the only person on the ship. Hutch had seen Meg once, from the back of a lecture hall. She'd been a tall woman, dark hair, lots of presence. Very sure of herself.

Hutch played it through, listened to the voice she remembered, not from the long-ago presentation, but because she'd played that same record any number of times. Meg had gone three times into the cloud, each descent deeper, each time encountering more electronic interference.

She hadn't come back from the third descent. A search had

revealed nothing, and on July 14, 2211, the *Pasquarella* was officially designated lost.

In the middle of the recording, Barbara's voice broke in. '*Transmission for you, ma'am. From Serenity.*'

She switched off the recording. 'Put it up, Barb.'

As soon as she saw Audrey's face, she knew there was bad news. '*Hutch,*' Audrey said, '*we lost contact with the* Quagmor *at 0014 hours 24 February. The AI went down without warning. They found an artifact yesterday in the vicinity of the Bumblebee and were investigating. The* Heffernan *has been diverted and will arrive in the area in three days. Record from* Quagmor *is attached.*'

Her stomach churned. It was possible there was nothing more to it than a communication breakdown. Then she watched the attached report.

NEWSDESK

PITCHERS, CATCHERS REPORT TO SPRING TRAINING
Forty-six Teams Start Today

STRANDED ORCA RESCUED IN PUGET SOUND

AMERICAN HIGH SCHOOL STUDENTS STILL LOSING GROUND
Who Was Churchill? Nobody Knows

GOMORRAH COUNTY RESIDENTS SUE TO CHANGE NAME

MASKED ROBBER WEARS NAME ON ARM
Tattoo Leads to Arrest

ORBITAL AMUSEMENT PARK GETS OKAY
ZeroGee Will Open in Two Years

UNN SURVEY: HALF OF ALL AMERICANS BELIEVE
ASTROLOGY WORKS

WHO WILL BE ONE-HUNDREDTH PRESIDENT?
Campaign Gets Under Way in Utah, Ontario

BASEBALL: MOVE TO OUTLAW ENHANCEMENTS
GAINS STEAM
Evidence Mounts of Long-term Damage

GREAT GATSBY FIRST EDITION SELLS FOR 3.6
MILLION

IBC WARNS OF STRONGER HURRICANES
Southern Coast Overdue for Big One

4

On board the *William B. Jenkins*.
Tuesday, February 25.

Except for one person, the research team on the *Jenkins* was delighted to be diverted. The fact that an omega had veered into a planetary system might mean they were close to finding the grail, a living alien civilization. A real one, something more exotic than the Angels, who were pretechnological barbarians, or the Noks, who were industrial-age barbarians. The exception was Digby Dunn, who would ordinarily have joined in the general elation. But Digby was in love with the captain. Her name was Kellie Collier, and Digby's passion for her was both intense and unrelenting.

On the whole, it had been a painful experience. Love affairs always include an element of discomfort; it is part of what makes them life-changing ventures. But this one had been extraordinarily difficult. Passengers may not touch the captain. Bad for morale and all that. Impossible situation, Digger. We'll just have to wait until we get clear. Be patient and everything'll be fine.

She smiled, that gorgeous, alluring smile, rendered even more seductive because she was trying to make it impersonal, friendly, understanding. Lose my job, she'd added on occasion when he'd tried to press her.

They'd been headed back to the station when the call came. We've got an omega changing course. Turn left and find out what's going on. See what it's after.

So Digby, an anthropologist by trade, but riding as a volunteer with a survey mission that was gathering information about local stars and planetary systems, pretended to be pleased, exchanged platitudes with everybody, and aimed pained glances at Kellie.

'Sorry,' she told him. 'But look, it'll be quick. In and out, see what's there, and then back to Broadside. We're only talking a couple of extra weeks.'

She was tall and lovely with soft black skin and luminous eyes and she made every other woman in his life seem hopelessly dull. Ah yes, how he'd like to take her out on an expedition to unearth a few ancient cookpots. But he resigned himself to making an occasional grab, which she usually – but not always – declined with stern disapproval. 'Be patient,' she told him. 'Our time is coming.'

The *Jenkins* was more than three thousand light-years out, and they held the current record for going farther from Earth than any other ship. They'd been away from Broadside almost a year. It had been a long and lonely voyage by any standard, broken only by an occasional rendezvous with a supply vessel.

A rendezvous was always a special occasion. There had been a push at the Academy to automate replenishment, to send the sandwiches in a ship directed only by an AI. Asquith had been unable to see the point of sending a captain along since it cost a great deal more, and it was hard to visualize a situation in which human judgment might be needed. But somebody apparently understood what seeing a fresh face could mean when you were out in the deeps.

Jack Markover had thrown his weight into the fight by threatening to quit and hold a news conference if they took the human captains off the run. The commissioner had backed down, pretended it had been someone else's idea, and it had been quietly put aside.

Jack was the chief of mission. He was a little man with a hawk face and too much energy. He loved his work and, if he'd been forced to follow through on his threat, would not have survived. He talked about retirement a lot, usually during the gray hours when the *Jenkins* was in hyperflight, and the hours were long and quiet. But Digger knew he'd never step down, that one day they'd have to haul him off and lock him away.

Digger had never quite figured out what Jack's specialty was. He was from the American Midwest, a quiet, dedicated type with doctorates in physics and literature. There seemed to be no field of human knowledge in which he did not speak as an expert. Acquainted with all, he was fond of saying, knowledgeable in none.

The comment could hardly have been less true. Where Digger knew the ground, the man inevitably had his facts down. He was the only person Digger knew who could explain Radcliffe's equations, quote *Paradise Lost*, discuss the implications of the *Dialogues*, play Mozart with panache, and hold forth on the history of the Quraquat.

Kellie loved him, Digger thought of him as the grandfather he'd never known, and Mark Stevens, who usually piloted the supply ship, was fond of saying the only reason he agreed to keep doing the flights was to spend a few hours with Jack Markover every couple of months.

The fourth member of the research team was Winnie Colgate. Winnie had been through a couple of marriages. Both had expired, according to Winnie, amiably under mutual agreement. But there was an undercurrent of anger that suggested things had not been so amiable. And Digger suspected that Winnie would be slow to try the game again.

She had begun her professional life as a cosmologist, and she periodically commented that her great regret was that she would not live long enough to see the solutions to the great problems: whether there was a multiverse, what had caused the Big Bang, whether there was a purpose to it all. Digger thought they were adrift in a cosmic bingo game; Jack could not believe stars and people had happened by accident. Winnie kept an open mind, meaning that she changed her opinions from day to day.

She was blond, quiet, affable. It was no secret that she was entranced by Jack, would have taken him into her bed, but Jack was something of a Puritan about sex, didn't believe you should do it outside marriage. In any case, he behaved like Kellie, apparently convinced that his position as head of mission would in some way be compromised if he started sleeping with the staff.

Digger wished for it to happen, because it would have eased his way with Kellie. But, unhappily, Jack held his ground and respected Winnie's virtue.

Jack Markover had spent half his career on these missions, and had come to doubt the wisdom of his choice. He'd staked everything on the glorious possibility of making the first major contact. There was a time when it had seemed easy. Almost inevitable. Just get out there and do it. But that had been during an era of overt optimism, when the assumption had been that every world on which life was possible would inevitably develop a biosystem, and that once you got a biosystem you would eventually get tribal chiefs and math teachers. It was true that the habitable worlds orbiting the sun's immediate neighbors had been sterile, but that had seemed like no more than a caprice.

Now he wondered whether they'd all simply read too much science fiction.

He knew what his reputation was. Hi, Jack, find any little green men yet? He had, after each of the last two missions, gone home determined not to come out again. But it was like a siren call, the sense that he might quit just one mission too soon. So he knew that, whatever happened this time, whatever he might think about retiring to Cape Cod, he'd be back out again, poking a new set of worlds. Hoping to find the big prize.

To date, during the past year, they had looked at seventy-nine systems, all with stable suns. The stated purpose of the mission was strictly survey. They were accumulating information and, especially, noting planets that might become future habitats without extensive terraforming. They'd found one life-supporting world, but the life-forms were microscopic. In his entire career, across thirty-five years, Jack had seen only nine worlds on which life had gotten a foothold and been able to sustain itself. There'd been two others on which conditions had changed, an atmosphere grown too thin, a passing star scrambling an orbit, and the life-forms had died out. And that was it.

On each of the living worlds, the bioforms were still microscopic. He had never gone to a previously unvisited world and seen so much as a blade of grass.

The omega was approximately 41,000 kilometers through the middle, big as these things went. It *had* turned, had adjusted course, was *still* turning. It was also decelerating. You could *see* it because the cloud had lost its spherical shape. As it decelerated, sections of mist broke loose and fountained forward.

The turn was so slight as to be barely discernible. Jack was surprised it had been detected at all. Observers must have been watching the object over a period of months to make the determination. Then he realized that, because it was approaching a planetary system, the Academy would have been paying special attention.

The *Jenkins* spent several days doing measurements and collecting readings, sometimes standing off at thousands of kilometers, sometimes pushing uncomfortably close to the cloud front. The numbers confirmed what Broadside had: It *was* angling into the planetary system.

It wasn't hard to find the target.

If the braking continued at the present level, and the turn continued as it was going, the omega would shortly line up on a vector that would bring it to a rendezvous with the third planet.

The *Jenkins* was still too far away to see details. But Jack reported to Broadside. 'Looks like a December 14 intersect, Vadim,' he told them. 'We'll head over there and take a look.'

* * *

It was their custom to name each terrestrial world they investigated. Although the names were not official, and each planet would continue to be referred to in formal communications by a numerical designator attached to its star's catalog number, unofficially it was easier to think in terms of Brewster's World, or Backwater, or Blotto. (Brewster had been Winnie's companion in her first foray to the altar. The world got its name because it had achieved tidal lock, so the sun, viewed from the surface, 'just sat there, doing nothing.')

It was Kellie's turn to name the new one. 'This might turn out to be a special place,' she said. 'When I was a kid we lived near Lookout Point in northern New York. I loved the place. We used to go there and have picnics. You could see the Hudson in the distance.'

'So you want to call it Lookout Point?'

'Lookout would be good, I think.'

And so Lookout it became.

The ship made a jump to get within an AU, and began its approach. They were still much too far for the telescopes to make out any detail. But they discovered immediately that no electronic envelope surrounded the world.

That news produced mixed feelings. Like everyone else, Digger would have liked to see a world with an advanced civilization. It had never happened, and it would be a huge achievement. On the other hand, there was the cloud. Better, he told himself, it should be empty, and the cloud being drawn by unusual rock formations. Or by ruins, like at Moonlight.

By the third day, the disk that represented Lookout was still only a bright sprinkle of light to the naked eye. In the scopes, however, it was covered with clouds. The only visible surface was blue. An ocean. 'It has a big moon,' said Winnie, watching the data come in from the sensors. 'Two moons, in fact.'

The presence of a large moon was thought to be critical to the development of civilizations. Or, for that matter, of large land animals.

The filters reduced the reflection and they were watching two disks and a star, the larger several times the diameter of its companion. The star was the second moon, which was probably a captured asteroid. They brought the images up to full mag and concentrated on the big moon, looking for signs that someone had been there. But they were still too far away. A building the size of Berlin's Bergmann Tower would not have been visible at that range.

It was a strange feeling. How many times had they approached worlds like this, literally praying for an earthwork, for a wall, for a light on the sea? And tonight – it was just short of midnight GMT – Digger hoped they would see only the usual barren plains.

The clarity of the images grew. Lookout had white cumulus clouds. Continents. Archipelagoes.

The continents were *green*.

They shook hands when they saw that. But it was a muted round of celebration.

The poles were white, the oceans blue.

'Looks like Earth,' Winnie said, as if she were pronouncing sentence.

On the fourth day they were able to pick up physical features, mountain ranges, river valleys, large brown patches that might have been plains. A section of the night side was visible, and they searched it eagerly for lights, but saw nothing.

They slept in shifts, when they slept at all. Usually, they dozed off in the common room, and left only to head for the washroom or to get something to eat. They began imagining they saw things. Someone would sit before a monitor tapping it with a pen, observing that there are lines here, looks like a building, or something there, in the harbor, maybe improvements. At one point, Winnie was convinced she could make out a mountain road, and Digger claimed he saw wakes at sea, maybe from ships. Kellie wondered whether she hadn't spotted a dam on one of the rivers, and Jack saw changes in the color of the land that suggested agricultural development.

But in the growing clarity of the telescopes, everything faded, save forest, jungle, rivers, and coastline. The arc of the night side remained dark.

There was a substantial cloud cover, and storms were everywhere. Blizzards covered the high northern and low southern latitudes, a hurricane churned through one of the oceans, and lightning flickered in the temperate zones. Rain seemed to be falling on every continent. Bill did the usual measurements and posted the results. The planet was about 6 percent smaller than the Earth. Axial tilt twenty-six degrees. (Axial tilt was another factor that seemed to be significant if a world was to develop a biosystem. All known living worlds ranged between eighteen and thirty-one degrees.)

According to Bill, the atmosphere would be breathable, but they'd be prudent to use bottled air. The air at sea level was notably richer in oxygen content than the standard mix. Gravity was .92 standard.

The smaller moon had a retrograde movement. Both satellites were airless, and both were devoid of evidence that anyone had ever landed on them. Seventy percent of the surface was liquid water. And Lookout had a rotational period of twenty-two hours, seventeen minutes.

They went into orbit, crossed the terminator onto the night side, and almost immediately saw lights.

But they weren't the clear hard-edged lights of cities. There was smoke and blurring and a general irregularity. 'Forest fires,' said Jack. 'Caused by lightning, probably.' He smiled. 'Sorry.' Though probably he wasn't.

Thirty minutes later they were back on the daylight side. There were no major cities. The night was dark as a coal sack. Jack sat down, visibly relieved, visibly disappointed, and sent off yet another report to Vadim, information to the Academy. 'No sign that the world is occupied. No lights. Will look more closely.'

'So why is the cloud coming this way?' asked Winnie.

* * *

They made several orbits and saw nothing. They zeroed in on numerous harbors and rivers, looking for any sign of improvement and finding none. There was no visible shipping, no indication of a road anywhere.

They were about to send off another message informing Broadside that the Academy need not concern itself with Lookout when Digger heard Jack's raspy uh-oh. He glanced at the screens, which were showing nothing but night. 'I saw lights,' said Jack.

'Where?' Digger knew that Jack had written the world off. He was not going to get excited again. Not about Lookout.

'They're gone,' said Jack. 'We passed over. They're behind us. But they were there.'

'Bill?'

'Realigning the scopes now.'

The alpha screen, the prime operational monitor, went dark, and then came back on. *'I've got it,'* said the AI.

Several lights, like lingering sparks. But they didn't go out.

'Fires?'

'What are we getting from the sensors?' asked Winnie.

Bill switched over, and they saw several hazy, luminous rings. 'Somebody's got the lights on,' said Digger. He looked over at Kellie.

'Could be,' she said.

It wasn't London, thought Digger. But it was sure as hell something.

'What's the ground look like?' asked Winnie.

Bill put the area on display.

The biggest of the continents stretched from pole to pole, narrowing to an isthmus in the southern temperate latitudes before expanding again. The lights were located on, or over, the isthmus.

It was about four hundred kilometers long, ranging between forty and eighty kilometers wide. It was rough country, with a mountain range running its length, lots of ridges, and three or four rivers crossing from one ocean to the other.

Digger didn't know what he was supposed to feel. He was

along on the mission, and he was dedicated to it like Jack and Winnie. But unlike them, he hadn't expected to see anything. Nobody ever saw anything. It was a rule.

'How could we have missed that?' asked Winnie.

'It's still raining down there,' suggested Bill. *'Visibility hasn't been very good.'*

'Lock it in, Bill. I don't want to have trouble finding it again when it gets out into the daylight.' Digger went back to the viewport and stared out at the long dark curve of the planet. There wasn't a light anywhere to be seen. Well, they'd come around again a few more times before it would be dawn over the target area. Maybe the cloud cover would go away and they'd get a good look.

And then they'd zero in by daylight.

They didn't see the lights again. But the weather cleared toward dawn, the target area rotated out into the sun, and Digger looked down on a long jagged line that traveled the length of the isthmus. A *road*! It couldn't be anything else.

Simultaneously Kellie announced she could see a city. 'One of the harbors,' she said, bringing it up on the monitor.

'Here's another one.' Winnie pointed at the opposite side of the isthmus. And another here, where the isthmus widens into the southern continent. And two more, where it reaches up into the northern land mass.

Cities crowded around harbors, cities spread out along an impossibly crooked shore line, cities straddling both sides of rivers. There was even a city on a large offshore island in the western sea.

The telescope zoomed in, and they saw creatures on the road, large awkward beasts of burden that looked like rhinos. And humanoids, equally awkward, wide around the middle, waddling along, with reins in their hands and hats that looked like sombreros.

'I'll be damned,' said Jack. 'They're actually there.'

They had pale green skin, large floppy feet (had their ancestors been ducks?), and colorful clothing. It was red and gold and deep sea blue and emerald green. Winnie counted six digits rather than five, and thought their scalps were hairless. They wore baggy leggings and long shirts. Some had vests, and everything was ornamented. There were lots of bracelets, necklaces, feathers. Many wore sashes.

'My first aliens,' said Kellie, 'and we get Carpenter.' That was a reference to Charlie Carpenter, the creator of the Goompahs, an enormously popular children's show. And the aliens did, in fact, look like Goompahs.

'Incredible,' said Winnie.

Somebody laughed and proposed a toast to Charlie Carpenter, who'd gotten there first. They were looking at the traffic on the central road just outside a city that stood on the eastern coast. While they shook their heads in amusement, Jack switched the focus and brought up a building atop a low ridge near the sea. It stopped the laughter.

The building was round, a ring of Doric columns supporting a curved roof. It glittered in the sunlight, which was just reaching it, and it looked for all the world like a Greek temple.

'Say what you like,' said Digger. 'But these people know their architecture.'

They counted twelve cities in all, eight through the isthmus, two on the northern continent, one in the south, and one on the island. It was sometimes difficult to determine where one city ended and another began because, remarkably, they saw no walls. 'Maybe it's a *nation*,' said Kellie, who'd come down from the bridge to share the moment of triumph. 'Or a confederacy.'

There was a similarity in design among all of them. They'd clearly not been planned, in the modern sense, but had grown outward from commercial and shipping districts, which were usually down near the waterfront. But nevertheless the cities were laid out in squares, with considerable space provided for parks and avenues.

The buildings were not all of the elegance of the temple, but there was a clean simplicity to the design, in contrast to the decorative accoutrements worn by individuals.

The cities were busy, crowds jostling through the commercial areas, hordes of the creatures doing that curious duck-walk, little ones chasing one another about, individuals relaxing near fountains. And Jack realized with a shock that the natives had running water.

'Can we tell how big they are?' asked Winnie.

'*Smaller than they look,*' said Bill. '*They would on average come up to Jack's shoulders.*'

There were a variety of structures, two-story buildings that might have been private dwellings, others that looked like public buildings, shops, markets, storage facilities. Three ships were tied up at the piers, and a fourth was entering the harbor as they watched. Its sails were billowing in the wind, and sailors scrambled across its decks.

The architecture was similar everywhere. If it lacked the Doric columns of the seaside temple, it possessed the same simple elegance, straight lines, vaulted roofs, uncluttered cornices. *Just the thing*, Digger thought, *that would attract an omega*. And he was struck by how much better the cloud's sensing equipment was than the *Jenkins*'s.

The cities were surrounded by agricultural areas, squares of land given over to one crop or another, orchards, silos, barns. A few rhinos, and other smaller creatures, grazed contentedly.

Gradually the farms gave way to forest.

Beyond the northern cities, the woods grew thick, and broke on the slopes of a mountain range that rivaled the Alps. Beyond the peaks lay jungle, and the jungle, as it approached the equator, became desert. In the south, the cities stood on the edge of more mountains, which proceeded unbroken for thousands of kilometers, all the way to the ice cap.

Where were the other cities?

Digger didn't realize he'd asked the question aloud until Jack commented that it looked as if the isthmus was the only populated section on the planet. The other continents looked empty. The land above and below the isthmus looked equally empty.

They searched the oceans for ships and found none other than those in the coastal waters near the cities. 'Looks,' said Kellie, 'as if they stay in sight of land.'

'Look at this.' Digger pointed at two of the rivers that crossed the isthmus. 'A lock.'

They zoomed in and saw that it was so. 'They have to get ships over the high ground in the middle of the isthmus,' said Jack. 'So they use a system of locks to raise them, then get them back down to sea level.'

Kellie raised a congratulatory fist. 'The Goompahs are engineers,' she said. 'Who would've thought?'

Jack was getting ready to make his report. 'They'll want to know about the population.' He looked around at his colleagues. 'What do you think?'

Anybody's guess. Winnie brought the cities up one by one. The northernmost was on the western coast, and it was probably the smallest of the group. It could lay claim to a couple of spectacular buildings. The larger of the two was set in front of a pool and looked very much like the main admin building on the Academy grounds. It was long, low, only three levels, made of white stone. It was probably a bit smaller, but the same architect might have designed both.

The other structure was round, like the temple by the sea, but bigger, with more columns. It appeared to be open to the elements. And something that might have been a sun disk stood at the apex of its roof. It looked out across a park.

Crowds were pressed into the commercial section, which was too narrow. The avenues curved and wandered off in all directions. They were lined with buildings of all sizes and shapes. *Minimum twenty thousand*, Digger thought. *Probably closer to twenty-five*. The other cities appeared to be larger. Say an average population fifteen to twenty percent more. Make it thirty thousand for each. That was a conservative estimate. And it gave, what?

'Three to four hundred thousand,' Winnie told Jack.

He nodded. Kellie said the estimate was a bit low, but Digger thought she had it about right. Jack agreed and went across the corridor to record his report.

One of the sailing vessels was making its way northward up the coast on the western sea. It was under full sail, and it looked like an eighteenth-century frigate. No Roman galleys for these guys. Or Viking boats. They clearly had no use for oars.

On the other hand, they hadn't learned how to make an outboard motor.

'The question,' said Jack, 'is what we do now?'

It was night on the isthmus again, but a clear night this time, and they could see the cities spotted with lights. They were barely discernible, flickering oil lamps probably, but they *were* there.

'We wait for instructions,' said Jack. 'They'll probably send some contact specialists.'

'I hate to bring this up,' said Digger, 'but where are the contact specialists coming from?'

'The Academy, I assume.'

'It's a nine-month flight.'

'I know.'

'The cloud is only nine months away. When they get here there won't be anybody to contact.'

Jack looked uncomfortable. 'If they get underway without wasting any time, they'll have a couple of weeks before the cloud hits. In any case, Hutch can get back to us within a couple of weeks and let us know what she intends. Meantime, I don't think there's much for us to do except sit tight.'

Kellie frowned. 'You don't think we should go down and say hello?'

'No,' said Jack. 'The Protocol requires us to keep hands off. No contact.'

'Nothing anybody can do,' said Winnie.

Digger frowned. 'Doesn't the policy say something about extraordinary circumstances?'

'As a matter of fact, no.'

ARCHIVE

Vadim, we have a lowtech civilization on Lookout. On the third world. It's confined to a small area in the southern hemisphere. What do you want us to do?

—Jack Markover
February 26, 2234

LIBRARY ENTRY

'Where are you going, Boomer?'

'I'm headed to the Chocolate Shop.'

'Can I go along? It's my favorite place in the whole town.'

'Sure. As long as you promise not to eat any. It's not good to eat between meals.'

'I know, Boomer. You can count on me.' (Wink, wink at the audience.)

—*The Goompah Show*
All-Kids Network
February 25

5

On board the *Patrick Heffernan*, near the Bumblebee Nebula.
Thursday, February 27.

'Nothing,' said Sky. They'd been searching the *Quagmire*'s last
known position for six hours. There was no sign of the ship, and
none of the hedgehog.

'It couldn't just have disappeared,' said Emma.

He wasn't sure whether the 'it' she was referring to meant the
ship or the hedgehog. But whichever, there didn't seem to be any
sign of either in the neighborhood.

Schuyler Capabianco was one of only two of the Academy's
twenty-three captains who were currently married, and the only
one whose wife was part of the onboard team. She was an astrophysicist out of the University of Arizona who claimed she'd never
have started taking Academy assignments had it not been for the
chance to be with her husband. He didn't believe it, but he was
happy to hear her say so.

Em had been optimistic for a happy outcome to the rescue
mission. She had never witnessed a fatal off-Earth incident, and
could not bring herself to believe one had happened there. A
rationale was hard to find, though. The most likely seemed to be
that a power failure had occurred, leaving the ship adrift, without

its long-range communication functions. Sky knew it was possible, but only remotely so.

When they'd arrived near the cloud and heard no distress signal, no radio call, they had both realized that the chance of rescue had become vanishingly small. Superluminals were designed so that the radio transmitter would be pretty much the last thing that went down.

There just weren't many things that could account for the silence other than catastrophe. Nevertheless they looked, but Bill reported no sign of the ship. '*It is not in the search area,*' he said.

Em and Sky didn't know either of the people on the *Quagmire*, but that didn't soften things any. There was a brotherhood among those who traveled the great deeps. A tradition had developed much like that among mariners in the dangerous early days on the seas: They were a band, they looked out for each other, and they grieved when anyone was lost.

The *Quagmire* was lost. The mission had become salvage rather than rescue.

'Must have been an explosion,' Emma said.

Sky looked off to starboard, where the omega drifted, dark and quiet. But it was too far away to be the culprit.

Emma folded herself into his arms. 'Damn,' she said.

'We knew all along it might be like this,' said Sky.

'I suppose.' She snuffled, wiped her eyes, pulled away from him, and cleared her throat. 'Well,' she said, 'there's probably no point hanging around here. What we should do is try to get a look at what happened.'

That got his attention. 'How do you suggest we do that?'

They slipped into hyperspace, rode the quiet mists, and jumped out again before Sky could finish his coffee. '*Right on target,*' Bill announced. They had traveled 104 billion kilometers, had gotten in front of the light wave from the search area, and could now look back at the place where the hedgehog and the *Quagmire* had been. Bill unfolded the array of dishes that served as the ship's telescope and aimed it at the region.

They were seeing the area as it had been four days earlier. Had the telescope been more efficient, they could have watched the *Quagmire* approach the hedgehog, could have watched Terry Drafts and Jane Collins leave their ship and descend into the spines.

Emma posted the time at the *Quagmire* site, late evening on the twenty-third, exactly twenty-five minutes before communications had stopped.

It was after midnight on the *Heffernan*. He felt weary, tired, numb, but not sleepy. While they waited he sent off a preliminary report to Serenity. No sign of the *Quagmor*. Continuing investigation.

They talked about the incident. Odd that they'd just vanish. You don't think they might have just taken off? Or been grabbed by something? Sounded wild, but no stranger than simply dropping out of sight. Sky laughed at the idea, but asked Bill whether anything unusual was moving in the area.

'*Negative,*' said Bill.

Watching too many horror sims.

Emma gently pressed his arm. 'Coming up,' she said. He was watching the time. Just a minute or so.

The cloud was, of course, invisible at that range. (He couldn't help connecting the event with the cloud. Knew it would somehow turn out to be responsible.) But they were well away from it now. The distance between their present position and the site of the incident was seven times as great as the diameter of the solar system. 'I can't imagine what we'd expect to see at this range,' he said.

'We won't see anything, Sky. But there's a chance—'

'*Photons,*' Bill reported. '*Just a sprinkle. But they were right on schedule.*'

'So what's it tell us?' asked Sky.

'Explosion,' said Em. 'Big one.'

'Big enough to obliterate the ship? And the rock?'

'If we can pick up traces of it out here. Oh, yes, I'd say so.'

LIBRARY ENTRY

. . . Few of us now alive can remember when we looked at the stars and wondered whether we were alone. We have had faster-than-light transport for almost a half century, and if we have not yet encountered anyone with whom we can have a conversation, we know nevertheless they are out there, or have been there in the past.

More than a hundred people have given their lives to this effort. And we are now informed that, during the last fiscal year, roughly 2 percent of the world's financial resources have gone into this exploration of the outer habitat in which we live.

Two percent.

It does not sound like much. But it could feed 90 million people for a year. Or provide housing for 120 million. It could pay all the medical costs in the NAU for sixteen months. It could provide a year's schooling for every child on the planet.

So what do we have for our investment?

Sadly, we have nothing to put into the account books. It's true we have improved our plumbing methods and created lighter, stronger materials. We can now pack more nourishment into a convenience meal than we ever could before. Our electronics are better. We have lightbenders, which have proved of some use in crime prevention, and also of some use to criminals. We have better clothing. Our engines are more fuel-efficient. We have learned to husband energy. But surely all of this could have been had, at far less cost, by direct investment.

Why then do we continue this quest?

It is too easy to think that we go because of the primal urge, as Tennyson said, *to sail beyond the sunset.*

We pretend that we are interested in taking the temperatures of distant suns, of measuring the velocity of the winds of Altair, of presiding over the birth of stars. Indeed, we have done these things.

But in the end, we are driven by a need to find someone with whom we can have a conversation. To demonstrate that we are not alone. We have already learned that there have been others before us. But they seem to have gone somewhere else. Or passed into oblivion. So the long hunt continues. And in the end, if we are successful, if we actually find somebody out there, I suspect it will be our own face that looks back at us. And they will probably be as startled as we.

—Conan Magruder
Time and Tide, 2228

6

University of Chicago.
Thursday, March 6.

It had been almost four years, but David Collingdale had neither forgotten nor forgiven the outrage at Moonlight. The sheer mindlessness of it all still ate at him, came on him sometimes in the depths of the night.

Had it been a war, or a rebellion, or anything at all with the most remote kind of purpose, he might have been able to make peace with it. There were times when he stood before his classes and someone would ask about the experience and he'd try to explain, how it had looked, how he had felt. But he still filled up, and sometimes his voice broke and he fell into a desperate silence. He was not among those who thought the omegas a force of nature. They had been designed and launched by somebody. Had he been able to gain access to that somebody, he would have gladly killed and never looked back.

A blanket of snow covered the University of Chicago campus. The walkways and the landing pads had been scooped out; otherwise, everything was buried. He sat at his desk, his class notes open before him, Vivaldi's 'Spring' from *The Four Seasons* drifting incongruously through the office. He'd spent the night there not because he knew the storm was coming, although he did, but simply because he sometimes enjoyed the spartan ambience of his office. Because it restored reason and purpose to the world.

The classes were into their first period. Collingdale had an appointment with a graduate student at nine thirty, leaving him just enough time to get himself in order – shower and fresh clothes – and get down to the faculty dining room for a quick breakfast.

Life should have been good there. He conducted occasional seminars, served as advisor for two doctoral candidates, wrote articles for a range of journals, worked on his memoirs, and generally enjoyed playing the campus VIP. He was beginning to get a reputation as something of an eccentric, though. He'd discovered recently that some of his colleagues thought he was a bit over the side. Believed that the experience at Moonlight had twisted him. Maybe it was true, although he would have thought *intensified* to be the more accurate verb. His sensitivity to the subject seemed to be growing deeper with time. He could, in fact, have wept on cue, had he wished to do so, merely by thinking about it.

He'd become sufficiently oppressed by conditions that he worried he might be having an unfortunate effect on his students. Consequently, he'd tried to resign in midsemester the year before, but the chancellor, who saw the advantage of having someone with Collingdale's stature on the faculty, had taken him to a local watering hole for an all-night session, and he'd stayed on.

The chancellor, who was also a longtime friend, suggested a psychiatrist, but Collingdale wasn't prepared to admit he had a problem. In fact, he had acquired an affection for his obsession. He wouldn't have wanted to be without it.

Things got better for him this past Christmas when Mary Clank had walked into his life. Tall, angular, irrepressible, she had heard all the jokes about her name and laughed all of them off. Trade *Clank* for *Collingdale*? she'd asked the night he proposed. You must think I have a tin ear.

94

He loved her with as much passion as he hated the clouds.

She refused to be caught up in his moods. When he wanted to watch a sim, she insisted on a stroll through the park; when he suggested a fulfilling evening at a concert, she wanted to bounce around at the Lone Wolf.

Gradually, she became the engine driving his life. And he found the occasional day when he did not see her to be an empty time, something to be gotten through as best he could.

He'd always assumed that the romantic passions were practiced exclusively by adolescents, women, and the slow-witted. Sex he could understand. But together forever? That's our song? It was for children. Nevertheless he'd conceived a passion for Mary Clank the first time he'd seen her – at a faculty event – and had never been able to let go. To his delight, she returned his feelings, and Collingdale became happier and more content than he had ever been.

But his natural pessimism lurked in the background and warned him she would not stay. That the day would come when he would walk into the Lone Wolf alone, or with another woman on his arm.

Enjoy her while you can, Dave. All good things are transient.

Well, maybe. But she had said *yes*. They hadn't set a date, although she'd suggested that late spring would be nice. June bride and all that.

He squeezed into his shower. He had private accommodations, a bit cramped, but sufficient. Collingdale liked to think he was entitled to much more, that he was demonstrating to the university that he was really a self-effacing sort by settling for, in fact by insisting on, much less than someone in his position would customarily expect. A lot of people thought modesty a true indicator of greatness. That made it, at least, a prudent tactic.

When he'd finished he laid out fresh clothes on the bed. The sound system was running something from Haydn, but the HV was also on, the sound turned down, two people talking earnestly, and he was pulling on a shirt when he became aware that one of them was Sigmund Halvorsen, who usually got called out when a major scientific issue was in the news. He turned the volume up.

'—*is unquestionably,*' Halvorsen was saying in his standard lecture mode, '*a group of cities directly in its path.*' He was an oversize windbag from the physics department at Loyola. Mostly beard, stomach, and overbearing attitude.

The interviewer nodded and looked distressed. '*Dr Halvorsen,*' he said, '*this is a living civilization. Is it at risk?*'

'*Oh, yes. Of course. The thing is already tracking them. We don't have much experience with the omegas, but if our analyses of these objects are correct, these creatures, whatever they are, do not have much time left.*'

'*When will the cloud get there?*'

'*I believe they're talking about December. A couple of weeks before Christmas.*' His tone suggested irony.

Collingdale hadn't been near a newscast since the previous evening. But he knew right away what was happening.

A picture of the cloud replaced the two men. It floated in the middle of his bedroom, ugly, ominous, brainless. Malevolent. Silent. Halvorsen's voice droned on about 'a force of nature,' which showed what he knew.

'*Is there anything we can do to help them?*' asked the interviewer.

'*At this time, I doubt it. We're lucky it isn't us.*'

From his angle near the washroom door, the omega seemed to be closing in on his sofa-bed. 'Marlene,' he said, calling up the AI.

'*Dr Collingdale?*'

'Connect me with the Academy. Science and Technology. Their headquarters in Arlington. Audio only. I want to talk with Priscilla Hutchins.'

Her whiskey voice informed him that the connection had been made and a young woman's voice responded. '*Can I help you, Dr Collingdale?*'

'Director of operations, please.'

'*She's not available at the moment. Is there someone else you wish to speak with?*'

'Please let her know I called.' He sat down on the bed and stared at the cloud. It blinked off, and was replaced by a scattering of lights. The cities by night.

'—*any idea what we're looking at?*' the interviewer asked.

'*Not yet. These are, I believe, the first pictures.*'

'*And this is where?*'

'*The third planet – just like us – of a star that has only a catalog number.*'

'*How far is it?*'

'*A bit more than three thousand light-years.*'

'*That sounds pretty far.*'

'*Oh, yes. That's about as far out as we've gone. I'd venture to say the only reason we're there now is because somebody spotted the cloud moving.*'

Collingdale's line blinked. He took it in his sitting room. '*Dave.*' Hutch materialized standing on the throw rug. She was framed by a closet door and a plaque awarded him by the Hamburg Institute. '*It's good to hear from you. How've you been?*'

'Good,' he said. 'The job pays well, and I like the work.' Her black hair was shorter than it had been the last time he'd seen her. Her eyes were dark and intelligent, and she obviously enjoyed being an authority figure. 'I see things are happening.'

She nodded. '*A living civilization, Dave. For the time being. We released it this morning.*'

'How long have you known?'

'*We got the news two days ago, but we've suspected it for a while now.*'

'Well,' he said, unsure how to get where he wanted to go, 'congratulations. I assume there's a major celebration going on down there.'

'*Not exactly.*'

No, of course not. Not with a cloud closing in on somebody. 'What kind is it?' he asked, referring to the type of civilization.

'*Green deuce.*'

Nontechnological. Agricultural. But organized into cities. Think eastern Mediterranean, maybe four thousand years ago. 'Well,' he said, 'I'm delighted to hear it. I know there'll be some complications, but it's a magnificent discovery. Who's getting the credit?'

'*Looks like a technician at Broadside. And Jack Markover on the* Jenkins.'

That was a surprise. In the old days, it would have been someone higher up the chain. 'The cloud led you to it?'

'*Yes.*' She looked discouraged.

'They're saying December on the HV.'

'*Yes.*'

'Are you going to try to do anything for them? For the inhabitants?'

'*We're putting together a mission.*'

'Good. I thought you would. Do you have anything going, anything that can take out the cloud?'

'*No.*'

Yeah. That's what makes it all such a bitch. 'What are you going to try to do? What's the point of the mission?'

'*We'll decoy it. If we can.*'

'How?'

'*Projections. If that doesn't work, a kite.*' She allowed herself a smile.

'A kite?' He couldn't suppress a grin himself.

'*Yes.*'

'Okay. I'm sure you know what you're doing.'

'*Ask me in nine months.*' She tilted her head and her expression changed. Became more personal. '*Dave, what can I do for you?*'

He was trembling. The smartest thing he could do, the only thing he could do, was to stay out of it. The mission, round trip, would take close to two years. And it was likely to fail.

When it did, he would be happily married to Mary. 'When are they leaving?'

'*A few days. They'll be on their way as soon as we can get everybody on board.*'

'They won't have much time after they get there.'

'*We figure about ten days.*'

'Who's running it?'

'*We're still looking at the applications.*'

He ran over a few names in his memory, thought he knew who'd be trying to get on board. Couldn't think of anyone with better qualifications than he. 'What happens if the decoy doesn't work?'

'*We have some other ideas.*'

Decision time. 'Hutch—' he said.

She waited.

Two years away. Mary Clank, farewell.

'*Yes, Dave?*' she prompted.

'I'd like to go.'

She smiled at him, the way people do when they think you're kidding. '*I understood you were pretty well settled.*'

'I'd like to do this, Hutch. If you can see your way clear.'

'*I'll add your name to the candidates' lists.*'

'Thanks,' he said. 'I'd consider it a personal favor.'

She turned away momentarily and nodded to someone out of the picture. '*Dave, I can't promise.*'

'I know. What kind of creatures are they?'

She vanished and a different image appeared, an awkward, roundish humanoid that looked like something out of a Thanksgiving parade. Complete with vacuous eyes and a silly grin. Baggy pants, floppy shoes, bilious shirt. Round, polished skull. No hair save for eyebrows. Long thin ears. Almost elfin. They were the saving grace in an otherwise comic physiognomy.

'You're kidding,' he said.

'*No. This is what they look like.*'

He laughed. 'How many of them are there?'

'*Not many. They all seem to be concentrated in a group of cities along a seacoast.*' Again, something off to the side distracted her. '*Dave,*' she said, '*I have to go. It was good to talk with you. I'll get back within twenty-four hours. Let you know, up or down.*'

He had lunch with Mary, and she knew something had happened. They were in the UC faculty lounge, he with only twenty minutes before he was due to conduct a seminar, she with an hour to spare. His intention had been to say nothing until he had the decision from the Academy. But she sat there behind a grilled cheese and looked into him and waited for him to explain what was going on.

So he did, although he made it sound, without actually lying, as if Hutch had called him and asked whether he was available.

'They might pick somebody else,' he concluded. 'There's a lot at stake. It would be hard to say no.'

She looked back at him with those soft blue eyes, and he wondered whether he had lost his mind. 'I understand,' she said.

'I don't really have a choice in something like this, Mary. There's too much riding on it.'

'It's okay. You have to do what you think is right.' Steel in the ribs.

'I'm sorry. The timing isn't very good, is it?'

'You'll be gone two years, you say?'

'If I get picked, it would be closer to a year and a half.' He tried a smile but it didn't work. 'If it happens, I can probably arrange space for you. If you'd want to come.'

She nibbled at the sandwich. Considered it. He saw her wrestle with it. Saw those eyes harden. 'Dave, I'd like to, but I can't just take two years off.'

'It wouldn't be two years.'

'Close enough. It would wreck my career.' She was an instructor in the law school. There was a tear. But she cleared her throat. 'No. I just can't do it.' And there was a message there somewhere,

100

in her voice, in her expression. I'm yours if you want me. But don't expect me to hang around.

In that moment, filled with the smell of fresh-brewed coffee and cinnamon, he hoped that Hutch would pass over him, pick someone else. But he also understood he'd driven a spike into his relationship with Mary, that whatever happened now, things would never again be right.

Hutch called that night. '*You still want to go?*'

'When do we leave?'

'*A week from tomorrow.*'

'I'll be ready.'

'*I'm attaching a folder. It has all the information on the mission. Who'll be there. What we plan to do. If you have any ideas, get back to me.*'

'I will.'

'*Welcome aboard, David.*'

'Thank you. And, Hutch—'

'*Yes?*'

'Thanks for the assignment.'

He signed off and looked out across the lake. He lived on the North Shore. Nice place, really. Hated to leave it. But he'd already arranged to sublet.

ARCHIVE

Jack, for planning purposes, we will assume that we'll be unable to stop the cloud. The cloud will target the cities. See if you can come up with a way to move the population out into the country, preferably to higher ground, since they're all vulnerable to the ocean. We are going to try to master their language. To that end, we need recordings. Raw data should be forwarded to the *Khalifa al-Jahani* as soon as it becomes available.

Anything you can do without compromising the Protocol

101

will help. I'm informed you don't have lightbenders. We're sending a shipment from Broadside, but I'd be grateful if you didn't wait for their arrival to get started. Find a way to make things happen. Everyone here understands the difficulty that implies. Therefore, be advised that your primary objective is to get the job done. If it becomes necessary to set the Protocol aside, this constitutes your authority to do so.

We also need you to collect and run analyses of food samples. Forward any information you can get. What do they eat? Fruit, pizza, whatever. Any other data that might help us get them through this.

Time is of the essence. In view of the lag between Lookout and your other points of contact, you are free to use discretion.

—P. M. Hutchins
Director, Operations
March 6, 2234

7

Arlington.
Friday, March 7.

Hutch found a note on her desk, requesting she report to the commissioner's office immediately on arrival. She found him packing. 'Heading for Geneva,' he said. 'Right after the memorial service.'

'What's happening?' she asked.

'Political stuff. But they want me there. You'll be acting the rest of the week.'

'Okay.'

He looked at her. 'That's it,' he said.

'No special instructions?'

'No. Just use your best judgment.'

She'd been hit hard by the loss of Jane Collins and Terry Drafts. Hutch had known both, had partied with Jane and risked her neck with Terry. Standing on the lawn by the Morning Pool, listening to the tributes, she couldn't get the notion out of her head that both would show up, walk into the middle of things, and announce it was all a mistake. Maybe if they had found the bodies, it would have been easier.

The commissioner conducted the event with his usual charm and aplomb. Their friends and colleagues recalled fond memories of one or the other, and there was a fair amount of laughter. Hutch glanced up at the south wall, on which were engraved the names of all who had lost their lives over the years in the service of the Academy. Or, as she'd have preferred to put it, in the service of humanity. The list was getting long.

When her turn to speak came, she filled up. Tom Callan handed her a glass of water but she stood there, shaking her head impatiently. Poor way for a leader to behave. She began by saying that Jane and Terry were good people, and her friends. 'They were bright, and they went to a place that was dark and deadly and nobody knew. Now we know.

'I'm proud they were my colleagues.'

The hedgehog and the cloud had been on the same course, moving at the same velocity. The cloud was programmed to attack objects with perpendiculars, or even sharp edges. The hedgehog had been all perpendiculars. If Terry's surmise that someone else was monitoring the cloud was correct, why do it with a package designed in that particular way? Why not just throw an ordinary set of sensors out there?

What was going on?

The two objects had been separated by sixty thousand kilometers. Why put a surveillance package in front instead of alongside? And why so far away?

She made some calls. Everybody she could think of who'd been involved with the omegas. She put the same question to each: Was it possible that there'd been other hedgehogs accompanying other clouds? And that they hadn't been observed?

The answers: It was certainly possible. And at sixty thousand klicks, it was unlikely they'd have been noticed. The research vessels had been intent on the omegas. It had not been part of the routine to do long-range sweeps of the area.

By midafternoon she was satisfied it was worth an investigation.

'Barbara,' she said, 'record transmissions for Serenity and Broadside.'

'*Ready, Ms Hutchins.*'

She looked into the imager. 'Audrey, Vadim: Let's find out if some of the other clouds have a hedgehog. Assign whoever's available to take a look. Just nearby stuff. A few samples. Tell them if they find one, or anything remotely like it, to stay away from it. We don't want to lose anybody else. Let me know results ASAP.'

The various weatherman packages had sighted several more tewks, for a total of ten. They were concentrated in two widely separated areas, three near the Golden Crescent, four near the Cowbell.

The Golden Crescent, home to millions of aging stars, floated over her couch. Great smoky walls fell away to infinity. A class-G dominated the foreground, close enough to illuminate the clock. A luminous river of gas and dust ran across the back of the room.

She activated the program, and three bright objects appeared, one at a time, inward from the Crescent. One up here, one over there, one down center.

Then the image rotated, the Golden Crescent sank, the vast clouds moved around the walls, and the three stars lined up.

She had just watched the same process happen with the four tewks at the Cowbell. Except that there only three of the four had lined up. But it was enough.

It was almost choreographed. And it chilled her.

They were no closer to figuring out what was happening than they'd been when the first sightings came in a few weeks earlier. She suspected that, with Weatherman packages becoming operational on a regular basis, they were going to see more of these things.

She checked the time and shut the program down. Leave it to Harold to figure out. As acting commissioner she had more pressing matters to attend to.

Asquith had taken her aside after the memorial. It was her first experience as the Academy's chief decision maker, and he had apparently thought better of his intention to pass along no special instructions. 'Don't make any decisions,' he'd told her, 'other than those directly in line with Academy policy. Anything that requires judgment, defer it, and I'll take care of it when I get back.' He'd looked at her, realized what he'd said, and added, 'No offense.'

None taken. Asquith was too shallow for her to take his opinion of her capabilities seriously. The problem, of course, was that he wrote her evaluation.

She pushed it aside, called Rheal Fabrics, and told them to assemble the kite. They gave her the dimensions it would have while stored, which she added to the space requirements Marge's weathermaking gear would need.

The Lookout mission would require two ships. One would carry Collingdale and his team. The other would have to be a freighter, which meant she'd have to charter it. Oddly, the Collingdale ship was the problem. She needed something that could transport upward of twenty people, and the only thing available was the *al-Jahani*, currently undergoing a refitting. She'd have to hurry it along.

She'd briefed Asquith on what she intended to do. 'Maybe even worse than the direct attack by the omega,' she told him, 'is the aftermath. We don't know what it'll do to the atmosphere. Might be years before things will grow. That means a possibility of starvation for the natives. We're going to need to send out relief supplies.'

He'd sighed. 'Not our job, Hutch.'

But it would become theirs, and they both knew it. When the pictures started coming back of starving and dying Goompahs, the public would get upset, and the politicians would turn to the Academy. 'When it happens,' she'd told him, 'we better be ready.'

Next day he'd announced his Geneva trip. It hardly seemed a coincidence.

The *al-Jahani* was supposed to leave Friday. The logistics were set, and Collingdale and his people were en route. But Jerry

Hoskins, the Academy's chief engineer, had been dubious. Not enough time. The ship was due for a major overhaul, and Hutch wanted to send her on a two-year mission? But he'd see what he could do. So when Barbara informed her that Jerry was on the circuit, she got a bad feeling. *'Hutch,'* he said, *'we can't really get her ready in a few days.'*

'How much time do you need, Jerry?'

'If we drop everything else—?'

'Yes.'

'Three weeks.'

'Three weeks?'

'Maybe two. But that's the best we can do.'

'That won't work. They wouldn't get there in time. Might as well not go.' She had nothing else available. Damned stuff was all out in the boondocks. 'What's the worst that can happen if we go through with the launch?'

'You mean Friday?'

'Yes.'

'It might blow up.'

'You're kidding.'

'Of course. But I wouldn't guarantee it'll get where it's going.'

'Okay. No guarantee. Other than that, what are my chances?'

'It'll probably do fine.'

'Any safety concerns?'

'We'll do an inspection. Make sure. No, they'll be okay. They might get stranded. But otherwise—'

'—No guarantees.'

'—Right.'

'Okay. Jerry, I'm going to send a record of this conversation to Dave Collingdale. You inform the captain.'

Collingdale hadn't come in yet, so she left a message, describing the chief engineer's concerns. She told him reluctantly that it should add some spice to the flight. Then she sighed and headed for the commissioner's office to assume her new duties.

* * *

Her first appointment was with Melanie Toll of Thrillseekers, Inc.

Despite the capabilities of existing technology to create images that could not be distinguished from the originals, allowing virtual face-to-face conversations between people thousands of kilometers apart, people with business propositions still found the personal touch indispensable. Making the effort to cross some geography at personal inconvenience sent a message about how serious one was.

Serious. And here came Ms Toll of Thrillseekers.

Hutch gazed at her over the vast expanse of Asquith's desk. (The commissioner insisted she use his office when exercising his function.) She was young, attractive, tall, quite sure of herself. She wore a gold necklace and a matching bracelet, both of which acquired additional sparkle in the sheen of her auburn hair.

'Nice to meet you, Dr Hutchins,' she said.

'You're giving me more credit than I deserve.' Hutch shook her hand, listened to the light tinkle of the gold, and led her to a seat by the coffee table.

They talked briefly about weather, traffic, and how lovely the Academy grounds were. Then Hutch asked what she could do for her visitor.

Toll leaned forward, took a projector from her purse, and activated it. An image appeared of a young couple happily climbing the side of a mountain. Below them, the cliff fell away five hundred meters. Hutch could see a river sparkling in the sunlight.

Thrillseekers, Inc., took people on actual and virtual tours around the world and let them indulge their fantasies. Aside from dangling from cliffs, they rode golly balls along treacherous rivers, rescued beautiful women (or attractive men) from alligators, mounted horses and fought mock battles with bandits in the Sahara.

The projector displayed all this in enhanced colors, accompanied by an enthusiastic score, and over-charged titles. *Danger for the Connoisseur. The Ultimate Thrill-Ride.* The latter was a wild chase in a damaged flyer pursued by a man-eating cloud.

Moments later Hutch was racing down a ski slope, approaching a jump that seemed to have no bottom. '*Hold on to Your Socks!*' read the streamer. She couldn't help pushing back into her chair and gripping the arms.

'Well,' said Toll, snapping off the image just before Hutch would have soared out into space, 'that's what we do. Although, of course, you knew that.'

She smirked at Hutch, who, despite herself, was breathing hard. 'Of course, Ms Toll.' Steady yourself. 'That's quite a show.'

'Thank you. I'm glad you liked it.'

'How can I help you?'

'We're interested in Lookout. The place where the Goompahs are.'

'Really. In what way?'

'We'd like to put it on our inventory.' She crossed one leg over the other. The woman oozed sex. Even with no male in the room.

Marla, the commissioner's secretary, came in with a coffee service and pastries. She glanced at Hutch to see if she could proceed. Hutch nodded, and the woman filled two fine china cups and asked if there was anything else. There wasn't, so she withdrew. (Asquith didn't use an AI for secretarial duties because having a human signified his elite status within the organization. Very few people other than CEOs and heads of state had them. But there was no question that Marla added to the ambience.)

'How do you mean,' Hutch asked, 'put it on your 'inventory'?'

'We'd like to make the experience available to our customers. We'd like them to be on the ground when the cloud comes in, watch the assault, feel what it's like.'

'Ms. Toll, Lookout is three thousand light-years away. Your customers would be gone for almost two years. Maybe gone permanently.'

'No, no, no. We don't mean we'd literally ship them out. What we'd like to do is send a couple of our technicians to Lookout to record the attack, get the sense of what really happens. Then we'd construct an artificial experience.' She tried the coffee and nodded. It met with her approval. 'We think an omega program would do quite nicely.'

'And you'd like permission from me?' She wondered about that detail. Any world shown to have sentient life automatically came under the purview of the World Council, but its agent in such matters was the Academy.

'Permission and transportation,' said Toll.

Her instincts pushed her to say no, but she couldn't see a reason to refuse. 'Thrillseekers would have to pay their share of expenses.'

'Of course.'

'You'd have to agree not to make contact with the natives. But that shouldn't be a problem. We'd simply set you down on the other side of the globe.'

She shook her head. 'No, Ms Hutchins. I don't think you understand. The natives and their cities are the critical part of the equation. We'll want to record them up close. But I can promise we'll stay out of the way. They won't see us.'

Representatives from two of the major news organizations had appointments with her during the afternoon, and she suddenly realized why they were there. There was going to be more of this. *Let's get good shots of the Goompahs running for their lives.*

'I'm sorry, Ms Toll, but I don't think we can do it.'

Her pretty brow furrowed and Hutch saw that she had a vindictive streak. 'Why not?' she asked, carefully keeping her voice level.

Common decency, you blockhead. 'It puts the Protocol at risk.'

'I beg your pardon.' She tried to look baffled. 'They won't see us.'

'You can't guarantee that.'

She tried to debate the point. 'We'll keep out of the way. No way they'll know we're there. Our people will be in the woods.'

'There's also a liability problem,' Hutch said. 'I assume you expect these people to stay during the bombardment.'

'Well, of course. They'd have to stay.'

'That makes us liable for their safety.'

'We'll give you a release.'

'Releases have limited value in this kind of case. One of your people doesn't come back, his family sues you, and then sues us. The piece of paper isn't worth a damn in court if it can be shown we willingly transported him into an obviously dangerous situation.'

'Ms. Hutchins, I would be grateful if you could be reasonable.'

'I'm trying to be.'

Toll quibbled a bit longer, decided maybe she needed to talk with the commissioner, the *real* commissioner. Then she shook her head at Hutch's perversity, shook hands politely, and left.

She had a brief conversation with maintenance over contracts with suppliers, then went down to the conference room for the commissioner's weekly meeting. That was usually a scattershot affair, attended by the six department heads. Asquith was neither a good planner nor a good listener. There was never an agenda, although he'd left one for her this time. It was all pretty routine stuff, though, and she got through it in twenty minutes.

It didn't mention the Goompahs. 'Before I let you go,' she concluded, 'you all know what the situation is at Lookout.'

'The Goompahs?' said the director of personnel, struggling to keep a straight face.

She didn't see the humor. 'Frank,' she said, 'in December, a lot of them are going to die. Maybe their civilization with them. If anybody has an idea how we might prevent that, I'd like to hear it.'

'If we had a little more time,' said Life Sciences, Lydia Wu-Chen, 'we could set up a base on their moon. Evacuate them. At least get some of them out of harm's way.'

Hutch nodded. 'It's too far. We need nine months just to get there.'

'I don't think it's possible,' said Physics, Wendell McSorley.

'Did you see the pictures from Moonlight?' asked Frank, looking around at his colleagues. 'You have to find a way to stop the cloud. Otherwise, it's bye-bye baby.'

'There's nothing we can do about the cloud,' said Wendell.

'No magic bullet?' asked Lydia. 'Nothing at all?'

'No.'

Hutch described Tom Callan's idea. Wendell thought there was a possibility it might work. 'It would have helped if we'd been out there with it a couple of years ago, though. We've waited until the thing has *seen* the Goompahs.'

'The same thing,' said Hutch, 'could happen somewhere else next month. We need a weapon.'

'Then we need money,' said Wendell. 'Somebody has to get serious about the program.' He looked dead at her.

And that brought her back to the issue of food and blankets for survivors. She'd like to send medical supplies, too, but saw no quick way to find out what would be useful. So forget the medical stuff. The food would have to be synthesized, after they'd discovered what the natives would eat. But who would do it?

She had Marla put in a call to Dr Alva. Very busy, they told her. Not available. Who is Priscilla Hutchins again? But ten minutes later Marla informed her that Dr Alva was on the circuit. She looked impressed. 'And by the way,' she added, 'your three o'clock is waiting.'

Alva was wearing fatigues and seemed to be inside a makeshift lab. *'What can I do for you, Hutch?'* she asked. She did not sound annoyed, but there was no preliminary talk.

'You know about Lookout, Alva?'

'Only what I've read.'

'They're going to get decimated.'

'Are you going to warn them? At least let them know what's coming?'

'There's a mission leaving next week with linguists.'

'Well, thank God for that. I don't suppose that means we already have people on the ground who can speak with them?'

'Not yet. We just got there, Alva. But we're trying.'

'*I was concerned you'd want to keep hands off. You want my help overturning the Protocol?*'

'Actually, that's not why I called. We're going to ship supplies to them. We don't have any samples yet to work from, but as soon as I can get them, we're going to send food and blankets. And medical, if it's feasible. Whatever seems appropriate.'

'*Good. Maybe you'll be able to save some of them. What do you need from me?*'

'Advice. After I get the formulas, who would be willing to synthesize the food?'

'*Gratis?*'

'Probably. I'm going to try to get the Academy to spring for some cash, but I have my doubts.'

'*Your best bet is Hollins & Groat. Talk to Eddie Cummins over there.*'

'Where'll I find him?'

'*Call Corporate. Tell him you talked with me. That I'd consider it a personal favor. In fact, wait until tomorrow and I'll try to reach him and set things up. You've no idea what you're going to need, right?*'

'Not at this point.'

'*Okay. Let me see what I can do. If you don't hear from me, call him tomorrow afternoon. Your time.*'

Her three o'clock appointment was with the Rev. George Christopher, M.A.D.S., S.T.D. He represented the Missionary Council of the Church of Revelation. His group was currently the largest and most powerful of the Fundamentalist organizations in the NAU.

Christopher was right out of Nathaniel Hawthorne. Tall, severe, pious, eyes forever searching the overhead as if communicating with a satellite. The drawn-out diction that comes from too many years in the pulpit and causes people to think *God* has two syllables. He was pale, with a lean jaw and a long nose. He told her how glad he was to meet her, that in his view they needed some

113

fresh young blood in the Academy hierarchy, and he implied he was tight with Asquith.

In fact, he was. The Church was of course not a donor, but it had influence over people who were, and it wielded considerable political clout. The Rev. Christopher was an occasional guest at Asquith's retreat on Chesapeake Bay. 'Good man, Michael,' he said. 'He's done a superb job with the Academy.'

'Yes,' she agreed, wondering if there was a special penalty for lying to a man of the cloth. 'He works very hard.'

He settled back in one of the armchairs, adjusting his long legs, adjusting his smile, adjusting his aura. 'Ms. Hutchins,' he said, 'we are concerned about the natives on Lookout.' His lips worked their way around the verb and the two nouns. 'Tell me, is that really the name of the place?'

'No,' she said. 'It doesn't have a designator other than a number.'

'Well, however that may be, we are concerned.'

'As are we all, Reverend.'

'Yes. Of course. Are we going to be able to head off the disaster?'

'Probably not. We're going to try. But it doesn't look as if we have much chance.'

He nodded, suggesting that was the usual human condition. 'We'll ask our people to pray.'

'Thank you. We could use a little divine intervention.'

He looked up, tracked his satellite, and nodded again. 'I wonder whether you've ever considered how the clouds originated? Who sent them?'

Her flesh chilled. *Who*? Well, whatever. The truth was that hardly a day had gone by that she *hadn't* wondered about it, since that terrible afternoon thirty years ago when she'd watched the first cloud rip into Delta, rip into it because she and Frank Carson and the others had carved a few squares to entice it. And the thing had come like a hound out of hell.

'A lot of good people know what this is about,' he said. 'They've looked at the clouds, and they know exactly what is happening.'

'Which is—?'

'God is losing patience with us.'

Hutch didn't really have any comment, so she simply cleared her throat.

'I know how this sounds to you, Ms Hutchins – may I call you *Priscilla*?'

'Of course.'

'I know how this sounds, Priscilla, but I must confess that I myself find it hard to understand why God would have designed such an object into the universe.'

'It may not be a natural object, Reverend.'

'I suppose that's possible. It's hard to see how, but I suppose it could happen. I'm not a physicist, you know.' He said that as if he might easily have been mistaken for one. 'When you get an answer, please let me know. Meantime, I have to tell you what *I* think it is.'

'And what's that?'

'A test.'

'It's a pretty severe one.'

'There've been pretty severe ones before.'

Well, she couldn't deny that. Wars, famines, holocausts. It could be a tough world. 'May I ask how I can help you, Reverend?'

'Of course.' He rearranged his legs and studied her, and she understood he was making a judgment about how honest he could be. 'You're not a person of faith, I take it?'

Hutch didn't know. There had been times when she'd almost felt the presence of a greater power. There'd been times when things had gotten desperate and she'd prayed for help. The fact that she was sitting in this office suggested the prayers might have been answered. Or she might have been lucky. 'No,' she said finally. 'It looks pretty mechanical out there to me.'

'Okay. That's fair enough. But I want you to consider for a moment what it means to be a person who believes, who *really* believes, there is a Creator. Who believes without question that there is a judgment, that we will all one day have to face our Maker and render an accounting of our lives.' His voice had taken on a controlled passion. 'Think of this life as being only a taste of what is to come.' He took a deep breath. 'Priscilla, do these creatures know about God?'

For a moment she thought he was talking about Academy employees. 'The Goompahs?' she said. 'We don't have any information on them yet, Reverend.'

He looked past her toward the window, gazing at the curtains. 'They face decimation, and they probably do not have the consolation of knowing there is a loving God.'

'They might argue that if they had a loving God they wouldn't be facing decimation.'

'Yes,' he said. 'You would think that way.'

She wondered where this was going. 'Reverend Christopher,' she said, 'it's hard to see what we can do about their religious opinions.'

'Priscilla, think about it a moment. They obviously have souls. We can see it in their buildings. In their cities. And those souls are in jeopardy.'

'At the moment, Reverend, I'm more worried about their *bodies*.'

'Yes, I'm sure.' Note of sympathy. 'You'll understand if I point out there's far more to lose than simply one's earthly life.'

She resisted pointing out that the Goompahs had no earthly life. 'Of course.'

'It's strictly short-term.'

'Nevertheless—'

'I want to send a few missionaries. While there's still time.' His manner remained calm and matter-of-fact. He might have been suggesting they have a few pizzas delivered. 'I know you don't agree with all this, Priscilla. But I'm asking you to trust me.'

'The Protocol prevents it, Reverend.'

'These are special circumstances.'

'That's true. But there's no provision, and I have no authority to override.'

'Priscilla. Hutch. They call you *Hutch*, don't they?'

'My friends do, yes.'

116

'Hutch, I'm asking you to show some courage. Do the right thing.' He looked on the verge of tears. 'If need be, the Church will back you to the hilt.'

Right. That's exactly what the Goompahs need right now, to hear about hellfire and damnation. 'I'm sorry, Reverend.' She got up, signaling the end of the interview. 'I wish I could help.'

He got to his feet, clearly disappointed. 'You might want to talk this over with Michael.'

'His hands would be tied also.'

'Then I'll have to go to a higher authority.' She wasn't sure, but the last two words sounded capitalized.

Josh Keppler represented Island Specialties, Inc., a major player in communications, banking, entertainment, and retailing. Plus probably a few other areas Hutch didn't recall at the moment.

Anyone who sought an appointment with the director of operations was required to state his business up front. She assumed the commissioner ran things the same way, but if so, he hadn't passed the information along. It was becoming a long day, and she couldn't imagine anything Keppler would have to say that she was interested in hearing.

'Costume jewelry,' he said.

'I beg your pardon?'

'The Goompahs wear a lot of costume jewelry. It looks pretty good. Sort of early Egyptian.'

'I'm sorry. I don't think I'm following you.'

'The original stuff would be worth enormous money to collectors.'

'Why? Nobody's interested in what the Noks wear.'

'Nobody *likes* the Noks. People *love* the Goompahs. Or at least they will after we launch our campaign. And anyhow, the Goompahs are going to get decimated. That provides a certain nostalgia. These things are going to be instant relics.'

Keppler wore a white jacket and slacks, and he had a mustache – facial hair was just coming back into style after a long absence

– that did nothing for him. Add close-set dark eyes, hair neatly parted down the center of his skull, and a forced smile, and he looked like an incompetent con man. Or a failed lothario. Care to swing by my quarters tonight, sweetie?

'So Island Specialties is going to—?'

'—We're sending a ship out. It'll be leaving in about a week. Don't worry. We'll take care of everything, and we'll stay out of the way.' He was carrying a folder, which he opened and laid before her. 'This constitutes official notification. As required by law.'

'Let me understand this,' she said. 'You're sending a ship to Lookout. And you're going to—'

'—Do some trading.'

'Why not just reproduce the jewelry? You know exactly what it looks like.'

'Authenticity, Ms Hutchins. That's what gives it value. Each piece will come with a certificate of origin.'

'You can't do it.' She pushed the document back across the desk without a glance.

'Why not?'

'First of all, Lookout is under Academy auspices. You need permission to do this.'

'We didn't think there'd be a problem about that.'

'There is. Secondly, it would be a violation of the Protocol.'

'We're willing to accept that.'

'What do you mean?'

'We don't think it would stand up in court. The Protocol has never been tested, Ms Hutchins. Why would anyone suppose the Court of the Hague has jurisdiction out around Alpha Centauri?'

Well, he was probably right there. Especially if the Academy granted *de facto* rights by accepting his notification. 'Forget it,' she said.

Keppler tried to smile at her, but only his lips moved. 'Ms. Hutchins, there would be a considerable financial advantage for the Academy.' He canted his head to let her know that Island

Specialties was prepared not only to buy off the Academy, but her as well.

'Makes me wonder,' she said, 'if the cloud doesn't constitute one of the Goompahs' lesser problems.'

His expression continued to imply he was trying hard to be her friend. He grinned at her little joke. Flicked it away harmlessly to show he hadn't taken offense. 'Nobody will get hurt,' he said. 'And we'll all do very nicely.'

'Mr Keppler, if your people go anywhere near Lookout, we'll act to defend our prerogatives.'

'And what precisely does that mean?'

'Show up and find out.' In fact, she knew that Island would not be able to get a superluminal for that kind of voyage unless they could show Academy approval, or at least Academy indifference.

The commissioner considered public relations his primary responsibility. Eric Samuels, his PR director, routinely scheduled a press conference every Friday afternoon at four. Shortly before the hour she heard his cheery hello to Marla, then he rolled into the office, bubbly and full of good cheer, affecting to be surprised to find Hutch behind the desk, and did a joke about how the commissioner had never looked better.

He wanted her to sign off on a couple of press releases on matters of no real concern. She was surprised he didn't have the authority to handle them on his own. One of the world's top physicists was scheduled to visit the Academy the following week, and Eric wanted to make it an Event. Several new artifacts were going on display in the George Hackett Wing of the library. (That one brought a twinge. Thirty years ago George had stolen her heart and lost his life.) There was also an announcement of new software being installed throughout the Academy buildings to make them friendlier to visitors.

'Okay,' she said, signing with a flourish. She liked the feeling of power it brought. 'Good.'

'Did Michael leave anything for me?' he asked. 'You know, the

Goompahs? They'll be all over me today about Lookout.' Eric was tall, and would have been quite good-looking had he been able to convey the impression somebody was home. The truth was that he wasn't vacuous, but he did look that way.

'No,' she said. 'Michael didn't leave anything. But *I* have something for you.'

'Oh?' He looked suspicious, as if she were about to hand him an assignment. 'What's that?'

She activated the projector and a Goompah appeared in the middle of the office. 'Her name's Tilly.'

'Really?'

'Well, no. Actually we don't know what her name is.' She changed the picture, and they were in one of the streets of the city with the temple. Goompahs were everywhere. Behind shop counters, standing around talking, riding beasts that were simultaneously ugly and attractive (like a bulldog, or a rhino). Little Goompahs ran screaming after a bouncing ball.

'Marvelous,' he said.

'Aren't they?'

'How much of this stuff do we have?'

She shut the sound off, extracted the disk, and held it out for him. 'As much as your clients could possibly want.'

'Yes,' he said. 'The networks'll love it.'

More than that, she thought. If the public reacted the way Hutch knew they would, it would become politically very difficult for the government to decide the Goompahs were more trouble than they were worth and simply abandon them.

At the end of the day, she wandered down to the lab. Harold was in his office, getting ready to leave. 'Anything more on the tewks?' she asked.

'Well,' he said, 'we do have another one.'

'Really?'

'In the Cowbell again.'

'Still no star it could have been?'

120

'This was already lit when the package went operational. And we don't have a good picture of the area beforehand, so we really don't know. But it's a tewk. The spectrogram is right. Incidentally, one of the older ones shut down.'

'Okay.'

'The one that shut down: We don't know how long it was active because we don't know when it first began. Might have been a couple of weeks before the package started operating.' He tugged at his jacket, as though a piece of lint were hanging on. Finally, he gave up. 'There's something odd about that, too. About the way they switch off.

'Usually, a true nova will fade out. Maybe come back to life a couple times in any given cycle. Burn some more. But these things—' He looked for the right word. 'When they're done, they're done. They go off, and nobody hears from them again.'

'Like a light going out?'

'Yes. Exactly like that.' He frowned. 'Is it cold out?'

Hutch hadn't been outside since morning. 'Don't know,' she said.

'There's something else.' He looked pleased, puzzled, amused. 'The clouds tend to run in waves.'

'Old news, Harold.'

'Sometimes they don't, but the ones we've seen usually do. Now, what's interesting, we've detected some clouds near the tewks. If we assume they are also running in waves, then at least four of the tewks, and maybe all of them, happened along wave fronts.'

She looked at him, trying to understand the implications. 'You're telling me these are all attacks? We're watching worlds get blown up?'

'No.' He shook his head. 'Nothing like that. There's far too much energy being expended for that kind of scenario. All I'm saying is what I said: Wherever one of these explosions has happened, we're pretty sure a cloud has been present.'

'No idea as to what's going on?'

121

'Well, it's always helpful when you can connect things. It eliminates possibilities.' He smiled at her, almost playfully. 'I was wandering through the Georgetown Gallery last night.' He was checking his pockets for something. Gloves. Where were his gloves? 'I got to thinking.' He found them in a desk drawer, frowned, wondering how they could have gotten there, and put them on. He seemed to have forgotten the Georgetown Gallery.

'And—?' prompted Hutch.

'What was I saying?'

'The Georgetown Gallery.'

'Oh, yes. I have an idea what the omegas might be.'

She caught her breath. Give it to me. Tell me.

'It's only an idea,' he said. He glanced at the time and tried to push past her. 'Hutch, I'm late for dinner. Let me think about it some more and I'll get back to you.'

She seized his arm. 'Whoa, Harold. You don't drop a line like that and walk off. Have you *really* figured it out?'

'Give me a few days. I need to do some math. Get more data. If I can find what I'm looking for, I'll show you what they might be.'

LIBRARY ENTRY

'Go, *therefore, and teach all nations*.' The requirement laid on us by the Gospels is no longer as clear as it once was. Do the creatures we call Goompahs constitute a nation in the biblical sense? Are they, like ourselves, spiritual beings? Can they be said to have souls?

For the third time in recent years, we are facing the issue of an extraterrestrial intelligence, beings that seem to have a moral sense, and might therefore qualify as children of God. To date, we have delayed, looked the other way, and avoided the question that is clearly being put to us: Was the crucifixion a unique event? Does it apply only to those born of terrestrial mothers? Or has it application on whatever worlds the children of Adam may visit?

What precisely is our responsibility? It is no easy question, and we must confess we find no ready answer in the scriptures. We are at a crossroad. And while we ourselves consider how to proceed, we would remind those ultimately tasked with the decision, who have delayed more than thirty years since the first discovery on Inakademeri, that failure to act *is* a decision. The cloud is bearing down on the Goompahs, while we bide our time. The entire Christian community is watching. And it is probable that whatever precedent is set in these next few months will determine the direction of missionary efforts well into the future. If indeed we determine that the Gospels are not applicable off Earth, we should so state, loudly and clearly, along with the reasons why. If, on the other hand, they *do* apply, then we should act. And quickly. The clock is running.

—*Christianity Today*
April 2234

8

Union Space Station.
Friday, March 14.

Hutch sat quietly in the back of the briefing room while Collingdale talked to his people. There were twenty-five of them, xenologists, sociologists, mathematicians, and technicians. And, primarily, a team of twelve language specialists, whose job it would be to interpret the raw data sent back by the *Jenkins* crew, and to become proficient in basic Goompah.

The *Khalifa al-Jahani* was visible through the viewports. It was one of the Academy's older ships, and she recalled the engineer's cautions with misgivings. Probably be okay, but no guarantees. Collingdale had not been happy. But he'd accepted the reality of their position, and they'd passed the information on to the volunteers. None had opted out.

He was telling them that he planned to break new ground and he was pleased to have them with him.

'I've asked the *Jenkins* to get as many recordings as possible,' she'd told Collingdale earlier in the day. 'They're going to plant A/V pickups wherever they can. I've advised them to get the data and not worry too much about the Protocol unless the natives prove hostile. In which case they're just going to hunker down until you get there.'

'If they turn out to be hostile,' Collingdale had said, 'I doubt we'll be able to do much for them.'

That had brought up the question of equipment. How many pickups did the *Jenkins* group have to work with? It couldn't be many. They'd been doing routine survey work and, in the ordinary course of things, had little use for recording devices. They'd have to jury-rig some spare parts. In any case, there wouldn't be more than a handful.

She'd ordered a shipment sent over to the *Jenkins*, along with some lightbenders, including a capital unit that could be used to conceal their lander. None of that, however, would arrive for weeks. So it would be left, for the time being, to Jack Markover's imagination. She knew Markover, and could think of no one she'd rather have in the present position.

Collingdale had already talked individually with his team members, of course. But this was the first time they'd all been together. She was pleased to see that he refused to use the term *Goompahs*.

That had raised the question of a proper reference. Had it been visible from Earth, Lookout would have been located in Draco. But *Draconians* would never do. They were close to the Dumbbell Nebula but that didn't help much either. In the end, knowing she had no control over the matter, hearing the media going on endlessly about *Goompahs*, she put it aside. It was already too late.

Collingdale finished his preliminary remarks, which consisted mostly of an orientation and welcome aboard. He invited them to get ready to depart, but asked the linguists to stay a moment. They were, to Hutch's mind, the heart and soul of the operation. And she was pleased to see a substantial level of enthusiasm.

Judy Sternberg would be their director. Judy was an Israeli, a specialist in the intersection between language and culture, and a born leader. He introduced her, and she said all the right things. Proud to be working with them. An opportunity to make a major contribution. She knew they'd perform admirably.

Judy was no taller than Hutch, but she had presence. 'Ladies and gentlemen,' she concluded, 'we are going to rescue the Goompahs. But first we are going to *become* Goompahs.'

So much for getting rid of the terminology. She wished Jack Markover had come up with something else on those initial transmissions.

Collingdale thanked Judy and shook her hand. 'While we're en route to Lookout,' he told the linguists, 'we are going to break into their language. We are going to *master* it. And when we get there we are going to warn the natives what's coming. We'll help them evacuate their cities and head for the hills.' He allowed himself a smile at the expression. 'And we are going to help them. If it comes to it, we may be with them. We'll do what is necessary to save their rear ends.'

One of them raised a hand. Hutch recognized him from the manifest as Valentino Scarpello, from Venice. 'How,' he asked, 'are we going to do this? Why would they believe us?'

Valentino had a dazzling smile and leading-man features. Half the women in the group were already drooling in his direction.

'By the time we arrive on the scene,' Collingdale said, 'the cloud will be hanging over their heads. I don't think it'll be hard to persuade anyone.'

That brought applause. Someone had hung on the bulkhead a picture of a Goompah, with its saucer eyes and large vacuous smile. They were pets, and the Academy people, and maybe the whole world, were adopting them.

'It might be,' he added, 'that we won't need to hide behind the disguises. Hutch back there – Hutch, would you stand a moment please? – Hutch is doing what she can to get us past the Protocol. It's possible that, by the time we get to Lookout, we'll be able to walk in, say hello, and suggest that everybody just get out of town. But however that plays out, we *will* not stand by and watch them die.'

More applause.

'Thank you.' He exuded confidence.

When the linguists had gone up the ramp to the *al-Jahani*, she took Collingdale and Judy aside. 'I appreciate your spirit,' she said. 'But nobody stays on the ground when the omega gets there.' She looked both in the eye. 'We are not going to lose anyone out there. You guys understand that?'

'I was speaking metaphorically,' said Collingdale. 'We'll take care of them.' He looked at Judy for confirmation and Judy gazed at Hutch.

'Don't worry,' she said. 'We won't let anything like that happen.'

Then they were shaking hands. Good-bye. Good luck. See you in a couple of years. Hugs all around.

She was thinking about Thrillseekers, Inc., and the Church of Revelation, and Island Specialties. Yesterday there'd been four more, a clothing retailer who wanted to bring back some of the natives to use as models for a new line of Goompah fashions ('—and we'd save the lives of the models, don't forget that—') which, incidentally, looked not very much like the originals; a representative from the media giants, who were demanding an opportunity to record the destruction; a games marketer who wanted to develop a game that would be called *Omega*; and an executive from Karman-Highsmith who wanted to send a crew to get location shots for a sim that was already in the works. Major people involved.

Collingdale lingered while Judy boarded. Then he looked down into her eyes. 'Wish you were coming?'

'No,' she said. 'I've gotten too old for this sort of thing.'

While waiting for departure, she checked in with ops and got the latest status report from the *Jenkins*. It was a week old, of course, the time needed for hyperlight traffic to reach her from Lookout. That was another mistake, allowing the name *Lookout* to get around. It had become a joke for late night comedians, as well as a predictor of disaster. She saw now that they should have gotten on top of that right away. Should have given the sun a name, something like Chayla, and then they could have called the world Chayla III. And the inhabitants would have become Chaylans. All very dignified. But it was too late for that. It was her fault, but a smart Academy public relations section would have picked up on it right away.

There was nothing new from the *Jenkins*. They were still debating how best to go down and look around. She didn't envy Jack, who had some tough decisions in front of him. The ops officer pressed his earphones and signaled her to wait. He listened, nodded, and looked up. 'Commissioner on the circuit for you, ma'am.'

That was a surprise. 'I'll take it in the conference room,' she said.

He was seated on the deck of a yacht, a captain's cap pulled low over his eyes. '*Just thought I'd check in*,' he said. '*How are we doing?*'

'Fine. I see you didn't quite make Geneva.'

He smiled innocently. '*Will the* al-Jahani *get away on schedule?*'

'Yes, sir. They're packed and ready to go.' She paused. 'Why?'

'*Why do I want to know about the* al-Jahani?'

'Why run me through the parade?'

'*I thought it would be a good idea if you learned why there's a Protocol.*'

She sat down. 'You made your point.'

'*Good. Hutch, it's not just the Goompahs. We're talking about a precedent. If we break it at Lookout, wherever we find anyone we'll be baptizing, selling motorized carts, and dragging critters back to perform in circuses. You understand?*'

'You really think that would happen?'

'*It's hard to see how it wouldn't. I take it you told them no deal.*'

'All except the media. They're getting limited access. But not on the ground. How'd you know?'

'*I've already heard rumblings of formal protests. Good. I'm proud of you.*'

She'd always thought of Asquith as a man who'd avoid a fight at any cost. 'What chance do you think they have, Michael? The protests.'

'Zero to poor. Unless you give the game away.'

She just missed a flight to Reagan and, rather than wait three hours, she caught one to Atlanta, and then took the glide train to D.C. Just south of Richmond they ran into a snowstorm, the first in that area in ten years or more. It got progressively heavier as the train moved north.

It was late evening by the time she reached home, descending onto the landing pad through a blizzard. Tor was waiting on the porch.

She got out of the taxi and hurried through the storm. The door swung open, and he handed her a hot chocolate. 'Well,' he said, 'did we get everybody off safely for Goompah country?'

'I hope so. How's Maureen?'

'Asleep. She missed her mommy. I don't think she likes the way I read George.' That was a reference to George Monk, the garrulous chimp.

The hot chocolate was good. Inside, he had a blazing fire going. She set the cup down and shook the snow off her jacket.

'It's all over the networks,' he said. 'The talking heads don't think much of your chances.'

'They're probably right.' She was about to sit when the house AI (named for the chimp, or maybe it was the other way round) sounded the chime that indicated an incoming call.

'Who is it, George?' Tor asked.

'Academy watch officer. For Hutch.'

'That's odd,' she said. 'I can't imagine what that would be about.' Actually she could: Her first thought was that the *al-Jahani* had developed a problem already.

Jean Kilgore's face appeared on-screen. *'Hutch?'*

'Yes. What do you have, Jean?'

'I wanted to let you know Harold is in the hospital. Apparently it's serious.'

She needed a moment to understand. 'What happened?' she asked. 'How is he?'

'*Heart attack. They took him to Georgetown. It happened this afternoon.*'

'Do you have anything on his condition?'

'*No, ma'am. Only what I told you.*'

'Okay.'

'*He went home early. Said he wasn't feeling well.*'

'Thanks, Jean.' She was headed toward her closet for a fresh jacket.

'*Jenny Kilborn says he's been on heart medication for years.*'

'Yes,' she said. 'I know.'

'*But they didn't think it was that serious. If he was having trouble, he doesn't seem to have told anyone. Jenny talked with somebody at the hospital. Or maybe the police. I'm not sure which. They said his neighbor couldn't get her front door open because of the snow. He went over to help her dig out.*'

Great. Guy with a heart condition. 'Thanks, Jean.' She'd have to change her shoes. 'George, get me a cab. And connect me with that aunt of his, the one who lives in Wheaton.'

She couldn't get through to the aunt, whom she'd met once, years before. She was, as far as Hutch knew, Harold's only relative in the area. But the traffic director informed her she was offline. Apparently one of those people who did not carry a commlink. Well, Hutch could understand it. If she ever got clear of the Academy, she'd think about ditching hers.

All attempts to get information from Georgetown also went nowhere. '*He's been admitted,*' the hospital told her. '*Other than that we don't have anything at the moment.*'

Twenty minutes after leaving Woodbridge she settled onto the roof of the Georgetown Medical Center. She climbed out, momentarily lost her balance on the snow-covered ramp, and hurried down to the emergency room receiving desk.

The aunt was there, standing in a small circle of worried-looking people. *Mildred.* Her eyes were red.

Hutch introduced herself. Mildred smiled weakly, stifling tears. There was also a female cousin, a neighbor, a clergyman, and Charlie Wilson, one of the people from the lab. 'How is he?' she asked.

Charlie looked steadily at Hutch and shook his head.

NEWSDESK

RECORD COLD IN MIDWEST
Temperature Hits Fifty Below in St Louis

WCN SENDS PEACEKEEPERS TO MIDDLE EAST
Train Bombed by Iniri Rebels

TIDAL WAVE KILLS HUNDREDS IN BANGLADESH
Triggered by Collapsing Island

SINGH DEFEATS HARRIGAN FOR HUMAN CHESS CHAMPIONSHIP
First Off-Earth Title Match

DOCTOR ALVA ACCEPTS PERUVIAN MEDAL
Honored for Efforts During Bolus Outbreak

WOMAN KILLS FOUR IN NEW HAMPSHIRE BAR
Claims Devil Was On the Way to Snatch Their Souls

RECESSION ENTERS THIRD QUARTER
Unemployment Up Seventh Straight Month

SIX KILLED AT BELGRADE CONCERT
Grandstand Gives Way During Beethoven Fair

DEALY GUILTY
Billionaire Convicted On All Counts

Victims Demonstrate Outside Court
Civil Suits Pending
Faces Character Reconstruction

SANASI CALLED BEFORE CONGRESS
Expected to Take Fifth
Martin Says No to Deal

ALIENS IN DRACO
Primitive Civilization Under Cloud
Natives Resemble Goompahs

PART TWO
Goompahs

9

Arlington.
Saturday, March 15.

Harold never regained consciousness, and was pronounced dead at 4:32 A.M.

Hutch was still there when the word came, trying to provide what support she could to Mildred and the cousin. She notified the lab watch officer and listened while the doctor said he was sorry, there was really nothing they could have done.

He was 106. Mildred explained that the doctors had wanted to give him a synthetic heart a few years back, but he'd refused. She wondered why. He'd always seemed rational. And he had everything to live for: He seemed content with his work and was respected around the world.

'He was alone,' Mildred said. Tears leaked out of her eyes. She looked relatively young, but she was Harold's aunt so she, too, was past the century mark.

Hutch came out of the hospital under a sky still dark and cold, wondering why she hadn't seen it coming, why she hadn't stepped in. She'd never invited him to the house. Not once. Despite the fact they'd eaten lunch countless times, that she'd confided in him when she'd gotten frustrated with the job. And he'd always told her to calm down, everything would be okay. It'll pass. It was his favorite line. Everything passes.

Tor's parents lived in Britain, and her own father was long dead. Harold would have made a superb substitute grandfather for Maureen, if Hutch had only known. Had only *thought*.

So she stood in the access station, watching the last few flakes drifting across the rooftop. Probably windblown, she decided, suspecting the snow had stopped. Banks of the stuff were piled up around the landing pads.

Harold gone. It was hard to believe.

Her link sounded. It was Tor. '*What's happening?*'

'We lost him.'

'*I'm sorry.*'

'About a half hour ago.'

'*You okay?*'

'Yes. I'm on my way home now.'

'*All right. I'll have some breakfast waiting.*'

'No. Nothing for me, thanks. I'm not hungry.'

A taxi descended, a woman got out, and Hutch's commlink sounded, alerting her it was *her* cab. She climbed in, and the harness descended on her. And the thought she'd been pushing aside for the last two hours settled in beside her. Harold, what are the omegas?

A medical unit drifted down onto the far end of the roof, where the emergency pad was located. She gave the taxi her address and settled back.

It lifted off, turned south, and picked up speed toward the Potomac.

She usually worked a half day Saturdays, especially when things were happening, which was pretty much all the time. She'd been at her desk less than an hour when the report came in. The *Gallardo* had inspected a cloud out near Alpha Cassiopeiae and found another hedgehog. The circumstances were the same: It was out front, same course, same velocity. Six and a half kilometers in diameter. Preliminary scan suggested it was an identical object. The only thing different was its range from the cloud, only fifteen thousand klicks.

The two sites were hundreds of light-years apart.

She'd barely digested the information when the watch officer called with more. The local cloud had one too. Again it was identical in everything except range, which was forty-two hundred kilometers. Even the spines were set in an identical pattern. As if the objects had come out of the same mold. There was some minor damage, probably caused by collisions.

It looked harmless.

She sat several minutes studying the images and went down to the lab. Harold's office was empty, but Charlie Wilson was there, and a few of the technicians. It had been Hutch's experience that bosses are rarely loved, and whatever the employees might say, there was inevitably a sigh of relief when they moved on. Even when the movement was to a better world. But everyone had liked Harold. And the mood in the lab was genuinely depressed.

'You know why we needed him?' Charlie told her after she'd sat down to share a glass of pineapple juice. 'He was as big as any of the people who try to shoulder their way to the equipment. Which meant he could say *no*. He could keep things orderly. Who's going to refuse time on the systems now to Stettberg? Or to Mogambo?'

'You will, Charlie,' she said. 'And I'll back you up.' He looked doubtful, but she smiled. 'You'll do fine. Just don't show any hesitation. You tell them no, that's it. Let them know we'll call them if we get available time. Then thank them kindly and get off the circuit.'

He took a long pull at the juice without saying anything.

'Charlie.' She changed her tone so he'd see the subject was closed. 'I want to talk with you about the omegas.'

'Okay.'

'Last week, Wednesday, I think, Harold told me he thought he knew what they were.'

Charlie tilted his head, surprised. The reaction was disappointing. She'd hoped Harold had confided in him. 'He didn't say anything to you?'

'No, Hutch. If he had any ideas, he kept them to himself.'

'You're sure.'

'Of course. You think I'd forget something like that?' Harold's office was visible through a pane of glass. The desk was heaped with paper, disks, magazines, books, and electronic gadgets. Waiting for someone to clear them away, box them and ship them home. 'I just don't know what he was thinking, Hutch. But I can tell you one thing you might not know.'

'What's that, Charlie?'

'We matched the tewks with the omegas. With the waves. Or at least with the places where the waves should be if they're consistent.'

'He told me that. So there's a connection.'

'Apparently.'

And two of them with hedgehogs. Did all the clouds have hedgehogs? 'Charlie,' she said, 'these objects that we've spotted running in front of the omegas: They seem to be booby traps. Bombs. Is it possible that what you've been seeing is hedgehogs exploding?'

'No.' He shook his head.

'How can you be sure?'

'Did you look at the pictures from the *Heffernan*?'

Hutch hadn't. She'd read the report.

'The explosion that destroyed the *Quagmor* – Is that right? I keep hearing two different names for the ship – is nothing like what we see when one of the tewks goes off. It's on the order of difference between a firecracker and a nuke.'

'Okay,' she said. 'Just a thought.'

They went into Harold's office and looked through the stacks of documents. But nothing presented itself as particularly relevant. 'Charlie,' she said, 'I need you to go over everything he was working on. See if you can find anything new on the clouds. Or the tewks.'

'Okay.'

'Let me know if you find something.'

'Actually,' he said, 'we've already started.' Charlie was tall and rangy, with sandy hair and clear blue eyes. Unlike most of the researchers who came to the Academy, Charlie kept himself in decent physical condition. He played basketball with his kids on weekends, swam an hour a day in the Academy pool, and played occasional tennis. He lacked his boss's brilliance, but then so did pretty much everybody else.

'Okay,' she said. 'Stay with it. Let me know if anything turns up.' She started to leave but stopped short. 'What about the nova patterns, Charlie? Anything new on those?'

'You mean, about the way they line up?' He shook his head. 'Maybe if more of them get sighted, we'll have a better idea. But I think the notion there's a pattern is an illusion.'

'Really. Why?'

'They tend to bunch up in a relatively small space. When that happens, you can almost always rotate the viewpoint and get a pattern.'

'Oh.'

'And the sightings are probably confined to those two areas not because that's the only places they are, but because we don't have that many packages up yet and functioning. Give it time. There will probably be more. If there are, I think you'll see the patterns go away.'

LIBRARY ENTRY
Harold Tewksbury

. . . His achievements over an eighty-year career have been adequately chronicled elsewhere. He is one of the fortunate few whose work will survive his lifetime. But that is also on the record elsewhere. What mattered to me was his essential

141

decency, and his sense of humor. Unlike many of the giants in our world, he was never too busy to talk to a journalist, never too busy to lend a hand to a friend. It is entirely fitting that he died helping a neighbor.

Everyone who knew him feels the loss. We are all poorer this morning.

—Carolyn Magruder UNN broadcast
Sunday, March 16, 2234

10

Union Space Station.
Sunday, March 16.

Twice to the Wheel in a weekend.

Standing with Julie Carson, the ship's captain, Hutch watched the people from Rheal Fabrics pack the kite onto the *Hawksbill*. Eight large cylinders, each more than thirty meters in diameter and maybe half again as long, were clamped to the hull. These were described on the manifest as chimneys. They were, in fact, rainmakers. Four landers had been stored in the cargo bays, along with an antique helicopter whose hull was stenciled canadian forces. There was also an AV3 cargo hauler; a shuttle reconfigured to accommodate an LCYC projector, like the big ones used at Offshore and other major theme parks; a half dozen pumps; and lengths of hose totaling several kilometers. A second LCYC was already mounted on the underside of the ship.

The *Hawksbill* was not part of the Academy fleet; it was a large cargo carrier on loan from a major shipping company which had donated it for the current project with the understanding that they would get all kinds of good publicity. Plus some advantages in future Academy contracts. Plus a tax break.

Like all ships of its class, it wasn't designed to haul passengers, and was in fact limited to a pilot plus two. Or three, in an emergency.

The workers from Rheal were in the after cargo hold, running a final inspection on the kite before closing the doors. A cart carrying luggage appeared on the ramp and clicked through the main airlock. 'Dave Collingdale will direct the operation,' Hutch was explaining. 'Anything that has to do with the *Hawksbill*, you're in charge. Kellie will be there with the *Jenkins*. Do you know her? Yes? Good. She'll be switching places with you so you can help Marge get the rainmakers set up.'

'Which means,' said Julie, 'that she'll be taking the *Hawksbill* out to play tag with the omega?'

'Yes.'

'Okay,' she said. 'Whatever you guys want.'

Julie was an Academy pilot, about the same age Hutch had been when she'd taken her first superluminal out of the solar system. She'd had her license for a year, but she'd already acquired a reputation for competence.

Hutch felt a special kinship with her. She was the daughter of Frank Carson, who had dodged the lightning with her during their original encounter at Delta.

She was tall, like her father, same military cut, brown eyes, her mother's red hair. She also had her mother's conviction that there was no situation she could not handle. It was one of the reasons Hutch had offered her the assignment. She was facing a long time away with a limited social life, but it was a career-enhancing opportunity and a chance to show what she could do. The other reason was that she could pilot the AV3 hauler.

One of her passengers appeared at the top of the ramp. Avery Whitlock was one of a long line of philosophical naturalists who had come to prominence originally in the nineteenth century with Darwin and Thomas Huxley, and continued with Loren Eiseley, Stephen Jay Gould, and Esther Gold. He had silver hair, a long nose, and a timid smile. He was a black man, had grown up with all the aristocratic advantages, gone to the right schools, mixed with the right people. But he had a populist talent that shone through his work, and made him the most widely read scientific writer of his era. Eventually, Hutch knew, he would produce a history of the attempt to rescue the Goompahs. Succeed or fail, Whitlock liked the human race and would ensure that it, and the Academy, got just due for the effort it was making.

He looked out at the ship, and Hutch saw his jaw drop a bit. 'It's a behemoth,' he said. 'Really only room for two of us?'

Hutch grinned and shook his hand. 'Good to see you, Whit. And actually, if you count the captain, it holds three.' She introduced him to Julie, who surprised her by commenting that she was familiar with Whitlock's work. 'I especially liked *The Owl and the Lamp*,' she said. Whitlock beamed, and Hutch saw again that there was no quicker way to a writer's heart than by expressing admiration for his work.

Julie had her own views, it turned out, about avian evolution. Hutch listened for a couple of minutes, then pointed out that it was getting late. 'Of course,' said Julie.

'You'll have plenty of time on the flight,' she added.

'I had no idea,' Whitlock said, returning his gaze to the ship, 'that it would be so big.'

'It's pretty much all storage space,' said Julie. 'Living quarters are on the top deck.' A line of viewports was visible. 'Most of the rest of it has no life support.'

'Incredible. What are we carrying?'

'Some rainmakers and a kite,' said Hutch.

Marge Conway showed up moments later. She was a big woman, a onetime ballet dancer, though Hutch would have liked to see the guy who would catch her in his arms and give her a quick spin. More to the point, she was an accomplished climatologist. The years had caught up with her somewhat since the last time Hutch had seen her. Her hair had begun to show patches of gray, and a few lines had appeared around her eyes. But there was still something feline in the way she got around.

Julie took them on board and showed them their compartments.

Avery here, Marge there, sorry folks, they're a little cramped, but they're comfortable.

Hutch had been surprised when Marge announced she would make the flight personally. She didn't seem to mind that it would be a two-year mission. 'Once in a lifetime you get to do something like this,' she said, 'if you're lucky. No way I'm sending somebody else.' Her kids were grown, her husband had not renewed, and she'd explained she wanted to get as far from him as she could.

Hutch stayed with them until it was time to leave. This was of course a different kind of social arrangement from the *al-Jahani*, which had been a small community setting out. The onboard interplay there would be vastly different. Cliques would form, people would make friendships, find others with shared attitudes, and they'd have no real problem.

The *Hawksbill* would be nine months in flight with three people. At the far end, if they were sick of each other, Collingdale could make other arrangements to get them home. But for the better part of a year they'd be sealed together and they would *have* to get along. Hutch had interviewed Marge a couple of days earlier, to reassure herself, and she knew Whitlock well enough to have no qualms about him. They should be all right. But it would be a long trip, and she knew they'd be glad to see daylight at the other end.

While they got settled, she repaired to the bridge with Julie. 'One critical thing you should pass on to Kellie,' she said. 'This ship wasn't designed to go anywhere near omegas. The architecture isn't right, and it could draw the lightning. You hear what I'm saying?'

'Yes, ma'am. I will tell her.'

'She'll be captain during that phase of the operation. I don't care what anybody tells her, she will keep minimum range from the cloud. She'll have it in writing from me long before then, but it's maybe a little more convincing coming from you.'

'I doubt that,' Julie said. 'What's minimum range?'

'Two hundred kilometers is standard for this kind of vessel.'

'Two hundred klicks. Okay. I'll tell her.'

Hutch asked permission to sit in the pilot's seat, and inquired about Julie's parents. Her father was semi-retired, teaching at the University of Maine and still serving as a consultant to the Margaret Tufu Foundation. Her mother Linda was curator of the Star Museum, which contained the third largest collection of extraterrestrial artifacts in North America, behind the Academy Museum and the Smithsonian.

'Say hello for me,' Hutch said.

'I will.'

'I hope you're as good as they are.'

'Yes, ma'am. I am.'

It was the right reply. Hutch shook her hand and gazed at the console, at the navigation monitor to the pilot's right, at the orange ready lamp indicating energy buildup, and she felt again the awesome power of the drive units. Finally, realizing Julie was waiting for her to leave so she could get to her check list, she said good-bye.

She wished Marge and Whitlock success, and strode up the ramp and back into the Wheel.

Gregory MacAllister was waiting when she got home. Tor, who was a better chef than she was, had dinner on. Maureen was entertaining Mac by running in circles while a black kitten watched.

MacAllister was a big man in every sense of the word. He took up a lot of space. He was an intellectual linebacker. When he walked into a room, everyone inevitably came to attention. Mac was an international figure, an editor and essayist whose acquaintance with Hutch had begun when they were stranded together on Deepsix.

He'd become interested in the Goompahs and had called, asking whether he could talk with her about what the Academy intended to do on Lookout.

Hutch explained over the pork chops. She told him about the

147

limitations imposed by the Protocol, about her fears as to what would happen if they set the wrong precedent, about the hedgehogs.

When they finished, they retired to the living room and Hutch put up some pictures of the Goompahs. These were long-range, taken from telescopes on the *Jenkins* and on satellites. There were shots of temples, of the isthmus road and some of its traffic, of farms, of parks and fountains. 'Not bad,' Mac remarked from time to time, obviously impressed with Goompah culture. Hutch understood he was impressed because he hadn't expected much. Hadn't done his homework. 'I thought they were primitives,' he said.

'Why would you think that?' The screen had paused on a picture of three Goompahs, mom, dad, and a kid, probably, almost as if Jack had asked them to pose. A tree like nothing that ever grew on Earth rose behind them, and the images were filled with sunlight.

Mac made a face, suggesting the answer should be obvious. 'Because—' He looked up at one of Tor's paintings, a depiction of a superluminal cruising through moonlight, and paused, uncertain. 'Well, they look dumb. And they have a fifth-century society.' He glanced over at Maureen playing with her dollhouse. 'She has her mother's good looks, Hutch.'

'Thank you.'

'I guess the question at issue is whether the Goompahs are worth all the fuss being made over them.'

'They're worth the fuss,' said Tor. 'They're intelligent.'

MacAllister smiled. 'That puts them ahead of us.'

Gregory MacAllister was not the best-known journalist of the age, but he was certainly the most feared. Acerbic, acid-tongued, not given to taking prisoners, he liked to think of himself as a champion of common sense and a dedicated opponent of buffoonery and hypocrisy in high places. During the course of an interview the previous evening regarding the drive to make light-benders available to the general public, he'd commented that while people have the right to commit suicide, he saw nothing in the Constitution requiring the government to expedite matters. 'Invisible drunks,' he'd said. 'Think about it.' Then he'd added, 'The original sin was stupidity, and it is with us still.'

'Maybe it does,' said Tor. 'That's all the more reason to give them a chance.'

Hutch produced a cold beer for Mac, and wine for herself and Tor. Mac took a pull at the beer, expressed himself satisfied, and asked Tor why he thought the creatures were intelligent.

Tor rolled his eyes. 'You've seen their architecture. And the way they've laid out their cities. What more do you need?'

Mac's eyes usually darkened when he considered the issue of intelligent behavior. They did so now. 'Tor,' he said, 'the bulk of the human race shouldn't be allowed out by themselves at night. A lot of them live near parks, fountains, and even spaceports. But that's assigning worth by reflection.'

'You're not serious.'

Mac had liberated some chocolate cookies from the kitchen. He held one out for Maureen, who took it happily and told Mac he wasn't supposed to give any to Babe. That was the kitten, who showed no interest anyhow. 'Tor,' he said, 'most generations produce a handful of rational people who, so far, have been able to keep us going while everyone else spends his time falling into the works. Most people are programmed by the time they're six, and learn nothing worthwhile afterward.'

Tor made a sound indicating he was in pain. In fact, of course, he was used to Mac's exaggerations and would have expected no less.

But Hutch never got used to it. 'Are you suggesting,' she asked, 'that we should give an IQ test before rescuing someone, or some*thing*, in trouble?'

'Not at all. By all means, we should help anyone if we can reasonably do it. And the Goompahs do look worth saving. But I think you're facing a no-win situation.'

That surprised her. 'How do you mean?'

'You'll probably have to break the Protocol to do anything for them. I mean, you're even going to be shipping relief supplies. How do you possibly get them to these creatures without announcing your presence?' A look of genuine concern passed over his craggy features. 'If you *don't* succeed in helping them and a lot of them get wiped out, or they *all* get wiped out, you won't forgive yourself. And the Academy will take a beating.'

Tor nodded reluctantly. 'He's probably right, Hutch.'

She looked at Mac across the top of her wineglass. And then leveled her gaze at her husband. 'What would you two have me do? Just ignore them? Let them die by the thousands and not lift a finger?'

For a time no one spoke. Maureen looked at her oddly, as if Mommy had misbehaved. Babe the kitten came over and tried to chew on her ankle.

'I take it,' said Mac, 'that there really *is* no way of shutting down the cloud?'

'None that we've been able to figure out. There's never been enough money to fund a serious effort.'

Mac laughed. 'But there's enough money to underwrite the farming industries. And to provide tax breaks for General Power and Anderson & Goodbody.' He growled. 'The truth is that it's hard to justify spending money on a hazard that's so far off, Hutch. Or that's threatening somebody else. Still, I can understand the reluctance.'

She knew that. Mac had remained silent while major pundits laughed at Senator Blasingame, when he'd put together a bill demanding an extensive effort to find a way to neutralize the omegas. Blasingame had even made Hal Bodley's annual Boondoggle List. Mac might have been able to stem the tide had he gotten into the fight.

'We could have used you,' she said.

'Hutch, the sun's going to expand in a few billion years and wipe out all life on Earth. Maybe we should do something about that, as well.'

'Try to keep it serious, Mac,' she said.

'Okay.' He emptied his glass, trundled out to the kitchen, and came back with a refill. It was an uncomfortable moment, and Hutch suspected she shouldn't have said anything, but damn it, Mac's point of view was shortsighted. Maureen got a pulltoy out and she and the kitten retreated into the den.

Rachmaninoff's Concerto Number Two was playing softly in the background. Light swept briefly through the window as a flyer descended onto the landing pad they shared with the Hoffmanns.

'It strikes me,' Mac said, easing back into his chair, 'that it's not true. Or at least, it's not a *universal* truth.'

'What isn't, Mac?'

'That cultures get swamped when they encounter a more developed civilization.'

'Can you name an exception?'

'Sure,' he said. 'India.'

'They weren't swamped,' said Tor. 'But they were taken over.'

'That doesn't count. The Brits at the time were imperialists. That wouldn't apply on Lookout. But my point is that Indian culture survived pretty well. The essentials, their music, their marital patterns, their self-image, didn't change at all.'

'What about the Native Americans?'

He smiled. 'It's a myth, Hutch. They didn't collapse because they were faced with an intrinsically stronger culture. They were beaten down by a superior military. And maybe because their own cultural habits wouldn't allow them to unite.'

'Priscilla, if I felt the way you do, I wouldn't mess around with all these half measures.'

'What would you do, Mac?'

'I'd send the Peacekeepers out there and get them all out of the cities when the damned thing gets close. Get them behind rocks or in caves or whatever else they have until it passes. It only takes a day or so, right?'

'Mac, I can't do that.'

'Then you don't have the courage of your convictions.'

She glanced over at Tor. He was shaking his head at her. You know better than to take Mac seriously. Relax. Let it go.

'There is this,' pursued Mac. 'If you called out the troops, you'd have the satisfaction of knowing you gave it your best shot.'

Maureen had finished her cookie, leaving crumbs everywhere. Hutch let her head drift back for a moment, then got up and took Maureen's hand. 'Time for bed, Mo.'

'Too early, Mommy,' said the child, who began to fill up. She hated going to bed when they had company. She especially liked Mac. What on Earth was there about him that a child could love?

'We'll read for a while,' she said. 'Say good night to Uncle Mac.'

Maureen made a sad face at Mac. 'Good night, Uncle Mac,' she said. And she reached for him, and kissed his cheek.

'Good night, darling,' said Mac.

Hutch could hear them chattering away downstairs while she read to Maureen. Benny Rabbit makes friends with Oscar the Cat. Hutch would believe it when she saw it. But Maureen giggled and Babe the kitten joined them and stayed when Maureen fell asleep and Hutch turned out the lamp and went downstairs.

They were talking about Paxon Carbury's latest novel, *Morley Park*. It had gotten strong reviews, and Tor had liked it, but Mac was consigning it to the unwashed. 'It's just more adultery in the suburbs,' he said.

And that seemed to settle it. Tor made a few objections, tried to explain what he had liked about the book, then backed off. Mac asked Hutch whether she'd read it.

'No,' she said. 'I've been a little pressed lately.'

In the background, the commlink chimed. Hutch excused herself and went into the dining room. 'Who is it, George?'

'*Academy watch officer*,' said the AI.

She was beginning to hate these calls. A screen lit up. Actually it was Charlie. '*I hate to bother you at home*,' he said.

'Yes, Charlie, what have you got?'

'*You wanted to hear anything that came in on the hedgehogs.*'

'What happened?'

'*They found another one.*'

'Who?'

'*The Santiago. We don't have any details yet. But it's beginning to look as if they all have them. All the clouds, I mean.*'

'Yes, Charlie, I think you're right. Thanks. Let me know if you hear anything else.'

'*There is something else.*'

'Yes?'

'*We don't think the hedgehogs and the clouds are actually running at the same velocity.*'

'Oh? I didn't think any questions had been raised about that.'

'*They hadn't. The difference is so slight, it's hard to detect. Even now, we're not really certain. But it looks as if the hedgehogs are moving a bit slower.*'

'How much?'

'*Almost too little difference to measure. It's why we didn't pick it up at first. I mean, a cloud's not a solid object, so you don't really get—*'

'How much difference, Charlie?'

'*The escorts are slower by between four and five meters an hour.*'

'All of them?'

'*Two of them. We're still trying to get measurements on the others.*'

She didn't know what to make of it. It didn't sound especially important until she found herself telling Tor and Mac about it. And suddenly the lights went on and a chill ran through the room. 'Dumb,' she said, breaking into the middle of a sentence.

'What is?' asked Tor.

'Me. *I* am.'

'In what way, Priscilla?' said Mac.

153

'You know about the tewks. We think they all happen where there are clouds.'

'And—?'

'If each cloud has a hedgehog, and each hedgehog is running at a slightly slower speed so that the cloud eventually overtakes it—'

'Oh,' said Mac.

'The escorts are exactly the sort of things that the clouds seem to want to attack. Lots of right angles. Couple hundred of them.'

Tor was nodding. 'They're designated targets.'

'I think so,' she said. 'Has to be.'

Mac couldn't accept the idea. 'Not at those rates of closure. You're talking a couple of thousand years before the clouds catch the damned things.'

'But what's the point?' asked Tor. 'I don't get it.'

She reactivated her link. 'Charlie?'

'*Yes, Hutch?*'

'Contact Serenity. Tell Audrey the hedgehogs may be triggers.'

'*Triggers?*'

'Right. They go boom. And they initiate something.'

'Like what?'

'Like a tewk. Listen, I'll be in touch with her tomorrow. Meantime, I want her to start looking at sending a mission to push one of the damned things into a cloud. See what happens.'

'*I'll tell her.*'

'Explain that we'll want the whole thing done by robot. Nobody is to go anywhere near any part of the operation. Okay?'

'*Yes, ma'am. I'll pass it on.*'

She switched off. 'When you talk to her tomorrow—' said Tor.

'Yes—?'

'Tell her to pick a cloud that's well away from anybody's neighborhood.'

LIBRARY ENTRY

The stores are filling up with Goompah dolls, and we are becoming increasingly aware of the existence of these terminally cute off-world wobblies. Children cannot resist them. They are showing up in games and books. There is already an activist society devoted to their welfare. Yet they face possible extinction.

It may be necessary to lay the Noninterference Protocol aside. Indeed, it's hard to see how we can go to their rescue without doing so. But it would help if we defined the exception as a one-time only affair. Make it clear that we are not setting a precedent, and draw a line across which interested manufacturers, religious groups, charitable organizations, trading companies, and everybody else who'd like to use these creatures to play out their own fantasies and ambitions, may not venture.

—Gregory MacAllister
'How's the Jihad Going?'
Lost on Earth Interview, Monday, March 17

11

On board the *Jenkins*, in orbit around Lookout.
Tuesday, March 18.

> . . . *Be advised that your primary objective is to get the job done. If you find it necessary to set the Protocol aside, this constitutes your authority to do so* . . .
> . . . *Collect and run analyses of food samples* . . .
> . . . *Time is of the essence. In view of the lag between Lookout and your other points of contact, you are free to use discretion.*

In fact, Jack didn't like the idea of using discretion. Not in this kind of situation. It was purely political. No matter what he did, and how things turned out, he would be criticized. Any blame to be assigned would come his way, and credit would go to the Second Floor at the Academy. He'd been around too long not to know how these things worked.

After watching Hutchins's transmission, Winnie was exasperated, too. 'How,' she demanded, 'do they expect us to record conversations down there? For a start, where are we going to get recording equipment?'

'We might be able to rig some pickups,' said Digger.

157

It had required more than two weeks for their report to cross the interstellar gulfs, and the answer to come back. And their instructions had been a surprise. They were to attempt to establish contact with the Goompahs. They were to record conversations, if in fact these creatures actually conversed, and send the results back, where a team of linguists would work to break into the language. They were to get visuals of the creatures as they spoke, so that nonverbal cues could be included in the translation effort. And they were to provide whatever additional information they could to help ferret out meaning. And they were to do all this, preferably, while respecting the Protocol.

Preferably.

Bureaucratic double-talk.

Translation: Get the job done without compromising the Protocol. If you compromise the Protocol, and things go badly, you will be asked why you found it necessary to do so.

Markover knew Hutchins, had always thought he could trust her, but he'd been around too long not to understand how these things went.

There was good news: The air sample analyses they'd transmitted to Broadside had undergone additional tests. No dangerous bioagents had been found, and no toxins. That was no surprise: So far, experience indicated that diseases from one world generally had no effect on life-forms from another. (Just as creatures operating outside their own biosystem would have a hard time finding anything digestible.) They could, if necessary, operate for a short time outside the e-suits.

Jack and Winnie both had notebooks, which were, of course, equipped with audio recorders and projectors. These could be used as pickups. Kellie said she thought the ship could contribute three more units.

'So how do we go about this?' asked Winnie.

Jack could see only one way. 'I think,' he said, 'if you read between the lines, we just go down and say hello. See how they react.'

Digger reread the message. '*That's* not what I see between the lines.'

'What do *you* see?'

'The message literally says that we can ignore the Protocol. But she'd like us to use our imagination and find a better way.'

Jack liked to think of himself as the kindly old director. Patient, easygoing, willing to listen. And to an extent he was correct. But it wasn't true that he had no temper; he was simply quite good at not letting people see it. This business with Hutch's message, though, was exactly the sort of thing that drove him up the wall. Because she was laying out contradictory propositions. If she could think of a way to accomplish what she wanted without talking directly to the Goompahs, why didn't she say so? Or, if she couldn't, why not just tell him flat out to take care of things.

'Do you know of a better way?' he asked.

'No,' said Digger.

Winnie looked out the viewport, peering down into the sun-streaked atmosphere, as though she could find an answer out there somewhere.

'Well,' said Jack, 'barring any other ideas, I think what we do is go down and say hello. See how they react. Then we plant some pickups so we can start recording their conversations.' He swung around in his seat and looked at the transmission again.

'First thing we want to do,' said Jack, 'is to create an avatar. One of us to say hello.'

'All right,' said Winnie. 'You don't think we'd do better to have someone just step out and wave?'

'Too dangerous. Let's see what they do when they see the avatar.' He looked around. 'We need pictures of somebody who looks friendly.'

Winnie studied each of them as if that was no easy task. 'Who do you suggest?'

'One of the women,' said Digger. 'They'll be less threatening.'

159

Kellie was watching him carefully, her nose wrinkled, trying to restrain a smile. 'I think *you'd* be our best bet, Dig.'

'Me? Why?'

But he knew. Nobody had to say it. Digger possessed a slight approximation to their size and shape. He was a bit overweight, and somewhat less than average height.

'I think that'll work fine,' said Jack. 'So we let them take a look at the avatar. It waves and says hello, and if things go well, we shut off the visuals and, Digger, you step out of the underbrush and continue the conversation. Make friends on the spot.'

'First ambassador from Earth,' said Winnie.

Digger sucked in his belly.

Kellie beamed at him. 'I'm proud of you, Dig.' She circled him, measuring his dimensions. 'We should give him a large shirt. Yellow, I think. Green leggings. Nice floppy hat. Get you looking a little bit like one of the locals.'

That hurt. 'You think I look like a Goompah?'

'No.' Kellie laughed and gave him a hug. 'You're cuter than they are. And you have a great smile.' She paused and must have seen he was embarrassed. Her tone changed: 'Digger, you're easy to like.' She gripped his arm. 'If they'll respond to any of us, it'll be you.'

Digger conceded. 'Doesn't fool me for a minute,' he grumbled. 'And I don't waddle, you know.'

Kellie embraced him again. Longer this time. 'We know that, Dig.' Her eyes told him she meant it. Or, if he did waddle, it didn't matter to her. Either way, he guessed it was all right.

They produced the appropriate clothing, floppy everything, and he put it on, a bright yellow shirt that felt as if it was made from sailcloth, and baggy green leggings and sandals three sizes too big. Most of it, Kellie informed him, was made from blankets. The sandals had belonged to the previous skipper. A woman's red hat, origin unknown, came out of storage. Looked as if it had been with the ship for years.

When he was dressed they took pictures of him. 'Why not make me look like a Goompah?' he suggested. 'Why stop here?'

He half expected someone to remark that he already did. But Jack, reading his mind, only smiled. 'Because eventually,' he said, 'we'll have to be able to talk to them. The avatar needs to look like you. Not them.'

They made up the visuals and jury-rigged a projector by removing the heart of one of the VRs and connecting it to the power cells from a laser cutter. In the same way, they constructed three audiovisual pickups. They were clumsy and bigger than they'd have preferred. But the things worked, and that was sufficient for the moment. 'All set,' said Kellie, after they'd tested everything.

Below, it was early morning on the isthmus, a couple of hours before dawn. 'Who wants to come?' asked Jack.

'I guess I'm going,' said Digger.

And Kellie would pilot. 'Winnie,' he said, 'you hold the fort.'

She shook Digger's hand solemnly as he started toward the cargo bay. Good luck, Dig, the body language said. I'm with you, kid.

The cargo bay also served as the launch area. Digger's pulse picked up a few notches as they descended through the ship. He was telling himself to relax, don't worry, we're about to make history. Hello, Goompahs.

The lander was a sleek, teardrop craft. It had less capacity than the older, boxy vehicles, but it provided a smoother ride. They climbed in, and Kellie started the launch process.

Jack began dispensing advice. He was a good guy, but he was a bit too helpful. If we decide it's okay for you to show yourself, don't make any sudden moves. Try to smile. Nonverbals are different from culture to culture, but the Noks and the Angels both recognize smiles, so it can't hurt. Unless, of course, things are different here.

He continued in that vein despite all Digger's efforts to change the subject, until finally Dig simply asked him to stop. 'You're getting me rattled,' he complained.

'I'm sorry. Listen, Dig, everything'll be okay.'

Digger sat there in his native finery, feeling both foolish and scared. The Goompahs looked friendly. But he'd read about the Angels on Paradise, how harmless they'd looked, how *angelic*, before they tore two members of the Contact Society to shreds.

'I'm fine, Jack,' he said. 'I just wish I knew the language.'

They dropped through a cloudless sky. The ground was dark despite innumerable individual lights. But they were mere sparks in the night, like distant stars, a few in the cities, some on the isthmus road, and a handful along the docks and on anchored ships.

They had no way of concealing the lander, and though Kellie turned off all the lights, they were nonetheless descending through a cloudless moonlit sky. Kellie, up front in the pilot's seat, held up five fingers to signify everything was okay. 'All in it together,' she said.

Jack sat lost in thought. 'I wonder,' he said, 'if we could do this strictly through the use of avatars.'

'How do you mean, Jack?' asked Digger.

'Produce a native avatar and stick with it. We stay out of sight altogether.'

Digger thought about it. 'Eventually,' he said, 'it would have to talk to them.'

Jack made a pained sound. The avatar could not be made spontaneous. It could be programmed to deliver lines, but unless they knew how the Goompahs would react, there was no way to have it respond to them.

'Just as well,' Jack said. 'You look so good it would be a pity not to put you out there.' Har-har.

Digger sat in his chair, thinking how this was the gutsiest thing he'd done in his life. Except maybe for the time in high school when he'd gotten his courage together and asked Veronica Keating for a date. Veronica had passed – thanks but I'm tied up for the next couple years – but he'd tried. Next time out of the barn he'd done better. With somebody else, of course.

They picked up some wind as they descended. Digger would have liked to open a window to get a sense of what the sea and the forest smelled like. Of course, they couldn't do that. The atmosphere was breathable, but it was oxygen-rich. He didn't know what the effect of that would be over an extended period, but it couldn't be good.

Jack was looking at the map, trying to decide where they should set down. 'Here,' he said at last, indicating the isthmus road a short distance north of the city with the temple by the sea.

The temple, lost in darkness now, looked Greek. That made the city Athens. He smiled at the notion. Athenians as oversize green critters waddling around.

He couldn't see anything out the windows other than the stars and the lights on the ground.

'You all set?' asked Jack, trying to relieve the tension.

'I'll be okay.' He wasn't used to riding in the lander with the navigation lights out. It was hard to say why, but it was disquieting, as if they were sneaking up on an enemy stronghold. Kellie had done something to render the vehicle quieter than usual, had made it virtually silent.

'Be on the ground in two minutes, gentlemen,' she said. 'Activate your suits.'

Digger checked his harness and his converter, and complied. One advantage of a relatively earthlike atmosphere was that they didn't have to haul air tanks around. The converter would provide an air supply from the existing atmosphere. Jack switched his on, and Digger momentarily caught the glow of the Flickinger field in the moment of ignition. Then it faded.

He activated his suit, pulled on a vest, attached his converter, and wondered briefly if he should have brought some trinkets to hand out to the natives.

Below, lanterns floated through the dark, spread out, and vanished. Trees rose around him. Kellie held the vehicle aloft for a moment to ensure that the ground was solid, then let the weight settle. They were down in a glade, the first streaks of light showing in the east.

It was Digger's first time on a world that could really be said to be alive. He squeezed Kellie's shoulder and shook hands with Jack. They were now eligible to join the Corbin Society, whose membership was limited to people who had made a first landing on a world with life-forms big enough to be visible. The Society was named for the director of the Tar-bell mission, who, forty-five years before, had been the first to look out a window across extraterrestrial soil and see a live animal. In his case, it had been a large reptile, still the biggest land creature on record. It had inspected, then tried to eat, the lander.

Kellie turned on her e-suit. Her voice sounded in his link. 'It's almost dawn. By the time we get out to the road, it should be daylight.'

Jack's notebook would provide the projector. He pushed it into a vest pocket and handed the avatar disk to Digger. 'You hang on to this,' he said.

Digger nodded, released his restraints, and started for the airlock.

Kellie got out of her seat and pocketed the second notebook. 'You might want to use the washroom before we leave. It'll be a while before we get back here.' Their e-suits had no provision for disposing of bodily waste. Attachments were available but no one saw any need for them on this trip. Just get out, go to the road, say hello, and see how the locals respond. Then hustle back to the lander. Simple enough.

They went through the airlock and stood momentarily in the outer hatch. There was some fluttering in the trees, and the steady clacking of insects, but otherwise the forest remained quiet. They switched on dark lights. Digger would have preferred a regular lamp, but who knew what might be wandering around in the woods.

'Everyone ready?' asked Jack, climbing down onto sawtooth grass. He knelt, reacted with an *ouch*, and said, 'Be careful. It's sharp.'

In fact it was like a field of daggers. Digger squared his shoulders the way he had seen Jack Hancock do when facing danger in a dozen sims. He cautioned Kellie and stepped aside to let her pass. Then he fell in behind to bring up the rear.

They all wore pistols, just in case. Digger was qualified but unpracticed. He'd never before been on ground where there was a risk from local wildlife.

The line of trees was dark and quiet. Jack paused, looking for a break in the forest. Shrubbery, blossoms, vines, thorns, dead leaves, and misshapen trees crowded on them. Jack picked a spot and plunged in. Kellie followed, and Digger watched her plow through a spiderweb. Or something's web. Digger remembered reading somewhere that, so far, spiders had been found only on Earth. Even safely enveloped in the Flickinger field, he felt queasy about them.

It was slow going. The vegetation was thick, and the e-suits provided no defense against thorns and needles. The road was less than a half klick away from the landing site, but after an hour's time they were still struggling through heavy growth.

Winnie called from the ship twice to ask why it was taking so long. Jack, who usually stayed cool, told her that next time she should come and her grasp of the situation would improve.

Then he felt badly about growling at her and apologized. On his private circuit, he told Digger that he understood why she was worried, that anything could happen, that nobody really knew what kind of creatures might be loose in this forest.

That did nothing for Digger's state of mind.

Through breaks in the canopy of overhead branches and leaves, they saw the ship, a bright star moving through the fixed constellations. That alone, he realized, in a low-tech culture, could be enough to cause a major reaction.

The eastern horizon was getting bright. Behind him, in the

bushes, something moved, and there was a brief scuffle. But Digger never saw anything.

'Road,' said Jack.

At last. Digger came up beside him and looked out at it. It was really only a trail. But it had been laboriously cut through the forest, and it was wide enough for two wagons to pass side by side.

There was a low hill directly opposite. 'He should stand up there,' said Jack, referring to the avatar. 'On the crest. I'd say under the tree would be good.'

The tree looked more like an overgrown mushroom. Digger surveyed the area. To his left, north, the road proceeded another fifty meters or so before disappearing over the top of a hill. To his right, toward Athens, he could see for a considerable distance, maybe the length of a football field, before it curved off into the forest.

They crossed the road, climbed the hill, and hid themselves behind a clump of bushes with bright red blossoms. Digger handed over the disk, which Jack inserted into his notebook. 'Test run, Holmes?' he asked.

'Indubitably, old chap.'

The notebook was equipped with a projector on its leading edge. Jack aimed it toward the tree, which was about ten meters away, and punched a button. Digger's image, in green and gold and with his bright red hat, blinked on. He was standing a half meter in the air. Jack adjusted the picture, focused it, and brought the feet to Earth. Then he turned to Digger. 'Okay,' he said. 'I think we're in business.'

There were green trees, and pale gray growths like the big mushroom at the top of the hill. The wind sucked at them all, and when Digger closed his eyes, it sounded like any forest back home. Avery Whitlock had once written that all forests were alike in their essence, that there was a kind of universal forest that was a prerequisite for intelligent life. *Wherever sentience is found*, he'd predicted, *it will have come to fruition in a deep wood*.

Kellie produced the second notebook and assured Digger she would take pictures and record everything for his grandchildren. She apparently thought remarks like that would put everybody off the trail of what was really happening (or not happening) between the two of them. But Jack was too excited wondering what was going to come around the curve in one direction or over the hill in the other, to give a damn about onboard romance.

'*Traffic on the road.*' Winnie's voice. As planned, she was watching through the ship's scopes and satellites. (The ship by then was over the horizon and somewhere on the other side of the world.) As long as the sky stayed clear, the *Jenkins* would have them constantly in view. '*Looks like two of them. And a cart.*'

'Thanks, Winnie.'

'*And a few more behind. Three on foot. And a second cart. Make that two, no, three, more carts. They're coming from the south. About a half kilometer from you.*'

Around the curve.

They waited, listening to the wind until they heard the sounds of creaking wheels, snorting, heavy clop-clops. And music. Pipes and stringed instruments, Digger thought. And thumping on a drum. And voices in allegro, maybe a little high-pitched.

The song, if that was what it was, lacked the easy rhythms of human melodies. 'They're not exactly Ben and the War-birds,' Kellie observed.

Well, no. The voices were a bit lacking. But the critical news was that Digger hadn't heard anything yet that wasn't within the range of human capabilities.

'But you'll need women to do it,' commented Kellie.

A large animal rounded the bend, hauling a cart, and lumbered toward them. It was one of the rhinos they'd spotted from orbit, big, heavy, with long tusks, and a body shaped like a barrel. The eyes were larger than a rhino's, though; they were saucer-shaped and had the same sad expression that was so prominent a part of the inhabitants' physiognomy. The eyes turned their way, and

Digger got the distinct impression the beast could see them through their screen of shrubbery.

'Maybe it can smell us,' said Digger.

'No.' Kellie's voice had gone flat. The way it might if she perceived danger. 'Not through the e-suit.'

Jack activated the recorder in the notebook.

The cart was loaded with plants. Vegetables, maybe? Two Goompahs sat in the vehicle, singing at the top of their lungs. It was all off-key.

'I'm tempted to take my chances,' said Jack, 'and just go out and say hello.'

'Don't do it,' said Kellie.

And there came the three on foot. And the other three wagons. They were filled with passengers. Everybody was singing. They plucked on instruments that looked like lutes, blew into pipes, and pounded on the sides of the carts. They were having a roaring good time.

'They know how to travel,' said Kellie.

There were eleven Goompahs in all. 'Too many,' said Jack. 'Let them go.'

'Why?' asked Digger. 'They're in a good mood. Isn't that what we want?'

'If they turn out to be hostile, there are too many. I want to be able to get clear if things take a bad turn.'

Some had mammaries. All were clumsy. Hadn't evolution worked at all on this world? Digger couldn't imagine how they'd avoided predators.

The convoy passed, gradually climbed to the crest of the hill and disappeared beyond.

Ten minutes later they got their chance. They heard the crunch of footsteps coming over the hill. A lone pedestrian appeared at the top. He carried a staff and swung it jauntily from side to side as he started down.

He wore boots and red leggings and a shirt made of hide. A

yellow cap was pulled almost rakishly over one saucer eye. 'Ladies' man,' said Kellie.

The sky was clear. 'Anybody else on the road?' Jack asked Winnie.

'Not anywhere near you.'

It struck Digger that the fact the creature was traveling alone said a great deal about the kind of society in which it lived. In early Europe, strolling about the highways without an armed escort would have been an exercise in recklessness.

Digger felt Kellie's hand on his shoulder. Here we go.

Jack waited until the traveler was immediately adjacent. Then he switched on the projector. Digger's avatar appeared gradually atop the crest opposite, as if striding up from the far side, paused on its summit, and waved.

The traveler swung his large head in the avatar's direction. *'Hello, friend,'* the avatar said cheerfully, in English. *'How are you doing?'*

The Goompah stared.

The avatar raised its hand and waved again.

The Goompah's eyes widened, grew enormous.

The avatar started slowly down the slope.

The Goompah growled and showed a set of incisors Digger hadn't seen before. It retreated a step, but quickly found its back against a tree.

'How are you today?' the avatar asked. *'What a lovely day this is. I just happened to be in the neighborhood and thought I'd pop by. Say hello.'*

'Careful,' said Kellie.

The Goompah edged away from the tree, back in the direction from which it had come. It bowed its head, and Digger could see its lips moving although he couldn't hear any sounds. It was, if he was reading the signs correctly, terrified.

'What's happening?' asked Winnie.

Kellie told her to wait a minute.

The creature was shaking its head from side to side. It moaned

169

and choked and spasmed. It threatened the avatar with its staff. It waved its hands, odd gestures, signs almost.

'This isn't going well,' said Jack.

'*Where are you headed, friend?*' asked the avatar, oblivious of the effect it was having. '*By the way, my name's Digger.*' It waved yet again, in the friendliest possible fashion.

The Goompah opened its mouth and said '*Morghani,*' or something very much like it. Then it turned and sprinted back the way it had come, moving far more quickly than Digger would have thought possible. It swayed wildly from side to side, tumbled but picked itself up without breaking stride, charged up the hill at the end of the road, and disappeared behind it.

When it was gone, the avatar said, '*It's been good talking with you.*'

Kellie couldn't resist snickering. 'You *are* pretty fearsome,' she said, 'now that I think of it.'

Digger thought they should go back to the lander and rethink things. But getting back there would be a battle, and Kellie told him he was giving up too easily. Jack agreed and that was the vote that counted.

'The problem,' Jack argued, 'was that the image wasn't responsive. The thing got scared, and the avatar can't shrug, and say, "Hey buddy, it's okay, don't worry."'

'But who here can speak Goompah?' asked Digger.

'Don't have to,' said Jack. 'All we need is a rational reaction. A sign that we can deal with them on a one-to-one basis. Nonverbals will do it.'

'What are you suggesting?'

'We dispense with the avatar.'

It didn't matter. The second attempt, with Digger in the flesh trying to be friendly, went pretty much the same way. They passed on a couple of single travelers, selecting instead a group of four, bouncing along in a wagon pulled by one of the rhinos. Should have been enough to grant a sense of security to the proceedings. But they took one look at Digger, the real Digger, safely perched atop his hill so that a quick retreat was feasible, and went screaming back down the road, abandoning their wagon and the rhino.

'Well,' he told Kellie, 'I'm beginning to wonder if I'm not quite as charming as I always thought.'

'Eye of the beholder,' she said, turning to Jack. 'What do we do now?'

'I'm not sure.'

'How about walking in through the front door? Just stroll right into the city.'

'I don't think so.'

He asked Winnie to send a report to Hutch, informing her that initial attempts at contact had been unsuccessful.

'Do you want to say that we'll try again?'

'Yes,' he said, but Digger knew that tone. He'd decided it wasn't a good idea.

'Having successfully completed phase one,' said Kellie, 'we should turn our attention to figuring out how to plant the pickups.'

They brought up images of the cities and looked through them one by one. All had waterfront areas, and that's where the shops tended to be. And where the population clustered. 'I say we go into downtown Athens,' Digger said. 'How many pickups do we have? Six?'

'Five,' said Kellie. 'Including the notebooks.'

There was one other assignment: The Academy wanted information on Goompah nutrition. During the past two weeks, they'd seen the Goompahs eating a variety of fruits, vegetables, meat, and fish. (At least, that's what it looked like through the telescopes.) Some of the fruit they'd seen hung on trees in their immediate area. Red pears, large golden melons that looked delicious, small silver apples. They picked up samples of everything.

In addition to buildings that appeared to be ordinary cabins or dwellings for housing individuals or small families, there were structures clearly intended to be living quarters, but they were big, rambling places, with wings and upper floors, large enough to provide shelter to fifty or more. And the places looked occupied and busy.

When they had seen enough, they retired to the lander to await the coming of dark.

It didn't take long. A twenty-two-hour rotational period created a short day. Jack napped, while Kellie watched for intruders and Digger watched Kellie. But the woods stayed quiet, and the afternoon passed without incident. Winnie informed them that there was still occasional traffic on the highway, in case they 'wanted to try again.' She sounded serious. Digger half expected that the palace guard and the local militia would arrive to put a volley of arrows into whatever the thing was that had been seen terrifying travelers along the isthmus road. But the area remained quiet, and Winnie observed nothing that looked like a militia response.

Clouds gathered, and rain began to fall. By sunset it was a steady downpour. Ideal weather for strange creatures that needed to get out and do some lurking.

When night came, it grew absolutely dark. Back-of-the-basement locked-in-the-storage-bin dark. There wasn't a speck of light out there anywhere. There was no way to judge, of course, the quality of the locals' ability to see at night, but they did have large eyes.

Jack, however, had a substantial advantage: night goggles. Kellie got them out of the supply locker, and ten minutes later the lander, operating in silent mode, drifted through heavy rain over Athens and its harbor.

Athens was medium-sized, compared with the other Goompah cities. It was located on the eastern side of the isthmus. Four piers jutted out into the harbor, where a few ships lay at anchor. Tumbledown storage facilities lined the waterfront. Lights flickered in one or two of them. The streets were deserted. 'A part of Athens you don't usually hear about,' said Digger.

Jack smiled in the glow of the instrument panel. 'Nobody uses Doric columns to build warehouses,' he said. His tone suggested it was wisdom for the ages.

Kellie brought them down alongside one of the piers. Jack turned in his seat and looked back at Digger. 'Listen, if you want, *I'm* willing to do this.'

Digger would have been happy to turn the job over to him. But Kellie would never have approved, would have seen it as an act of cowardice. Jack was not young, was slow afoot, and would have a difficult time if the mission went wrong. This was a rare chance for Digger to show off. And he suspected there was no real danger. Goompahs were terrified of him, so what did he have to fear? 'You don't have the build,' he said laconically. 'Or the clothes.'

He stuffed the pickups and the notebooks into a bag and headed for the airlock. 'Be careful,' Kellie said. She surprised him with a quick embrace.

He slipped through the hatch, looked around, saw nothing moving, and stepped out onto the pier.

The sea was high, and the wind tried to push him into the water. The e-suit kept him comfortable but he knew it was cold out there.

He signaled to Kellie, and she began to pull away. '*Good luck, Champ,*' she said.

Digger hurried off the pier and slipped into a narrow street. There were small wooden buildings on either side, mostly sheds. But there was noise ahead: music and loud gargling sounds and pounding like the pounding he'd heard on the road. He rounded a corner and saw an open-front café.

It was half-empty, but the Goompahs inside were drinking, eating, dancing, and having a good time. The café was located in a dreary four-story stone building. A stout wooden canopy was erected to protect daytime patrons from the sun. He stood beneath it, peering into the interior, when two Goompahs he had not seen passed behind him and wandered into the café without giving him a second look.

173

He strolled closer, squeezing down inside his shirt and pulling his wide-brimmed hat down over his face.

The pickups, because they were jury-rigged, were of different sizes and shapes. Each had a strip of adhesive affixed that would allow him to attach it to a flat surface.

The café was an ideal spot, and the obvious flat surface was in the juncture of cross-fitting wooden beams supporting the canopy. Digger wandered casually close to it, and was able to stay out of sight of the customers while he put one of the notebooks in place. He'd have preferred to install it higher, where it would be less visible and out of everyone's reach. But it was reasonably well hidden, and he thought it would probably be okay for a while.

He withdrew into the shadows and away from the noise. 'Jack,' he said. 'I just planted number four. How's it look?'

'*Good. Perfect. One thing, we won't have any problem hearing them.*'

The area was lined with wooden stalls hung with skins. Rain poured down on them. Somewhere, down the street and around a corner, there was more noise. Another drinking establishment, obviously. He tried to look in a couple of the shops, but they were locked.

The streets were becoming a swamp. Occasionally, figures hurried along, bundled against the downpour, too intent on keeping dry to think much about strangers. One of these came out from behind a wall without warning and almost collided with Digger. The creature said something, glanced at him, and its eyes went wide. Digger smiled back and said, 'Hi,' in his best falsetto.

The creature shrieked.

Digger broke into a run, turned left behind a shed, cut across a muddy expanse of open ground, and found himself in a quiet street of stone-and-brick houses. He listened for a long moment, heard sounds of commotion behind him, but there was no evidence of pursuit.

'*How you doing?*' asked Kellie. He jumped at the sound of the voice.

'I just crashed into one of them.'

'*You're kidding.*'

'I never kid. I think the thing saw enough of me to realize I wasn't a local.' He couldn't altogether keep the pride out of his voice.

'*Are you okay now?*'

He found an alley and turned into it. 'I think so.'

'*If he gets too curious, just show him what you really look like.*'

'Har, har.' The sounds behind him were dying down. And the street remained empty.

'*Maybe you should just plant the pickups and get back here.*'

'Relax,' he said. 'Everything's under control.' But something was coming. Two animals, large-jawed, trimmer than the rhinos, sort of like fat horses. Two Goompahs rode them, bent against the storm. He hurried to the other end of the alley and came out on a street that was given over to more shops.

He found occasional bits of vegetable and meat or fish lying about. He recovered them and dropped them into sample bags, grateful for the Flickinger field that prevented his having to touch them. Some of the stuff looked repulsive.

He broke into a storage building, found an office, and planted one of Kellie's pickups. He got it up on a shelf, between vases, where it seemed relatively safe. The truth was that none of these devices could really be hidden. Later, when the shipment they'd been promised from Broadside showed up, they'd be working with units not much bigger than coins.

He hid the third pickup in a tree near a meat shop. And the fourth in a park, aimed at a couple of benches.

Two blocks away, there were buildings whose architecture had been taken seriously and which were therefore probably either public or religious. Or both.

Several of them had signs outside. The signs contained some hand-drawn pictures, of Goompahs, and of a boat, and, on another, of a torch. There was writing on all of them, delicate, slender characters that reminded him of Arabic.

175

He took pictures, then tried a door. It opened, and he stepped into a long, high-ceilinged hallway. No lights anywhere. No sounds.

The floor might have been made of marble. The walls were dark-stained wood, and suggested that the authorities were not without resources. Several sets of large doors lined the corridor. He opened one and looked in.

It might have been a theater-in-the-round. Or possibly an auditorium. A platform stood in the center of a large room, surrounded by several hundred oversize seats.

Perfect. Digger found a column, climbed atop a seat, and attached the last pickup, the remaining notebook, as high as he could, aiming it at the platform.

They tested it on the lander, and Jack pronounced it satisfactory.

Time to go back.

The rain had finally stopped, and Digger was within a block of the waterfront, moving through the shadows, when a pair of doors directly across the street banged open, light spilled into the night, and a crowd began to pile out. It was too late to duck, so he tried to squeeze down, to minimize his height, and kept going. But several were looking at him already. And the voices died off completely. 'I've attracted attention, Jack.'

'*You need help?*'

Sure. A lot of help Jack would be. 'No. Stay put. I think they they're wondering about my size.'

'*Yeah. It's probably not* de rigueur *in that neighborhood.*'

Digger wished he had a bigger collar to pull up. He stared at the street and kept walking, but he could feel their eyes on him until he got past them. He wanted to break into a run. He heard nothing behind him. No movement, no sound. It was eerie.

A Goompah appeared in front, coming in his direction. On the same side of the street. There was no way to get around him, no way to avoid being seen. The Goompah's eyes reacted, in a reflex

176

that was becoming painfully familiar. It squealed, turned, and fled. The shriek triggered the crowd, which joined in the screaming, but they were coming after him. Something sailed past his head.

That put Digger in the impossible position of seeming to chase the fleeing Goompah, whose cries must have been audible all over the waterfront.

They reached the end of the street, the Goompah barreling along in abject terror, Digger right on its heels. It turned right, the direction Dig needed to go to get to the pier where the rendezvous was to take place. But the creature, out of its mind with fear, fell down and rolled out of the way.

Digger was distancing the crowd. 'Jack,' he said, 'pier in three minutes.'

All five pickups passed their field tests, and they were recording that night. Digger watched and listened with satisfaction as the day's customers haggled and pleaded, criticized and pressed their hands to the tops of their skulls in dismay. They watched a supervisor behind a desk working with subordinates and occasionally reporting to others to whom he was responsible. They watched young Goompahs romp in a park while older ones sat on benches and carried on animated conversations. And they watched a seminar of some sort conducted from the stage in the public building. Digger was surprised how easy it became to interpret substantial passages of the conversation.

Meantime a fresh transmission came in from Hutch. When Jack saw it, he ran it for all of them.

'*Help is coming. The* al-Jahani *will have left by the time you receive this. Dave Collingdale is heading up the operation, and he needs as much information as you can get him. Particularly anything that will allow him to gain access to the language.*

'*Also, we're dispatching the* Cumberland *from Broadside to take supplies and equipment to you. It'll take off anybody who wants to go home. But it won't be able to leave for a few days yet. It looks as if it'll be about seven weeks before you'll see it.*

I hate to ask this of you, but it's essential that we keep somebody at the scene to learn whatever we can. So I need you to hang on there until it arrives. I know that's not exactly the mission plan, and it's an inconvenience to you. But you'll understand this is a special circumstance.

'Also, I need to know what you want to do. We have to maintain an Academy presence until the al-Jahani gets there. But that won't be until December. Do you want to stay on? Or do you want me to organize a relief mission? Jack, I'd prefer to have you stay, but I understand if you feel enough is enough. Let me know.

'The Cumberland *will be carrying shipments of lightbenders and pickups. Plant as many of the devices as you can. It's essential that we get the language down.*

'All data relating to the Goompahs should be designated for relay by Broadside directly to the *al-Jahani, and I'd appreciate it if you included me as an information addee.*

'Thanks, guys. I know this doesn't make you happy, but if it means anything, I'm grateful.'

There was a long silence when the Academy logo appeared on-screen. They looked at one another, and Kellie grinned. 'The aliens are lunatics,' she said. 'And the cloud is coming. Is there anyone who *wants* to go home?'

It wasn't exactly what Digger had hoped to hear.

In fact, there was one. 'I don't plan to spend the next year or so of my life out here,' Winnie told Jack. 'It'd be different if there were something constructive I could do. But I'm not needed. I'm ready to head out.'

So was Digger. But Kellie wouldn't be leaving, so he wasn't about to go anyplace. Digger let her see that he wanted to stay on, wanted to be part of a major achievement, and all that. The truth was, he wanted Kellie, and everything else was a sideshow. But with Kellie watching, he had no choice but to play the selfless hero. He knew her too well and understood clearly what would happen to her respect for him if he didn't stand up and do his duty.

He wished, as a compromise, he could think of a way to persuade Jack to go back to Broadside while he stayed here with Kellie. Don't worry about the details, big fella. We'll take care of anything that comes up. You go ahead and take some time off.

LIBRARY ENTRY

'You should never talk to strangers, Shalla.'

'Why not, Boomer? Some of the nicest people I know are strangers.'

'But if you know them, they're not strangers.'

'Oh.'

'Do you see what I mean?'

'Not really, Boomer. I mean, you were a stranger once. Should I not have spoken to you?'

'Well, that's different.'

'How?'

'I'm a nice person.'

'But how can I find out if I don't talk to you?'

'I'm not sure, Shalla. But I know it's not a good idea.'

—The Goompah Show All-Kids Network
March 19

12

On board the *Jenkins*, in orbit around Lookout.
Wednesday, March 19.

Bill did an overnight analysis of the food samples and told Digger
he probably wouldn't like any of the local cuisine. They forwarded
the results to Broadside and the *al-Jahani*.

They were having breakfast in the common room when Winnie
carried her tray in. 'I just saw something odd,' she said, sitting
down at the table with the other three. 'There's a parade of some
sort out on the road. Near where you were yesterday.'

'Really?' Jack rolled up a biscuit, dipped it into his egg yolk,
and finished it off. 'How do you mean, a parade?'

'Well, not really a parade. But a bunch of locals look as if
they're headed for the spot where you showed up.'

'Are you serious?' asked Digger.

'They're coming from the north. About twenty of them. The
guy in front is wearing a black robe.'

'They're probably just going through to Athens,' said Digger.

Jack looked interested. 'It's the first black robe we've seen.
These folks like bright colors.'

Kellie had been trying to finish her breakfast without getting caught up in the latest bout of Goompah mania. But she sighed. 'You think they came to see where the critter was?'

'Maybe. There's a bunch of wagons parked up the road a bit. We didn't have coverage this morning because of clouds, but I think these guys rode in on them. There are still a few back there. With the wagons. Looks as if they're waiting,'

'Bill—?' said Jack.

The screen lit up. There was indeed a Goompah in a black robe. He was approaching the spot where the avatar had appeared. Approaching in the sense, Digger thought, that he was coming up on it with great care. The crowd was trailing, but giving him plenty of room.

He carried a staff, and when he'd reached the spot on the road in closest proximity to the hill on which the avatar had stood, he stopped, planted the staff, leaned on it, and appeared to survey his surroundings. After a minute he looked behind, and one of the onlookers came forward. There was a conversation and some pointing.

'Looks as if Digger may have stirred something up,' Jack said.

Right. Digger did it.

A cloud drifted into the field of view.

'What do you think?' asked Kellie.

'It looks ceremonial.'

Winnie wondered whether anybody recognized any of the Goompahs.

Digger smothered a laugh. 'They all look alike. Can *you* tell them apart?'

'I haven't seen them up close. Not the way you have. I thought you might recognize one of the guys you talked to yesterday.' She put a slight emphasis on the verb, and she was obviously talking about the one who had been traveling alone and whom Digger now saw was indeed there, carrying a javelin.

'I have no idea,' Digger said.

'He's saying something,' said Kellie, meaning the one in the robe.

'I think he's singing,' said Jack. 'We should have left a pickup in the area.'

The marchers spread out on either side of the black robe, forming an arc centering on him.

'It's a chant,' said Winnie. 'Look at them.' They had all begun doing a kind of coordinated swaying.

'They're looking for *me*,' said Digger.

Jack leaned forward, intrigued. Digger, whose training should have produced the same curiosity, felt only a chill. 'It's a religious ceremony,' Jack said.

'Maybe we need to go back down,' said Winnie. 'Explain to them it's okay.'

Kellie's eyes shone. 'I'll be damned,' she said. 'They think they saw a god.'

'I doubt it,' said Jack.

The one in the robe shook down long sleeves and pulled a hood over his head. The javelin was held out for him to take. He made signs over it, lifted it, and waved it in a threatening gesture at the top of the hill. The chant ended.

Everyone stood quietly for another minute or so. Then he climbed the hill while the others watched with – Digger thought – no small degree of anxiety, and came finally to the spot where the avatar had stood. The one who'd been on the road, who'd carried the weapon, called out to him and he moved a couple of steps to his right. They seemed to agree that was the correct location. And without further delay, he brandished the javelin with practiced ease and plunged it into the ground.

He made more signs, drew his hands together, and looked at the sky. They all bowed their heads and closed their eyes. Their lips moved in unison. One of them crept up the hill and recovered the javelin. And they withdrew.

Down the hill and back along the road until they reached the waiting wagons. Into the wagons and headed north.

'I think,' said Digger, 'we've just seen a declaration of war.'

Jack was still looking ecstatic. 'I don't think so,' he said. 'I believe we've just watched an exorcism.'

* * *

They spent much of the next few days watching and listening to Goompah conversations. Winnie hung a sign on the bulkhead that said *It's Greek to me*. Each of the five channels allotted to the pickups had been routed in, but one had gone inactive. They'd seen a Goompah hand close over it, and then for a while all they could see was the grass. And finally the unit shut down. Somebody had probably hit it with a stick.

But they still had four links.

They listened and marked down phonetic impressions and bounced phrases off each other while Bill recorded everything, collapsed the signals into compressed transmissions, and fired them off every six hours by way of Broadside to the *al-Jahani*.

The language seemed straightforward enough. Some of the sounds were odd, lots of grunts and gargles, a load of aspirates and diphthongs. And nobody rolled their *l*'s like these guys. There was an overall harshness to the diction, but Digger didn't hear much that a human tongue couldn't reproduce. And they'd even deciphered a couple of words.

Challa, collanda appeared to be the universal greeting. Two Goompahs met, morning or evening, male or female, it didn't seem to matter: '*Challa, collanda*,' they would say.

Hello, friend. Kellie took to greeting her passengers with it, and soon they were all using it. *Challa*, Jack.

Digger discovered the sheer pleasure in reproducing some of the sounds he was hearing. He could roll his *l*'s and grunt with the best of them. He also began to discover something he hadn't known about himself: He had a facility for language. Next time he ran into some Goompahs he'd be ready. He wondered if things might have gone a bit differently had he been able to raise his hand and, in his jolliest demeanor, send the proper greeting: '*Challa, collanda*.'

But there wouldn't be a next time. Lightbenders were on the way, so when they went back down to set up more listening posts they'd be invisible.

Well, there was nothing to be done about it now. But he knew he'd be tempted to walk up to one of the Goompahs, no more than a voice in the wind, and say hello. Just whisper it and watch him jump.

He'd never worn a lightbender. They were prohibited to private ownership. A few had gotten out and become invaluable tools for criminals. But there was a National Lightbender Association claiming that people had a constitutional right to the devices. It struck Digger that once they became generally available everyone would have to wear infrared glasses to protect himself. Even imagining himself invisible bestowed a sense of both power and recklessness.

About a week after they'd gone down to the surface, Jack announced that a message had arrived from the Academy. 'We've got something else to look for,' he said.

Hutch's image appeared on-screen.

'*Jack,*' she said, '*This is a hedgehog.*' The screen divided and produced a picture of an object with triangular spikes sticking out all over it. An accompanying scale indicated it was six and a half kilometers in diameter.

'*To date, we have three reports of these objects. We have no idea what they are or what their purpose is. We do know that one of them exploded while it was being inspected by the Quagmor. If you can take a look around without compromising your main objectives, please do so. We'd like very much to know if your cloud has one. It'll be directly out front, running on the same course, at the same speed. The ranges between the objects and the clouds have varied out to sixty thousand klicks.*

'*So far, the things are identical. They have 240 sides. Lots of right angles. If you see one, keep a respectful distance. Don't go near it. We don't want an inspection; we just want to know whether it's there.*' She allowed herself a smile but Digger could see she was dead serious. '*Thanks,*' she said. '*Be careful. We don't want to lose anybody else.*'

The hedgehog remained a few seconds after Hutch's image

blanked, and then it, too, was gone, replaced by the Academy logo.

All those spines. Like stalagmites. But with flat tips. 'What is it?' asked Winnie. 'Do they have any idea?'

'You heard as much as I did,' said Jack.

Kellie looked thoughtful. 'I'll tell you what it might be,' she said. 'It looks designed to attract the clouds. Maybe somebody's been using them to get rid of the damn things. A cloud shows up and you give it a whatzis to chase.'

They all looked at her. 'It's possible,' said Digger. 'That might be *it*.'

Kellie's eyes shone. It was a pleasure to be first to solve a puzzle.

'Well,' said Jack, 'let's go see if we've got one.'

The cloud's shape had changed during the few weeks since they'd first seen it. It had become distorted, and was throwing jets forward and to one side, blown off by gee forces as it continued to decelerate and to turn. At the rate the thing was braking, Digger had trouble understanding how it managed to hold together at all. He was not a physicist, but he knew enough to conclude that the stability of the gas and dust, in the face of those kinds of stresses, demonstrated that this was no natural phenomenon. There were widespread claims by mystics, and even some physicists, who should know better, that the omegas were an evolutionary step, a means by which the galaxy protected itself from the rise of the supercivilization, the one entity that could raise havoc, that could eventually take control and force it away from its natural development.

It was a notion very much in play these days, fitting perfectly with the idea that the present universe was simply a spark in a vast hypersky, one of countless universes, afloat in a cosmos that was perhaps itself an infinitesimal part of an ever-greater construct. Grains of sand on a beach that was a grain on a much bigger beach . . .

Where did it all end?

Well, however that might be, the omega clouds were too sophisticated to have developed naturally.

'How do you know?' asked Kellie, sitting quietly looking out at the monster, while Digger went on about stars and universes.

He explained. How it held together. How it had long-range sensors far better than anything the *Jenkins* had. How it had spotted Athens from a range of 135 billion kilometers when they couldn't find it from orbit.

She listened, nodding occasionally, apparently agreeing. But when he'd finished, she commented that there were people around who'd argue that *Digger* couldn't have happened simply as a result of natural evolution. 'I think,' she said, 'you're doing the argument from design.'

'I suppose. But this is different.'

'How?'

'It's on a bigger scale.'

'Dig, that's only a difference in degree. Size doesn't count.'

He couldn't find an adequate response. 'You think these things are natural objects?'

'I don't know.' The cloud was misshapen, plumes thrown forward and to one side. It was a dark squid soaring through the night. 'I'm keeping my mind open.' Neither spoke for a minute. Then she said, 'I'm not sure which scares me more.'

'Which what?'

'Which explanation. Either they're natural, which leads to the conclusion that the universe, or God, however you want to put it, doesn't approve of intelligence. Or they're built and set loose. That means somebody who's very bright has gone to a lot of trouble to kill every stranger he can find.'

At their current range, Lookout's sun was only a bright star.

The *Jenkins* had begun a sweep when it had approached within 12 million klicks of the cloud. They moved steadily closer over the next three days but saw nothing.

On the fourth day of the hunt Kellie suggested they terminate.

'You're sure there's nothing there?' said Jack.

'Absolutely. There are a few rocks but that's it. Nothing remotely resembling the dingus.' She waited for instructions.

'Okay.' Jack's attitude suggested the hell with it. 'Let's go back to Lookout.'

Kellie directed them to belt down and began angling the *Jenkins* onto its new course. It was going to be a long turn and they'd be living with gee forces for the better part of a day. Consequently, she wasn't particularly happy. 'If I'd used my head,' she told Digger, 'I'd have arranged things differently. We could have been on a more efficient course at the end of the pattern. But I assumed we were going to find something.'

'So did I,' he said. 'If you're right, though, that the hedgehogs are lures, they won't be everywhere. Only close to clouds that are threatening something their makers are interested in.'

Jack sent off a message to Hutch, information copies to the *al Jahani*: '*No hedgehog at Lookout. Returning to orbit.*'

While they made the long swing, they decided to watch a sim together, and Kellie, at their request, brought up a haunted house thriller. Digger didn't have much taste for horror, but he went along. 'Scares me though,' he told them, making a joke of it, as if the idea were ridiculous, but in fact it did. He took no pleasure watching a vampire operate, and there'd been times even here, in the belly of a starship, maybe *especially* here, when he'd gone back through a dimly lit corridor to his quarters after that kind of experience and heard footsteps padding behind him.

The problem with the superluminal was that, even though it was an embodiment of modern technology, a statement that the universe is governed by reason, a virtual guarantee that demons and vampires do not exist, it was still quite small. Almost claustrophobic. A few passageways and a handful of rooms, with a tendency toward shadows and echoes. It was a place you couldn't get away from. If something stalked you through the ship's narrow corridors, there would be nowhere to run.

His problem, he knew, was that he suffered from an over-abundance of imagination. Always had. It was the quality that had drawn him into extraterrestrial assignments. Digger was no coward. He felt he'd proved it by going down on Lookout and sticking his head up. He'd worked on a site in the middle of the Angolan flare-up, had stayed there when everybody else ran. On another occasion he'd gotten a couple of missionaries away from rebels in Zampara, in northern Africa, by a mixture of audacity, good sense, and good luck. But he didn't like haunted houses.

The plot always seemed to be the same: A group of adolescents looking for an unusual place to hold a party decide to use the abandoned mansion in which there reportedly had been several ghastly murders during the past half century. (It wasn't a place to which Digger would have gone.)

There was always a storm, rain beating against the windows, and doors opening and closing of their own volition. And periodically, victims getting cornered by whatever happened to be loose in the attic.

He tried to think about other things. But the creaking doors, the wild musical score, and the tree branches scraping against the side of the house kept breaking through. Jack laughed through much of the performance, and energetically warned the actors to look out, it's in the closet.

Midway through, strange noises come from upstairs. Shrieks. Groans. Unearthly cries. Two of the boys decide, incredibly, they will investigate. *Only in the sims*, Digger thinks. But he wants them to stay together. The boy in the lead is tall, good-looking, with a kind of wistful innocence. The kid next door. Despite the silliness of the proceedings, Digger's heart is pounding as he and his companion climb the circular staircase, while the tempo builds to a climax. As they arrive at the top, another shriek rips through the night. It comes from behind the door at the end of the hallway.

The door opens, apparently unaided, and Digger sees a shadowy figure seated in an armchair facing a window, illuminated only by the flickering lightning. The second boy, prudently, is dropping behind.

Stay together. Digger shakes his head, telling himself it's all nonsense. No sensible kids would do anything like this. And if they did, they'd certainly stick close to each other.

And he found himself thinking about the hedgehog. They'd overlooked the obvious.

'What would it be doing way out there?' asked Jack.

Digger has used a cursor to indicate where he thought the object could be found. 'We assumed the cloud and the hedgehog were a unit. Where one goes, the other follows. But here, we've got a cloud that has thrown a right turn.

'The cloud's been turning and slowing down for a long time. Maybe over a year. But there's no reason to assume the hedgehog wouldn't keep going.'

'Original course and velocity?' said Jack.

'Probably.'

'Why would it do that?' asked Winnie.

'Why *any* of this? I don't know. But I bet if we check it out, we'll find it where the cloud would have been if it hadn't decided to go for a walk.'

Kellie's dark eyes touched him. Go to it, big boy.

'Why not take a look?' he asked. 'It's not as if we have to be anywhere tomorrow.'

They found it precisely where Digger had predicted. It was moving along at a few notches under standard omega velocity. As if the great cloud still trailed behind.

LIBRARY ENTRY

The discovery of escort vehicles with the omegas reveals just how little research has been done over the past thirty years on this critical subject. What other surprises are coming? And how many more lives will be sacrificed to bureaucratic inertia?

—The London *Times*
March 23

13

On board the *Heffernan*, near Alpha Pictoris, 99 light-years from Earth.
Friday, April 4.

The Pictoris hedgehog made it six for six. They all have one.

It was twenty-eight thousand kilometers in front of the cloud. Its diameter was the standard six and a half kilometers. 'Report's away,' Emma said.

Sky didn't like going anywhere near the damned thing. But they'd asked for volunteers, told him they'd probably be okay, but to be careful, don't take any unnecessary chances, and keep your head down. Emma had said not to hesitate on her account, and the *Heffernan* was the only ship in the neighborhood.

Ordinarily Sky loved what he did for a living. He enjoyed cruising past ringed giants, lobbing probes into black holes, delivering people and supplies to the ultimate out-of-the-way places. But he didn't like the clouds. And he didn't like the hedgehogs. They were things that didn't belong.

They were far enough away from Pictoris that the only decent illumination on the object was coming from their probe.

'*Its magnetic field matches the signature of the other objects,*' said Bill.

'Ajax is ready to go,' said Emma.

There was no known entry hatch anywhere, so Drafts would have chosen a spot at random. Which is what the *Heffernan* would do.

Emma and Sky were looking forward to celebrating their sixteenth anniversary the next day, although they hadn't been married precisely sixteen years. Participating in experiments with the new hypervelocity sublight thrust engines had alternately speeded them up and slowed them down, or maybe just one or the other. He'd never been able to figure out relativity. He just knew the numbers didn't come together in any way he could understand. But it didn't matter. He'd had a lot of time with Emma, and he was smart enough to appreciate it. She'd told him once, when they were still a few months from their wedding, and were eating dinner at the Grand Hotel in Arlington, that he should enjoy the moment because the day would come when they'd give anything to be able to return to that hour and relive that dinner.

It was true, of course. Everything was fresh and young then. They hadn't yet learned to take each other for granted. When he was tempted to do so now, he reminded himself that the life he had wouldn't be forever, and if he couldn't go back to the Grand Hotel when his romance with Emma was still new, when the entire world was young and all things seemed possible, it was equally true that he'd remember the hedgehog, and how they'd stood on the bridge together, watching it come close, a piece of hardware put together by God knew what, for purposes no one could imagine. A *bomb*. But it was still a moment that he savored, because he knew that, like the Grand Hotel, he would one day give much to be able to return.

Sixteenth anniversary. How had it all gone by so quickly?

'Relativity.' She laughed.

'*Recommend Ajax launch*,' said Bill.

'Okay, Bill. Keep in mind that we want it to snuggle up very gently. Just kiss it, right?'

'*Just a smooch*,' said Bill. He appeared beside them, wearing a radiation suit and a hard hat. Protection against explosions. His idea of a joke.

'Okay,' Sky said. 'Launch Ajax.'

Warning lamps blinked. The usual slight tremor ran through the ship. '*Ajax away. Time to intersection: thirty-three minutes.*'

'Okay, Bill. Let's leave town.'

They accelerated out. Sky directed the AI to maintain jump capability, which required firing the main engines throughout the sequence to build and hold sufficient charge in the Hazeltines.

It was the first time in all these years that he'd been in this kind of situation, not knowing well in advance whether he'd have to jump.

'Out of curiosity—' she said.

'Yes?'

'On the jump, can you override Bill? If you had to?' The jump engines couldn't be used until they were charged. That usually required twenty-eight minutes off the main engines. Any attempt to do a jump prior to that risked initiating an antimatter explosion, and consequently would be refused by the AI.

'We could do a manual start if something happened to Bill.'

'You know,' she said, 'I suspect that's what the hedgehog is loaded with, too.'

'Antimatter?'

'Yes. That would explain the magnetic field.'

'In what way?' asked Sky.

'Containment envelope. It's probably what happened to Drafts. He did something that impaired its integrity.'

Sky shook his head. Who'd have expected anything like that out here?

Emma was an astrophysicist. When he'd warned her that marrying someone who took a superluminal out for months at a time might not be a smart move for her, she'd said okay, that she'd really wanted a tall blond guy anyhow, good-bye. And he'd tried to recover ground, said he wasn't entirely serious, didn't want to lose her, just wanted to be sure she knew what she was getting into.

It had taken almost two years to get the joint assignment to the *Heffernan*, but it had happened, largely because the Academy had a policy of trying to keep its captains happy.

They were both on the bridge, sharing, after all these years, their first moment of danger. The danger was remote, fortunately, but it added a dash of spice to the experience.

'*Ajax has closed to four klicks*,' said Bill. '*Contact in eleven minutes*.'

They could see Ajax, which looked like an insect, wings and legs spread, angling toward the spiked surface.

'Is it going to work?' asked Sky.

'If it's what we think it is, Ajax will find the frequency and interfere with the magnetic belt. That should be enough. If it isn't, it'll start cutting the thing up with its lasers. One way or another, yes, it should work.'

Sky listened to the innumerable sounds the ship's systems routinely make, whispers and sighs and clicks and the ongoing background thrum of the engines, boosting them to ever-higher velocities.

They talked occasionally about retirement, about her getting a job at home, maybe having the child they'd always promised themselves. Can't really do that if you're bottled up inside a container all the time. Virtual beaches are all right for adults, but a kid needs real sand.

Emma, reading his thoughts, nodded. 'Time for something new?' she suggested.

'I don't know,' he said uncertainly.

'There *is* this, Sky. Where else could we be this useful?'

Can't hug her. Not while under acceleration. So he reached over and took her hand.

'*Five minutes*,' said Bill. '*We are ready to jump on command*.'

One of the screens carried the cloud, its image captured live through the telescopes. Sky thought the omegas possessed an ethereal kind of beauty. Not this one, because it was too dark, there wasn't enough light hitting it. But when they got lit up by sunlight, they were actually very striking. He grinned at the unintentional pun.

Emma couldn't see it. She thought they were the embodiment of pure malevolence. A demonstration that there were devils loose in the universe. Not the supernatural kind, of course. Something far worse, something that really existed, that had left its footprint among the stars, that had designed booby traps and sent them out to kill strangers.

Sky had grown up with the notion that evil inevitably equated to stupidity. The symbol of that idea was embodied in the fact that superluminals were not armed, that no one (other than fiction writers) had ever thought of mounting a deck gun on an interstellar vessel.

It was a nice piece of mythology. But mythology was all it was.

'*Two minutes.*' Bill loved doing countdowns. There was a picture of him on the auxiliary screen, sitting in an armchair, still safely tucked inside his suit, and with his helmet visor down.

'Bill, ready to bail if we have to.' There was no way to be sure the energy levels of the hedgehog were all the same.

'*We are QBY,*' he said. Ready to go. Bill favored the official terminology. He sometimes admitted to Sky that he regretted that starship life was so peaceful. He talked occasionally, and wistfully, of running missions against alien horrors that were determined to destroy civilization, to overrun Berlin and all it stood for. (Sky could never tell for sure when Bill was kidding.) The AI wished for pirates and renegade corporations, hiding in the dust of giant clouds. Clouds, he added, hundreds of light-years across, clouds that would make the omegas look like puffs of mist on a summer breeze.

Bill, *this* Bill, had a poetic streak. Sometimes he went a bit over the top, but he did seem to have a passion for flowers and sunsets and the wind in the trees. All a facade, of course. Bill had never experienced any of that, wasn't even self-aware if you believed the manual. Furthermore, although the Academy AIs were compatible, and in fact most people thought there was really only *one* Academy AI, which sometimes simply got out of contact with its various parts, Sky knew that Bill was different on different ships. Sometimes the manifestation was withdrawn and formal, seldom showing up visually, and then usually in dress whites; on other vessels, on the *Quagmire*, for example (which Sky had piloted on a couple of missions), he'd been young, energetic, always advancing his opinion, usually in a jumpsuit with the ship's patch on his shoulder. The *Heffernan* AI was philosophical, sometimes sentimental, inclined to quote Homer and Milton and the Bible. And apparently a fan of melodrama.

Sky was one of the few Academy captains who believed that a divine force functioned in the universe. He'd heard Hutch say one time that the notion of a God was hard to accept out here because of the sheer dimensions of the cosmos. Richard Feynman had made a comment to that effect. *'The stage is just too big.'* Why create something so enormous? Why make places so far away that their light will never reach the Earth?

But that was the reason Sky believed. The stage is *immense* beyond comprehension. The fallacy in Hutch's reasoning, he thought, was the assumption that the human race was at the center of things. That *we* were what it was all about. But Sky suspected the Creator had made everything so large because He simply liked to create. That's what creators do.

'Twenty seconds,' said Bill.

He watched the package move in. The hedgehog was rotating, slowly, once every thirty-seven minutes. The others rotated at different rates. It depended on the gravity fields they'd passed through.

'Ten.'

It closed and snuggled in against one of the object's 240 sides.

'*Contact.*'

'Very good, Bill.'

'*Thank you, sir.*'

He looked over at Emma.

'Bill,' she said, 'proceed with Ajax.'

'*Proceeding.*' And, a moment later: '*Lockdown.*' The magnetic couplers took hold. There had been a possibility that might have been enough to detonate the thing, but Emma hadn't thought so. If it had no more stability than that, it would have gone up long ago. Objects drifting through interstellar space are bathed by particles and gravitons and you name it.

'You know,' said Emma, 'I think I'm going to enjoy blowing this son of a bitch to hell.'

'There's nobody in it.'

'Doesn't matter.' She looked over at him. Her eyes were green, and they were smoldering. She didn't share his faith in a benign creator, but she felt that the universe should be a place of pristine beauty and wonder. And most of all it should be neutral, and not loaded against intelligence. We're the only reason there's any point to it, she believed. Unless there's someone smart enough to look at it, and appreciate its grandeur, *and do the science*, the universe is meaningless.

'Are we ready to pull the trigger?' Sky asked.

'Just enjoying the moment,' she said.

'Fire when ready, babe.'

She checked the status board. All green. 'Bill,' she said.

'*Locked and loaded.*'

'Proceed to degauss.'

'*Activating.*' His image vanished. He was all business now.

Sky watched the time tick off. 'Would the reaction be instantaneous?' he asked.

'Hard to say. But I'd think so.'

'*I do not detect a change in the object's magnetic signature.*'

'Doesn't work?' asked Sky.

'Let's give it a little more time.'

The hedgehog was getting smaller as the *Heffernan* continued to withdraw.

'*Still no change,*' said Bill.

'Maybe it's not antimatter?'

'It might be that we don't have enough energy to shut it down. Or that we haven't calibrated correctly. Or who knows what else? It's not exactly my field.' She took a deep breath, 'You ready to go to phase two, Sky?'

'Yes. Do it.'

'Bill?'

'*Yes, Emma?*'

'Activate the blade.' The laser.

'*Activating blade.*'

'Can you enhance the picture?' Sky asked.

'*Negative. We are at maximum definition now.*'

Emma had told him it would probably take time, but Sky kept thinking about Terry Drafts poking a laser into its shell. The record showed that once you did that, things happened pretty quickly. But some parts of the object might be more vulnerable than others.

Sky was beginning to amuse himself thinking how the Academy might say okay, it's obviously not going to work, go back in and retrieve the unit when it went, erupted in a white flash.

ARCHIVE

No one denies that the effort to find a way to dispose of the omega clouds is of value. But they do not constitute a clear and present danger. They are in fact so remote a hazard that it remains difficult to understand why so many continue to get exercised over the issue. At a time when millions go hungry, when repairing environmental damage is exhausting vast sums of money, when the world population steams ahead, we can ill afford to waste our resources on a threat that remains so far over the horizon that we cannot even imagine what the planet will look like when it arrives. The Council and the Prime Minister need to set their priorities, and live with them despite the shifting political winds.

—Moscow International
April 5

14

Arlington.
Monday, April 4.

'Asquith never really looked happy, except when VIP visitors were present. This morning, which was rainy, gloomy, and somehow tentative, was momentarily devoid of VIPs. The commissioner was making the kinds of faces that suggested he was tired of hearing about problems that didn't go away. 'So we know the hedgehogs – can't we get a better name for them, Hutch? – are bombs. Tell me about the one that's going to pass close to us. Tony's going to be over this afternoon, and I need some answers. What happens if it goes off?'

Tony was the ultimate VIP: the NAU's funding liaison with the Academy.

'You don't have to worry about it, Michael. It's as far away as the cloud is. It can't hurt us.'

'Then why are we worried about it?'

'We aren't worried in the sense that it can do any damage to us. Not at its current range. Maybe in a few centuries.'

'Then why do we care about it?'

'Because we don't know its purpose.'

'So we're talking a purely academic issue? Nobody's at risk?'

'No.'

He'd gotten up when she came into the room. Now he eased himself back into his chair. 'Thank God for that,' he said. He motioned her to a chair. 'Why would anybody be putting bombs out there?'

'We think they're *triggers*.'

'Triggers. Bombs. We're arguing terminology.' He rolled his eyes. 'What do they trigger?'

'The clouds.'

'What's that? How do you mean? The clouds blow up?'

'We don't really know yet, Michael. But I think it's something like that. I think you get a special kind of explosion.'

'How many kinds of explosions are there?'

She sat down and tried to get the conversation onto a level at which she could handle it. 'The reason they're important,' she said, 'is that if these things turn out to be what they seem to be, they may give us a way to get rid of the clouds.'

'By blowing them up.'

'Yes. Maybe. We don't know.' She felt good this morning. Had in fact felt pretty good for the last few days. 'We need to find out.'

'So what precisely do you propose?'

'We need to run a test.'

He nodded. 'Do it.'

'Okay.'

'But not with the cloud.' The local one.

'We won't go near it.'

'Good.' He took a deep breath. 'I'd be grateful if it worked.'

'As would I, Michael.'

'I guess you've noticed the Goompahs have been getting popular.' His tone suggested that was a problem.

Of course she'd noticed. Everywhere she looked there were Goompah dolls, Goompah games, Goompah bedding. People loved them. Kids especially loved them. 'Why is that bad news?' she asked innocently. But she knew the reason.

'There's a growing body of opinion that the government hasn't done enough to help them.'

'I'm sorry to hear it.'

'They'd like to keep the media away. In case things go badly.'

'*They* being the president and the Council.'

He nodded. Who else? 'They're afraid there'll be graphic pictures of Goompahs getting killed in large numbers.'

'Too bad they're not insects.'

He didn't pick up the sarcasm. 'Anything but these terminally cute rollover critters.'

'The media say they'll be there.'

He made a sound in his throat that resembled a gargle going awry. 'I know. But there's no way to stop them. If our little experiment works out, though, the problem will be solved.' He looked happy. As if the sun had come out in the office. 'Make it happen, Hutch.'

'Wait a minute,' she said. 'Michael, I think we've had a communication breakdown. Even if it works, we aren't going to be able to use the technique to help the Goompahs.'

Shock and dismay. 'Why not? I thought that was the whole point.'

'The whole point is to get control of the clouds. To forge a weapon.' She tried to sound reassuring. 'I'm sorry I misled you. But the cloud at Lookout is too close.'

'How do you mean?'

'If we get the result we expect, we're going to learn how to destroy the damned things. But we expect a very big bang. Trigger the cloud at Lookout, and you'd fry them all.'

'How can you know that before you've run the test?'

'Because I'm pretty sure I've seen other clouds explode. I know what kind of energy they put out.'

And suddenly he understood. 'The tewks.'

'Yes.' She'd put it all in the reports, but it was becoming clear he didn't read the reports.

'All right,' he said. He was still disappointed and he let her see it. 'Let me know how it turns out.'

'Okay.' She started to get up, but he waved her back down. Not finished with you yet.

'Listen, Hutch. I've gone along with everything you've wanted to do. We sent out Collingdale and his people. We sent out the kite. And we're sending meals, for God's sake. We'll be broke for three years after this. Now you owe me something.

'We've gotten some help from the Council on this. So we need to play ball with them. I'm going to tell Tony we'll go all out to save the poor bastards. That's what they want, by the way. Save them. Divert the goddam cloud. If you can't blow it up, make your kite work. Make it happen.

'If you don't, if the cloud hammers them, we'll all be in the soup.'

Hutch kept her voice level. 'Michael,' she said, 'we've had thirty years to figure out how to do something about the omegas. The Council felt safe because the danger seemed so far away. It didn't occur to them that political fallout might come from a different direction. I personally don't care if they all get voted out. But we are trying to save the Goompahs. We were trying to do it before it became politically popular.'

She was at the door, on her way out, when he called her back. 'You're right, Hutch,' he said. 'I know that. Everybody knows it. Which is why the Academy will look so good if we can pull these fat little guys out of the fire.'

'Right,' she said, and let it drop.

ARCHIVE

'Senator, we've all seen the pictures of the cloud at Moonlight. Is there anything at all we can do for the Goompahs?'

'Janet, we are moving heaven and earth to help. Unfortunately,

206

we haven't yet learned how to turn these things aside. The first shipload of supplies will be leaving day after tomorrow. We're doing everything we can.'

—Senator Cass Barker, Press Conference, April 4

15

On board the *al-Jahani*, in hyperflight.
Wednesday, April 23.

There were too many people on the mission. Collingdale had heard that the entire scientific community had wanted to go, despite the distance to Lookout. And Hutch had accommodated as many as she possibly could. That was a mistake. They were going to have to work as a team, and he had the unenviable task of trying to organize, mollify, control, and entertain a task force that included some of the biggest egos on the planet. There were historians and xenologists and mathematicians and specialists in other lines of inquiry of which he'd never heard. Every one of whom thought of him/herself as a leading light in his or her field. And they were going to be locked up together until late November.

Frank Bergen was a good example of the problem. Frank expected everyone to take notes whenever he spoke. Melinda Park looked stunned if anyone took issue with any of her opinions, even those outside her area of expertise. Walfred Glassner ('Wally' behind his back) thought everyone else in the world was a moron. Peggy Malachy never let anyone else finish a sentence. The others, save Judy Sternberg's linguists, were no better. Before it was over he was convinced there'd be a murder.

They comprised the Upper Strata, the scientific heavyweights.

Bergen was, in his view, the only one of them who really mattered. After everybody else had debarked onto the *Jenkins*, he would make the flight with Kellie Collier to try to distract the omega. Bergen, who was short, dumpy, arrogant, was sure the plan would succeed if only because anything he touched always succeeded. They had at their disposal visual projections, and if those didn't do the job, they had the kite. One way or the other, he assured anybody who would listen, they'd get rid of the thing. He sounded as if he thought the cloud wouldn't dare defy him.

In fact, it seemed to Collingdale that the only other ones crucial to the mission were the linguists. They were all kids, all graduate students or postdocs, save for their boss, Judy Sternberg.

They were already at work with the data forwarded by the *Jenkins*, trying to decipher and familiarize themselves with basic Goompah. He'd have preferred to double their number and get rid of the giants-in-their-field. But he understood about politics. And Hutch had maintained that it was impossible to find, in a few days' time, an adequate supply of people, no more than five and a half feet tall, with the kind of specialized skill they needed, who were willing to leave home for two years. She had done the best she could and he'd have to make do.

They were indeed of minimal stature. Not one of the twelve, male or female, rose above his collarbone.

It had been an ugly scene, those last few days before departure. He'd never seen Hutch lose her temper before, but it was obvious she was under pressure. You have to understand the reality, he'd told her, and she'd fired back that politics *was* the reality.

Nonetheless, they were doing as well as could be expected. The Upper Strata had settled in and seemed to have achieved an amicable standoff with each other. And the linguists were hard at work on the daily flow of recordings. They were both enthusiastic and talented, and he expected that, by the time they arrived on-station, he'd have people able to speak with the natives.

He'd been trying to master the language himself but had already fallen far behind the young guns. His lack of proficiency surprised him. He spoke German and Russian fluently and, despite his fifty-six years, had thought he'd be able to pace the help. Within the first two weeks he'd seen it wasn't going to happen. But maybe it was just as well. Staying ahead of the old man provided an incentive for them.

The incoming data consisted of audiovisual recordings. The pictures weren't very good. Sometimes the conversations took place entirely out of view of the imager. On other occasions, the Goompahs walked out of visual range while they talked. Even when the subjects stayed still, the angles were usually less than ideal. At this early stage, in order to have a reasonable chance to understand, the linguists needed to be able to *see* what was happening. But they were getting enough to match actions with talk and, still more important, with gestures.

Most of the Upper Strata were looking forward to putting on lightbenders and walking unseen among the population. They would try to do what they'd done on Nok, penetrate the libraries, eavesdrop on conversations, observe political and religious activities. But Nok was a long time ago. They'd all been young then. And Collingdale had already noticed a reluctance among them to learn the language. He knew what would happen: They'd put it off, finding one pretext or another to avoid the effort. And when they got to Lookout they'd be asking to borrow one of the linguists, somebody to go down and interpret.

It was clear that whatever was to be accomplished on this mission would be done by Judy's team.

When he'd heard the conditions under which he would be making the flight, he'd almost changed his mind about going. But he had asked Hutch for the assignment, and he didn't feel he could back away. Moreover, he hoped that Bergen was right, that the cloud would be turned aside, and that they would beat the thing. He desperately wanted to be there if it happened.

* * *

211

They were making some progress in figuring out the syntax, and they had already begun to compile a vocabulary. They had words for *hello* and *good-bye, near* and *far, ground* and *sky, come* and *go*. They could sometimes differentiate among the tenses. They knew how to ask for a bolt of cloth, or to request directions for *Mandigol*. (Nobody had any clue where *that* was.)

There was some confusion about plurals, and they were mystified by pronouns. But Judy was there, reassuring them that time and patience would bring the solutions. Her plan called for the establishment of a working vocabulary of at least one hundred nouns and verbs by the end of their first month on board, and a basic grasp of syntax by the end of the second. They'd achieved the first goal, but the second was proving elusive. At the end of the second month, no English would be permitted in the workroom. At the end of the third month, they would speak Goompah exclusively, everywhere on the ship, except when communicating with home.

Several objected to that provision. How were they to talk with their fellow passengers? To Collingdale's immense satisfaction, Judy replied that was the problem of the passengers. It would do Bergen and the others good, she said, to begin hearing the native language. They're supposed to be learning it anyhow.

The Upper Strata, when it heard the idea, dismissed it out of hand. Utterly unreasonable. They had more important things to do. Not that it mattered. But Collingdale didn't want more division and in the end he was forced to intervene and insist, in the interests of peace, that Judy back down. The surrender was disguised as a compromise: English, or other non-Goompah languages, would be spoken by the linguists outside work hours when members of the Upper Strata or the captain were present, or at anytime during any emergency.

Collingdale did his best to appease Judy by including in the declaration that he henceforth considered himself a member of the language team, and would be bound by their rules, except when his duties made it impractical.

* * *

The only other functioning culture that had been found during the decades of interstellar travel was on Nok. It was the right name for the world. The inhabitants were in the middle of an industrial age, but they'd been up and down so many times they'd exhausted most of their natural resources. They were always at war, and they showed no talent whatever for compromise or tolerance.

The research teams had experienced massive problems there during the first couple of years because everybody who wanted a lightbender just checked one out and went down to the surface. They were forever running landers up and down with consequent waste of fuel. They had people fighting over e-suits, trying to monopolize the language specialists, and arguing constantly about the no-contact policy. A substantial number maintained it was immoral for the Academy to stand by while the idiots made war on one another, and huge numbers of noncombatants were killed. It happened all the time, the wars never really ended until everybody was exhausted, and as soon as they got their breath back they started up again.

The level of animosity among the researchers rose until it became apparent that the human teams weren't able to rise much above the level of the Noks. It was as if the Protocol should have been working the other way, shielding humans from the less advanced culture.

There was no evidence of conflict at Lookout, but once again they were facing the intervention issue. Except this time they were prepared to confront the natives, if it seemed prudent.

Not everyone on board was in agreement with that policy. Jason Holder, who described himself as the world's only exosociologist, had wasted no time taking Collingdale aside to warn him that contact would cause extensive harm in the long run, that if the Goompahs could get past the Event on their own, they'd be far better off if we kept out of it. 'Sticking our noses in,' he'd said, 'all but guarantees they'll be crippled.'

When Collingdale asked how that could be, he'd trotted out

the usual explanation about the clash of civilizations, and how the weaker one always, *always*, went down. 'The effects might not be immediately noticeable,' he'd said, 'but once they understand there's a more advanced culture out there, they lose heart. They give up, roll over, and wait for us to tell them the Truth, provide dinner, and show them how to cure the common cold.'

'But we won't let them become dependent,' Collingdale had said. 'We won't be there after the Event.'

'It'll be too late. They'll know we exist. And that will be enough.'

Maybe he was right. Who really knew? But the natives weren't human, so maybe they'd react differently. And maybe Holder didn't know what he was talking about. It wouldn't be the first time an authority had gotten things wrong.

Judy Sternberg was a little on the bossy side, and she ran her operation like a fiefdom. She laid out each day's assignments in detail, added projects if time permitted, and expected results. She might have run into some resentment except that she didn't spare herself.

Her specialty was, she explained, the interrelationship between language and culture. 'Tell me,' she was fond of saying, 'how people say *mother* and I'll tell you how their politics run.'

Like Hutch, she was a diminutive woman, barely reaching Collingdale's shoulders. But she radiated energy.

They'd been out more than five weeks when she asked whether he had a moment to stop by Goompah Country, which was the section of the ship dedicated to the linguists, housing their work-rooms and their individual quarters. 'Got something to show you,' she said.

They strolled down to B Deck, started along the corridor, and suddenly a door opened and a Goompah waddled out and said hello. Said it in the native tongue. '*Challa*, Professor Collingdale.'

Collingdale felt his jaw drop. The creature was realistic.

'Meet Shelley,' Judy said, trying to restrain a smile.

Shelley was even shorter than her supervisor. In costume she was wide, green, preposterous. Her saucer eyes locked on him. She adjusted her rawhide blouse, tugged at a yellow neckerchief, and held out a six-fingered hand.

'*Challa*, Shelley,' he said.

She curtsied and pirouetted for his inspection. 'What do you think?' she asked in English. The voice had an Australian lilt.

'We haven't done much with the clothing yet,' said Judy, 'because we're not really sure about texture. We'll need better data. Preferably samples. But by the time we get there, we'll have our own team of Goompahs.'

'Well,' he said, 'it looks good to me, but I'm not a native.'

She smiled. 'Have faith. When we go down, nobody will be able to tell us from the locals.'

Shelley took off her mask, and Collingdale found himself looking at an amused young blonde. Her figure in no way resembled Goompah anatomy. And he was embarrassed to realize he was inspecting her.

'I suspect you're right,' he told Judy.

He sent a twenty-minute transmission to Mary, describing what they were doing, and telling her how much he'd have enjoyed having dinner with her tonight on the *al-Jahani*. 'It's very romantic,' he said, smiling into the imager. 'Candlelight in the dining room, a gypsy violinist, and the best food in the neighborhood. And you never know whom you're going to meet.'

None of it made much sense, except that she would understand the essential message, that he missed her, that he hoped she'd wait for him. That he regretted what had happened, but that it was a responsibility he really couldn't have passed off.

He had been getting messages from her every couple of days. They were shorter than he'd have preferred, but she said she didn't want to take advantage of Hutch's kindness in providing the service and run up the bill on the Academy. It was enough to satisfy him.

This was the only time in his life that he'd ever actually believed himself to be in love. Until Mary, he'd thought of the grand passion as something adolescents came down with, not unlike a virus. He had his own memories of June Cedric, Maggie Solver, and a few others. He remembered thinking about each of them that he had to possess her, would never forget her, could not live without her. But none of it had ever survived the season. He'd concluded that was how it was: A lovely and charming stranger takes your emotions for a ride, and the next thing you know you're committed to a relationship and wondering how it happened. He'd even suspected it might turn out that way with Mary. But each day that passed, every message that came in from her, only confirmed what now seemed true. If he lost her, he would lose everything.

While he was composing the transmission to Mary, Bill had signaled him there was a message from Hutch.

'*Dave*,' she said, '*you know about the hedgehogs.*' She was seated behind her desk, wearing a navy blouse, open at the neck, and a silver chain. '*It's beginning to look as if all the clouds have one. Jenkins tells us there's one at Lookout. The cloud has fallen away from it since it angled off to go after the Goompahs.*' The imager zoomed in on her until her face filled the screen. Her eyes were intense. '*It gives us a second arrow. When Frank uses the projectors, instead of just giving it a cube to chase, let's also try showing it a hedgehog. If one doesn't work, maybe the other will.*

'*Hope everything's okay.*'

He was appalled to discover that some of his colleagues were actually looking forward to the coming disaster. Charlie Harding, a statistician, talked openly about watching a primitive culture respond to an attack that would certainly seem to them 'celestial.'

'The interesting aspect,' he said, 'will come afterward. We'll be able to watch how they try to rationalize it, explain it to themselves.'

'If it were a human culture,' commented Elizabeth Madden, who had spent a lifetime writing books about tribal life in Micronesia, 'they would look for something *they'd* done wrong, to incur divine displeasure.'

And so it went.

It would be unfair to suggest they were all that way. There were some who applauded the effort to get the natives out of the cities, get them somewhere beyond the center of destruction. But anyone who'd seen the images from Moonlight and 4418 Delta (where the first omega had hit) knew that a direct strike by the cloud might render irrelevant all efforts to move the population.

Most nights, before retiring, he sent angry transmissions off to Hutch, damning the clouds and their makers.

She seemed curiously unresponsive. Yes, it was a disaster in the making. Yes, it would be helpful if we could do something. Yes, getting them out of the cities might not be enough. She knew all that, lived with it every day. But she never mentioned giving the Academy a kick in the rear to try to jump-start something.

They had good pictures of several of the isthmus cities, identified by latitude. Their names were not considered a critical order of business by the linguists, but since they would probably not survive the Event, it seemed appropriate to get past the numbers. Collingdale wondered which of them would turn out to be *Mandigol*.

The cities were attractive. They were spacious and symmetrical, the streets laid out in a pattern that suggested a degree of planning mixed in with the usual chaotic growth that traditionally started at a commercial area and spread out haphazardly in all directions. Unfortunately, the patterns of the Goompah cities were exactly what would draw the cloud.

Markover's people had commented on a general style of design that had approximated classical Greek. They were right. Whatever one might say about the clownishness of these creatures, they knew how to lay out a city, and how to build.

The center of activity in the cities was usually near the waterfront area. But he saw parks and wide avenues and clusters of impressive structures everywhere. Bridges crossed streams and gulleys and even, in a couple of places, broad rivers. Roads and walkways were laid out with geometric precision.

Buildings that must have been private homes spread into the countryside, thinning out until forest took over. He spent hours studying the images coming from the *Jenkins*. The place wasn't Moonlight, but it was worth saving.

LIBRARY ENTRY

The notion that a primitive race, or species, is best served by our keeping away from it, is an absurdity. Do we refrain from assisting remote tribes in South America or Africa or central Asia when they are in need? Do we argue that they are best left to starve on their own when we have wheat and vegetables to spare? To die by the tens of thousands from a plague when we have the cure ready to hand?

Consider our own blighted history. How much misery might we have avoided had some benevolent outsider stepped in, say, to prevent the collapse of the Hellenic states? To offer some agricultural advice? To prevent the rise to power of Caligula? To suggest that maybe the Crusades weren't a good idea, and to show us how to throw some light into the Dark Ages? We might have neglected to create the Inquisition, or missed a few wars. Or neglected to keep slavery with us into the present day.

The standard argument is that a culture must find its own way. That it cannot survive an encounter with a technologically superior civilization. Even when the superior civilization wishes only to assist. That the weaker society becomes too easily dependent.

The cultures pointed to as examples of this principle are inevitably *tribal*. They are primitive societies, who, despite the claims made for their conquerors, are usually imposed on by well-meaning advocates of one kind or another, or are driven off by force. One thinks, for example, of the Native Americans. Or the various peoples of Micronesia.

However one may choose to interpret terrestrial experience, it is clear to all that the Goompahs are an advanced race. It is true that their technology is at about the level of imperial Rome, but it is a gross error to equate civilization with technology. They are, for the most part, peaceful. They have writing, they have the arts, they appear to have an ethical code which, at the very least, equals our own. A case can be made that the only area in which we excel is in the production of electrical power.

There is in fact no reason to believe that a direct intervention on behalf of the Goompahs would not be of immense benefit to them. Especially now, when they face a lethal danger of which they are not even aware. To stand by, and permit the massive destruction of these entities in the name of a misbegotten and wrongheaded policy, would be damnable.

The Council has the means to act. Let it do so. If it continues to dither, the North American Union should take it upon itself to do something while there is yet time.

—*The New York Times*
Wednesday, April 23, 2234

16

On board the *Hawksbill*, in hyperflight.
Saturday, April 26.

Julie, Marge, and Whitlock had become friends. The women called him Whit, and they talked endlessly about omegas and cosmology, elephants and physicists, Goompahs and God. The days raced by, and Julie began to realize she had never been on a more enjoyable journey. It was almost as though her entire life had been spent preparing for this epochal flight.

Whit consistently delivered odd perspectives. He argued that the best form of government was an aristocracy, that a republic was safest, and that a democracy was most interesting. Mobs are unpredictable, he said. You just never know about them. He pointed out that during the Golden Age, the worst neighbor in the Hellespont had been Athens. On the major knee-bending religious faiths, he wondered whether a God subtle enough to have invented quantum mechanics would really be interested in having people deliver rote prayers and swing incense pots in His direction.

Marge had been reserved at first, had seemed always buried with work. But gradually she'd loosened up. Now the three of them plotted how to save the Goompahs, and make sure that the

Academy was funded afterward so that it could learn to deal decisively with the omegas.

Julie wanted to see an expedition put together to track the things to their source. There'd been plans for years to do just that. The old Project Scythe, for one. And then Redlight. And finally, in its early stages, Weatherman. But it was expensive, the target was thought to be near the core, thirty thousand light-years away, and the resources were simply not there.

'We'll only get one chance to beat these things,' Whit said, referring to the omegas. 'The time spans are so great that people get used to having them around. Like hurricanes or earthquakes. And eventually we'll try to learn to live with them. So if we don't succeed on the first attempt, the window will close and it won't get done.'

'But why does it have to be us?' Julie asked. 'Why not some-body six centuries from now?'

'Because we're the ones who lived through the shock of discovery. For everybody else, it'll be old stuff. Which means people will still be sitting in London and Peoria complaining about why the government didn't do something when the cloud shows up to shut *them* down.'

Although he lived in a society of renewable marriages and, in many places, multiple spouses, Whit was a romantic. At least, that was the impression Julie had gotten after reading *Love and Black Holes*, his best-known collection of commentaries on the human condition. True love came along only once in a lifetime, Whit maintained. Lose her, or him, and it was over. Everything after that was a rerun. Julie assumed that Whit, who wasn't married, had suffered just such a loss and never recovered. She was careful not to ask about it, but she wondered who it had been, and what had happened. And, eventually, if the woman had any idea what she'd let get away.

Whitlock was tall, with a lined face, one of those faces that had been lived in. He had white hair, and exuded dignity. The rejuvenation treatments had come along too late to do him much good, but he didn't seem to mind. He told her he'd lived the life he wanted and had no regrets. (That was clearly a falsehood, but a brave one.) He was on board because Hutch liked him and liked his work. There'd been a battle about his coming, apparently. Whit wasn't a serious scientist, in the view of many, and consequently was not on the same level as others who would have liked the last seat on the mission. Julie had heard that Hutchins had taken some heat for giving it to him.

He asked Julie whether a lightbender would be made available to him when they got to Lookout because he wanted to go down to the surface and actually *see* the Goompahs. He was even working with some of the people on the *al-Jahani*, trying to familiarize himself with their language, but he confessed he wasn't having much luck picking it up. 'Too old,' he said.

He had turned out to be a dear. He did not assume a superior attitude, as she'd expected when she first saw his name on the manifest. He was already taking notes, not on what was happening on the *Hawksbill*, but on his own reaction to learning that an intelligent species was at risk. At Julie's request, he'd shown her some of his work, and had even gotten into the habit of asking for her comments. She doubted he really needed her editorial input, but it was a nice gesture, and she had quickly learned he wanted her to tell him what she really thought. 'Doesn't do any good to have you just pat me on the head and say the work is great,' he'd said. 'I need to know how you really react, whether it makes sense. If I'm going to make a fool of myself, I'd prefer to keep the fact in the ship's company rather than spread it around the world.'

He had a habit of referring to humans as smart monkeys. They were basically decent, he told her one evening in the common room when they were talking about the long bloodbath that human history had been. 'But their great deficiency is that they're too easily programmed. Get them when they're reasonably young, say five or six, and you can make them believe almost anything. Not only that, but once it's done, the majority of them will fight

223

to the death to maintain the illusion. That's why you get Nazis, racists, homophobes, fanatics of all types.'

Marge Conway's assignment was to assume the cloud would arrive over the isthmus precisely on schedule, and to find a way to hide the cities. She would do so by generating rain clouds. If a blizzard had concealed a city on Moonlight, there was no reason to think storm clouds wouldn't have the same effect on Lookout.

If the mission to shoo the cloud away succeeded, her job would become unnecessary. Marge was one of those rare persons who was primarily concerned with overall success, and didn't much care who got the credit. In this case, though, she couldn't conceal that she longed to see her manufactured clouds in action.

Marge admitted that she'd gotten the appointment not because she was particularly well thought of in her field, but because of her connection with Hutchins. She'd worked on a number of projects for the Academy, but had never before been on a superluminal. She didn't even like aircraft. 'The ride up to the station,' she told Julie, 'was the scariest experience of my life.' Julie wasn't sure whether to believe her or not because the woman didn't look as if *anything* could scare her.

'We have one major advantage,' Marge commented. 'Nobody expects us to get the job done.'

'Hutch does,' said Julie.

Marge didn't think so. 'Hutch puts on a good show. She knows that Moonlight might have been an anomaly. She's seen the clouds in action, and I doubt she thinks anything can turn them aside.'

'Then why are we being sent out?'

'You want the truth?' said Whit.

'Please.'

'Because the politicians want to be able to say they made a serious effort. If we don't try this, and a lot of Goompahs die, which they almost certainly will, the public's going to be looking for whose fault it is.'

Whit's statement cast a pall over things because he was usually so optimistic.

Marge asked him why he thought the decoy wouldn't work.

'Because somebody else tried it. We don't really know who, although we suspect it was the Monument-Makers. Somebody tried to save Quraqua at one time by building a simulated, and very square, city on its moon. At Nok, they put four cube-shaped satellites, each about two kilometers wide, in orbit. Both places got hit anyhow.'

'Sounds definitive to me,' said Marge.

'Maybe they waited too long,' said Julie.

'How do you mean?' asked Whit.

'At both places, the decoys were too close to the targets. By the time the cloud picked them up, it would already have been locked on its objectives. Lots of cities on both worlds.'

Whit considered it. 'You may be right,' he said. 'But we'll be showing up at the last minute, too. It's not as if we're getting there with a year to spare.'

Dead and buried, she thought. He must have seen her disappointment because he smiled. 'But don't give up, Julie. There's a decent chance the rain makers will work.'

Whit wanted to look at the cloud-making equipment, so in the morning Julie took them down to the cargo bay, which required everyone to get into an e-suit because it was in vacuum.

The bay itself looked like a large warehouse. Marge and Whit had not been off A Deck, which was the only area of the ship maintaining life support. It had therefore been easy for them to forget how big the *Hawksbill* was until they stood gazing from prow to stern, down the length of an enclosure filled with four landers, an AV3 heavy-duty hauler, and an antique helicopter. The rainmakers were attached to the hull. Julie took them into the airlock and opened up so they could see them. They resembled large coils.

'They're actually chimneys,' Marge said. 'When they're deployed, they'll be three kilometers long. Each of them.'

'That's pretty big.'

'As big as we could make them.'

Avery Whitlock's Notebooks

One of the unfortunate side effects of organized religion is that it seeks to persuade us that we are inherently evil. Damaged goods.

I've watched volunteers work with kids injured in accidents; I've seen sons and daughters give over their time to taking care of elderly parents. There are a thousand stories out there about people who have given their lives for their children, for their friends, and sometimes for total strangers. We go down to the beach to try to push a stranded whale back into the ocean.

Now we are trying to help an intelligent species that cannot help itself. Whether we will pull it off, no one knows. But of one thing I am certain: If we ever start to believe those who think God made a race of deformed children, then that is what we will become.

And who then would help the Goompahs?

17

On board the *Heffernan*, near Iota Pictoris, 120 light-years from Earth.
Monday, April 28.

Sky stayed well clear of the hedgehog. Since he'd watched the one at Alpha Pictoris explode, he'd gained a lot of respect for the damned things.

Emma was beside him, enjoying a mug of beef stew. The aroma filled the bridge. 'Bill,' he said, 'send the packages.'

He sensed, rather than heard, the launch. '*Packages away,*' said Bill.

The hedgehog was forty-four thousand kilometers in front of the cloud.

'Withdraw to five thousand kilometers.'

Bill swung the *Heffernan* around and retreated as directed.

'Keep the engines running.'

The AI smiled. He was on-screen, seated in his armchair. '*We are ready to accelerate away, should it become necessary.*' He looked off to his left. '*Sky,*' he said, '*we are receiving a transmission from the Academy. From the DO.*'

Emma smiled. 'That'll be another warning to play it safe,' she said.

'Let's see what she has to say for herself, Bill.'

The overhead screen blinked on, first the Academy seal, a scroll and lamp framing the blue Earth of the United World, and then Hutch. She was seated on the edge of her desk.

'*Emma,*' she said, '*Sky, I thought you'd be interested in the preliminary results we're getting. It looks as if, when these things blow up, they're not ordinary explosions. I can't explain this exactly, but I suspect Emma will be able to. The energy release is sculpted. That's the term the researchers are using. They think it's designed for a specific purpose.*

'*We hope, when you're finished out there, we'll have a better idea what the purpose is. And we appreciate what you've been doing. I know it's not the most rousing assignment in the world.*'

She lifted a hand in farewell, the seal came back, and the monitor shut down. Sky looked at his wife. '*Sculpted?*'

'Just like the lady says,' said Emma. 'Think of it as a blast in which the energy doesn't just erupt, but instead constitutes a kind of code.'

'To do what?'

She gazed at the image of the omega, floating serenely on the auxiliary screen. 'Sometimes,' she said, 'to excite nanos. Get them to perform.'

The packages arrived in the vicinity of the hedgehog and opened up. Twelve sets of thrusters assembled themselves, collected their fuel tanks, and circled the hedgehog. At a signal, each located the specific site it had been designed for and used its set of magnetic clamps to attach itself. The twelve sites had been carefully chosen, because on this most uneven object, the thrusters lined up almost perfectly parallel with each other. They would function as retrorockets.

'*Everything's in place,*' said Bill. '*Ready to proceed.*'

'Execute, Bill.'

The thrusters fired in unison. And continued to fire.

Satisfied, Sky got himself a mug of Emma's soup.

'You do good work, darling,' she said.

'Yes, I do.' He reclaimed his seat and slowly put away the soup. Bill screened the figures on deceleration rate, the fuel supplies left in the retros, and attitude control.

There had been some concern that the magnetic clamps would set the device off, but that had happily not occurred.

They were in a dark place, in the well between stars, where no sun illuminated the sky. It wasn't like a night sky seen from Earth. You knew you were far out in the void. There was no charm, no bright sense of distant suns and constellations. The only thing he felt was distance.

'*Retro fuel running low,*' said Bill. '*Two minutes.*'

The important thing was to shut them all down simultaneously, and not let one or more run out of fuel and cause the others to push the thing off-course.

'Bill, where will we be if we shut down with thirty seconds remaining?'

'*The hedgehog will have shed 30 kph.*'

'Okay. That means the cloud will overtake it when?'

'*In sixty days. June 27.*'

'Good. Let's do it.'

'I don't like these things, Em.' He pushed himself out of the chair.

'Nor do I,' she said.

He gazed down at the navigation screen, which had set up a sixty-day calendar and clock, and begun ticking off the seconds.

'I'm going to turn in.'

She nodded. 'Go ahead. I'll be along in a minute.' She was looking at the cloud. It was dark and quiet. Peaceful. In the vast emptiness, it would not have been possible to realize it was racing through the heavens.

'What are you thinking, Em?'

'About my dad. I remember one night he told me how things changed when people found out about the omegas.'

'In what way?'

'Until then,' he said, 'people always thought they were at the center of things. The universe was made for us. The only part of it that thinks. Our God was the universal God and He even paid a visit. We were in charge.

'I never really thought that way. I more or less grew up with the clouds.' She touched the screen, and the picture died. 'I wish we could kill it,' she said.

LIBRARY ENTRY

The omegas are a footprint, a signal to us that something far greater than we is loose in the galaxy. Once we used our churches to demonstrate that we were kings of creation, the purpose for it all. Now we use them to hide.

—Gregory MacAllister
'The Flower Girl Always Steals the Show'
Editor-at-Large, 2220

18

On board the *Jenkins*.
Tuesday, May 6.

'Never saw anything like it,' said Mark Stevens, the captain of the *Cumberland*, as he docked with the *Jenkins*. He was referring to the omega. 'Damned thing's got tentacles.'

That was the illusion. Jack explained how the braking maneuver tended to throw it around a good bit, tossed giant plumes forward as it slowed down. And more plumes out to port as it continued a long slow turn. 'Gives me the chills,' said Stevens.

Jack Markover was a Kansas City product, middle-class parents, standard public school education, two siblings. He'd gotten engaged right after high school, an arrangement heartily discouraged by his parents, who had assumed all along that he'd go to medical school, succeeding where his father had failed.

Jack and the young woman, Myra Kolcheska, eventually ran off, sparking a battle between the families that ultimately erupted in full-blown lawsuits. Meantime, the subjects of the quarrel both lost their nerve at the altar. Let's give it some time. See how it plays out. Last he'd heard, she was married to a booking agent.

Jack never got close to medicine. For one thing, he had a weak stomach. For another his mother was a hypochondriac and he always felt sorry for the doctor who had to listen to her complaints. He suspected that doctors' offices were full of hypochondriacs. Not for him, he'd decided early on.

He'd gone to the University of Kansas, expecting to major in accounting, but had gotten bored, discovered an affinity for physics, and the rest, as they say, was history. No big prizes and no major awards. But he was a gifted teacher, good at getting the arcane out there on the table where students could either understand it or at least grasp why no human being anywhere could understand it. And now he'd acquired a place in history. He was the discoverer of the Goompahs. He could write his memoirs and toss down scotch and soda for the rest of his life if he wanted.

The Cumberland brought fuel, food, water, wine, all kinds of electronic pickups, some spare parts for the ship, and assorted trinkets that someone thought could be used as gifts to win over the natives. They consisted mostly of electronic toys that blinked and donged and walked around. Stevens smiled while he showed them to Jack. 'Not exactly in the spirit of the Protocol,' he said.

Jack nodded. 'We won't be using them.'

The big item in the shipment, other than the pickups, was a set of six lightbenders. 'Did you bring one for the lander?' asked Kellie.

Stevens looked blank. 'For the lander? No, I don't think so.' He opened his notebook and flipped through. 'Negative,' he said. 'Was there supposed to be one?'

'Yes,' said Jack. 'They assured us it would be here.'

'Somebody screwed up. I'll look around in the hold. Maybe they loaded it without making an entry, but I doubt it.'

He went back through the airlock while Jack and Digger grumbled about bureaucrats. It took less than five minutes before his voice sounded on the commlink. *'Nothing here.'*

'Okay,' said Jack.

'I'll let them know. Get them to send it out right away.'

'Please.'

'Right. No point in the individual units if you can't cover the lander.'

Stevens finished unloading and announced that he'd be starting back to Broadside that evening. Schedule's tight, no time to screw around. And he laughed, implying that the same bureaucrats who hustled him back to Broadside in a mad rush would keep him waiting a week.

He had dinner with them, and irritated everybody by referring to the Goompahs as *Goonies*. Thought it was just impossibly funny. 'That's what they're calling them back at Broadside,' he said. And then, looking around at the others, 'Who's going back with me?'

They'd talked about it at length. Two years was a long bite out of anyone's life. It apparently never occurred to Kellie to ask to be relieved. The *Jenkins* was her ship, and if it was staying, she was staying. Jack saw himself as mission director and, like Kellie, felt an obligation to remain. He also expected to go back eventually as a celebrity. Books would be written about Lookout, and biographies about him. 'If we handle this right,' he told Digger, 'we can save a few of these critters and go back with our tickets punched.'

And Digger could imagine no conditions under which he would abandon Kellie. Or, for that matter, Jack, whose opinion of him mattered.

So only Winnie was leaving. 'Family obligations,' she explained, not without a sense of guilt.

When the dinner ended, they said goodbye, companions of the past fifteen months. 'Don't get caught in the storm,' Winnie told them, as she delivered embraces to all and disappeared through the airlock.

Stevens was telling Kellie something about the hyperlink arrangements. He wished them luck, and he, too, made his exit. The hatches closed, and they heard the muffled clangs of the docking grapplers.

Then the *Cumberland* was drifting away. And they were alone.

* * *

233

Transmissions from David Collingdale ('Jahanigrams') had been arriving regularly, spelling out what the linguists didn't know, which was a lot, and what they needed Jack to do when the lightbenders arrived. More and better recordings. More pictures to provide context for the conversations. Recordings of the natives in various situations, at play, at worship, haggling over prices, and, trickiest of all, during courtship. The Jahanigrams became a major source of amusement.

They also received a transmission from the *Hawksbill*. A tall, dark-haired woman, just beginning to go gray, identified herself as Marge Conway. '*I'm bringing some equipment with me,*' she said, '*to try to create a cloud cover over the cities.*' She was wearing a baseball cap, which she tugged down over one eye. Digger suspected she'd been an athlete of some sort in her younger days. '*The equipment will be stealth technology stuff. The Goompahs won't be able to see it unless they get right on top of it.*

'*I need a favor. I'd like you to scout the area for me. Find eight places where I can lock down my gear. These places need to have a few trees, at least. The more the better, actually. They should be as remote from populated areas as possible. And preferably four on either side of the isthmus, although that's not a necessity. They should be spread out, to the degree it's practical. I appreciate your help. By the way, I'd also be grateful if you could have Bill do some weather scans of the isthmus and offshore waters. Get me as much climate information as you can.*

'*Thanks. I'm looking forward to working with you on this. With a little bit of luck, we should be able to pull off a rescue.*'

'And I bet she will,' said Jack.

In the morning they tried out the lightbenders. Jack was the only one of the three who had any experience with the devices. He opened the packages, took them out, and removed several pairs of goggles. 'So we can see each other,' he said, pointedly holding them up and then laying them on a table.

The lightbender consisted of a set of transparent coveralls and a wide belt. The belt buckle doubled as both control and power unit.

Jack pulled on the coveralls, added a wide-brimmed safari hat, smiled at them, and touched the buckle.

Digger watched with pleasure as Jack faded from sight. The process took about three seconds during which he became transparent, then vanished completely. Except for his eyes. They looked back at him from the middle of the chamber. More intensely blue and bigger than he'd ever noticed. And disembodied.

'My irises, to be precise,' Jack said. 'The system is selective. Has to be. If it blanked out your eyes, you wouldn't be able to see. So it isn't perfect.'

'I'll be damned,' Digger said. 'You know, I've seen it in the sims, but actually standing in a room when it happens—' He started thinking about the possibilities of being invisible.

'That's why they don't sell them down at the mall,' said Kellie, reading his expression.

She and Digger strapped on the gear. She faded away and Digger looked down at his body, found the appropriate stud on his belt, slid it sideways, and watched himself vanish. A wave of vertigo swept through him.

'It'll seem a little strange at first,' said Jack's voice.

Kellie's dark eyes were full of mischief.

'Take a pair of goggles,' said Jack, 'so we can see each other.' One of them rose from the table, apparently on its own, and went over the blue eyes. The goggles vanished and the eyes came back. 'Ah,' Jack said, 'that's better.' The other two pairs also levitated, and one floated over to Digger. He took it and put it on.

The light in the room dimmed, but two shimmering silhouettes appeared.

'You'll need to be careful about walking until you get used to things. You can see the ground, but you can't see your feet. At least not the way you're accustomed to seeing them. Sometimes they're not where you think they are. People have broken ankles. And worse.'

Kellie popped back into the light. 'I'm ready to go,' she said.

'You know' – Digger smiled – 'you could get into a lot of trouble with one of these things.'

'Try your luck, cowboy,' Kellie said.

The *Cumberland* had also brought a substantial supply of pickups. They looked like large coins. *Wilcox Comm. Corp.* was engraved on the head, with an eagle symbol, and a reproduction of their headquarters on the flip side. They were powered, like the e-suits, by vacuum energy, and consequently could be expected to perform for indefinite periods of time. The back side would adhere, according to the directions, to virtually any solid surface.

They put about thirty of them into a case and stored it in the lander. It was late evening on the *Jenkins*, late afternoon on the isthmus. 'Let's try to get some sleep,' said Jack. 'We'll go down first thing tomorrow.'

When everyone had retired, Digger stopped by the bridge, saw that Kellie wasn't there, and knocked gently on her compartment door.

'Who is it?' she said.

'Me.'

The door opened slightly. She stood tying her robe. 'Yes, Dig?'

'I love you, babe,' he said.

'I love you, too.' She made no move to open wider.

'You know,' he said innocently, 'you never know what might happen on these surface trips.'

'They can be pretty dangerous,' she agreed.

He reached in, touched her hair, pulled her forward. She complied, and their lips brushed softly. She came forward the rest of the way on her own, crushed her mouth against his, and held on to him. He was acutely aware of her heartbeat, her breasts, her tongue, her hair. His right hand pushed against the nape of her neck, sank down her back, cupped one buttock.

And she backed away. 'Enough,' she said.

'Kellie—'

'No.' She put a hand on his shoulder, restraining him. 'Once it starts, you can't get it stopped. Be patient.'

'We have been,' he said. 'We just signed up for, what, another year or so out here?'

She looked at him a long moment, and he thought she was going to bring up Captain Bassett, which she often did when this topic arose. Captain Bassett had begun sleeping with one of his passengers on a run in from Pinnacle or some damned place. The other passengers had found out, the Academy had found out, and Bassett had been fired. Conduct unbecoming. Violation of policy. Once a captain engaged in that sort of behavior, he, or she, could no longer expect to be taken seriously by the other passengers.

But on this occasion, Captain Bassett didn't surface. Instead Kellie withdrew into her room and waited for him. He followed her in and closed the door. The bed was still made; a lamp burned over her desk. A book was open. She watched him for a long moment, as if still making up her mind. Then she smiled, her eyes narrowed, and she did something to the robe.

It fell to the deck.

Kellie took them back to the glade they'd used on their first landing, descending through a rainstorm and arriving shortly before dawn. They packed up a supply of water and rations and got ready to move out. After they were off the lander, Kellie would take it offshore to a safe place and wait until called. Jack and Digger activated their e-suits but, at Jack's suggestion, not the lightbenders. 'Let's wait until we're out of the woods,' he said.

'Why?' asked Digger. 'Aren't we taking a chance on being seen?'

'It's still dark, Dig. All you'd do is make it more difficult to walk. It's tricky in these things until you get used to them.'

'You guys need anything,' Kellie said, 'just give me a yell.'

They waved, turned on their wristlamps, and climbed out into the night. The grass was wet and slippery. Jack led the way to the edge of the trees and plunged in. Digger hesitated and looked back. The lander waited patiently in the middle of the clearing. The lights were off, of course, and the sky was dark. More rain was coming.

He knew Kellie would stay put until her passengers were safely clear. The east was beginning to brighten. Jack turned and waved him forward. He was really enjoying his role as leader and light-bender expert. The lander lifted, the treads retracted, and it rose silently into the sky.

Thirty minutes later they were out by the side of the road. Jack told him it was time to 'go under,' which, it turned out, was the standard phrase for switching on the lightbender. It had a disparate ring for Digger.

He touched his belt, felt a mild tingle as the field formed around him, held out his arm, and watched it vanish. When he looked up, Jack was also gone. He activated his goggles and his partner reappeared as a luminous silhouette.

They turned south. Toward Athens.

There were already travelers abroad. Two Goompahs appeared riding fat horses. They were gray, well muscled, with snouts, and ugly as bulldogs. 'Everything in this world,' said Digger, 'seems uglier than at home.'

'Cultural bias?'

'No, they're ugly.'

One of the Goompahs carried a lantern. They were engaged in a spirited conversation, which included growls and thwacking their palms together and jabbing fingers at the sky. They passed Jack and drew alongside Digger and suddenly grew quiet. To Digger's horror, the closer of the two had raised his lantern and was looking in his direction. Staring at him.

The animals sniffed the morning breeze, but they wouldn't be able to detect any unusual scents because the e-suits locked everything in. Still, it was a trifle unsettling, especially when one of the beasts turned its head and also looked at Digger.

'Your eyes, Dig,' said Jack. 'Close your eyes.'

He put his hand in front of them and began backing away. The riders exchanged remarks, and Digger was sorry he didn't have a recorder running because he could guess the meaning. Harry, did you see that? You mean that pair of little blue eyes over there?

Harry rode to where he'd been standing and looked in all directions. They exchanged a few more comments and the one without the lantern detached a switch from his saddle. Just in case something had to be beaten off.

Digger had to restrain a laugh at the weapon. But he actually did hear a word repeated by the second rider: *Telio*. The name of his companion?

Digger was tempted. *Challa, Telio*. But he could guess how the pair of them would react to a voice coming out of the air. He compromised by trying to memorize the features of the one who might be Telio. It was difficult because they all looked alike. But he marked down the creature's nervous smile, a battered left ear, and the shape of nose and jaws. *Maybe we'll have a more opportune moment.*

Over the next hour, they encountered several groups and a few lone pedestrians. There were both males and females on the road, and Digger noted that one of the females was alone on foot. The area was apparently safe.

They began to see scattered dwellings. The forest gradually died away and was replaced by farms and open fields. They stopped to watch a female working just outside a small building on a mechanical device that might have been a spinning wheel. An animal, a two-legged creature that looked like a goose with an extraordinarily long bill and protruding ears, waddled out the door, looked in their direction, got its neck stroked, and nibbled at something on the ground.

Digger backed off a few steps. 'You sure we're invisible to the animals?' he asked.

The creature's ears came up.

'Yes. But it's not deaf. Stay still.'

He'd learned to squint, thereby reducing the amount of exposed iris.

They passed a building that might have been a school. Inside, young ones scribbled on stiff gray sheets.

The room was decorated with drawings of trees and animals. Thick sheets, covered with characters they could not read, were posted around the walls. He could imagine the messages. *Square Roots Are Fun* and *Wash Your Hands After Going to the Bathroom*.

There was never a moment when you could say that you were entering the city. The fields contracted into parks, buildings became more frequent, and traffic picked up.

They were approaching a stream. It ran crosswise to the road, which narrowed and became a bridge. Jack examined the construction and took some pictures. Planks, crosspieces, bolts, beams, and a handrail. It looked sturdy. A wagon rumbled across, coming out of the city, and the bridge barely trembled.

A lone female was approaching. Jack and Dig always stopped when traffic of any kind was in the vicinity and they did so now. But she looked in their direction, and her lips formed an 'o' the way humans do when they're puzzled. She was looking curiously down at Jack's legs.

And Digger saw that he'd pushed against a melon bush. The melons were bright yellow and big as balloons and maybe a trifle ripe. The problem was that Jack had backed against them and lifted one so that it seemed to be defying gravity.

'Watch the melon,' he told Jack, who eased away from it.

The melon slowly descended, the branch picked up its weight, and the plant sagged.

'Doesn't look as if this being invisible,' said Digger, 'is all it's cracked up to be.'

The female wore wide blue leggings, a green pullover blouse, and a round hat with a feather jutting off to one side. She looked dumbfounded.

Something moved behind him. Wings flapped, and Digger turned to see a turkey-sized bird charging out of a purple bush. It raced clumsily across the ground, stumbled once or twice, and launched itself into the air.

The female watched it go and moved her lips. It wasn't quite a smile but Jack knew it had to be. Smiles seemed to be universal among intelligent creatures. Noks did it. The Angels on Paradise did it. He'd heard somewhere that even whales did it.

She advanced on the melon, studied it, touched it, lifted it. After a moment she let it swing back down. Jaw muscles twitched. Then she casually turned and continued on her way.

'Better be more careful,' said Digger.

'How bad was it?' asked Jack.

'It was afloat.'

Ahead, the road passed through farmland, rolling fields filled with crops, plants and trees in long rows, green stalks and something that looked like bamboo. Other fields lay fallow. Occasional buildings with a slapdash appearance were scattered across the landscape. Some were barns. Others were the huge, sprawling structures in which large numbers of Goompahs lived. They appeared sometimes singly, sometimes in clusters of three and four.

It was clear that they were home to communal groups, although what divided them from other groups or bound the individuals together remained a mystery. As they continued on, this type of structure became more frequent, but occupied smaller segments of land. And there were individual homes as well. Parks began to appear. The road became busy, and eventually expanded into a thoroughfare. Shops lined both sides.

Some public buildings possessed a level of elegance almost rivaling that of the temple. But most were of a more pedestrian nature, austere and practical. All were filled with the creatures, who leaned out windows and exchanged comments with the crowds outside. Young ones played in doorways, others frolicked on rooftops. Everybody seemed to be having a good time.

'Partyville,' said Jack.

Most of the shops were flimsy structures, plaster or wood with awnings hung over them. A few were brick. The shelves were well-stocked with fabrics, fish, wine, clothing, jewelry, cushions, animal skins, and every other conceivable kind of product.

'They have money,' whispered Jack. 'Coins. A medium of exchange.'

It was a chaotic scene. Merchants hawked products, customers pushed and shoved to get close to the counters. A quarrel broke out in front of what appeared to be a weapons shop. Everywhere Goompahs haggled over prices and commodities.

The coins Jack had seen were spread across the counter of a fabric shop. Hadn't been picked up yet by a careless proprietor. Behind him were displayed woven spreads and shirts and trousers and even a few decorative wall hangings.

It occurred to Digger that a coin would make a dazzling souvenir.

He hesitated. Everybody was so tightly packed together. But therein lay safety, right? In this crowd, who'd notice getting bumped by an invisible man?

'Jack,' he said. 'Wait here.'

'Wait, Dig. Where are you going?'

'I'll be right back.'

The battle at the weapons shop had not gotten past a lot of screaming and yelling. But it had cleared an area for him to pass through. The weapons shop had bows, arrows, knives, and javelins on display. They looked mostly ornamental, something gawdy to hang on the wall and maybe claim you'd taken from a fallen enemy.

His path to the coins took him directly past the squabbling Goompahs, who were hurling threats and making gestures at each other. Digger got jostled by one of the combatants, who turned in surprise and looked for the offender. 'Kay-lo,' he growled, or something very much like it.

The largest of the coins was about the size of a silver ten-dollar piece. It looked like bronze. A plant or tree was engraved on it, and a series of characters around the edge. In God We Trust. It was roughly made, the product of a primitive die, but it would be a priceless artifact to take home.

'*Don't do it, Digger.*' Jack's voice was stern.

'It won't hurt anything.'

'*No.*'

'It'll help the translators.'

Silence. Jack was thinking it over.

Digger would have liked to leave something in exchange, another coin, preferably, but he had nothing like that available. He'd think of something later. Come back tomorrow. Behind him, the combatants were drifting apart, issuing a few final threats before calling the whole thing off.

He scooped up the ten-dollar piece and turned quickly away.

The shopkeeper screeched. The sound stopped Digger cold because he thought he'd been too quick to be observed, thought the shopkeeper had been distracted by the dispute.

But he was staring directly at Digger. And beginning to babble. Others turned his way and moaned.

'Digger,' said Jack. 'Your hand.'

To the Goompahs the coin must have been afloat in the air. Part of it, the part covered by his hand, would have been missing altogether. He tried to adjust his grip, but it was too big. He was about to slip it into his vest when a large green paw tried to close over it. The thing held on and he couldn't let go. One of the creatures growled, and another barged into him. Somehow one got hold of his belt. They went down struggling and suddenly the one with his belt let go, drew back with a terrified expression, and howled. The coin got knocked away.

They were shrieking and squealing and scrambling desperately to get away from him. He realized to his horror that he was visible. They were screaming '*Zhoka!*' over and over, and the pitch was going high. He didn't know what it meant but it was obviously not good.

He got his hands on his belt, turned the lightbender field back on, and was relieved to see that it still worked. He tried to scramble away from the mob. But the Goompahs were running for their lives. Jack cried out and damned him for an idiot. Digger was knocked sideways and trampled. He went down with his hands over his head, thinking how there's no safe harbor in a stampede for an invisible man. He took kicks in the ribs and head, and something that felt like a pile of lumber fell on him.

When it was over, he staggered to his feet. The street was empty, save for a few injured Goompahs trying to drag themselves away. And Jack's ghostly form lying quite still.

Digger hurried over to him and killed the e-suits. Jack's head lolled to one side. He tried mouth-to-mouth. Pounded on his chest.

Nothing.

A last lingering Goompah blundered into them, fell, moaned, and got up running.

LIBRARY ENTRY

. . . Other people have families. I have only my work. The only thing that I really ask of this life is that I do something at some point that my colleagues consider worth remembering. If I can be reasonably assured of that, I will face my own exit, however it may come, with serenity.

—Jack Markover
Diary, March 4, 2234
(Written shortly after discovering the Goompahs)

19

On the ground at Lookout.
Tuesday, May 6.

Other than reactivate the lightbenders, Digger didn't know what to do. He told Kellie that Jack was dead, but she didn't have to ask him how it happened because he poured it out. *Damned coin. All I did was pick up a coin and they all went crazy. My fault. He's dead, and it's my fault.*

'*Take it easy, Digger,*' she said. '*Sometimes things just go wrong.*' A long pause. '*Are you sure?*'

'Yes I'm sure!'

'*Okay.*'

'He told me not to do it.' He was sitting in the middle of the street. It was dusty and bleak. There was still a crowd of the things, and every time he moved, the dust moved, and the Goompahs groaned and pointed and backed away.

'*Where is he now?*'

'Right where he fell.' In broad daylight. On the street. A couple of the Goompahs had been hurt, and others were creeping cautiously closer, trying to help, probably asking what happened.

'*We have to get him out of there.*'

'He's a little heavy.' Even in the slightly reduced gravity,

Digger couldn't have gone very far with him. Jack's face was pale. The features, which had been twisted with agony when Digger first got to him, were at rest now. There was no heartbeat and his neck appeared to be broken. 'I've tried everything I can, Kellie.'

'*Okay, Digger. You have to keep calm.*'

'Kellie, don't start on me.'

She ignored the comment. '*You* want *me to come?*'

'No. Stay with the lander.'

'*I mean, with the lander.*'

'No. My God, you'll panic the town.'

'*Can you commandeer a cart maybe? Get him to a place where I can get to you?*'

'You're talking about a cart with no driver going down the street?'

'*You're right. I don't guess that would work.*'

'Not hardly.' The crowd was closing in again. He hoisted the body onto his back and staggered off with it toward an alley.

'*Digger, I feel helpless.*'

'Me too.' Digger was crushed by guilt. Actually, he told himself, *they* killed him. The stupid Goompahs. Who would have thought they'd react the way they did? Damned things were dumber than bricks.

The alley ran between the backs of private homes on one side and what looked like shops on the other. It was empty. He stumbled on and told Kellie what he was doing. 'I'll stay here with him until it gets dark,' he added. 'Then we'll do what we can.'

He set Jack down but saw immediately there was going to be too much traffic. Goompahs coming from the far end, and a couple angling off the street he'd just left. There were some fenced spaces behind the shops, and he chose one and hauled Jack inside.

'I'm okay,' he told Kellie.

He settled down to wait. Kellie would have stayed on the circuit with him, but he was in no mood for small talk, and she got the message and signed off. Digger sat wishing he could go back and change what he'd done. It was a horrible price to pay for a moment's stupidity.

He could see past a chained door into an area that contained a couple of urns and shelves filled with pottery. Goompahs thumped around inside, but no one ever came out into the yard. For which he was grateful.

The sun crossed the midpoint overhead and slipped into the western sky. Voices drifted down the alley. Doors opened and closed, animals brayed and slurped, and once he heard someone apparently beating a rug.

Jack's body began to stiffen.

He talked to Jack during the course of the afternoon, but quickly broke off when he found himself apologizing. No point to that. Instead he promised to do what he could to make the mission successful. That's what Jack would have wanted, and Digger would make it happen. It was the only way he could think to ease his conscience.

The rain clouds that had been threatening the area off and on all day grew dark and ominous, but in the end there were only a few sprinkles, and they blew away.

The streets became noisier as darkness fell. The relatively subdued crowds haggling over prices were replaced by Goompahs out to enjoy the evening. Traffic in the alley stopped. For a while oil lamps burned in the shop, but they went out as the first stars appeared. Doors closed and bolts rattled home.

Kellie checked with him occasionally. He'd calmed down during the course of the day, had gone back and forth between blaming the Goompahs and himself, would have liked to pass off responsibility, but kept coming back to the warning from Jack. *Don't do it.* Jack had known what would happen.

It was almost midnight before he decided the attempt could be made in relative safety. Even then a few Goompahs were still hanging about in cafés.

'*On my way,*' said Kellie.

They caught a break. She came in from the sea, and as far as Digger could tell, no one saw the lander descend over the rooftops. The Goompahs in the cafés were singing and laughing and having a good time, and they stayed in the cafés. Kellie hovered high, above rooftop level, and threw down a line. Digger looped it around his harness and secured it beneath Jack's arms. When he was ready, he took a deep breath. Dangling from a lander wasn't his idea of a good time. 'Okay,' he said. 'Ready to go.'

She found a deserted beach and took it back down. When they were all on the ground she climbed out, embraced him, looked sadly at Jack, and embraced him again. 'I'm sorry, Dig,' she said.

They returned him to the *Jenkins* and conducted a memorial service. Jack had not been affiliated, but he'd occasionally commented that he would have liked to believe in the idea of a God who so loved the world – so they read a few appropriate passages out of the Bible. And they said good-bye to him.

When it was finished Kellie told him to get a drink, and she would take care of putting the body in storage. In the light onboard gravity, that wouldn't be a problem, so he gratefully accepted the offer.

While she was below, he opened one of the bottles that Mark had brought in the day before – it seemed like a different age now – and poured two glasses, setting one aside.

It occurred to him that he had his wish – that he was finally alone with Kellie.

He filed a report in the morning, accepting full responsibility. But he kept the statement general, not mentioning the coin, merely stipulating that he'd been momentarily careless and been consequently detected, and that the crowd had panicked. He added that he understood they would probably want to pull him out. If that was their decision, he would comply. But he asked that he be allowed to stay on, to finish the mission.

Meantime, there were pickups to be distributed around the

isthmus. They returned to the glade, but when Digger started to leave, Kellie announced her intention to go with him.

'Too dangerous,' he said.

'That's exactly why you need someone else along.'

They argued about it, but Digger's heart was never in it, and after he felt he'd convinced her of his basic willingness to go it alone, he agreed, and they started out.

By midday they were back at the scene of the riot. The garment district. Life had returned to normal, and if the Goompahs were talking about the previous day's events, it was impossible to know. The merchant from whom he'd tried to pilfer the coin was still at his stand, and seemed immersed in hawking his wares.

'Let's get some recordings,' said Kellie, all business, and probably determined not to let him think about yesterday.

A couple of blocks west of the shopping district lay an area dominated by parks and public buildings. One of the structures had signboards outside, rather like the ones you might still see near small country churches in the southern NAU. They took pictures and went inside.

A broad hallway with a high, curving roof ran to the rear of the building. There were large doors on both sides, and a few Goompahs wandering about, lost in the sheer space. Goompah voices came from one of the side rooms.

Digger looked in and saw several gathered around a table. They might have been debating something, but it was hard to tell. Goompahs seemed to put more energy into speaking than humans did. The laughter was louder, the points were made more vociferously, the negotiation was more demonstrative. In this group, voices were raised, and tempers seemed frayed.

'Fight coming,' said Kellie.

Digger doubted it. 'I think they just like to argue.'

'They don't hide their feelings, do they?'

'Not much.' Digger walked quietly into the room and planted a pickup on a shelf that was crowded with scrolls, aiming it so it got a decent view of the table. Then they went back out into the hall.

'Bill,' Digger said. 'First unit's up. How's reception?'

'*Loud and clear. Picture's five by. What's the argument about?*'

'One of them was cheating at poker.'

'*Really? Do they play poker here?*'

Digger grinned. 'Bill has no sense of humor.'

Kellie squeezed his arm. 'Sure he does. He did that last line deadpan.'

They went into other buildings and placed more pickups. They set a few around some of the shops and hid others in the parks.

The parks were everywhere. They were furnished with gorgeous purple blooming trees and cobblestone walkways and flowering plants in a stirring array of colors. There were benches, low and wide, impossible for either Digger or Kellie to use, but perfect for the locals. And there were statues, usually of Goompahs, sometimes of animals. One, depicting several winged Goompahs, formed the centerpiece among a group of walkways. The subjects were displayed in licentious poses. They wore no clothes, although genitals were discreetly hidden. The females, they could now confirm, *did* have breasts on the order of human mammaries.

'Incredible,' said Digger, just before a cub – what did you call a young Goompah? – crashed into him and sent them both sprawling. But none of the adults noticed anything unusual. The pup squalled and pointed at the spot where Digger had been standing and looked puzzled. A female helped him to his feet and chattered at him. Watch where you're going, Jason.

Two teams of seven players engaged in a game that looked remarkably like soccer. On another field, riders on the fat horses careered about, chasing a ball and apparently trying to unseat each other, using paddles as swatters. Small crowds gathered to watch both events. At the swatting-match, it was hard to tell whether it was an individual sport or teams were competing. If the latter, Digger could see no way to distinguish the players. But the crowd got involved, jumped up and down, stomped their feet, and cheered loudly whenever someone fell out of his saddle.

Kellie was moving too quickly for him. Digger had not entirely adjusted to using the lightbender. Not being able to see his own body, but only a luminous silhouette, still threw him off-balance. He hadn't been aware that he watched his feet so much when he walked.

'You all right, Dig?' Kellie asked.

'Sure,' he said. 'I'm fine.'

They were walking near the north end of the park, an area lined with fruit trees. In fact, Athens almost seemed to have been built within a huge grove. Greenery was everywhere, and edibles just hung out there waiting for someone with an appetite. No wonder these creatures seemed to have so much time for leisure.

'This place might be like some of the South Sea islands,' said Digger. 'Everything you need grows on the vine, so nobody has to work.'

They spent the afternoon trying to analyze how the city functioned. *This* looks like a public building, probably the seat of government. And *that* is maybe a courthouse or police station. (Digger had seen a uniformed functionary going in.) I'd say that's a library over there. And look at this, a Grand Square of some sort, where the citizens probably gather to vote on issues proposed by the town council. 'You think they vote here, Digger?'

'Actually,' he said, 'I doubt it. Place like this will probably turn out to be run by a strongman of some sort.' Around him, the shops seemed prosperous, the Goompahs content. Other than the one uniform, there was no sign of armed guards. 'Still, you never know.'

They peeked through the windows of a two-story building and saw rows of Goompahs sitting on stools, copying manuscripts.

They visited a blacksmith, watched an artisan crafting a bracelet, and got stranded in a physician's quarters when someone unexpectedly closed a door. They tried to abide by Jack's dictum that the natives not be allowed to see unexplainable events. So they sat down in the presence of the physician and his patient, and waited for their opportunity.

The patient was a male with a bright blue shirt. He was apparently suffering from a digestive problem. It was then that Digger first noticed the ability of the natives to bend their ears forward. While the patient answered questions, his doctor did precisely that. They left a pickup.

Later, they wandered through the markets near the waterfront. This was the same area that Digger had visited on that first night, when he'd placed the original set of pickups. The shops were decorated with brightly colored linens and tapestries. Pennants flew from rooftops. There were quarrels, beggars, some pushing and shoving, and once they saw a thief get away with what looked like a side of beef. So maybe Athens needed some policing after all.

Barter was in effect, as well as the monetary system.

Several times, Digger brushed up against the creatures. It was hard to avoid. What was significant was that the Goompahs, after they'd bounced off empty space, stared at it in surprise, moved their jaws up and down and muttered the same word. It was always the same. *Kay-lo*. The same thing the Goompah in the quarrel had said. He filed it away as an expletive, or as *strange*.

Two buildings on opposite sides of an avenue each contained a raised platform, centered among rising rows of benches. Concert halls? Places for political debate? Theaters in the round? They were empty at the moment.

'I'd like to see the show,' he told Kellie.

'We can come back this evening,' she said, 'and take a look.'

It was time to go see the temple.

It stood atop a crest of hills on the southern edge of the city, gold now in the approaching sunset. They climbed a road and finally a wide wooden staircase to get to it.

It was bigger up close than Digger had expected, round and polished, without ornamentation other than an inscription over the front entrance. Doric columns. A winged deity guarding the approaches, and watching over an ornate and lovely sundial, as though she were keeper of the seasons.

Walkways curved around the building and arced out to the highest point of the promontory, overlooking the sea. There were a goodly number of Goompahs, some simply strolling along the paths, others wandering among the columns and through the temple itself. There was no mistaking the sacred tone of the place. Voices were lowered, heads bowed, eyes distant. It was there that Digger first felt a serious kinship with the Goompahs.

A young one was being taken to task by a parent for breaking into a run and making a loud noise. A pair, male and female, approached the front entrance hand in hand, drawing closer together. Digger saw one bent with age struggle to kneel on the grass, lift a hinged piece of stone (by a ring installed for the purpose), and put something beneath it. *Money*, Digger thought.

An offering?

Moments later, a child who'd been with him retrieved the object. Or retrieved part of it.

'What do you think?' Digger asked.

Kellie's hand was on his arm. 'Don't know. Passing the torch, maybe. Bury in sacred ground and recover. Pass it on beneath the eyes of the gods. Probably leave part of it for the religious establishment.'

The winged deity was about three-times life-size, and, unlike the ones in the park, this one was clothed. The wings were larger, sweeping, regal. She – there was no question it was female – carried a torch which she held straight out from her body. Save the wings, the figure shared all the physical characteristics of the natives, but Digger would never have considered calling her a Goompah.

They mounted the steps. Digger counted twelve. And he thought immediately of twelve months, twelve Olympians, twelve Apostles. Was all this stuff hardwired into sentient creatures everywhere?

The columns were wide, maybe twice as far around as he could have reached. The stone felt like marble.

The interior was a single space, a rotunda. The ceiling was high, possibly three stories, and vaulted. A stone platform, perhaps an altar, stood in the central section. Other statues gazed down at them. None had wings, but all shared a sublime majesty. They wore the same leggings and pullovers and sandals as the locals, but in the hands of the sculptors they'd become divine effects. One male divinity looked past Digger with a quiet smile, a female watched him with studied compassion. Another, more matronly, female cradled a child; a large warrior type was in the act of drawing a sword.

Not entirely without conflict, were they?

An older deity, with a lined face and weary eyes, bent over a scroll. A girl played a stringed instrument. And a male, overweight even for a Goompah, was transfixed in the act of laughing. He seemed somehow most dominant of all, and he set the mood for the place.

'Are you thinking what I am?' Kellie whispered.

That all this was going to be destroyed? That the circular shape of the temple was unlikely to save it because it was much too close to the city? 'You know,' he said, 'I'm beginning to get annoyed.'

The floor was constructed from ornately carved tiles. There were geometric designs, but he could also see depictions of the rays of the sun and images of branches and leaves. There were more columns in the interior. These were narrower, and they were decorated by the now-familiar symbols of the Goompah language. They moved through the temple, taking pictures of everything.

The worshipers walked quietly. No one spoke; the only sounds came from the wind and the sea and the periodic scream of a seabird. In the west, the sun was sinking toward the horizon.

An attendant passed through, lighting oil lamps. 'It's getting late,' Kellie said. 'You ready to go back?'

Digger nodded. He removed a pickup from his vest, kept it

carefully hidden in his hands, until he'd inserted it in the shadows between a column and a wall. 'Last one,' he said.

'You think there's much point, Dig? I don't think anybody here says anything.'

'It's okay. The atmosphere of this place is worth recording and sending back.'

But he knew they wouldn't capture the atmosphere on disk. Hutchins, sitting in her office three thousand light-years away, would never understand what this place felt like.

They stood a moment between two columns and watched a ship pass. Digger tried to remember what the ocean looked like to the east. How far was the next major landfall?

'Traffic must all be up and down the isthmus,' said Kellie. 'North and south.'

Not east and west. There was no evidence the Goompahs had been around the world. Strictly terra incognita out there.

The visitors to the temple were filing away; Digger and Kellie were almost alone. The lamps burned cheerfully, but their locations seemed primarily designed to accent the statuary.

Digger looked at the flickering lights, at the figure of the woman and child. What was the story behind that? The images were aspects, he knew, of the local mythology. Of the things that the Goompahs thought important. This was information that Collingdale would want to have.

The place was different in some ineffable way from houses of worship at home. Or even from pagan temples.

They paused again before the winged figure at the entrance. 'Somebody here studied under Phidias,' said Kellie.

Digger nodded. Creature from another world that he was, he could still read dignity and power and compassion in those features. And the torch that she held spoke to him.

He looked back into the rotunda. At the laughing god.

The isthmus road seemed unduly long on the return, and Digger was weary by the time they reached the lander. Night had fallen, and he was glad to shut off the lightbender and the e-suit and collapse into his seat.

Kellie gave a destination to Bill, and they lifted off and turned seaward. 'How we doing?' she asked, reminding him that his bleak mood was still showing.

'Good,' he said. 'We're doing fine.'

For a long moment he could hear only the power flow. 'You going to be all right?' she asked.

He looked out at scudding clouds, bright in the double moonlight. 'Sure.' *Don't do it, Digger.* He was okay. A little down, but he was okay. 'Where are we going?'

'There's an island. Safe place to spend the night.'

'Alone with Collier on an island,' he said. 'Sounds like a dream.'

'You don't sound as if you mean it.'

'I'm all right,' he insisted. 'This island. Does it have a name?'

She thought a moment. 'Utopia,' she said.

LIBRARY ENTRY

The great tragedy confronting us here is not that the Goompahs, to use the common terminology, face massive destruction, although that is surely cause enough for sorrow. But what makes me sad is that they may pass from existence without ever having understood the supreme joy that accompanies the life of the spirit. They have lived their lives, and they have missed the heart of the matter.

—Rev. George Christopher
The Monica Albright Show
Wednesday, May 7

256

PART THREE
Molly Kalottuls

20

On board the *al-Jahani*, in hyperflight.
Tuesday, June 10.

The news of Markover's death had delivered a jolt, reminding everyone on board that the operation on which they were embarked had its unique dangers.

A few members of the research team had known him. Peggy Malachy had worked with him years earlier, and Jason Holder recollected signing a petition that Markover had sent around, though he could not recall the issue. Jean Dionne remembered him from a joint mission years before. 'Good man,' she told Collingdale. 'A bit stuffy, but you could depend on him.'

Collingdale had been on a weeklong flight with him once. He remembered Markover as aggressive, arrogant, irritating. Although he wouldn't have admitted it even to himself, he was relieved he wouldn't have to deal with him at Lookout.

The linguists were getting torrents of raw data from the *Jenkins*. They'd broken into the language, and were in the process of constructing a vocabulary that by then numbered several hundred nouns and verbs. They understood the syntactical structure, which resembled Latin, verb first, noun/subject deeper in the sentence. They had the numeric system and most of its terms down. (Base twelve, undoubtedly a reflection of the fact that Goompahs had twelve digits.) They knew the names of about forty individuals.

The city that Markover had called Athens was *Brackel* in the language of its inhabitants.

Brackel.

Whatever else you could say for the Goompahs, they had tin ears.

The residents of *Brackel* were *Brackum*. Well, Collingdale thought, there you are.

Two other cities for which they had names were *Roka* and *Sakmarung*. The planet, their word for Earth, was *Korbikkan*, which (as at home) also meant *ground*. They lived *in* it, and not *on* it, implying they had no sense of the structure of things. Their name for the sea was *bakka*, which also meant *that which is without limit*.

They had a complex conjugal system of shared spouses, which Collingdale and his team of specialists hadn't quite figured out yet. *Brackel* seemed to be home to approximately twenty-eight community groups. Spouses within a group had free access to each other, although it appeared they settled on a favorite or two, and only had relations with others to keep up appearances or morale or some such thing. It wasn't an area in which Collingdale was interested, but some of his experts were already making lascivious jokes.

Offspring from one group could, on maturity, become a member by marriage of specified other groups. But the choices were limited to prevent genetic damage. It was a cumbersome system, which would, he suspected, eventually give way to monogamy. Holder wasn't so sure, pointing out that similar systems were still in use in remote places at home.

They had not established whether the same system was in use in the other cities, although preliminary evidence suggested it was.

Life among the Goompahs seemed to be pretty good. Apparently, the crops all but grew themselves. Digger Dunn was still dithering about getting a reliable climate analysis, but it looked as if the temperatures ranged from cool to balmy.

The Goompahs talked a lot about politics, leading Holder to conclude that the general population participated in government. Whether the city was an aristocracy or a democracy, or some variant, was still impossible to say. Although some of Collingdale's people were entranced at the prospect of finding out, it was not a detail that particularly concerned the director.

And that fact puzzled him. He'd thought that his reason for coming, aside from managing a rescue, was to learn about the Goompahs. But he'd lost interest. In fact, he'd begun to suspect that he'd never really cared all that much. He gradually began to realize that he'd come because of the cloud.

His xenologists had insisted from the beginning that he warn the *Jenkins* people not to establish contact with the natives under any circumstances. They all seemed to think nobody else should say hello, but that it was okay for them to do it because only they knew how to do it correctly.

He'd warned them that policy had not changed to the degree that they should expect to sit down over dinner with the natives. (They still hadn't agreed on an appropriate term of reference for the aliens. *Goompahs* set his teeth on edge. *Brackum* was limited to the inhabitants of *Brackel*. Peggy Malachy liked to call them Wobblies. Collingdale began trying to encourage the use of *Korbs*.)

Shelley Baker invariably looked amused when they talked about limiting or barring communication. She said nothing in front of the others, but she'd told him privately that the omega made all the difference. 'We're going to *have* to talk with them,' she said. 'If nothing else, we have to be able to tell them to get out of the cities.'

Mary sent a message every couple of days. She kept them short, well within Academy guidelines. She'd tell him about a show she'd seen, or how she'd run into some old school friends downtown. Or how she still went to Chubby's, but the sandwiches had tasted better when he was there.

He replied in kind. He was busy, and sometimes couldn't think what he wanted to say. But he enjoyed switching on the system and imagining she was in the room with him. He told her about the work they were doing, how he'd been tweaking the visuals they were going to use to get rid of the cloud. And that he was trying to learn the Goompah language. 'We can make the sounds,' he said. 'Judy says we got lucky. Now it's just a matter of doing the work.'

Seeing her, listening to her voice, sometimes happy, sometimes wistful, fed his hatred for the omega. He took to spending time in the VR tank, where he conjured up the view from Lookout, as it would be in late November, when the cloud would be prominent in the skies. Vast and ugly, torn by its own gee forces, it would be coming in over the western ocean, visible only at night, rising shortly after the sun went down, growing larger and more terrifying with the passage of time.

It was obvious Judy was worrying about him. She occasionally joined him in the tank, when she thought he was getting too moody. 'The clouds aren't personal,' she insisted. 'Whoever, whatever, did this, it happened a long time ago. Who knows what the purpose was? But I'll bet, when we find out, if we ever find out, we'll discover it's more stupidity than venom.'

'You're kidding,' he told her, as they stood together on the shore near *Brackel* and looked up at the omega. He saw it as pure malice. And while he was not a violent man by nature, he would happily have taken the lives of the engineers that had put these things together.

But she was serious. 'Whatever it was, it's long dead. The machinery keeps working, keeps pumping them out, but the intelligence behind them is gone. And it couldn't have hated us. It didn't know us. It just—' She stopped. 'I'm not sure I'm making sense.'

He gazed up at the cloud, quietly unfolding across the star fields. 'Judy,' he said, 'I don't know how else to explain these things other than as an act of pure evil.'

'Well,' she said. 'Maybe.' She shrugged and looked out to sea, and he thought how attractive she was. More so there on the beach than in the confines of the ship. He wondered at the capability of women to take on part of the beauty of their surroundings.

But he could not keep his eyes long off the cloud. He yearned to be able to reach up and strike the thing out of the sky.

Judy was barely out of her twenties. She had a Ph.D. in anthropology, specializing in primitive religions, from the University of Jerusalem. Her reputation for linguistic capabilities had brought her to Hutch's attention. Collingdale had heard she was also a pretty good equestrienne.

Her parents, she told him, had been horrified when she volunteered for the mission. Nobody else crazy enough to go. Get yourself killed. There'd been a pretty big blow-up, apparently.

At her worksite she'd mounted pictures of several of the Goompahs for which they had names. Goompahs used a string of names, of which two defined the conjugal group and the region of birth. The others appeared to be individual and arbitrary.

To Collingdale they all looked alike. But Judy laughed and said there were clear differences. This one had a large chin, that one a weak mouth. She even claimed she could distinguish personality traits and moods: Kolgar was gruff, while Bruk was amiable.

She'd mastered enough of the language to be able to carry on a respectable conversation, though not with Collingdale, who'd fallen far behind. He could commit some of the words to memory, and knew how to say *hello, fish, cold, night, home*, and another dozen or so terms. If he were stranded he might even have been able to ask for the local equivalent of coffee, which was a brewed hot drink called *basho*. Sounded Japanese to his ears.

But she encouraged him and told him he was doing fine. And he took pride in the fact he was light-years ahead of his peers. Bergen, Wally Glassner, and the others couldn't have gotten the time of day.

They were still having trouble with the syntax. But there was plenty of time, and Judy was more than satisfied with their progress, so Collingdale was pleased.

They were at a point at which most of the data coming in from the *Jenkins* was repetitious, but Judy's team was becoming more practiced at setting it aside, at finding the constructions that helped them solve the inner workings of the language.

There were all kinds of sites where they'd have liked to see pickups. But the quantity of units was limited. And they were all in *Brackel*. They had only verbal descriptions of the other cities.

Requests to Digger not only indicated target sites, but also designated which surveillance units could be moved elsewhere. A transmission still took several days to reach the *Jenkins*, and moving the pickups around took more time. It was cumbersome, but they were making progress.

There was no information yet about local religions. Collingdale had no idea how old the civilization on the isthmus was. Had it been preceded by something else? What did the Goompahs know about the rest of their world?

Digger wanted to know whether he should use his own judgment about the pickups. Plant them, let them sit for a bit, and then move them around rather than wait for instructions.

Yes, you nit. Do whatever you can to get as much coverage as possible.

But that didn't work out either. A feed that had become interesting suddenly went dark and by the time they could direct him to get it back up and working, the line of inquiry had dried up.

Most of the cities seemed to have a library. They were getting pictures of Goompahs sitting down to read, but Collingdale and Judy couldn't see the materials. Invade one of those places, they told Digger. We need to find out what they're reading. Send pictures of the scrolls. Sometimes he wondered whether Digger had any imagination at all.

Judy made suggestions where the surveillance units might be placed for maximum effect. She pointed out that they'd gotten next to nothing whatever from the interior of the temple. Nothing ever happened on the main platform, the altar, whatever it was, except that one of the worshipers occasionally got up and stood on it in a pious manner and looked around.

Inevitably they ended back on Collingdale's beach, where he stared out at the dark sea – the wine-dark sea – while she stood by to ensure he wasn't alone.

A few cities along a seacoast. Widespread literacy. Sailing vessels. A peaceful society. Probably participatory government. Apparently universal education. Not bad, actually.

He wondered whether the human race had just encountered its first serious competitor. The *Korbs* would need an industrial revolution and all that. But if they could skip the Dark Ages, and the assorted other imbecilities that people had come up with, they might leapfrog ahead pretty quickly.

And the omega. They'd have to get past that too.

'They've got a lockup,' Judy announced without warning.

'A jail? How do you know?'

'Somebody got tossed in.'

'Do you know why?'

'No. I think he was trying to steal some fish. Got caught, the shopkeeper chased him down, and somebody came and took him away. So there *is* a police presence of some sort.'

They also had a series of terms for what seemed to be political leaders. There was a *kurda*, and a *krump*, and a *squant*. But they were unable to get equivalences for them. They were in charge, but whether a *kurda* was a king, a representative, a ward boss, or a judge, there was simply no way to know.

With so many young people on board, social life on the *al-Jahani* was active. It didn't usually get rowdy, but there was a fair amount of partying and VR games. The older members of the mission, anxious to get away from the noise, took to congregating in a storage area on C Deck, near the shuttle bay, where they talked about the mission, their careers, and the omegas. They worried

265

about whether they'd get to Lookout in time, and reminisced about the old days.

Collingdale had traveled with most of them before. And if they'd become cranky over the decades, they were nonetheless good people. They'd endured months and sometimes years digging on Quraqua and Pinnacle, or cataloging the systems within a couple of hundred light-years of Earth until we knew the diameter, weather, and mass of every world in the neighborhood. A couple had been at Deepsix when it had blooped into the gas giant Morgan. They had a history of getting results. Melinda Park, for example, had served four years on Serenity, a space station assignment that would have driven Collingdale completely around the bend. But she'd directed efforts to determine the laws of planetary formation and had won an Americus for her efforts.

Ava MacAvoy, who'd been with him at Moonlight, was there. And Jean Dionne, with whom he'd once conducted a romance that had been a kind of shooting star, lots of flash and then an eruption and nothing left. Except regrets. Nevertheless, or possibly because of that fact, they'd remained friends. Their captain was Alexandra Kyznetsov, who had also been at Moonlight, lobbing nukes from this very ship. She'd been embarrassed at the way things had turned out and assured Collingdale immediately after departure that she'd brought no bombs this time.

It would not have been correct to say that during the passing months they'd become a tightly knit group. In fact they didn't agree on much. Some thought the basic mission was to study the society on Lookout (before it got obliterated?) while others thought the intent of the mission was to get ready to set up a rescue effort. Although how the latter was to be done was unclear.

Some argued that, under the circumstances, they should forget the Protocol and make contact with the Goompahs, while others maintained it would do far too much harm. There was disagreement over how the basic research should be handled, who should be allowed down on the surface, what the priorities were, and how best to make decent coffee using the onboard equipment.

'*Basho,*' said Collingdale.

'I'm sorry?' said Elizabeth Madden, who'd been complaining about the coffee in Alexandra's presence, but who had no idea what Collingdale was talking about.

'*Basho.* Coffee. You'll have to get the language right if you want to prosper on the surface.'

Madden was the most outspoken of those who wanted to maintain the isolation policy. She was a small woman who always spoke in a level tone, never got excited, and seemed to have a mountain of facts to support any position. There was a quality in her manner that implied, without her saying so, that her opponents merely needed to hear the reality of a situation to see the foolishness of their position. She occupied the Arnold Toynbee chair at King's College, London. Her husband Jerry, also a xenologist of considerable reputation, had accompanied her, and usually led the opposition.

She was alarmed when she first heard that Judy Sternberg was having the pickups moved around.

'Unconscionable risk,' she maintained. 'We were lucky the first time. It would have been prudent to wait until *we* were on the scene.'

Judy shrugged. 'I can't see that any harm might be done.'

She closed her eyes and sighed. 'If the *Korbs* so much as become aware that we exist,' she said, 'their entire worldview will change.' Their natural development would be set aside, she argued, and they would become dependent, at least in their philosophy and probably in their development of technology.

'Ridiculous,' said Judy.

'They'll wind up on reservations! There has never been an exception to the general law.'

Madden didn't explain which law, but there was no need to do so. Somebody-or-other had laid down a manifesto that a civilization could not survive collision or integration with, or even a bit of jostling by, a more advanced culture.

'If we don't intervene directly,' said Judy, 'there won't be enough of them left for a reservation.'

'That's an exaggeration, Judy. You know it and I know it. We've survived at least one of these things at home, and other worlds have survived God knows how many. It kills off *individuals*, and that's regrettable. But it will not kill off the culture.' They were sitting in the area they'd fixed up in cargo, which someone had nicknamed the Oxford Room. 'Our obligation is to save the culture. To give them their chance to evolve.'

Well, maybe she was right. But Lookout was not a global civilization. It was a handful of cities, positioned on a narrow strip of land between major oceans. The cloud was coming and when the destruction was over, maybe the archeologists could go in and look at what was left of the culture. And the xenologists could go home.

Raw data poured in. Collingdale sent his analyses on to Hutchins, with information copies to the *Jenkins*.

The package went out daily at the close of day. They were, he thought, making excellent progress.

He had just finished sending off a message to Mary, exulting over how well the effort was going, when Judy asked him to come by the workroom.

He hurried up to the B Deck conference room that the linguists had taken over. Judy was there with a couple of her people, Terry MacAndrew from the Loch Ness area, and Ginko Amagawa from Yokohama.

She handed him a printout. 'We just found this,' she said. 'Thought you might be interested. It's from a conversation on a park bench.'

It was in Goompah, but using English letters. Nobody tried to translate it for him, and Collingdale felt the force of the compliment. He had to translate it however word by word:

'*ROM, HAVE YOU NOTICED THAT HARKA AND KOLAJ ARE MISSING?*'

'*YES. THREE NIGHTS NOW. WHAT DO YOU THINK?*'

'*I DON'T KNOW WHAT TO THINK. I HAVE NEVER HEARD OF ANYTHING LIKE THIS.*'

'IT SCARES ME.'

'IT SCARES ME TOO, ROM.'

Collingdale's first thought was that two of the young ones had been kidnapped. Or two lovers had eloped. Did Goompahs elope?

'We're not sure what *Harka* and *Kolaj* refer to. But we think they may be stars.'

'Stars?'

Judy glanced at Ginko. Ginko's eyes were dark and worried. 'We think they've just seen the cloud, Dr Collingdale.'

ARCHIVE

Nobody here can understand how it happens that a race virtually confined to a limited land area, sealed off both north and south by natural impediments, has managed to maintain what is clearly a peaceful existence. There are no armies, no walls, no battle fleets. No indication that anyone even carries weapons other than what might be expected for hunting purposes.

We are not yet certain, but early indications suggest the cities are independent, that there is no formal political framework, but that somehow they coexist peaceably.

This framework is difficult to understand in light of the fact that the Goompahs are clearly carnivores. Hunters. They do not appear to have a history extensive enough to explain the amity in which they live. We would also like to understand why they find Digger such a fearsome creature.

We share the sense of loss at Jack's death. But I would be remiss not to commend Digger and Kellie, without whom we'd be flying blind.

—David Collingdale
Hyperlight Transmission
June 9

21

On the ground at Lookout.
Friday, June 13.

. . . Invade one of the libraries. *We need to find out what they're reading. Get access to the scrolls.*

The *Frances Moorhead* arrived in the middle of the night with the industrial-size lightbender, which would hide the lander. Kellie and Digger thanked the captain, and transferred Jack's body. That was an ordeal that reopened wounds and left Digger wandering aimlessly through the ship after the *Moorhead* had gone.

He'd received a sympathetic message from Hutchins shortly after the incident. She was sorry, shared their grief, don't blame yourself, bad things happen. But she didn't know everything, didn't know Jack had warned him to stop, didn't know Digger was going to lift the coin.

'She never really asked for the details,' he told Kellie. 'She must know I left stuff out.'

'I'm sure she does. But the Academy needs heroes.' She looked at the lightbender and looked at him. 'She's giving you a chance, Dig.'

Kellie saw to it there was no time for him to sit around feeling sorry for himself. They tied the unit into the lander's systems, connected field belts around the hull, ran a successful test and headed for the surface.

Kellie trusted him. Had it been someone else, she might have been frightened. The prospect of being caught out there alone, weeks away from the nearest base, with a guy who was coming emotionally apart, would have been unnerving for anyone. But she'd known Digger a long time.

This wasn't their first flight together, and though she'd been aware from the beginning of his interest in her, she hadn't taken him seriously until the beginning of this mission. She wasn't sure what had changed. Maybe she'd gotten to know him better. Maybe it was that he hadn't embarrassed her by becoming persistent. Maybe it was that she'd simply realized that he was a good guy. In the end, she'd come to enjoy just being with him.

But the way in which Jack had died was a nightmare. And the ironic aspect of the event was that she wasn't sure she wouldn't have made a grab for the coin herself. Mistakes happen. And if you get unlucky, there's a price to be paid. It doesn't make you culpable, she told herself, and occasionally, when it seemed necessary, Digger.

She was glad to see the library request come through. It provided a challenge and gave him something else to think about.

The most accessible means of entry into the center of *Brackel* was through the harbor. But she couldn't simply set down in the water, even with the lightbender field protecting the lander. Its treads would create twin depressions in the water, an effect that would startle any witnesses. So they waited until the sun went down. When it was reasonably dark, Kellie came in over the harbor, past a vessel anchored just offshore (there was a light in a forward cabin but no other sign of life), and descended a few meters away from a deserted pier.

Digger was beginning to feel like an old hand. He slipped into the gear, turned on the Flickinger field, switched on his converter, put his laser cutter into a pocket, and activated the lightbender. Kellie climbed into her own gear and followed him out the airlock onto the pier.

He looked back at the lander. Its ghostly silhouette rose and fell in the incoming tide. Kellie directed Bill to move it well out into the harbor. They watched it go, then turned toward the city.

It was a bright, clear night. The big moon was overhead; the smaller one was rising in the west. It wasn't much more than a bright star.

Digger led the way through the harbor area. Lights were going on, cafés filling up, crowds roaming the streets. They had four pickups, two for the library, and two, as Digger said, 'for a target of opportunity.'

The target of opportunity showed up when they passed the two structures they'd thought of as theaters-in-the-round. Both were busy. Oil lamps burned out front, signs were prominently displayed, and the locals were pushing their way in.

'Care to stop at the theater first, my dear?' asked Digger.

'By all means,' she said. 'We can do the library in the morning.'

They chose one and took pictures of the signs, several of which featured a female Goompah with a knife, her eyes turned up. (When a Goompah turns those saucer eyes to the heavens, one knew that great emotions were wracking his, or her, soul.)

They waited until most of the patrons were inside before they joined the crowd.

The circular hall was three-quarters filled. Most of the patrons were in their seats; a few stood in the aisles holding conversations. Most Goompah conversations were animated, and these were no exception. That they kept looking toward the stage indicated that they were discussing the show. Stragglers continued to wander in for several minutes. Kellie and Digger stayed near the entrance, where they had room to maneuver.

Oil lamps burned at the doors, along the walls, and at the foot of the stage.

'What do you think?' asked Kellie, pressing a finger against the pickups, which were in his vest.

'I think Collingdale would *kill* to have a record of whatever's about to happen.'

'My feelings exactly.'

They waited until everyone seemed to be settled, then picked an aisle, moved in close, and squatted. An attendant went through the auditorium extinguishing some of the lamps. There was no reasonable place to attach a pickup, so Digger simply aimed it manually.

The show was a bloodbath.

At first Digger thought they were going to see a love story, and there was indeed a romance at the heart of the proceedings. But all the characters other than the principals seemed angry with everyone else for reasons neither of the visitors could make out. An early knife fight ended with two dead. Swords were drawn later and several more perished. One character was hit in the head and thrown off the stage to universal approval.

The action was accompanied by much music. There were musicians down front, manning wind and string instruments and a pair of drums. Onstage, the characters danced and sang and quarreled and made love. (Much to Digger's shock, there was open copulation about midway through. The audience, obviously moved, cheered.) Later there was what appeared to be a rape. With Goompahs it was hard to be sure.

The music jangled in Digger's ears. It was all off-key. It banged and rattled and bonked, and he realized there was more to it than the instruments he'd seen. There was something like a cowbell in there somewhere, and noisemakers clanked and clattered.

Eventually, the female love interest gave in to temptation a second time, either with a different character, or with the same character wearing different clothes. Digger couldn't make it out until the end, when three apparently happy lovers strode off arm in arm. Hardly anyone else was left standing. The audience pounded enthusiastically on any flat surface they could find.

'*Romeo and Juliet* with a happy ending,' said Kellie.

Romeo, Frank, and Juliet, Digger thought. Nevertheless, in his view, a distinct improvement. Digger liked happy endings.

The crowd drifted out. Some headed for cafés, others strolled into connecting streets. Everyone was on foot. No carriages rolled up, no horses.

It had gotten late. There was a sundial in front of the theater, but that obviously wouldn't work at night. He wondered how the locals scheduled a show. When the moon touched the sea? Sunset plus time for dinner plus time to walk in from a half kilometer away?

Anyhow, he had gotten it all on the pickup. They returned to the lander and sent it off to the *al-Jahani*, wondering how it would be received there.

They stayed in the lander, in the harbor, overnight. It was hard to sleep, because it was the middle of the afternoon their time.

Despite everything, despite his culpability in Jack's death and his sympathy for the Goompahs, he had never felt more alive. Kellie had fallen into his arms like ripe fruit, and he knew beyond any doubt that whatever happened out here he would take her home with him.

She lay dozing inside a blanket while he considered how well things were turning out and fought off attacks of guilt over the fact that he felt so good. It was possible his career might be over; he might be sued by Jack's family and possibly barred from future missions by the Academy. But whatever happened, he was going to come out ahead.

After a while he gave up trying to sleep and opened a reader. He scanned some of the more recent issues of *Archeology Today*, then tossed it aside for a political thriller. Mad genius tries to orchestrate a coup to take over the NAU. But he couldn't stay with it and eventually ran part of the show they'd watched that evening. The Goompahs seemed less childlike now.

'The audience loved it.' Kellie's voice came out of nowhere.

'I thought you were asleep.'

'More or less.'

'It was all pretty matter-of-fact,' he said. 'Nobody seemed shocked.'

She shrugged. 'Different rules here.'

'I guess.'

She rearranged herself, trying to get comfortable. 'But you know, if I was reading the story line right – it's hard to be sure of anything – but I thought they reacted pretty much the same way we would have. You could pick out the villain, and they didn't like him. They approved of the young lovers. Even if there were three of them. They were silent during the killings. Holding their breath, it seemed to me.'

Digger had had the same reaction.

'What did you think of the score?'

He laughed. 'Not like anything I've heard before.'

They went to the library next day. It was a battered L-shaped gray stone building set along two sides of one of the smaller parks just a block from the theater. They found a signboard posted inside the heavy front doors. Several pieces of parchment were displayed, on which someone had listed about two hundred items. 'Maybe it's an inventory of the holdings,' suggested Kellie.

They took a picture and drifted into a large room given over to reading. Nine or ten Goompahs sat at tables, poring over scrolls. A couple more were standing before boards to which notes were attached. (Looking for a ride home?) Another examined a map at the back of the room. A couple of the readers were making notes. To do that, it was necessary to go to the librarian, secure a pot of ink and a pen, and do it right there at his station, where he could watch, presumably to ensure you didn't have any sloppy habits. You used your own parchment, which was sometimes attached to a piece of wood and resembled a clipboard, and sometimes rolled inside a cylinder.

Digger noticed that the windows were screened with metal crosspieces and supported heavy shutters. Unlike many of the public buildings he'd seen, this one could be locked and bolted at night.

There were two librarians, both male. Both wore black blouses and purple leggings. Otherwise, they were not at all alike. One was older, obviously in charge. He moved with deliberation, but clearly enjoyed his work. He was constantly engaged in whispered conversation with his patrons, helping them find things, consulting a wooden box in which he kept sheaves of notes. None of the material seemed to be in any kind of order, but he kept dipping into it, rummaging, and apparently coming up with the desired item, which he would wave in the air with satisfaction before showing it to those he was assisting.

His name, or perhaps his title, was Parsy.

His aide was equally energetic, eternally hustling around the room adjusting chairs, rearranging furniture, flattening the map, talking with clients. He had something to say to everyone who came or went.

Between them they kept a close watch on the readers. Their primary function, Digger suspected, was to make sure no one got away with a scroll.

Kellie wanted to look at the map. 'Back in a minute,' she said. 'Don't go away.' He followed. The map was of the isthmus, and it looked reasonably accurate. The cities were marked and labeled, and he noted the symbols that represented *Brackel*. The map ended beyond the most northern and southern cities. *Terra Incognita*. A few islands were included. Digger remembered one, a big one to the west. Utopia, which they were using as a base for the lander, was not on the map, although it should have been. Beyond the big western island, he thought, lay the edge of the world.

He took more pictures, then resumed wandering through the room, looking over the rounded shoulders of the readers. The texts were, of course, hand-written.

The scrolls were not laid out on shelves, as printed books might have been. They were kept in a back room, secure from potential thieves. A visitor consulted the list at the front door, filled out a card, and submitted it to one of the two librarians, who then retreated into the sanctum sanctorum. Moments later, he emerged with the desired work. Judging by labels, many of the books required multiple scrolls, but it appeared only one scroll at a time could be had. And, of course, nobody checked one out and took it home.

The inner stack was closed off. It was a small room, located immediately behind Parsy's desk, and sealed off by furniture so that no one could get near it without being seen by him. It had no windows and no other exit, save into a private washroom. Its walls were lined with cubicles, in which lay the scrolls. The cubicles were marked with a few characters. *Biography*, Digger thought. *Northern Isthmus Travel. Literature. Mystery.* There were altogether approximately two hundred labeled volumes, comprised of roughly three times as many scrolls.

Digger, maybe for the first time since he'd been a child, took a moment to reflect on the pure simple wonder of a collection of books. Throughout his life he had always had immediate access to whatever book he cared to look at, to whatever body of knowledge he wished to explore. Everything humans knew about the world they lived in was within fingertip reach.

Two hundred books.

Literacy appeared to be widespread. The readers did not seem, in any way he could determine, to belong to a higher class than the Goompahs strolling the streets. He recalled the school he and Jack had come across outside *Brackel*. Outside *Athens*.

They were planning to wait until the place closed, and then begin the recording session. It was late afternoon, they'd been away from the lander for ten hours, and Digger discovered a need to relieve himself. It would have been easy enough had it been dark. Just find a remote street corner, shut the systems off, and go. But it was still daylight. They'd not been using the sacks that allowed one to dispose of waste inside the suit because then it became necessary to haul it around, and neither of them cared to do that. Just organize things properly, Jack had always maintained, and you won't need it.

Right.

Digger was thinking how he'd like to grab some of the scrolls and run. He entertained an image of a group of scrolls apparently leaping into the air and streaking for the exit on their own.

'You okay?' asked Kellie.

'Looking for a washroom.'

'Good luck.'

He found it at the rear of the building. There was only one for the general public, apparently intended for both sexes. He pushed through the door and entered a small room, equipped with a floor-level drain and some wide benches. No commode. You sat on a bench, if need be. The room was occupied, but only by one individual. Digger waited until it was empty, killed the e-suit, did the deed (listening anxiously for footsteps outside, trying to plan what he'd do if he got caught, knowing he couldn't just reactivate the unit without making a mess of himself).

But he got through it okay. Just in time, though. The door was opening as he hit the switch. Flickinger field on. Light-bender on. Goompah in the room, standing uncertainly in the doorway, as if he had just seen something out of the corner of his eye.

All kinds of firsts were being set here. First person to watch an alien theatrical production. First to visit a library. First to use a washroom.

He smiled and walked out into the corridor, forgetting that, to an observer, the door opened of its own volition. He realized what he'd done just as he started to close it behind him. Two more Goompahs were coming, one of each sex. The door caught their attention and he moved away from it, leaving it ajar. They looked at it, looked at each other, did the Goompah equivalent of a pair of shrugs, and went in.

Digger returned to the reading room, found a chair toward the rear, and sat down to wait.

Closing time. The last of the readers was waddling toward the door. When she was gone, the librarians took a quick look around, straightened chairs, picked up some loose pieces of the hard crackly material that passed for notepaper, and arranged their own stations. Parsy went into the back room, counted the scrolls, opened a logbook, and signed it. His colleague, whose name seemed to be Tupelo, put out the oil lamps, closed and bolted the shutters, and retrieved a wooden padlock from his desk.

Kellie was visibly impressed by it. 'They're not entirely without technology,' she said.

'No big deal,' said Digger. 'The Egyptians had them four thousand years ago.'

Tupelo closed the stack room door and lowered a bar across it. Digger had feared they might padlock the room, and he was primed to try to lift the key. But it didn't happen, and he was feeling that he was home free when someone knocked at the front door. The librarians opened up and a small, evil-looking beast was led in on a leash. The creature looked like an undersized pig, except that it had fangs, fur along its jaws and across its skull, and a line of quills down its back. It snorted and showed everyone a healthy double row of incisors. Its master, a brightly-ribboned female, moved in with it while the two librarians finished checking around to be sure everything was attended to.

'That what I think it is?' asked Kellie.

The animal's red eyes came to rest directly on Digger, and it commenced to pull at its leash. Its master spoke to it and the thing looked away momentarily and growled. Then its head swung back.

'As soon as she turns it loose,' said Kellie, 'things are going to get tense.'

The librarians filed out through the front door. The female

280

looked around the darkened room, apparently puzzled by the beast's behavior. Digger watched her kneel beside the animal and stroke its neck.

'Our chance,' he told Kellie. He edged toward the stack room, raised the bar, and signaled Kellie to get inside. When she'd gone through, he followed and pulled the door shut.

Simultaneously he heard a shout. Then, unmistakably, the beast was galloping across the reading room. They heard it slam into the stack room door, which Digger was holding shut.

More voices outside. Howling and scraping.

Then someone was tugging on the door. Digger backed away from it, looking around for a weapon, seeing nothing except the scrolls. The commotion outside continued until finally he heard the female's voice. Kellie produced a pistol and was about to thumb it on when the door opened. But the animal was tethered again.

Parsy held up a lamp and stepped into the room. Tupelo was speaking, probably trying to explain how the bar happened to be in the raised position.

The animal, fortunately, was being held back.

They looked in all directions. Obviously, no one was hiding there. When the animal continued to growl and show its teeth, its master kicked it. The thing whined but quieted. They dragged it clear, the door swung shut and the bar banged down.

'I guess we're in here for the duration,' said Digger.

'We can cut our way out if we have to,' said Kellie.

They listened to receding voices. Then came the familiar charge across the room by the little pig, and lots of snuffling outside their door. But the thing wasn't trying to tear it down this time.

Digger heard the front door open and close.

'What was the plan again?' asked Kellie.

The animal whined.

'No problem,' he said. 'When they come tomorrow to secure the doggie and open up, we'll just stroll out.'

The lightbender field faded, and she was standing before him.

'Have you considered the possibility,' she asked, 'that tomorrow may be Sunday?'

There were, in fact, 587 scrolls. They were tagged and divided into fourteen cubicles. Digger set up a lamp and worked one cubicle at a time, taking them out singly, logging the marking on the cubicle and on the tag for each scroll. When they were ready to start, one held the pickup, the other handled the scroll. And they began to record the Complete Available Works of the Goompahs.

Digger once again wished he had command of the language, and promised himself he would learn it, promised himself he'd read at least one of the texts in its original form before he went home.

They were surprised to discover some illustrations: animals and plants, buildings, Goompahs, maps. Other segments might have been mathematical, but since they didn't know what the local numbering system looked like, or the mathematical signs, they couldn't be sure (other than some sections devoted to geometry).

The paper used in the scrolls was of a textured quality, appealing to touch, but thick enough to limit the length of the work that could be placed on a single dowel.

The dowels were made of wood or copper. A few of the scrolls were contained within protective tubes that had to be removed before the parchment could be unrolled. The printing itself was simple and unadorned. Like the architecture, Digger observed.

They worked through the night. There was a brief rain storm around midnight. The creature at the door whined once in a while, scratched occasionally, but never went away.

They watched the time, and when they knew the sun had been up for a half hour or so, and could hear the unmistakable sounds of traffic outside, they decided they were pushing their luck, shut down the effort, and put everything back.

In time they heard noises at the front, heard the doors open, and someone took the beast away. It protested, the caretaker protested, and there was much pawing and scratching at the wooden floor. And then everything went quiet for a while. Eventually the stack door opened, courtesy of the younger Goompah, and they passed out into the musty, sunlit reading room.

'I feel as if we owe this guy a good turn,' said Digger.

Kellie was a glowing wraith in his goggles, gliding between chairs and tables. 'If we can figure out a way to turn that cloud aside,' she said, 'you'll have done that. And more.' The library was empty save for the aide. 'What did you have in mind?'

'When this is over—'

'Yes?'

'—And we know how things stand, I'd like to leave something for him. He'd never know where it came from. A gift from the gods.'

'Leave what, Dig?'

'I don't know. I'm still thinking about it. These folks like drama.'

'Oh.'

'Maybe something from Sophocles. Translated into Goompah.'

LIBRARY ENTRY

'Are books important, Boomer?'

'Reading them is important.'

'Why?'

'Because they take us places we can't get to otherwise.'

'Like where, for instance?'

'Like China, when they were building the Great Wall. Or Italy, when they were discovering that the world could be explained rationally. Or Mars when McCovey and Epstein first walked out the door.'

'That sounds pretty exciting, Boomer.'

'There's someplace else too, that's especially important.'

'Where's that? Ohio?'

'Ohio, too. But I was thinking that it's the only way you have of getting behind someone else's eyes. It's the way we found out that we're really all the same.'

—The Goompah Show
All-Kids Network
May 21

22

On board the *al-Jahani*, in hyperspace.
Monday, June 23.

It was the first day of full-time basic Goompah. The change came easier than anyone would have dreamed. Of the entire group of trainees, only two seemed to be struggling with the spoken languages, and even they could order food, ask directions and understand the bulk of the response, comment that it was going to rain, and inquire whether Gormir would be home in time for dinner.

They'd been speaking Goompah almost exclusively in the workroom since mid-May. And now Judy and her *Shironi Kulp*, her Elegant Eleven, were ready to excise all English from their vocabularies for the balance of the outbound flight, save when they had something that had to be passed on to the *makla*. The word meant *outsider*, she confided to Collingdale. It was the closest they could get to *barbarian* in Goompah.

They were permitted one sim per day. But teams had been assigned to translate the English so that even the entertainment was offered in the target language. An honor code was in effect, and violators were expected to turn themselves in.

Collingdale was present when Juan Gomez admitted to an

infraction within an hour of converting to the new system. Juan explained himself in Goompah, and Collingdale couldn't follow. Something to do with Shelley. The penalty was mild, a requirement to do an extra translation from one of the *Brackel* Library texts. A heroic poem, Judy explained.

Collingdale tried to restrict himself to Goompah in the presence of the *Kulp*. He was making progress, and he enjoyed impressing his young wards. They never ceased looking surprised, and he began to suspect they didn't have a high opinion of his intellectual abilities, or, for that matter, of those of the Upper Strata in general. 'Too locked in to their mental habits to be taken seriously,' Judy said with a perfectly straight face. 'Except you of course.'

'Of course.'

'It is a problem,' she said. 'People live longer all the time, but they still freeze up pretty early. Flexibility goes at thirty.'

'You really think so?'

'Lost mine last month.'

However that might have been, they called him in on that first full Goompah day and bestowed on him the *Kordikai* Award, named for an ancient Goompah philosopher famed for constructing what humans would have called the scientific method.

Had his support for them been tentative, that act alone would have won him over. They were the best people he'd ever worked with, young, enthusiastic, quick learners, and, perhaps, most important of all, they believed in what they were doing, saw themselves as the cavalry riding in to help an otherwise-doomed people. When the time came, when the cloud darkened the skies and frightened the wits out of the Goompahs, the *Kulp* would arrive, one for each of the eleven cities (by then they knew that the southernmost pair were a single political unit), their alienness hidden within Judy Sternberg's exquisite disguises. They would go in, do a few hightech magic tricks, claim the gods had sent them to warn of approaching disaster, and urge the inhabitants to clear out. Head for the high ground.

What could go wrong?

'*Challa*, Dr Collingdale.' They shook his hand and told him they intended the *Kordikai* to become an annual award.

But speaking Goompah more or less full-time was one thing to talk about and something else to do. The breakfast is good. There's a fruit bowl on the table. I am reading an interesting book. They had the lines down. And all quite effectively, except, of course, that they really needed to engage with native speakers. As things were, the conversation remained hopelessly superficial. It is nice out. Your shoes are untied. I am a little red pencil box.

'*Pay-los*, Dr Collingdale.' Good-bye. See you around. Until next time.

And *that's* what could go wrong. There would be all kinds of nuances that they were not going to pick up because there was no one to tell them where they were getting it wrong.

At dinnertime, he went into the dining room. Five of the *Kulp* were at a corner table. He wandered over and, in his measured Goompah, asked them how it was going.

It was going well.

Had they encountered any problems?

Boka, *Ska* Collingdale. *Friend* Collingdale. *Mr* Collingdale. *Acquaintance* Collingdale. Who really knew?

But they'd learned much since Digger and Kellie had penetrated the library.

The cities were significantly older than anyone had assumed. Their roots went back at least five thousand years. If that were so, how did one explain that they were still sitting on the isthmus? Why had they never expanded into the rest of their world? What had happened to them?

Prior to the foundation of the first city, which the Goompahs believed to be *Sakmarung*, the world had belonged to the gods. But they had retreated to the skies, and had left the isthmus, the *Intigo*, which was also their word for *world*, to the mortal beings, created by a mating between the sun and the two moons; between

Taris, who warms the day; Zonia, who brightens the night; and the elusive Holen, who flees and laughs among the stars.

The Goompahs had started with a ménage à trois, and several of the experts suspected there was a connection with the tradition of multiple husbands and wives in each connubial group. Collingdale knew that mythology inevitably comes to reflect the aspirations and ideals of any society.

They'd acquired illustrations of eleven gods and goddesses, and it had not been hard to match them with the sculptured figures in the temple at *Brackel*. There were deities charged with providing food and wine, laughter and music, the seasons and the crops. They maintained the sea, saw to the tides, controlled the winds, maintained the cycle of the seasons. They blessed the births of new arrivals and eased the final pains of the dying.

Jason Holder pointed out to him that, although their duties were similar to those of earth-born deities, there was a subtle difference. The gods at home had given their bounty as a gift, and might withdraw it if they were miffed, or out of town, or jealous of another deity. The *Intigo*'s gods seemed to have a responsibility to make provision. It was not quixotic, but rather an obligation. It almost seemed as if the Goompahs were in charge.

Also significant, Holder continued, there was no god of war. And none of pestilence. 'All of the deities represent positive forces,' Jason said. But he admitted he didn't know what to make of that fact, except that the Goompahs seemed remarkably well adjusted.

The artwork from the library texts revealed much about how the Goompahs saw their gods. They did indeed embody majesty and power; but there was also a strong suggestion of compassion. One of the deities, Lykonda, daughter of the divine trio, had wings. And she always carried a torch. So they knew who welcomed mortals at the entrance to the temple. There was as yet no indication that the natives believed in an afterlife, but Jason predicted that, if they did, Lykonda would be on hand to welcome them to their reward.

The cities formed a league whose political outline was vague.

But they had a common currency. And neither Judy's people nor Hutch's analysts back home found any mention of defense needs. Nor did the available Goompah history, sketchy though it may have been, indicate any kind of conflict that humans would have described as war. *Ever*.

Well, some intercity disagreements had sent mobs from one town to the outskirts of another, where they threw rocks or, in one celebrated incident, animal bladders filled with dyed water. There had been occasional fatalities, but nowhere was there a trace of the kind of mass organized violence that so marred human history.

There had even been a handful of armed encounters. But they'd been rare, and the numbers involved had been small. Collingdale could by no means claim to have a complete history of the *Intigo*. Still, this seemed to be a remarkably peaceful race. And a reading of their philosophers revealed a subtle and extraordinary code of ethics that compared favorably with the admonitions of the New Testament.

The Goompah world appeared to be limited to the isthmus and the areas immediately north and south. Their sailing vessels stayed in sight of land. There was no indication whether they'd developed the compass. They had apparently not penetrated more than a few thousand kilometers in any direction from home. They had not established colonies. They showed no expansionist tendencies whatever.

The Goompahs possessed some scientific and engineering ability. Judy's team had found a book devoted to climatology. Most of its assertions were wrong, but it revealed an underlying assumption that climatic fluctuations had natural causes, and if one could assemble the correct equations and make valid observations, weather prediction would become possible.

Some among them suspected they lived on a sphere. No one knew how they'd figured that out, but a number of references to the *Intigo* described it as a globe. Occasionally the adjective *world-circling* was attached to *ocean*.

The team had recovered and partially translated thirty-six books from the *Brackel* Library. Of the thirty-six, thirteen could be described as poetry or drama. There was nothing one might call a novel, or even fiction. The rest were history, political science – their governments were republics of one form or another – and philosophy, which had been separated from the natural sciences, itself no small achievement.

The Upper Strata made an effort to join in the spirit of things. They prepared lines and committed them to memory, so the common room filled up with Goompah chatter.

Challa this and *Challa* that.

Frank Bergen wished everyone *mokar kappa*. Good luck. Literally, *happy stars*. They could find no Goompah word for luck or fortune, so they'd improvised. Dangerous, but unavoidable.

When Wally offered a chocolate brownie to Ava, she had the opportunity to deliver her line: '*Ocho baranara Si-kee.*' *I am in your debt.*

Ava smiled, and Wally, fumbling pronunciation, replied that her blouse looked delicious.

Jerry Madden told Judy that he hoped she found success in all her endeavors, delivering the line from memory. And getting it right.

She replied that things were going quite well, thank you very much, and that his diction was excellent, rendering the last word in both Goompah and English.

Jerry beamed.

Elsewhere, Peggy got a suggestion from Harry Chin: 'When stuck,' Harry told her, 'you can fall back on *karamoka tola kappa*.'

Peggy tried it, beat it up a bit, and finally got it right.

'Excellent, Peg,' he said. 'We may draft you into the unit.'

'Of course. And what does it mean?'

"May the stars always shine for you."

Dinner was served with a Goompah menu, although the food was strictly terrestrial. While they ate, Alexandra, trying to use the language, told Collingdale something. But she butchered it, tried again, and threw up her hands. 'You have a message from the DO,' she said, finally.

It was simply a status report. Hutchins had rounded up the assistance of a few more experts in a half dozen fields, and shown them the recordings and the texts from Lookout, and she was forwarding their comments. Her own covering remarks were short and to the point. *You might especially want to pay attention to Childs's observations on the arrangement of the statuary in the temple. Billings has interesting things to say about the recurrence of the number eleven, although there's probably nothing to it. Pierce thinks he's isolated a new referent for the dative case. Hope all's well.*

What struck him was that she said it all in Goompah. And got most of it right. Not bad for a bureaucrat. 'Alexandra,' he told the captain, 'the woman has something going for her.'

Much the same thing happened when the daily transmission came in from the *Jenkins*.

'*David, we got another show for you last evening.*' Digger did it in Goompah. Collingdale hadn't known anybody on the *Jenkins* was making the effort.

Digger went on to explain they'd recorded a drama for which the *al-Jahani* already had the script. He smiled out of the screen, signaling that he understood quite well the value of *that*. An unparalleled chance to tie together the written and spoken versions of the language.

Magnificent, Digger, thought Collingdale.

'*We've also relocated some of the pickups to* Saniusar. *They're all designated, so you won't have any problem sorting them out. Raw data is included with this package.*

'*One more thing. I'm trying to translate* Antigone *into Goompah. But we don't seem to have the vocabulary. I don't know how to say* glorious, forbidden, fate, brooding, *and a bunch more. I've included the words. If any of your people have time, I'd appreciate the help.*'

Antigone?

Alexandra looked over at him, her forehead creased. 'Why?' she asked.

He shook his head. 'I've no idea, but it sounds like a decent exercise.'

Collingdale was in the shower, preparing to call it a day, when Alexandra's voice broke in with a general announcement: '*Attention, please. This is the captain. We are going to jump back into sublight for a few hours. There is no problem, and no reason to be concerned. But we'll be performing the maneuver in two minutes. Please get to a restraint.*'

Two minutes? What the hell was going on? She sounded calm and reassuring, but that was what most alarmed Collingdale. This was an unscheduled stop, so obviously something was wrong.

'*Everyone please find a harness and settle in.*'

It struck him that it was probably almost the first back-to-back English sentences he'd heard all day.

'*It's nothing serious,*' she said when he called.

'It's an unscheduled jump, Alex. That sounds serious to me.'

'*We're only doing it as a precaution. Bill picked up an anomaly in the engines.*'

'Which engines?'

'*The Hazeltines. That's why we're making the jump. It's routine. Anytime they so much as burp, we go back to sub-light.*'

'In case—'

'*—In case there's a problem. We don't want to get stuck where no one can find us.*'

'What kind of anomaly?'

'*Rise in temperature. Power balances.*'

He had no idea what that implied. 'I thought the engines were shut off while we were in hyperspace.'

'*Not really. They go into an inactive mode. And we run periodic systems checks.*' She paused. '*Actually, we've been getting some numbers we don't like for the last week.*'

'That doesn't sound good.'

'*It may not be a problem. On the other hand, we rushed the* al-Jahani *into service. Maybe before it was ready.*'

'We going to be okay?'

'*Oh, sure. There's no danger to anybody.*'

'You're sure?'

'*Dave, if there were any risk whatever to the passengers, any risk, I'd shut her down and call for help. Now, get into your bunk. I have work to do.*'

Hyperflight is a disquieting experience, an apparently slow passage, at about ten knots, through unending fogbanks. For reasons he didn't entirely understand, he had begun to think of his relationship with Mary in much the same way.

His communications with her had dropped off somewhat. His fault, really. Nothing new ever happened on the *al-Jahani*, other than the progress they were making understanding the Goompahs. At first he'd told her about that, but her replies suggested the stories about *zhokas* and temples and Goompah revels were not exactly at the center of her interests.

So now, at least, he had some real news to report. We are back out under the stars, he told her, and they look good. You don't appreciate them when you see them every night.

He'd been cooped up for more than three months. It was already the longest nonstop flight he'd made, and it would be another half year before they arrived at Lookout. 'All sense of movement is gone, though,' he said. 'We're at almost 1 percent of lightspeed, but we seem to be frozen in space.'

Becalmed in an endless sea.

One-third of the way to Lookout. He tried to say it aloud in Goompah, but he didn't know how to express fractions. Or percentages. Did Goompahs have decimal points?

They must if they'd designed and built the temple.

And his mind ran on: How would you say *jump engines* in Goompah? *Molly* was *jump*. No reason he couldn't use it as an adjective. And a machine, a mechanism, like the hand-cranked pump they used to get water into their plumbing system, was a *kalottul*. Hence *molly kalottuls*, literally *jump machines*. Without their *molly kalottuls*, how long would it take to get to *Brackel*?

It occurred to him that he was putting all this into the transmission. But it would scare her, even though he'd assured her there was no danger. Still, he went back and deleted it. He finished up, telling her they would be on their way again shortly. And that he missed her.

He didn't tell her that he thought he was losing her. That he felt every mile of the void between them. Not the void as it was counted in light-years. But as in *distant*, *remote*, *hidden*.

The laughter was gone.

When he'd completed the transmission and sent it off, he went back to the problem he'd set himself. How long to travel to Lookout at current velocity?

They were still about eighteen hundred light-years away. At one light-year per century.

Better have a good book ready.

Alexandra came back on-line: '*Dave, you can tell your people we're okay. Just running some tests now. We'll be getting under way again within an hour.*'

'We're clear?'

'*Well,*' she said, '*we've got some worn valves and a feeder line, and the clocks have gotten out of sync. We've checked the maintenance reports, and they never got to them in port.*'

His first reaction was that heads would roll. And it must have shown when he told her that he hoped they'd be able to get to Lookout without any more problems.

'*You can't really blame the engineers, Dave. Everything was being rushed to get us out of there. Actually, it should have been okay for a couple more runs. But you can never really be sure. I'm talking about the valves and the feeder line now. The clocks we've already taken care of. And I'm replacing the line. The valves, though, are something else. Heavy work, in-port stuff.*'

We can't do much about them, except take it easy on them the rest of the way.'

'How do you take it easy on a jump engine?' he asked.

'You say nice things to it.'

'Alex, let me ask you again—'

'There's no risk to the ship, David. These things are engineered so that at the first hint of a serious problem it jumps back into sublight and shuts itself down. Just as it did this morning.' Her voice changed, became subdued. 'Whether we get to Lookout or not, that's another story.'

LIBRARY ENTRY

'How far is the sky, Boomer?'
'It's close enough to touch, Shalla.'
'Really? Marigold said it's very far.'
'Only if you open your eyes.'

—The *Goompah Show*
Summer Special, All-Kids Network
June 21

23

On board the *Heffernan*.
Friday, June 27.

'Electrical activity picking up inside the omega,' said Sky. It was getting close to the hedgehog.

'*Estimated time fifty minutes,*' said Bill. The rate of closure was just over 30 kph.

The *Heffernan* had backed away to 80 million klicks, the minimum range set by Hutchins. They were watching by way of a half dozen probes running with the omega, and they were maintaining jump status so they could leave in a hurry if the need arose. That used a substantial quantity of fuel and would require all kinds of refitting when they got back to Serenity. But that was the point: They were making sure they would get back.

'I don't know how big this is going to be,' Sky told Em, 'but they've got my attention.'

The overhead monitor carried a picture of the omega as seen from the monitors, a wall of churning mist streaked with bursts of incandescence. The cloud was usually dark and untroubled, but now it almost seemed as if the thing was reacting to the chase. Sky was glad to be well away from it.

Other displays provided views of the hedgehog and the forward section of the omega. He watched the range between them growing shorter. Watched the flow of black mist across the face of the cloud, the electricity rippling through its depths.

Emma refused to commit herself about what would happen. 'Large bang,' she said. Beyond that, the data were insufficient. It was all guesswork. That was why they were out here doing this, to find out.

The cloud seemed almost to have a defined surface. Like a body of water rather than mist. Sky had looked at some of the visuals from researchers who had snuggled up against omegas and even on a couple of occasions penetrated them. The clouds looked thick enough to walk on.

A flash of lightning, reflected through the monitors, lit up the bridge. The pictures broke up and came back. 'Big one,' he said.

The hedgehog had seemed enormous when the thruster packages had closed in on it two months before. Six and a half kilometers wide. Skyscraper-sized spines. Seen against the enormous span of the omega, it might have been only a floating spore.

More heavy lightning.

'Bill,' said Sky, 'let's buckle in.'

The AI acknowledged, and the harnesses descended around them.

'You know,' said Emma, 'about twenty years ago they towed an old freighter up to one of these things and pushed it inside. One of the Babcock models. Looked like a big box.'

'What happened?'

'It got within about twenty klicks before a bolt of lightning took it out. All but blew it apart.'

'At twenty klicks.'

'Yep.'

'Won't be long for our guy.' He tried to relax. Theirs was an unsettling assignment. God knew they were far enough away to have plenty of warning, and they could jump out of danger. But Hutch had explained there was a risk, they just didn't know, she would understand if they'd just as soon pass on the assignment. In case the worst did happen, they were maintaining a moment-to-moment on-line feed to Serenity.

The range shortened to twenty kilometers, the range of the freighter, and then to fifteen. The cloud flickered, and Sky could have sworn he heard a rumble, but that was, of course, impossible, so he didn't say anything but just watched the gap continue to close.

At twelve klicks Bill reported that electrical activity inside the cloud had increased by a factor of two over its normal state.

At ten, a lightning bolt leaped out of the roiling mist and touched the hedgehog. Embraced it.

One of the imagers went out. 'I think it hit the package, too,' said Emma.

The hedgehog was by then so close that none of their angles showed separation. It was almost into the cloud.

A second bolt flickered around the hedgehog, licked at it, seemed to draw it forward. The mists churned. And the hedgehog slipped inside.

The pictures coming from the probes showed nothing but cloud. He checked the time. Sixteen forty-eight hours. Adjust for signal lag and make it 1644.

They waited.

Ragged bolts ripped through the cloud. It brightened. And then it began to fade.

'Well, Em,' said Sky, 'that was something of a bust. Do we go around the other side to see if the hedgehog comes out?'

Emma was still watching the screens. 'Not so fast,' she said.

For several minutes the omega grew alternately brighter and darker. Lightning flowed along its surface like liquid fire. Then it began to shine.

And it went incandescent.

One by one, the feeds from the accompanying probes died.

Emma's eyes looked very blue.

'Bill,' said Sky, 'be ready to go.'

'*Say the word, Sky.*' The engines changed tone.

It was becoming a sun.

'What's happening to it, Em?'

'I have no idea,' she said.

'Bill, has it exploded?'

'*I don't think so. The sensors are gone, but the remotes haven't detected a shock wave.*'

'That's good.'

'Readings are off the scale,' said Em.

He shut down the monitors.

'*Sky, do you wish to leave the area?*'

'This is goofy,' said Em. 'How can we not be getting a shock wave?'

'I have no idea.'

'It shouldn't be happening. I can't be sure because everything we have is blown out. But the way it was going, I'd guess it's putting out the light-equivalent of a small nova. Without the explosion. Without the blast.'

'Is that possible?'

'We'll see what the measurements look like. Meantime, yes, I'd say we're watching it happen.'

'I don't think I understand.'

'Think flashbulb,' she said. 'And tell Bill we should go.'

LIBRARY ENTRY

. . . And then there are those who say there is no evidence of the existence of God.

Think about the universe. To understand how it works, one must grasp the significance of light. It is the speed limit, the boundary, the measure of physical reality. We use it as a metaphor for knowledge, for intelligence, for reason. We speak of the forces of light. It is so bound up in our souls that we think of it as the very essence of existence. And yet there is no definable necessity for a

300

physical force that can be observed by sense organs. By eyes. If there is proof anywhere of an involved God, it is the existence of light.

—Conan Magruder
Time and Tide

24

24

Woodbridge, Virginia.
Sunday, June 29.

Hutch sat on a rocker on the front deck watching Maureen and Tor tossing a beach ball back and forth. Maureen's tactic, when she had the ball, was to charge her father, giggling wildly, while he ran for cover. But she inevitably lost control of the ball, popping it in the air or squirting it sideways or kicking it into the rosebushes.

It was an early-summer day, filled with the sounds of a ball game a couple of blocks over, and the barking of Max, their neighbors' golden retriever, who wanted to get out to play with Maureen, but they weren't home and nobody was there to unlatch the screen door. So Max whined and barked and snuffled.

The warning from Alex, from the *al-Jahani*, had come in only moments ago. *If you have an alternate plan, you might want to implement.*

Yes, indeed. Send in the second team.

Alex was citing a fifty-fifty chance that she could make it to Lookout. But Hutch knew she didn't really believe that. Captains were expected to be both accurate and optimistic. It was a tradition that probably went back to Odysseus. But it didn't take much insight to see how she really felt.

The problem was that, other than the *Hawksbill*, there was no alternate plan. If the *al-Jahani* broke down, she'd have nothing left but the kite.

Maureen was charging her daddy again, trying to raise the ball over her head. Max was barking. Somebody must have just belted a long one at the ballpark because the crowd was roaring. Maureen tripped over her own feet and went rear end over beach ball. She came up screaming, rubbing her eyes. Tor hurried to her side and scooped her up and returned her to the deck, where Hutch soothed her and checked her for scratches and handed her a glass of lemonade.

'You all right?' Tor asked.

It took a moment before she realized he was talking to her and not to Maureen. 'Sure. Why do you ask?'

He sat down beside her and looked at her in a way that said she was wearing all her emotions.

She shrugged. 'Maybe it'll get there. Sometimes I tend to assume the worst.'

Tor nodded. 'That's what I've always heard about you.'

Maureen was trying to gulp her lemonade. 'Take your time, sweetie,' said Hutch.

Cathie Blaylock came out of her house across the way, waved, picked up something on her deck, and went back inside. Maureen put the lemonade down, said, 'Daddy, again,' and started tugging at her father's knee. Ready to go another round.

'You don't have anybody you could send after them?' he asked. 'Pick them up if they get in trouble?'

'No,' she said quietly, 'nobody who could do that and get them to Lookout on time.'

'So what are we going to do?'

'Only one thing we can do.'

'And what's that?'

'Hope our luck holds. And alert Digger that he might have to get inventive.'

* * *

While she was on the circuit, the watch officer told her that the results from the *Heffernan* had just come in.

Hutch held her breath. 'What happened?'

'*It lit up*,' he said. '*The cloud became a torch.*'

'Is it a tewk?'

'*Too soon to tell. The lab just got it. But they're pretty excited.*'

Two hours later she had confirmation from Charlie. '*No question,*' he said. '*It's the same spectrogram.*'

ARCHIVE

COSMIC MARKER. It now appears that the omega clouds, which have mystified scientists for thirty years, and have spawned a whole new branch of research, may be only an experimental device themselves. Although their purpose remains unclear, according to Dr Lee MacElroy of the International Research Center in Edinburgh, they may well be part of an experiment gone awry.

—*Science News*
June 30

LIBRARY ENTRY
Priscilla Hutchins's Diary
(Reaction to above)

MacElroy never got anything right in his life.

—July 3

25

Lookout. On the ground at *Brackel*.
Wednesday, August 13.

Digger had become fascinated by the Goompahs, had learned to enjoy the shows, would have gone down every day to mingle with the crowds, to visit the temple, to stand outside the cafés, wishing he could take a place at one of the tables and join in the conversation.

Kellie told him he had cabin fever. But it was more than that. He had never been anywhere before where the inhabitants seemed to enjoy themselves so thoroughly. The nights were filled with laughter and music, and the downtown area played host each evening to happy crowds.

So they took the lander down regularly, and, to the extent they were able, mixed with the locals. Some nights they strolled along the beaches. Others, they went to concerts and visited sporting events, and sometimes they just sat in one of the parks.

Had they been able to set aside the coming storm, and the haunting memory of Jack's death, it would have been a golden time. Kellie was bright and upbeat. She shared his fascination, had picked up enough of the language to understand much of what was going on around her. And he knew that the day would come when he'd look back on these evenings with a sense of wistfulness and loss.

The omega had by then become visible in the sense that a small patch of stars had gone missing. Occasionally Digger overheard conversations about it, conversations that grew more frequent as the weeks passed and more stars blinked out. The Goompahs admitted to each other that they'd never seen anything like it. There was no record of any such occurrence in the histories, and Digger could see they were getting nervous. He wondered how they'd be when it filled the sky.

The thing rose at night a few hours after sunset, and dropped into the sea just before dawn. And the Goompahs watched.

Where was *Melakar*?

Where was *Hazhurpol*?

Behind the cloud, he was tempted to tell them. They're there, and if you folks know what's good for you, you'll start thinking about packing up and heading for the hills.

It might have been the sense that Athens, *Brackel*, with its theaters and its parks and its scrolls, was approaching its demise: It might have been this realization that drove him through its streets like a ghost, savoring its life and its fragile beauty.

Kellie tried to slow him down. She told him he was becoming obsessed. Maybe, she said, he should think about going back. Going home. Get away from there.

But he would not do that. Wouldn't consider it.

Kellie thought the kite might work. She knew Hutchins well and had a lot of confidence in her. Digger didn't point out that Hutchins hadn't hidden her feeling that the *al-Jahani/Hawksbill* mission was a long shot.

Now that they could wrap a lightbender field around the lander, it was much easier getting in and out of *Brackel*. Kellie usually brought them in among the orchards and open ground on the north side of the city. One day, she picked instead a glade a short distance off the isthmus road. 'Breaks the monotony,' she said, as the invisible craft descended.

Digger looked at the woods, hunting for Goompahs, but Kellie reassured him. 'Bill can't see anybody down there,' she said. 'It's okay.'

Any*body*.

It was, as far as he could recall, the first time.

He expected this to be an interesting evening. Even more popular among the Goompahs than the theater was an event that was part lecture, part free-for-all. A speaker, usually a visiting authority of one kind or another, attempted to present a point of view on a given topic while the paying customers engaged him in open debate. (Or agreed with him, as the case might be, though, in Digger's experience, it seldom was.) The visitor might be discussing the health benefits of sunlight, an abstract ethical issue of one kind or another, the merits of a drama that had recently been hooted out of town, or a supernatural visitation she had undergone and which had led to a spiritual awakening and the sure and certain knowledge that the members of her audience were groping through moral darkness and needed to get their act in order. It was all great fun, and Digger was often left in doubt whether any of the Goompahs on either side of the issue were serious. The attendees paid for the privilege, the speakers looked for subjects that would provoke outrage, and everybody had a good time.

They were called *sloshen*, for which there is no completely accurate English translation. Call it a felicitous quarrel, a happy argument, a glorious difference of opinion.

That evening's guest speaker, according to notices that had been posted for several days, would be Macao Carista, who was described as a cartographer. Macao was from *Kulnar*, a city immediately northwest of *Brackel*. According to the displays, she was widely known throughout the *Intigo*.

While lingering several days earlier in the lobby of the building that would be used for the presentation, Digger had overheard enthusiastic patrons commenting that she always brought maps of places to which no one had ever journeyed, or sometimes of which no one had even heard.

She used the evenings, apparently, to talk about her travels, describing various kinds of fantastic creatures she'd seen, armored *terps* as tall as she was, *bandars* that spat venom at a range exceeding the diameter of the hall (which was considerable), flying *solwegs*, talking *bolliclubs*. Last time out, she was reported to have described two-headed Goompahs, which she'd seen on an island in the eastern ocean. One head, she'd said, always spoke the truth, and the other always lied. But you never knew which was which.

And there was *Yara-di*, the city of gold.

And the bridge across the bottomless *Carridan* Gap, built by unknown hands, using engineering principles beyond the grasp of any alive today. The bridge was so long that, when she crossed on the back of a *berba*, it had taken three days.

She'd spoken of the *Boravay*, the carnivorous forest, from which no traveler, save Macao, had ever returned.

'Sounds like a hell of a woman,' said Kellie.

Goompah, thought Digger. *She's a Goompah. Not a woman.*

A strict and formal decorum was observed during the *slosh*. No hooting, no raised voices. 'If the honored speaker would pause for a moment,' one might say, 'before we wander farther into confusion—'

It was a cool night. A brisk wind blew off the sea, and management needed several fires to warm the hall to a comfortable level. Macao was obviously popular because Goompahs filled the building, and sat talking quietly to one another while they waited for her to appear.

The audience, about two hundred strong, were seated above the stage, amphitheater style, but restricted to three sides. Kellie and Digger, who had long since planted a pickup near the stage, lurked in the roped-off section, well out of the way. At the appointed hour, two workers pulled a large armchair into view, made a great deal of fuss getting it aimed in the proper direction, and returned with a frame on which Digger assumed Macao would put her maps. Then they brought out a roll of animal skin and leaned it against the side of the chair. They added a table and a lighted oil lamp, and when they had everything arranged to their satisfaction, they scurried off. A bell tinkled, the audience quieted, and a Goompah in red and gold entered from the side. He placed his palms together, the equivalent of bowing to the audience. Digger missed part of his comments, but it came down to, Welcome, ladies and gentlemen, please give a hand to our world-traveling guest, Macao Carista.

The audience rapped politely on any available flat surface, and Macao made her entrance. To Digger's eyes she was pretty much indistinguishable from the other females. She wore a bright yellow blouse with fluffy sleeves. Green leggings. And animal-hide boots. A gold medallion hung on a purple ribbon about her neck.

'Well,' she said, 'this looks like a desperate bunch.' And they were off and running. Macao, it seemed, had just returned from a long overland journey to the north. Through the desert and beyond the jungle where, she claimed, it grew cooler again. She regaled her audience with tales of the mystical *Lyndaia*, where the gods had placed the first Goompahs; of attack *bobbos* and the flying *groppe*, and a giant *falloon*, which had half a dozen slithery tentacles, and 'only last year, as we all know, dragged a full-masted ship to the bottom.' And finally she spoke of *Brissie*, the city on the edge of forever. 'From its towers, one can see the past and the future.' She recognized a hand in the audience. 'Please give us your name,' she said.

'Telio. And what did *you* see, Macao?'

'Do you really wish to know, Telio?'

The questioner had a smashed ear. It was the same Telio he'd seen on the isthmus road what now seemed a long time ago.

'Yes,' he said. 'Tell us.'

'Be aware first that I looked to the west, to the past. What's past is done, Telio. There's no point gazing that way.'

'So what did you see?'

311

'Well.' Feigning reluctance. 'In the east, I saw a world filled with gleaming cities. Where our ships crossed the seas, and no part of the *Intigo* was hidden from us. Where travelers could find (something) wherever they went.'

Digger and Kellie were off to one side, but at the edge of the stage. They were getting everything – Macao, Telio, and the audience reaction. Dave Collingdale's people would love this.

'Orky,' said someone in the audience. A female. 'Crossed the seas to *where*?'

'Oh, yes,' Macao said. 'That *is* the question, isn't it?' She hadn't sat down yet in the chair. She was using it instead as a prop. She circled it, gazed at her audience from behind it, leaned on its arm. Played to the expectant silence. 'What do you think is on the other side of the sea?'

'There is no other side,' the questioner said. 'The sea goes on forever. There may be other islands out there somewhere, but the sea itself has no end.'

'How many believe that?'

About half the hands went up. Maybe a bit more than half.

Macao fastened her gaze on the questioner. 'The sea is (something),' she said. 'It never stops. That sounds like a lot of water.'

Orky made the rippling sound that passed for laughter among Goompahs. A few pounded on chair arms. 'If the sea has an end, what kind of end is it? Does the water simply stop? Is there a place where you can fall off, as Taygla says?' Macao, obviously enjoying herself, *flowed* across the stage. 'It's really an interesting question, isn't it? It almost seems there is no satisfactory answer to these things.' She got up, opened the roll of animal skin, and withdrew a map, which she put on the frame. This was an attempt at cartography on a much larger scale than anything they'd seen at the library, which had been limited to the area in and around the isthmus. Her map showed icy regions in the south and deserts to the north, both correct. But it showed a western continent much closer than it actually was, and the big pole-to-pole continent a few thousand klicks east was missing altogether.

But the map contained a shock. 'Wait here,' he told Kellie.

'What?' she whispered. 'Where are you going?'

He was already up on the stage, moving behind Macao, until he stood directly in front of the map. It reminded him of those sixteenth-century charts that showed personified clouds blowing in different directions, or whales spouting. There were no whales or animated winds on this one. But it *did* have what appeared to be a graphic of a human being. A male.

It was at the bottom of the chart, riding a winged rhino.

It wasn't done in sufficient detail to know for sure that it was human. But it was close. Eyes, mouth, and ears were all smaller than a Goompah's. It had pale brown skin, and it looked a lot better than the natives. Its clothing was standard, a loose-fitting shirt and leggings. And it carried something that looked like a harpoon.

'The sad thing is,' Macao was saying, 'we really don't know whether Orky is right or wrong. We don't know whether this map is right or wrong.' She advanced without warning in Digger's direction and he had to scramble clear. Damned things were quicker than they looked.

'It's one of us,' Digger told Kellie.

'What is?'

'On the chart.'

Macao paused in front of the map, pretending to study it, but they could see her eyes look away while she considered what came next. 'In fact, we don't even know what lies beyond the *Skatbrones*.' Digger had heard the term before and believed it referred to the mountain range that sealed off the northern continent from the *Intigo*.

'We come here and talk about all manner of curious beasts, some of which I've actually seen, and some of which not. But not one of you knows which is true and which an imagining. And I put it to you that that is not a supportable state of affairs.'

'It's not a perfect representation,' Digger continued. 'Arms are too long. Feet are too much like their own. But it's close.'

A cup of water and an oil lamp stood on a table beside Macao. Digger decided she looked good in the glow of the lamp. Large malleable ears. Supple arms. Cute in the way, maybe, that a giraffe was cute. If her features were less than classic, they were nonetheless congenial and warm. Her eyes swept across him and seemed for a heart-stopping moment to linger. As if she *knew*.

More hands were going up. She recognized one.

'I'm Koller. It's true we can't see far, Macao; but it's impious to talk the way you do. The gods (something, something) these things for a reason.'

'And what is the reason, Koller?'

'I don't know. But we should (something) the will of the gods. You come here and make up these wild tales, and I wonder whether the gods laugh to hear what you say. I'm not sure I want to be sitting this close to you when we all know that a bolt could come through the roof at any moment.'

She smiled at him. 'Koller, I think we're safe.'

'Really? Have you looked at the sky recently?' And with that Koller got up, made his way into the aisle, and left the building.

'Well,' Macao said. 'I hope nobody gets (something, but probably 'singed') when it happens.'

The audience was silent, except for a couple of nervous laughs.

'The thing is,' said Digger, 'it looks like us, but not quite. And it's sitting on one of those rhinos. But the rhino has wings.'

She had to go look for herself. When she came back she touched his arm. 'Never see the day one of those things could get off the ground,' she said.

'That's what I'm wondering about.'

'How do you mean?'

'It's obviously a mythological beast.'

'So you think—'

'—The guy that looks like us is a mythological beast, too.'

'Hey,' she said, 'he looks like you, not me.'

So the next question was, what sort of mythological beast?

Considering the way everyone had panicked whenever they'd caught a glimpse of Digger, he thought he could guess.

'I actually *have* done a fair amount of far traveling,' Macao was saying. 'There are a lot of strange things out there. Some strange things in here, too.' She said it lightly, and they pounded their appreciation. 'If you go out the front door of this place and turn left, and walk a few hundred paces, there's a park. It's called *Bin*lo, or *Bop*lo—'

'*Bar*lo,' someone said from the third row.

Digger suspected she'd known all along. '*Bar*lo.' She tasted the word on her tongue, rolled it around in her mouth, smiled, and took a coin out of her sleeve. 'Later this evening, when we're finished here, if your way home leads through *Barlo* Park, stop a minute, and consider that *this* is the world that we know.' She held the coin so it flashed in the lamplight. '*This* small piece of metal encompasses the entire known world. Where we live. It's the isthmus, and the land up to the *Skatbrones,* and the Sunrise Islands, and the Seawards, and the Windemeres, and the shoreline as far as we can see. And south to the Skybreakers. Every place where we've walked.' She gazed curiously at it. 'And the park is the world beyond. The great darkness into which we've cast no light.

'We boast of our maps, and we call ourselves (something). We pretend to much knowledge. But the truth is that we are gathered around a fire' – she lifted the lamp, and watched shadows move across the room – 'in a very large and very dark forest.' She turned the stem and the light flickered and died. 'I can't bring myself to believe there's an infinite amount of water in the world. But maybe I'm wrong.' Someone was trying to get her attention. 'No,' she said, 'let me finish my thought. We live on an island of light. What extends beyond us in all directions is not the sea, but our own ignorance.' The lamp blinked back on, as if by magic. 'Persons like me can come before you with the most preposterous stories, and no one really knows what is true and what is not. In fact, despite everyone's (something), there really *is* a *falloon.* It doesn't

315

actually gulp down ships.' She moved to the edge of the stage, gazing out over her audience. 'As far as I know.'

Digger and Kellie moved cautiously around the stage so they could see better.

'I've seen it with my own eyes,' she continued. 'Yet when I tell you about it, you assume that I make it up. Why? Is it because you have evidence to the contrary? Or because you *expect* me to invent such tales?

'Each year, in the spring, the citizens of *Brackel* celebrate the founding of their city. *Kulnar*, which is, of course, older by several hundred years, celebrates in midwinter.'

Several of the audience stood to repudiate her remark. Someone flung a scarf into the air. The question of which city was older was obviously a matter in dispute, and advocates were present for both claims.

Macao let it go on for a bit, then waved them to order. 'The truth is, nobody really knows which city is older. But it's of no consequence.' Her audience quieted. 'However—' She drew the word out. '—That we have been here so long, and know so little, even about our own history, is to our discredit.' Digger could hear a cart passing outside.

She held up a scroll. 'This is Bijjio's *Atlas of the Known World*. It's accurate, as far as anyone knows. But it is really no more than a few introductory remarks and a lot of speculation.' She paused and took a sip of the water. 'We all know the story of Moro, who sailed east and returned from the west.'

An arm went up in back. 'My name is Groffel.' The speaker swelled with the significance of what he was about to say. 'You're not going to tell us the world is round, I hope?'

'Groffel,' she said, 'it's time we found out. Found out if there really are lands over the horizon. If there really are two-headed Goompahs. But we need support. We need *you* to help.'

There were shouts. 'The Krolley mission,' someone said. And: 'They're lunatics.' And: 'My honored friend should open his mind.'

A voice on the far side, near the wall: 'I assume, Macao, we're talking about contributions.'

She waited until her audience had subsided. 'We are talking about an *investment*,' she said. 'We are talking about our future, about whether we will still be wondering about these issues a hundred or six hundred years from now.' She seemed to grow taller. 'I don't say who's right and who's wrong. But I do say we should settle the matter. We should find out.

'Three ships will make the voyage. Like Moro, they will travel east, into the sunrise. They will record whatever islands they encounter, and eventually they will return over *there*.' She pointed toward the back of the auditorium. West. A murmur ran through the audience.

'But why now? When the signs are bad?'

Kellie stirred. 'Signs?' she asked. 'Does he mean the cloud?'

Another voice: 'How long will it take?'

'We estimate three years,' she said.

'And on what is the estimate based?'

'The size of the world.'

'You know the size of the world?'

Another smile. 'Oh, yes.'

'And how big is it?'

'It is a sphere, 90,652 *gruden* around the outside.'

'Really?' This was Orky again. 'Not 653?'

'Round it off a bit, if you like.'

Someone in back stood up. 'You've measured it?'

'In a manner of speaking. I have seen it measured.' She waited for the laughter, got it, let it die away, and added: 'I am quite serious.'

'And was it done with a measuring rod?'

'Yes,' she said. 'Actually it was done with *two* measuring rods.' She was completely in control. 'Scholars placed rods of identical lengths at *Brackel* and at *T'Mingletep*. Who knows how far *T'Mingletep* is from here?'

'A long walk,' said someone in back. But he didn't get the laughter he expected, and he sat down.

317

'That's right. Although it's on the western sea, it's almost directly south of *Brackel*. And the distance has been measured. North to south, it is precisely 346 *gruden*.' Digger had seen the term *gruden* before, but until that moment he had no idea whether it was the length of someone's arm or a half dozen klicks.

'The shadows cast by the rods were measured through the course of the day. The shadows are longer in *T'Mingletep*. And the difference in lengths between *T'Mingletep* and here makes it possible to calculate the size of the world.'

'It's too much for me,' said Orky.

Whether 90,000 *gruden* seemed outrageously big or too small to the audience, Digger couldn't tell. But he knew the experiment, of course. It was similar to the one performed by Eratosthenes, who got very close to the size of the Earth in 240 B.C.

They were silent for a time, and she recognized a big Goompah in the front row. 'Klabit,' he said. 'Macao, I don't know whether it's round or not. But if it really *is* round, wouldn't the water run off? Wouldn't the ships themselves fall off when they got far enough around the curve?'

Macao let them see the question had stopped her. 'I don't know the answer to that, Klabit. But the ground between here and *T'Mingletep* is curved. That's established beyond doubt.' She looked out over her audience. 'So the truth is, nobody really knows why the water doesn't run off. Obviously, it doesn't happen, or there'd be no tide tonight.' (Laughter.) 'I admit I don't understand how the world can be round, but it seems that it *is*. I say, let's find out. Once and for all. Let's send the ships east over the ocean and watch to see from which direction they return.'

Her audience had become restive. Macao left the stage and went out among them. 'The mission will cost a great deal of money. The funds from this evening, after I've taken my expenses—'

'—of course—' said a voice on the far side.

'—of course. After that, I will contribute the proceeds to the effort. This is your opportunity to become part of the most significant (something) expedition ever attempted by our two cities.

'But they need something more than money. They need volunteers. Sailors.' She paused and looked down at Telio. 'It will be a dangerous voyage. Not something for the faint of heart. Not something for the unskilled.'

'I fish for a living,' said Telio.

'Just what they need. I'll send your name over.'

The audience laughed. Someone commented that Telio was lucky to have gotten such an opportunity.

Macao was back on her stage. She held up her hands. 'Velascus talks about the defect each of us has, implanted by Taris, to prevent our being perfect. For *you*—' she looked at one of the Goompahs off to her left – 'it is perhaps too great an affection for money. And for Telio over there, it may be a (something) toward jealousy. For me, perhaps, it is that I have no sense of humor.' (Laughter.) 'But for each of us it is there. The *individual* defect. But there is another flaw that we all share, that we share as a community.

'You remember *Haster*?'

Yes. They all did.

'What's *Haster*?' asked Kellie.

'No idea.'

'The colony failed within three years. As did the several attempts that preceded it. Why do you suppose that is? Why have so many efforts to move abroad been abandoned?'

There were several older children seated in the rear. One of them stood to be recognized. 'It is wild country beyond the known lands,' she said. 'Who would want to live there?'

'Who indeed?' echoed Macao. 'And I put it to you that herein lies our fatal defect. Our common flaw. The characteristic that deters us. We love our homeland too much.'

When the last of the lights had gone out, and the cafés had emptied, Kellie and Digger wandered the lonely walkways that bordered the sea at the southern edge of the city. They were wet, and the Flickinger field produced by the e-suits was notoriously slippery underfoot, especially in such conditions. It didn't seem to matter what sort of shoes he wore. He turned it off, and gasped in the sudden rush of cold salt air.

Kellie heard his reaction and guessed what he had done. She followed his lead. 'It's lovely out here,' she said.

The sea was rough. It roared against the rocks and threw spray into the air. A sailing ship, squat and heavy, lay at anchor. Lights poured out of the after cabin, and Digger could see a figure moving about inside.

'Do the Goompahs have the compass?' asked Digger.

'Don't know.'

'Does Lookout have a magnetic north?'

'Yes, Dig. About twelve degrees off the pole. Why? Does it matter?'

'If they don't have a compass, how will they navigate on that round-the-world jaunt they're talking about?'

'Sun by day, stars by night. Shouldn't be all that difficult. Except I don't know how they'll get past the eastern continent. They'll have the same problem Columbus did.'

It was too dark to be able to make out where the horizon met the sky. Digger tried to visualize the sea east of Athens. He remembered a couple of big islands out there, and a few smaller chunks of land beyond. Then it was open ocean for several thousand kilometers.

He understood why the Goompahs had never crossed their oceans. How long had it taken before Leif Eriksson and the longboats made the run across the Atlantic? But it seemed odd that there'd been no serious effort to explore the continent on which they lived. It was true there were natural barriers, but they had sail, and they had easy access by water. They weren't in the classic Greek situation of being penned in an inland sea.

They wandered out onto a wooden pier, and Kellie's hand lay gently on his hip. It was a floating pier, and some of the planks were loose or missing. They kept going until they reached the far end, where they stood listening to the ocean. A few gulls were in the air. The universal creature. Any world that produced oceans and living things eventually produced gulls. Swamps gave you crocodiles. Forests always had wolves. Living worlds were exceedingly rare, but their creatures were remarkably alike. Which after all made sense. How many different ways are there to make a fish? The variations were almost always limited to details.

A lantern moved across the deck of the ship.

He liked this place. It felt a bit like an island lost in time. 'You know, Kellie,' he said, 'I wish there were a way we could talk with her.'

'With whom?'

'With Macao.'

'Forget it,' she said. 'You'd scare the devil out of her.'

LIBRARY ENTRY

The oddest thing about the entire evening was the image on the map. Except that his skin color was a bit light, the guy on the winged rhino looked like my uncle Frank.

—*Jenkins* Log
Captain's entry

26

Lookout. On the ground at *Saniusar*.
Saturday, September 6.

More surveillance devices had arrived, and Kellie and Digger had spread them throughout the isthmus this time, instead of confining them to *Brackel*. *Saniusar*, the northernmost Goompah outpost, was the last of the cities to receive its allotment.

It occupied the shores of a bay and was surrounded by a ring of picturesque hills, which grew progressively higher until they ascended finally into towering mountains.

Beyond the mountains lay dense jungle, and beyond the jungle lay a broad desert, extending for thousands of kilometers, well north of the equator. Digger was beginning to understand why the Goompah world ended on the north at *Saniusar*.

'But they have ships,' protested Kellie. 'I can understand why they haven't crossed the seas. But running up and down the coast shouldn't have been a problem.'

'Don't be so sure. How far did the Greeks go?'

'But they were hemmed in. Couldn't get beyond the Mediterranean.'

They'd been wandering the streets of Goompah cities like the wind, unseen, irrelevant. He missed Jack, and he missed being able to sit down with friends, and he missed being able to party.

He had been relatively isolated before. But it had always been in some desolate spot, remote from everything, with maybe a couple of technicians who spent all their time talking about the local grade of sandstone, or the level of humidity at a given latitude. But here, with Kellie, he was surrounded by a vibrant community whose energy crackled through the cities every day and lit up the night, and he was cut off from it all.

He touched her luminous form, her arm, her shoulder. The mild vibration projected by the external surface of the e-suit was reassuring. She moved beneath his fingers and folded herself into him. Everything was accessible through the field except her lips, which were shielded behind the hard bubble that covered her face.

They were standing outside a double-domed building on the edge of the city, looking north toward a tangle of river and valley and granite. A few of the natives were wandering about, some working, some playing with young ones, some just walking. To the west, over a few hilltops, the sea was bright and cool.

'I love you, Kellie,' he said.

Her body moved against him. She was laughing.

'What's funny?'

'At the moment,' she said, 'your choices are limited.'

'I don't know.' He switched his e-suit off. The smell of salt air swept in. Lovely stuff. 'I saw some pretty good-looking females at the park yesterday.'

The tingle blinked off with her suit. 'I love you, too, Digby,' she said.

'I wish I could see you.'

'Maybe tonight, if you behave.'

He found her lips, and they stood quietly for several moments, enjoying each other. 'Kellie,' he said, 'I'd like very much if you would be my wife.'

She stiffened, simultaneously pulling him forward and pushing him away.

He wondered if anyone else had ever proposed to an invisible woman.

'Digger,' she said, 'I'm honored.'

That didn't sound good.

'I'm not sure it would work.'

He switched off his goggles, and the spectral form vanished. Only those dark eyes remained. 'You wouldn't have to quit,' he said. 'It wouldn't mean your career. We could work something out.'

The wind off the sea was cold. 'It's not that.'

'What's the problem?' he asked.

Her eyes narrowed. He'd long since become accustomed to disembodied eyes, and had discovered that they did actually reflect mood and emotion. He'd always assumed that only happened in the context of a complete facial expression. 'Digger, I'd like very much to marry you—'

'—But—?'

'I'm not interested in any short-term arrangement. I don't want to commit myself to you and discover that a few years from now everything's changed and we head our own ways.'

He pulled her back into his arms. All resistance was gone, and he was surprised to notice her cheeks were damp. 'You want me to sign an agreement that I'd renew?'

She thought it over. 'No,' she said. 'I wouldn't ask that. Wouldn't do any good anyhow. I just—' She trembled. It seemed out of character. 'In my family, we don't believe in doing things halfway. You commit, or you don't. If you commit, don't expect that if you change your mind in five years, I'm going to shake hands and say let's be friends.'

He was holding her tight by then. And he wanted very much to see her, but there were too many Goompahs drifting around. 'It would never happen, Kellie. I love you. I want you to be my wife. Forever. No time off. No letting the lease run out.'

'You're sure?'

'Yes.'

'And you'll feel the same way when we get home?'

'Of course.' He pressed his lips against hers. 'You're a hard sell.'

'Yes I am. And if you don't mean any of this, the price'll be high.'

Aside from distributing pickups, they'd also roamed through the cities recording engraved symbols, statuary, architecture, whatever seemed of interest. They'd found a museum in *Mandigol*, filled with artifacts excavated from beneath existing cities. So there were Goompah archeologists.

They'd found several academies, or colleges, the most extensive of which was located in *Kulnar*, the home of Macao. *Mirakap*, an island city that was actually part of *T'Mingletep*, hosted concerts almost nightly. They'd recorded several, some purely instrumental, others employing singers. The Goompahs, by the way, conceded nothing to humans in the range of their voices. On the *al-Jahani*, Collingdale and his people seemed to have a higher estimation of native music than did Digger and Kellie.

They watched sailboat races at *Hopgop*, on the northeastern shore, and track events at *Sakmarung*. In all these places, the café was king. Everyone retired at the end of the day to the assorted bistros and taverns, and the evenings slipped away in laughter and conversation.

Life was good on the isthmus. The land was fertile, the sea full of fish, and it didn't look as if anyone had to work very hard.

'They've been around as long as we have,' Digger commented on one of the reports to the *al-Jahani*. 'But technologically, they've gone nowhere. Does anybody have any kind of explanation at all?'

They didn't. There were a couple of people with Collingdale, Elizabeth Madden and Jason Holder, who thought that Goompahs simply weren't very smart. The fact that they could use tools and build cities, they argued, didn't mean they could manage an industrial revolution.

326

But if they hadn't progressed technologically, they were doing well politically. All the cities had representative governments, although the machinery was different from place to place. *Sakmarung* had a single executive, chosen by a parliamentary body from among its number. He (or she) served for two local years and could not under any circumstances reassume the post. The parliamentary body was elected by a free vote of the citizenry. Collingdale thought everyone was granted the franchise, but that question was still open.

Mandigol took the classical Spartan approach: It had two executives, with equal power, who apparently kept an eye on each other. *Brackel* elected a parliament and an executive council, not unlike the world government at home. There was no indication of political unrest, no inclination to make war, no poverty-stricken Goompahs in the streets.

On the whole, thought Digger, *they've done pretty well. Of course, it helps when you can pick your food off the trees on the way home.*

'Maybe it's the Toynbee idea,' said Digger.

'Who's Toynbee?'

'Twentieth-century historian. He thought that, for a civilization to develop, the environment has to be right. It has to offer a challenge, but not so much of a challenge that it overwhelms everybody. That's why you get progress in China and Europe but not in Micronesia or Siberia.'

But Goompahs were not humans. And who knew what rules applied? Yet the shows, the parks, the temples, the late nights on the town: The Goompahs *seemed* human in so many ways. *They were,* he thought, *what we might have chosen to be, if we could.*

But what was the secret?

They were capable of quarrels and scuffles. He'd seen a few. They had thieves. The locked doors at the libraries and other places that held objects of value demonstrated that. But their females thought nothing of walking the streets at night. And there were no armies.

'Their society's not perfect,' said Kellie. 'But they're getting a lot of it right.'

'Could it be the DNA?' he asked.

'You mean a peace gene?' She shrugged. 'I have no idea.'

'I mean an *intelligence* gene. Technology or not, I'm beginning to wonder if they're smarter than we are.'

Two statues stood atop the twin domes. They appeared to be representations of two of the deities they'd seen at the temple in *Brackel*: the elderly god, the one who'd had the scroll; and the young female with the musical instrument. 'Mind and passion,' suggested Kellie.

All the temples they'd seen – each city seemed to have one, and there'd been a few out in the countryside – were roofed, but were otherwise left open to the elements. It was always possible, at any time of day or night, to enter a temple.

A few visitors wandered among the columns that supported the twin domes. The gods seemed to have been assigned separate quarters there. They were seated or standing or, in a couple of cases, reclining on benches. The effect created was less distant and majestic than they'd encountered elsewhere. These were the gods at home, informal, casual, come on in and have a drink.

Along the walls, they were depicted helping children ford a river, calming a stormy sea, holding a torch high for travelers lost in a forest. That was Lykonda, her wings spread wide to keep the chill of the night from her charges. From the scrolls, they knew a little about her. She was described as the defender of the celestial realm, although they did not know why she held that exalted title. She was the guardian of knowledge, champion of the weak, protector of the traveler. Mistreat a stranger and answer to Lykonda. Elsewhere they found the laughing god, who was apparently in the middle of delivering a punch line to a group of convulsed Goompahs.

'When a god tells a joke,' whispered Kellie, 'who's not going to laugh?'

* * *

Another deity, whose name they did not know, wielded a sword.

'*Look!*' Kellie stopped in front of the frieze. He wore a war helmet, held a staff with a fluttering pennant in one hand, and raised his weapon in the other. He looked enraged, with demonic creatures swarming toward him. The attackers were armed with spears and cudgels. Brute weapons.

Digger caught his breath.

The demonic creatures—

—Looked reasonably human. Like the figure on the winged rhino.

'Their noses are a little long,' said Kellie, speaking into a sudden silence.

As were their limbs. And they had claws rather than fingernails. Their hair was straggly, trailing down their backs. Their expressions breathed malevolence and treachery. They were male and female, and they very much resembled the demons one found in fifteenth-century art.

'We been here before?' asked Digger.

A group of birds scattered out of a tree, regrouped, and fluttered off to the west.

'Well,' said Kellie, 'I guess we know why they went screaming into the night when you showed up.'

The land beyond the temple rose through broken country toward the *Skatbrones*, the Goompah name, not for a single range, but for the vast mountainous north. A few homes dotted the lower slopes, and there were a couple of orchards. The lander had been left on a remote crag.

Kellie summoned it, and they boarded it from the temple grounds, taking a chance. But she kept the starboard side toward the sea so that no one could see the airlock open.

They climbed in and closed the hatch. Kellie took them up and headed back to the crag. Digger shut his systems down, and when they landed he happily grabbed a hot shower, changed clothes, and collapsed into his chair. After Kellie had her turn in the washroom, Bill served dinner. To her delight, Digger produced candles and a bottle of red wine from the *Jenkins*'s store. 'Whatever made me think,' she said, 'that you weren't very romantic?'

'I majored in romance,' he said. 'It's why women have chased me so persistently all these years.'

'I understand completely. Pour the wine.'

He'd have preferred champagne, but their small store was long since gone. And he'd have liked something a bit more elegant for the occasion than meat loaf, but the lander had its limits. He filled their glasses, lit the candles, proposed a toast to his lovely fiancée. They closed the viewports so that no light would leak out, and enjoyed an evening that Digger knew he would remember forever.

The following night, they flew over the city.

Digger loved riding in an invisible aircraft. They kept the lights doused inside, and when he looked out, there were no stubby wings and no hull. It reminded him of his early boyhood, when he'd ridden the glide trains from Philadelphia to Wildwood, New Jersey. They'd crossed the Delaware River en route, on a bridge whose span and girders and trusses weren't visible from inside the train. Sitting in his seat with his parents across from him, Digger (who had been *Digby* then, and no nonsense about it) had loved to look out at the sky and the river, and pretend the car wasn't there, pretend he was an eagle. It had been a long time, and he hadn't thought about those rides, those *flights*, for thirty years.

The city lights were dim by human standards. Oil lamps here and there. Candles. A couple of open fires. Yet they were warm and inviting, illuminating a place of magic. A place he'd want to come back to one day, when the crisis was over.

Romeo and Juliet was playing that night, would play for the next three evenings. The actual title was *Baranka*, and it was indeed a tale of lovers from feuding families. Baranka was the

330

girl's father, portrayed as an essentially decent but strong-willed character who cannot get past his own anger at his perceived enemies.

Reading it in a language he hadn't begun to master, Digger couldn't make a judgment as to its quality, but he was struck by the degree to which it dealt with familiar issues. When he'd mentioned it to Kellie, she'd commented that they'd been talking about a sense of humor as a universal among intelligent creatures, and she suggested the most characteristic universal could turn out to be programmed stupidity.

He wondered whether a translation might not play one day in New York and Berlin.

'How do you feel?' she asked, breaking a long silence.

'Good.' He thought she was referring to their new status.

'Really?' She seemed surprised.

'What are we talking about, Kel?'

She grinned. 'How's it feel to be the enemy of the gods?'

'Oh.' He produced an image of the frieze. The resemblance to humans was uncanny. 'Not so good, actually.' He raised his voice a notch. 'If you're listening out there, whatever I did, I didn't mean it.'

Kellie's eyes glowed. 'You think there are human-style critters around here somewhere?' she asked.

He thought about it. 'Don't know.'

'It occurs to me,' she said, 'that if there are, the cloud could be a godsend for them.'

'In what way?'

'If it were to wipe out the Goompahs, it might clear the boards for the second wave.'

'The monkeys.'

'Yes. Maybe.'

'From the look of things,' he said, 'I don't think it would be an improvement.'

They landed and strolled among the crowds, and even went into a Goompah café, turned off the e-suits, and sang with the customers. It was great fun, and Digger yearned to shut down the lightbender as well and tell them he and Kellie were there and they liked a good time as much as anybody. Despite the isolation, they made it a special evening. At the end, with the omega back in the sky, and the lights going out, they returned to the lander and flew back to the crag. It overlooked the temple, a jagged piece of rock with sheer walls dropping away on all sides. And it was glorious in the light of the big moon. Farther north, the hills and ridges gave way to dark forest. The city was quiet, little more than a few smoldering lights in the night.

They got out of the lander. There was a stiff wind out of the west, and Bill was predicting rain sometime during the early-morning hours. But when you're tucked safely inside a Flickinger field it doesn't matter much. They were still out there when the storm came. It was an exhilarating feeling, to be caught up in the wind and the rain, with the temple below and Kellie holding tight. But when the first lightning flickered across the sky they decided the situation called for prudence. They lingered momentarily in each other's arms, and Digger turned off her field. Before she could react she was drenched.

She pushed him away and ran for the lander.

He followed happily, using his remote to switch on the navigation lights. Her clothes had become transparent.

It was still dark when he came fully awake. He listened and heard a distant sound. Felt it in the lander.

Voices.

Chanting.

Kellie was asleep beside him. He lifted himself carefully out of the blankets, but couldn't see anything from inside. He pulled on his e-suit and went out into the night. It was coming from the temple grounds.

He walked to the edge of the crag and looked down. There were torches and movement. And the chant.

But it was impossible to see what was happening.

His experience with the Goompahs told him that they weren't big early-morning risers.

He went back inside and woke Kellie.

There was a pair of Goompahs wearing black hoods and robes and carrying torches, led by another in white. It immediately felt like *déjàvu*, here they come again, where's the javelin? And sure enough, there it was, hauled along by a bearer.

The crowd had grown. Someone was playing a set of pipes, and the marchers were chanting, although Digger could catch only an occasional word. *'Darkness.' 'Righteousness.' 'Your glory.' 'Help.'*

Help.

Help us put a new roof on the temple?

Help us in our hour of need?

They were crowded together. Digger and Kellie kept a cautious distance.

The three robed figures moved along one of the walkways, staying in step, not military precision, but practiced nevertheless. The crowd fell in behind. He estimated it at several hundred, and they were joining in the chant and becoming more enthusiastic.

The rain had cleared off, and the stars were bright and hard.

The procession moved through a patch of woods and issued finally onto a beach. When Digger got there, well in the rear, the three leaders had thrown off their sandals and advanced a few paces into the surf. They spread out into a semicircle. The one in white looked older than the others, and he wore a wide-brimmed white hat.

'Creature of—'

The onlookers had gone quiet. They all stayed back out of the water.

'—the night—'

Digger suddenly realized he hadn't brought a pickup. He had no way of recording this.

'—*Depart*—'

They got as close as they could, moving down into the wet sand, leaving footprints. But it was too dark for anyone to notice.

The marchers were looking out over the sea—

No, in fact they were looking *up*. At the black patch, which was sinking toward the northwestern horizon.

'—*Hour of need*—'

A large wave rolled in, and the one in the white robe floated over the top.

He raised his arms and the night fell silent. He stood several moments, and it seemed to Digger he was hesitating. Then he went a step or two farther out. The bearer appeared alongside him and offered the javelin. He took it and held it aloft. His lips moved. Trembled.

More Goompahs were arriving at every moment, some coming from the temple area, others arriving from the far end of the beach. But they were all silent.

He aimed the javelin in the direction of the omega, jabbed at it a few times, and handed the weapon off to one of the others. And as Digger watched in growing horror, he strode out into the waves, his robes floating, until at last *he* was floating. Then he was swimming, struggling to move forward against the tide. The sea tried to push him back, but he kept going and at last he got beyond the breaking waves.

He continued swimming for several minutes.

And he disappeared.

The one who had received the javelin stripped off his outer garment to reveal a white hood and robe. He raised the weapon over his head, and called out to Taris, the defender of the world.

'We beg you accept our (something). And protect us from *T'Klot*.' The hole. The omega. 'Malio takes our plea to your divine presence. Hear him, we beg you, and extend your hand in this our time of need.'

LIBRARY ENTRY

Religion is like having children, or taking medicine, or eating, or any of a thousand other perfectly rational human activities: Taken in small doses, it has much to recommend it. One need only avoid going overboard.

—Gregory MacAllister
'Slippery Slope'
Editor-at-Large, 2227

27

On board the *al-Jahani*, in hyperspace.
Wednesday, September 17.

Six months and three days out. Collingdale had expected his people would be climbing the walls by then. But they were doing okay. It was true that some of the early enthusiasm had worn thin, but that might have been because there was less to be gleaned from the stream of data coming in from the *Jenkins*. By and large, they had recovered an extensive vocabulary, and they understood the syntax. From there on, mastering the language would be largely a matter of pronunciation and nuance.

Once they'd gotten on top of things, Judy had cut back on the Goompah-only requirement. They'd derived some serious benefits from the restriction, but it had lost its charm quickly and, despite the early compromises, it had begun to strain relations between the *Shironi Kulp* and the other passengers. In a nonstop voyage of record-breaking duration, it just wasn't a good idea. So the linguists continued to limit themselves to Goompah in the workshop, but they had long ago become free to use whatever language they liked, with the provision that they were to regard Goompah as their native tongue, and to resort to it as the language of choice.

It had worked well.

The brief tensions that had appeared subsided, the Goompah jokes lost their edge, and Collingdale noted a decrease in the resentment that *everyone* on board had developed toward him and Judy.

Well. There you were. But, as he'd explained to Alex, and to several others, Judy had had a job to do, and the language policy had been the best way of getting it done.

They'd extracted a series of Goompah aphorisms from the library material, which were posted on a bulkhead in the work room. *Deal justly with your neighbor.*

Assist the weak.

Be kind to all.

Everyone was invited to add to the collection, and Collingdale stopped to scribble one that he'd come across in a treatise of the teachings of Omar Koom. (That first name brought a smile. Were there also Goompahs somewhere named Frank? Or Harriet?)

The principle that he'd added to the collection: Accept no claim without evidence.

He liked that. Where's the proof? I'm from Missouri.

How peaceful would the history of his own world have been if that idea were universally accepted? Yet these were the same creatures who exorcised demons and had allowed one of their own to walk into the sea in an effort to head off the cloud. It hadn't taken much analysis to confirm that was what it had been about, the idiot ceremony that Digger had watched.

Well, humans weren't very consistent either.

He stood a few moments studying the list. Enjoy your life because it is not forever. Whatever gives pleasure without injuring another is to be sought, but let no pleasure become so ingrained that it overcomes reason. Beware addictions; the essence of the good life is a free exercise of the will, directed by reason.

Beware addictions.

Judy was talking about eventual publication. *Goompah Wit and Wisdom.* Might be a best-seller one day.

He admired their utilitarian approach to life. Beauty equated

338

to a kind of simplicity. Suiting the form to the purpose. No frills. They'd never have approved of Renaissance cathedrals or Main Line mansions. Keep a clear eye on what is important and do not get caught up in the frivolous.

It was, he thought, mundane stuff. But it had a ringing clarity and lacked the Puritanical sense of guilt that this sort of code would have had back home. If you get something wrong, fix it and move on. Do not weep for that which is beyond your control.

Accept responsibility. Bring no one into the world whom you are not prepared to love and nourish.

He wondered how a society that seemed to put no limits on sex managed that?

One of the linguists had become romantically involved with Ed Paxton, a mathematician, and the captain had performed the wedding. Collingdale had always found mathematicians dull, methodical, and unimaginative. Why anybody would marry one, he could not understand. He'd wondered why evolutionary forces hadn't wiped the breed out.

Paxton had seemed typical of the tribe, but he had conquered the heart of Marilyn McGee, an attractive blonde who had shown a penchant for winning the shipwide chess tournaments.

Another wedding was in the works, this time between two of the linguists. There was talk of doing a Goompah ceremony. Digger had captured a couple of isthmus weddings for the record, so they had models. And Judy was already designing a costume for the captain. Everybody involved would need an appropriately styled hat, and the only projected change would be a substitution of the Judeo/Christian God for Taris, Zonia, and Holen.

They'd also done a few Goompah sing-alongs. Those had become popular with everyone. And they'd staged two native dramas.

Judy had collected eight Goompah dramas from the scrolls, and two more that Digger had recorded. Two were tragedies in the classic sense; the others were like something out of the Baines

Brothers, with lots of slapstick, characters running into walls, getting caught *en flagrante*, and constantly falling down.

The shows frequently involved the audience. In one, a staged brawl spilled over into the front rows, where the patrons got caught up in the battle. Characters chased each other through the aisles. One comedy was apparently interrupted midway when bandits, fleeing from authorities, raced down a center aisle with bags of coins. One of the bandits tossed his loot to a patron, who was then set on and dragged off by the authorities. The audience loved it, and the human observers needed time to recognize that it was all rehearsed.

Another show stationed a medical unit at the rear of the theater. Periodically, when someone fell down onstage, or walked into a chair, the actors called out '*Gwalla timbo*,' which translated roughly to *medical team*. The *gwalla timbo* would then gallop forward, bearing stretchers and splints, collect the injured party, plunk him unceremoniously onto the stretcher, and charge back out, usually dropping the patient en route. It was hilarious.

He would have liked to spend an evening in a Goompah theater with Mary.

They also watched three funerals. The dead were wrapped in sheets and interred in the ground in the presence of family and friends. The mourners did not give in to weeping or other signs of hysteria, although several had to be helped away, and two collapsed altogether.

Collingdale and the linguists listened closely to the ceremonies. The blessings of the gods were invoked in two, and religious references did not show up at all in the third. There was no talk at any of them of a hereafter or suggestions that the deceased had gone to a better world, leading the humans to suspect that the Goompahs did not believe in an afterlife. He suggested to Judy that she advise her people not to mention the fact in personal messages home. 'No point stirring up the missionary society,' he said.

340

They also were able to interpret the signs that Jack and Digger had seen on the schoolroom wall on their first visit. It had been somewhat difficult because the characters were stylized. But they read *THINK FOR YOURSELF* and *SHOW ME THE EVIDENCE.*

They had a record of one class in which the students were learning basic arithmetic. They were operating off a base twelve. Which meant that $14 + 15 + 29$, but there are actually 33 items in the result. Ed explained it to him, but it gave Collingdale a headache, and he simply nodded yes when asked if he understood. It didn't really matter anyhow.

He was impressed by the fact that widespread literacy seemed to exist. That was no small accomplishment when one considered the paucity of reading materials.

There was a priest class, whose actions Digger had recorded on several occasions.

Think for yourself.

There was no visual record of the sacrifice made at *Saniusar*. Digger had said there were several hundred locals in attendance. Pretty sparse crowd when you think of it, in a town with a population they'd estimated at around thirty thousand.

That was 1 percent for a service intended to invoke salvation for the city. 'It tells me,' Frank Bergen said, 'that these critters don't take their religious obligations very seriously.'

The one aspect of life on Lookout that Collingdale found unsettling was the open sexuality. That struck him as stranger even than the cleric who had gone into the ocean. Scheduled orgies could be found most nights in most cities. With signs inviting participants to pop by. The Goompahs no longer looked like the happy innocents of the early days.

Hutch had also been surprised and had told him she would have liked to bury it for the time being, but the news had already gotten out. A number of politicians and religious leaders had expressed their shock. If you could do orgies at city hall, what kind of society were you running? No wonder they didn't have time to conduct wars.

The general public, Hutch thought, seemed to be taking it in their stride.

He was still in the workroom looking at the Goompah aphorisms when Bill broke in. '*Incoming for you, David,*' he said. '*From the* Hawksbill.'

Julie Carson was about an hour and a half away via hyperlight transmission.

One of the screens lit up with the *Hawksbill* seal, then Julie appeared. '*Dave,*' she said, '*I wanted to say thanks for the material on the Goompahs. We're getting an education. Whit, by the way, is trying to learn the language, but I don't think he's having much luck.*'

Collingdale felt a sudden bump and heard the steady thrum of power in the bulkhead change tones. It grew louder. And became erratic.

'*He thinks they're more advanced than we are.*' Julie smiled. At least he thought she had. Her image disintegrated, came back, and began to roll over. '*He says they're less violent and less hung up about sex. I've watched them pop one another in the street, and they don't seem less violent to me. They just look funnier when they fall down.*'

The screen went blank. The captain's voice broke in: 'Everybody please get to a harness. We'll be making a jump in *less than one minute. I say again . . .* '

Collingdale's heart sank. They were still ten weeks from Lookout.

ARCHIVE

We now know that the creatures the media have been so blithely referring to as *Goompahs*, with all the innocence and unsophistication that term implies, in fact worship pagan gods, practice an equivalent of human sacrifice, and engage in unrestrained sex. Margaret, this is shocking behavior, utterly beyond belief. It demonstrates the absolute depravity of the Nonintervention Protocol. Do these unfortunate creatures possess souls? Of course they do, or they wouldn't be seeking their Creator. But they're being misled, and they need to be shown the truth. I urge everyone who's out there watching today to get in touch with their congressman, to write to the Council, to demand that the Protocol be declared null and void.

When you think about it, Margaret, it's already too late for a lot of them. A disaster of major proportions is about to overtake them, and large numbers of them are going to their judgment utterly unprepared. We have an obligation to act, and it seems to me if we fail to do so, we will share their guilt.

—Rev. George Christopher
The Tabernacle Hour

28

On board the *al-Jahani*.
Wednesday, September 17.

They were out under the stars again.

'No chance?' he asked Alexandra, pleading with her, *demanding* that she come up with *something*.

'I'm sorry, David,' she said. 'It's *kaput*.'

They were moving at 20,000 kph. Crawling. 'How about if we just try it? Just make the jump back? See what happens.'

Alexandra was about average size, came up maybe to Collingdale's shoulder. She lacked the presence of some of the other female captains he'd known, did not have the knack of putting iron into her voice when she needed to, did not have Priscilla Hutchins's blue gaze that warned you to back off. Nevertheless she said no, and he understood that she would not risk the ship.

She was blond, with good features, not beautiful, but the kind of woman you knew you could trust if you were in trouble. Under normal circumstances she was congenial, easygoing, flexible. 'Overriding,' she said, 'would pose a severe risk to the ship and the passengers, and we will not do it.'

There wasn't much jiggle room that he could see. He argued

for a couple of minutes before reluctantly conceding. 'I'd better let Julie know.'

'I've already sent a message to the *Hawksbill*. They should be getting it in about' – she checked the time – 'an hour.'

'How about Hutch?'

'I thought you'd want to do that.'

Yes. The crash-and-burn transmission.

First he needed to inform the passengers. He did it from the bridge, telling them what they'd undoubtedly already guessed, that they were stranded, that help would be coming, but that all possibility of moving on to Lookout was gone. 'I'm sorry,' he said. 'We took our chances, and it looks as if we lost.' He paused and shrugged helplessly. 'I'm not sure yet how long we'll be here. Broadside has been notified. They'll send over a relief mission, but the captain tells me it's going to take a few weeks to get to us, at best. So everybody make themselves comfortable.

'I should add, by the way, that there's no danger.'

He sent the bad news to Hutch from his quarters, keeping it short, nothing but the facts. Engine burnout. Going nowhere. We've let Broadside know. Everybody's safe. We have plenty of air and food. He tried to sound upbeat, knowing the news would hit her hard. There was nothing she could do, of course. She was too far. There'd be no rabbits out of the hat this time, like the ones at Deepsix and on the *chindi*.

The next message went to the *Jenkins*. 'Digger, we won't be coming. Jump engines blown. I'm going to try to arrange transportation for myself on the *Hawksbill*. But you better assume everything's up to you. You need to figure out a way to get the Goompahs to evacuate the cities prior to the hit.'

Then he considered what he wanted to tell Julie. He started by calling Alexandra, who was back on the bridge. 'If we ask them to come here, to us, do they lose enough time that we endanger their mission?'

Alex looked tired. '*Hard to say, Dave. If they get lucky and find us right away, it shouldn't be a problem. But the jumps are*

346

imprecise. You know that as well as I do. And especially under these conditions.'

'What conditions do you mean?'

'They're already in hyperspace. They're going to have to jump out, figure out where they are, set a new course, and come get us.'

Damn. He looked out his portal at the stars. He could see the Tyrolean Cloud that, according to Melinda Park, was a hundred light-years across, filled with burning gas and young stars. At their present speed, the *al-Jahani* would need five million years just to go from one end of the cloud to the other. 'Thanks, Alex,' he said.

He switched over to the AI. 'Bill, message for the *Hawksbill*.'

'Ready to record, David.'

The *Hawksbill* was a cargo hauler with a total passenger capacity of two. They already had two. They'd need Marge, so Whitlock would have to come aboard the *al-Jahani*, trade places with Collingdale.

How the hell could he say that? Julie, it looks as if the *al-Jahani* is out of action. I need you to pick me up. I know there's a space problem, but we don't really need the poet.

No, best not insult Whitlock. Julie seemed to like him.

He wrote his ideas down, made a few adjustments, activated the system, and read it to her, trying to look spontaneous. Then he told Bill to send it.

Next he tracked down Judy. 'Let's get everybody together,' he said. 'We need to talk.'

The mood on the ship was bleak. The frustration was fed not only by the perceived importance of the mission, but by the depth of individual commitment. These were people who'd invested a year and a half of their lives. His group of linguists, his *Goompahs*, had spent seven months working to acquire the language, had done so, had actually believed they were going to go into the *Intigo* and rescue tens of thousands of the natives. The others, the senior personnel, the Upper Strata, were watching an unparalleled opportunity, a chance to observe a functioning alien civilization, go south.

'What are you going to tell them?'

Before he could answer, his link vibrated against his wrist. 'Collingdale,' he said.

'*Dave.*' Alexandra's voice. '*I've got a delegation of your people up here.*'

He looked at Judy. 'You know about this?'

She shook her head. 'No.'

The bridge was off-limits except to a few specified persons, or by invitation. It was supposed to be the one place in the ship to which the captain could retreat from social obligations. When Collingdale and Judy got there, all eleven of their linguists were either crowded inside or standing around the open door.

Harry Chin tried to take Judy aside.

'After we clear the bridge,' she snapped.

But Harry showed no inclination to be put off. 'Listen, we've got too much invested in this to just sit here.'

Collingdale had never been a good disciplinarian. In fact he had relatively little experience with difficult cases. The people he'd led on past missions had always been mature professionals. Tell them what you needed and they produced. They might question authority on occasion, but the tone was subtle. *This* felt like mutiny.

But Judy never hesitated. 'Listen,' she said, raising her voice so they could all hear. 'The decision's been made. Everyone go back to the workroom. We'll talk there.'

Mike Metzger had been standing beside Harry, lending support. He was tall and reedy, usually the epitome of courtesy. A muscle in his neck was twitching, and his expression was a mixture of anger, regret, nervousness. He turned and looked at David. 'Can't you do something?' he asked.

It wasn't clear whether he was talking about remaining stalled in the middle of nowhere, or returning to the workroom. But he was close to tears.

Terry MacAndrew put an arm around his shoulders to calm him. 'Judy,' Terry said, lapsing into the Scottish burr that David had only heard previously when Terry drank too much, 'we've talked it over. We're all willing to take the chance. And we know *you* are.'

'You've all agreed to this.'

'Right. We say we should move ahead. Take our chances.'

'Really.'

'The stakes are too high just to sit here.'

"The stakes are too high"? You've been reading too many novels.'

Terry glanced back at Alex, who was out of her seat, standing by one of the navigation panels, looking bored and annoyed. 'We're too close to quit now. Bill thinks we'd be okay if we tried it.' He turned toward Alex. 'Isn't that right, Captain?'

She dismissed him and spoke to Collingdale. 'As I told you earlier, David, if we go back in and the system breaks down, which it is threatening to do, we'll stay in there.' She looked around at the others. 'Permanently. That's not going to happen to my ship. Or to my passengers. Bill has nothing to say about it.' Her eyes came back to Collingdale. 'Please get your people off my bridge.'

The reply from the *Hawksbill* arrived shortly after midnight. Julie's message was simple and direct: '*On our way. We can make room for one more.*'

ARCHIVE

Alex, sorry to hear about the problem. I'm sending the *Vignon*. They'll do a temporary fix to get you running again. But everybody, including you, will be evacuated to the *Vignon* before attempting transit. Let Bill bring it in.

Good luck. Frank.

—Broadside transmission
September 18

PART FOUR
Chimneys

29

Lookout. On the ground at *Kulnar*.
Friday, September 19.

They were sitting on the docks watching the Goompahs get ready to launch their round-the-world mission. Three ships stood in the harbor, flags flying, masts filled with bunting. A band was banging away. The sailors were saying good-bye, it seemed, to the entire population of the *Intigo*. Small boats waited alongside the piers to ferry them out to the ships. Bouquets were being tossed, and on at least two occasions celebrants fell off the piers and had to be rescued. Various dignitaries, including Macao, were making speeches. In the midst of all this a message came in from Dave Collingdale.

'. . . *You better assume everything's up to you. You need to figure out a way to get the Goompahs to evacuate the cities prior to the hit.*'

Up to me? Digger listened to a more detailed report from Alex to Kellie, describing how the *al-Jahani* was stranded in the middle of nowhere, of how they were safe and not to worry, but that they wouldn't be going anywhere for a while.

'Well,' said Digger, 'at least they're okay.'

'Dig,' she said, 'what are we going to do?'

353

Somehow or other, Digger had half expected something like this would happen. Hutch had warned him, and he remembered the old line that anything that can go wrong will go wrong. It had been on his mind for weeks, a dark possibility that he kept trying to push away. But the sad reality was that his options were limited.

'We can't work miracles,' she said. 'And when they have a few minutes to think about it, they'll realize that.'

Digger watched something splashing out in the harbor.

'We should ask for specific instructions, Dig. Don't let him lay this on your back.'

'The *Hawksbill* is still coming,' he said.

'Yes.'

'Maybe they can decoy it. If they can do that, there's no problem.' He listened to the murmur of the sea. The band was starting up again, and more flowers were flung into the air.

Kellie's silhouette was seated a couple of meters higher up on a grassy slope. They were well out of the way of the crowds. 'I'm sorry, Digger,' she said.

The night before, they'd listened to Goompahs talking about *T'Klot*. The hole in the sky.

'*There's a rational explanation,*' some were saying. And others, that it was the work of *zhokas*. Devils.

'*I don't like it.*'

'*I don't care as long as it stays in the sky.*'

'*They were saying down at Korva's that the priests think it's coming here. That the gods are angry.*'

'*Is that possible?*'

'*I don't know. Not too long ago I'd have thought a hole in the sky couldn't happen.*'

'*I wonder whether it's not because of all the immorality.*'

'*What immorality?*'

'*Well, you know, children don't have much respect for their elders anymore. And a lot of people say there are no gods.*'

'*Are there gods?*'

'*I'm beginning to think not.*'

The omega was located in a constellation the Goompahs called *T'Gayla*, the Reaver. It consisted of an arc of six stars that they thought looked like a scythe.

Several of the departing sailors broke away from the crowd, wobbled out onto the pier, and climbed into the boats that would take them to the waiting ships. There was much waving of colored filigrees and throwing of seeds, not unlike the custom of tossing rice at newlyweds. The band picked it up a notch.

Digger felt sorry for them. Like Columbus, they were attempting an impossible journey. Columbus had thought the planet considerably smaller than it actually was. Isabella's retainers knew better, and that was the reason they'd resisted underwriting the voyage. Had North America not been there, the great mariner would probably have disappeared somewhere at sea and become a different kind of legend.

The Goompahs had the dimensions down, even if many of their well-wishers refused to believe the world was round. But once again there was a major continent blocking the way. Two, in fact. There *was* an east–west passage through each, long chains of rivers and lakes, but finding their way would be an impossible task for the voyagers.

He watched, suspecting none of the sailors would see home again. His old friend Telio was among them, with his smashed left ear and his lopsided smile. He was hefting a bag made of animal skins, ready to go on his great adventure.

By midafternoon the sailors were all aboard. The ships were the *Hasker*, the *Regunto*, and the *Benventa*. The *Charger*, the *Spirit*, and the *Courageous*. They hoisted anchor, put up sail, and, accompanied by cheers and drums, started toward the mouth of the harbor. There was a ridge several hundred meters north of the piers, and another crowd had gathered there, where they could get a better view as the ships stood out to sea.

'We shouldn't be doing this,' said Digger.

'Letting them go?' asked Kellie.

He nodded. 'They're going to die out there.'

She looked at him a long moment. 'It's what noninterference means.'

'You know, we have authorization to intervene.'

'Not for something like this. Listen, Dig, you want to jump in and figure out a way to turn them around, I'm with you. But I think they should be left to find their own way. Build their own legends. One day this'll be part of their history. Something they can be proud of. They don't need us involved in it.'

He gazed sadly after them. 'The day will come when the crews on the ships will be praying for someone to step in.'

She had gotten closer to him, and her hand rubbed his shoulder. 'This is why I love you, Dig. But it's not our call. Even if it was, what would you do? Give them a map of their world? Maybe throw in the compass? Where do you stop?'

Digger had no idea. He wondered what human history would have been like had someone arrived to shut down, say, the Persian Wars. Handed us a printing press and some lenses and spiked the gunpowder. Would we really be worse off? There was no definitive answer, but he knew that, in this time, at this moment, he wanted to reach out to the three ships, now rounding the spit of land at the north end of the harbor.

They were silent for a time. The wind blew across them. The crowd began to break up. 'Look at it this way,' she said. 'As the situation is right now, the ships probably have a better chance of surviving than the people left behind. They'll be well away when the cloud gets here.'

'That's a consolation.'

'Well, what do you want me to say?'

'I still think we should warn them,' said Digger.

'God's position.'

'How do you mean?'

'You can intervene for a short-term benefit. But it might not be advantageous over the long haul.'

'We're not going to get metaphysical, are we?'

She lay back on the soil and stared up at the sky.

Digger got to his feet and looked toward the city, spread out across a range of hills behind them. And at the mountains beyond. 'I think we have to make another attempt to talk to them.'

He heard her sigh. 'Instead of just waylaying somebody on the road,' she said, 'how about we select a likely candidate this time?'

'Macao,' he said.

She nodded.

They had lost her in the crowd. How did you go about finding someone in a nontech city? You couldn't look in the directory, and there was no way to ask without scaring the citizens half to death.

They tried scouting the lecture circuit. But they found no advertising, no placards, nothing that suggested Macao was on the schedule.

'We don't even know for certain that she lives here,' grumbled Digger. 'She might just have been here for the launch.'

'No,' said Kellie. 'In *Brackel*, she was listed as Macao of *Kulnar*. This is her home.'

'Or maybe where she was born. But okay. Let's assume you're right. How do we find her?'

'There has to be a way to communicate with people. To pass messages around.'

Digger thought about it. How did you get a message to Cicero? You wrote it out on a piece of parchment and sent it by messenger, right? But where could they get a messenger?

They called it a night and took the lander out to Utopia, where they were safely alone.

In the morning, as they were getting ready to return to *Kulnar*, he asked Kellie whether he could have the silver chain she wore as a necklace.

'May I ask why?'

'I want to give it to another woman.'

357

She canted her head and regarded him with a combination of amusement and suspicion. 'The nearest other woman is a long walk, Digger.'

'I'm serious,' he said. 'It's important. And when we get home, I'll replace it.'

'It has sentimental value.'

'Kellie, it would really help. And maybe we can figure out a way to get it back.'

'I'm sure,' she said.

On the way into the city, he retrieved one of the pickups and attached it to the chain. 'How's it look?'

'Like a pickup on a chain.'

Actually, he thought it looked pretty good. If you didn't look too closely, the pickup might have been a polished, dark, disk-shaped jewel. It was the way a Goompah would see it.

They found the local equivalent of a stationery store. It carried ink, quill-style pens, parchment of various thicknesses, and document cylinders. Because the weather had gotten cool, a fire had been built in a small metal grate in the middle of the floor. Its smoke drifted out through an opening in the roof. It wasn't Segal's, but it was adequate to their needs.

'So where do we get a messenger?' asked Kellie.

'Macao's an entertainer,' he said. 'They should know her at the public halls.' He disliked stealing merchandise, but he put the store in his mental file beside the *Brackel* Library, for future recompense. He lifted two cylinders, a pen, a pot of ink, and some paper that could be rolled and placed inside. Then they went next door to a shop that sold carpets, and made off with some coins.

The public buildings that hosted *sloshen*, shows, and other public events, were lightly occupied at that time of day. They picked one and looked in. Except for a couple of workers wiping down the walls, it seemed empty.

They found a room with a table, closed the door, and sat down to write to Macao.

The cylinders, which were made of bronze, were about a third of a meter long. They were painted black with white caps at either end. A tree branch with leaves for decoration on one, birds in flight on the other. What would one of these be worth at home?

'What do we want to say?' asked Digger. 'Keep in mind that I can't write the language very well.'

'I don't see why we should write anything,' said Kellie. 'All we want to do is find out where she lives.'

Sounded reasonable to him. He twisted the caps and opened both cylinders, but stopped to wonder whether the messenger might look inside. 'Better put something in there,' he said. He sat down at the table, pulled one of the sheets toward him, and opened his ink pot. *Challa, Macao,* he wrote. And, continuing in Goompah: *We've enjoyed your work.* He signed it *Kellie* and *Digger*.

She smiled and shook her head. 'First written interstellar communication turns out to be a piece of fan mail.'

He inserted the message, twisted the cylinder shut, put the caps on, and reached for a second sheet. *Please deliver to Macao Carista,* he wrote.

They found an inner office occupied by a Goompah who seemed to have some authority. He was installed behind a table, talking earnestly to an aide, describing how he wanted the auditorium set up for that evening's performance. They were staging a show titled *Wamba*, which rang no bells for Digger.

Shutters were closed against the cool air. A pile of rugs was pushed against one wall, and a fire burned cheerfully in a stove. A pipe took the smoke out of the building.

While the Goompahs were engaged in their conversation, Digger moved to the side of the table, keeping the cylinder inside his vest, where it remained invisible.

'Up there, Grogan,' said the Goompah behind the desk.

Grogan? Another peculiar name for a native. Kellie snickered. The sound was loud enough to escape the damping effect of the suit and attract the attention of the Goompahs. Puzzled, they looked around while she held one hand over her mouth, trying to suppress a further onset. *Grogan*. Digger, watching her, felt a convulsion of his own coming on. He fought it down and took advantage of the distraction to slip the tube onto the table, along with three of the coins he'd taken. With luck, it would look like a piece of outgoing mail.

'It must have been the fire,' said Grogan.

The one behind the table scratched his right ear. 'Sounded like a *chakul*,' he said.

That brought a second round of snorts and giggles from the corridor, where Kellie had retreated. Digger barely made it out of the office himself before exploding with laughter. They hurried through the nearest doorway into the street, and let go. A few passersby looked curiously in their direction.

'This being invisible,' said Digger, when he could calm down, 'isn't as easy as it's supposed to be.'

With Jack's death, they'd shed the policy of not splitting up. Their increasing familiarity with the cities of the *Intigo* might have caused them to become careless, but Kellie had pointed out that they had commlinks, that if either of them got into trouble, help was always nearby.

So they divided forces. Digger would stay near the office, watching to see what happened to the message they'd left, while Kellie would post another one at a second likely location. Eventually, they hoped, one or the other would get delivered.

But the prospect of hanging around the nearly empty building all day did nothing for his state of mind.

When she'd left, and he'd gone back inside, he saw that the coins had vanished and the message had been moved to the edge of the table. That was encouraging. But the cylinder remained untouched through the balance of the morning, and he began to wonder whether he should have marked it URGENT.

There were several other visitors, including a female who exchanged sexual signals with the office occupant and then, to

Digger's horror, closed the door and proceeded to engage him in a sexual liaison. All this occurred despite the fact there were others immediately outside who could not possibly have misunderstood what was happening.

Digger, unhappily, was forced to watch.

There was much gasping, clutching, and slobbering. Clothes went every which way, and the combatants moaned and laughed and sighed. There were protestations of affection, and when, midway through the proceedings, somebody knocked, the manager politely told him to come back later.

When it was over, and the female gone, the message remained. The occupant of the office, whose name Digger now knew to be Kali – unless *Kali* was a derivative of *lover* or *darling* – threw some wood on the fire and settled back to his paperwork.

Digger opened a channel to Kellie and told her what had happened. '*Valor above and beyond,*' she said.

She had planted her message, she told him, only to see it get tossed aside. She'd recovered it, and the coins, and had gone to a third location.

Kali left several times to wander through the building. Digger stayed with the cylinder, and was leaning against the wall, bored, when Kellie called to say her message was on the move.

'*I'll let you know what happens,*' she reported. '*Meantime I think you should stay put.*'

Kali came back and went out again. Kellie was by then following the messenger, who'd been given one of the three coins. '*I guess we overtipped,*' she said.

'*Crossing the park. Headed north.*

'*Messenger's a female. Really moves along. I'm having all I can do to stay up with her.*

'*Threatening rain.*

'*Uh-oh.*'

Digger was watching Kali trying to stay awake. 'What do you mean 'uh-oh'?'

'*She's gone into a stable. Talking to somebody.*'

One of the workers came in and began straightening up the office, working around Kali. Digger waited in the corridor, but he kept an eye on the cylinder.

'*Digger, they're bringing out a* berba. *One of those fat horses.*
'*She's getting on.*'

'The messenger?'

'*Yes. And there she goes, trotting off into the park. Bye-bye.*'

'How about grabbing one of the critters for yourself?'

'*You think anybody would notice?*'

Digger had a vision of a riderless *berba* galloping through the park. 'I don't know.'

'*Believe me, it wouldn't be pretty.*'

'If you can keep the animal in sight, Kellie, I'll try to have Bill follow her.'

'*The park is the one immediately west of where you are. She's headed north.*'

'Okay. Hang on. I've got a channel open to Bill now.'

Bill acknowledged his instructions. Meanwhile, the cleaning person finished up and left. It was a perfunctory effort. Kali never stirred.

Bill was on the circuit to Kellie: '*Can you describe the animal?*'

'*It's got big jaws. It waddles when it runs. And it looks like all the rest of them.*'

'*Color. What color is it? There are a lot of Goompahs down there riding around.*'

'*Green. It was green. With a big white splash across its rear end.*'

'*Wait one.*'

Kali shook himself awake, wandered outside, looked at the sundial that dominated the area in front of the main entrance, and came back in.

'*I can't find the animal,*' said Bill.

'*Damn.*'

'*I need more information. Several of them look like the one you describe. How about the messenger? Any distinguishing characteristics?*'

'*She's a Goompah.*'

'*Good. Anything else? What color's her jacket? Her leggings?*'

'*White. White jacket. No, wait. Yellow. I think it was yellow.*'

'*Leggings?*'

'*White.*'

'*You sure?*'

'*Yes.*' But she'd hesitated.

Bill insisted there was no rider wearing yellow and white atop a beast of the description Kellie had given. But it didn't matter. Near the end of the afternoon, Kali bundled up the cylinder with some other papers, glanced curiously at it, shrugged, picked up a bell to summon an assistant, and handed him everything. The assistant made a further distribution. The cylinder and a couple of other items ended in the hands of a young Goompah with a bright red hat.

Digger, having learned from Kellie's mistake, noted his clothing, noted also that Kali kept the three coins, and followed the creature out of the building.

'*Mine's on the way,*' he reported. The big items in the description were the red hat and a violently clashing purple scarf, a combination that should be easily visible to the naked eye from orbit.

The messenger stopped for a cup of the heated brew that passed locally for tea. He engaged in a loud conversation with a couple of others. He wasn't anxious to go home, he told them. His mate, wife, *zilfa*, was still angry. They laughed and took turns offering advice on how he should handle it. One of the comments translated roughly to '*Show her who's boss.*' When he'd finished, they agreed to meet tomorrow, and he picked up his deliveries and headed across the street into a stable. Minutes later, he saddled up and headed north.

'*I've got him,*' said Bill.

Macao lived in a brick cottage on the northern side of the city. It was a long walk, mostly uphill, and they were exhausted when they arrived. By then, Bill reported, the cylinder had been delivered.

The cottage was one of several set at the edge of a dense forest. There was a small barn in the rear, and a modest garden probably given over to raising vegetables. The sun was down, and the first stars were in the sky. An oil lamp flickered through closed, but imperfectly fitted, shutters. Black smoke rose out of a chimney.

Something yowled as they approached, but nothing challenged them. A gentle wind moved against the trees. They heard voices farther along the crest, sporadic, sometimes laughing or shouting. Digger could make out only part of it. 'Kids,' he said.

Goompah kids.

They paused under a tree facing the house. Something moved against the light.

'I think it should be just one of us,' said Digger.

Kellie agreed. 'Has to be you,' she added.

'My personality?'

'Right. Also your language skills.' He felt her hand on his wrist, restraining him. 'Maybe you should kill the lightbender.'

Digger took a deep breath and thought of the demonic, foul creatures being dispatched by the god with the sword. They all looked like him and Kellie. So how best approach her? Demon or disembodied voice?

He turned off the device. 'I don't look so terrible, do I?'

'You look ravishing, love.'

'All right. Let's try it this way. She is, after all, enlightened.'

'Yes. Absolutely.'

'Can't go wrong.' He walked up to the front door, which was a bit low for him. It was constructed of planks laid side by side, painted white, and polished with a gum of some sort. 'First contact,' he told Kellie. And he knocked.

'Who's there?' He recognized Macao's voice.

Footsteps approached the door.

'Digger Dunn,' he said.

'Who?'

'I was at your *slosh* in *Brackel*, and I listened to you speak at the launch. Could I ask a question, please?'

A bolt was thrown, and the door swung out. Her eyes locked on him. He'd expected a screech in those first moments, screams followed by bedlam, neighbors on the way, animals howling, torches in the night, God knew what. He was prepared at the first indication of panic to hit the switch and wrap himself again in the lightbender.

But she laughed. And when he stayed where he was, half-shrouded in darkness, she reached back and produced an oil lamp. She held it up to inspect his face. And the laughter died.

'Is that *real*?' she asked, staring and beginning to breathe irregularly. She was gripping the door, hanging on to it for support.

'*Roblay culasta.*' I'm a friend. He didn't budge. Did nothing she could interpret as threatening. 'Macao,' he said. 'I know my appearance is strange. Frightening. I'm sorry. I come from very far.'

She stared. Her mouth worked but nothing came out.

'From beyond the sea,' he said. 'It's important that we speak.'

She sighed and staggered back into the room. She wore a bright yellow blouse with rolled-up sleeves and a pair of red shorts that hung to her knees. Digger hesitated, edged forward, saw that she was on the verge of collapse, and reached for her arm.

She did not react.

He took hold of it and eased her into a chair.

'*Still got the old charm,*' said Kellie.

Macao needed a couple of minutes. She opened her eyes, looked at Digger, and instinctively turned her face aside as though he were too horrible to behold. He tried his most winning smile. 'I won't harm you, Macao,' he said softly. 'And I'm not a *zhoka*, even though I look like one.'

She quailed in his presence. 'Don't hurt me,' she said, in a tiny voice.

365

'I would never do that.' He eased the door shut, found cups and a flagon of wine on a table, and poured some for her. She shook her head no. He was tempted to try it himself. 'No,' she said. Her voice was barely audible. 'Lykonda, protect me.'

'I, too, have great affection for Lykonda,' he said.

She simply sat there, limp as a wet towel, staring at him, as if she'd retreated into some far corner of her mind.

'Macao, I'm sorry to frighten you. But it's important that we talk. About *T'Klot*.'

Her jaw muscles tightened, and he again thought she was going to pass out.

'I've come to try to help you.'

It was a pleasant home. Fireplace, several chairs, plank floor, a looking glass, a table, and a shelf with several scrolls. The shutters were flanked by thick blue curtains. A second room, opening off the back, was dark. 'I will leave in a few minutes, Macao. Because I know that is what you wish. But first I need you to listen to me.'

She tried to speak, but the words wouldn't come.

'It's all right,' he said. 'I'm a friend.'

She got her breathing under control. And finally looked directly at him. 'I did not see you,' she said, 'at the *slosh*.' And she laughed. The sound touched a few notes that sounded hysterical, but she held on. 'Why have you come?'

'The hole in the sky,' he said, forgetting himself and using English. '*T'Klot*.'

'Yes.' She glanced past him at the door. It was supposed to be furtive, he thought, but maybe Goompahs weren't good at that sort of thing. 'Is it the creation of Shol?'

'Who's Shol?'

'*You* are Shol.'

'No. No, Macao. I am Digger, and Shol didn't create the hole. But it is very dangerous.'

'If you are not Shol, not a *zhoka*, what are you?'

'I'm somebody who's come a long way to help you, Macao.

366

Let me tell you first that, in *Brackel*, you were right. The world *is* round.'

'Is that *true*?' A light came into her eyes. And she seemed to recover herself. 'Is that *really* true?'

'Yes,' he said. 'It's really so. But it's not why I'm here.'

She started to ask the obvious question but, probably fearful of the answer, stopped.

The chairs were made from interwoven strips of hide on a wooden frame. They were a bit low for Digger, but they were more than sufficiently wide. 'May I?' he asked, glancing at a chair facing her.

She made no move to say no, so he lowered himself into it. 'The Hole presents a serious hazard. To everyone in the *Intigo*.'

She glanced at the cup of wine and he passed it to her. She took it, gazed into it as if assuring herself that it would not snatch away her soul, and put it to her lips. 'You may have some,' she said, 'if you wish.'

The universal. Share a drink with someone and bond. Would it prove to be true in all cultures? He poured a few drops into a second cup and raised it to her. 'To your courage, Macao,' he said.

She managed a smile.

He held the cup to his lips and tasted the brew. It was bitter. 'It's actually a cloud,' he said, 'a vast storm. It will arrive in ninety-three days, and it's going to wreck the eleven cities.'

Ninety-three of the shortened days at the *Intigo*. Eighty-six standard days on board the *Jenkins*. The target date was December 13.

It was the most painful conversation of Digger's life. Macao was terrified, and the news wasn't helping. 'It'll bring tornadoes and lightning and high water and rocks falling from the sky and we don't know what else.'

In spite of everything, she managed a half smile. *If you don't know, who would?*

She was struggling to control her emotions. And he found his respect for her growing. How many of the women back home

367

could have sat more or less calmly conducting a conversation with a demon?

'Rocks cannot fall from the sky,' she said.

'Believe me, they can.'

'Then why can I not see them?'

'I don't understand the question.'

'There are no rocks in the sky. If there were, surely we would see them.'

'The rocks are very far away. And hidden in the cloud.'

'How far?'

How to translate 30 million or so kilometers into a number she could understand? '*Very* far,' he said.

'The sky is only a shell. What you are telling me is incomprehensible.'

'Macao,' he said, 'what are the stars?'

'Some say they are the light from the celestial realm, which we can see through holes in the shell.'

'But you don't believe it?'

'No.'

'Why not?'

'It does not seem to me to make sense.'

'Good for you. What do *you* think the stars are?'

'I do not know.'

'Okay,' he said. 'I want you to take my word that the hole in the sky is dangerous. That, when it comes, it will bring great suffering. Your people, the people across the *Intigo*, must get away from the cities, must get to higher ground. If they cannot do this, they will die.'

Her eyes cut into him. 'Despite your words, you are, after all, a manifestation of evil.'

'I am not.'

'If you are not, then stop this thing that you say is coming. Surely you are able to control a hole. Or a cloud. Or whatever it is.'

'It's a cloud.'

'Only a cloud? And you, with all your power, cannot brush it aside?'

'If I could do that, do you think I would be here asking for help?'

She looked at him and shuddered. 'I don't understand any of this. Who are you, really?'

'Macao,' he said, 'in *Brackel* you talked about lands beyond the seas. And about giant *falloons* and attack *groppes* and flying *bobbos*—'

'*Bobbos* that attack and *groppes* that fly—'

'Pardon?'

'You had it backward.'

'Sorry. Memory fails.'

'*Bobbos do* fly.'

'Oh.'

'Ordinary *bobbos* fly all the time. They are in the trees outside at this very moment.' She injected an adjective after *ordinary* that he did not understand. Probably something like *run-of-the-mill.* 'How could you not know?'

'That *bobbos* fly? Because I'm not from around here.' He gazed intently at her. 'I wouldn't know a *bobbo* from a seashell.' He put the cup down. 'You talked, in *Brackel*, about the city from which people can see the past and the future.'

'*Brissie*,' she said.

'Yes. *Brissie*.' He leaned forward, watched her push back in her chair, and immediately retreated. 'Macao, we are looking at two possible futures now. If you are willing to trust me, you can save your people. Or, if you cling to the superstition that brands me as something out of the dark, then you and all that the *Korbikkans* have built, will be destroyed.'

'In ninety-three days, you say?' Her voice shook.

'Yes.'

More wine. 'And I am to do what?'

'Warn them.'

'They will not believe me.'

'Who will not?'

'Everyone. People are afraid of *T'Klot*, but they would not believe that a supernatural messenger has come to me with this news.' She looked at him carefully. 'Of all persons here, me especially.'

'And why is that?'

'Because I am a professional storyteller. An exaggerator of considerable reputation.' A bit of pride leaked into her voice.

'I will go with you.'

'No!' It was almost a shriek. 'That would be the worst thing you could do.'

Time for another tack. 'Do you know the mayor?' The *booglik*.

'I've met him once.'

'Can you get in to see him?'

'Possibly.'

'Do so. Tell him what I've told you. Tell him, when the time gets close, he has to get his people out of *Kulnar*. Have them take several days' supply of food and clothes. And blankets. Go to high ground. Any who fail to do so will almost certainly be lost.'

She folded her hands in the manner of one praying. 'It's no use,' she said. 'He won't listen to me. It's ridiculous.' A tear ran down her cheek. It surprised him to realize she had tear ducts.

'Digger Dunn,' she said. 'Is that really your name?'

'Yes.'

'It is a strange name.'

He fumbled in his jacket, and found Kellie's necklace. 'I have something for you.' He held it out to her. 'It will bring you good luck.'

She looked at it uncertainly, as if it might bite. Gift from a *zhoka*. But at last she took it, and while she drew the necklace over her head, Digger tried the most harmless smile of which he was capable. 'It looks lovely,' he said. 'Like you.'

'Thank you.' She pressed her fingertips against the pickup. 'I have never seen anything like this. What is it?'

'There is only one in the world.' In a sense, it was true. 'It was made especially for you.'

Macao gazed at herself in the looking glass. She turned back toward him, pleased, frightened, uncertain. 'Thank you,' she said. 'Digger Dunn.'

He nodded.

'For everything,' she added.

LIBRARY ENTRY

The general public seems surprised that the Goompahs are so much like us. They had expected aliens to be, well, *alien*. As if their mathematics should be incomprehensible, as if they would develop from something other than a hunter-gatherer society, as if they would not need shelter from the storm, as if they would not love their children.

Indeed, they have all these things, and a great deal more. They have selfish politicians, they have squabbles, they even enjoy ball games.

There are, of course, some differences. To our eyes, they look odd. They do not seem interested in traveling far from home, to the extent that they hardly know what lies a few hundred kilometers beyond their seacoasts and their borders. They have primitive religious notions. And they seem to have some ideas about sex that most of us would frown on. At least, if anyone's looking.

Maybe it's time to recognize them for what they are, spiritual siblings. If one could sweep the differences in appearance and technology aside, who could doubt that many of us would feel quite comfortable in *Brackel*, the city that our researchers still insist on calling Athens? And it's probable that these creatures of a far world would enjoy themselves thoroughly in Georgetown, or out on the Mall.

The Goompahs, the *Korbikkans*, as they call themselves, join us and the Noks as the only known living civilizations. The Noks quarrel constantly. The Korbikkans seem to have found a way to live in peace. How can we look at either of them and not see ourselves?

—C. W. Chrissinger
Staying the Course

30

The imager on Macao's necklace was apparently facing her skin, so they got no picture. It seemed likely that she lived alone. They heard no conversation during the evening, just the sounds of someone moving around, pouring water, playing one of the stringed instruments. The wind blew against the side of the cottage, and forest creatures hooted and twirped. Doors opened and closed, the bolt rattled, and occasionally someone sighed.

It was the rattles that got Digger. How many times could she check the lock? And the sighs. Well, he could understand that. She'd just had a visit from a *zhoka*, and if the Goompahs shared the standard earthly tradition, that the devil could be very smooth, all Digger's charm might not have helped.

Most surprising, they both thought, was that, when he'd left, she had not run screaming into the night. Had not gone to a friend or neighbor to describe what had happened.

They were listening from Utopia. Digger was emotionally exhausted. Almost as if *he* had just gone through an unexpected meeting with a demon. He'd gotten a shower as soon as they arrived, and sat wrapped in a robe, listening to Macao move around her cottage.

'If it were me,' said Kellie, 'I'd be out of there and headed for my mother's. Or something. Anything to get with other people.'

The omega was rising. It was approaching too slowly to make out any real change in its appearance from night to night. But when he compared images from a couple of weeks earlier, he could see the difference. And the Goompahs, more attuned to watching the night sky than he was, knew it was growing.

He pushed his seat back and drifted off. Digger usually woke two or three times during the night, but this time he slept straight through until Bill woke him shortly after dawn. '*Macao is up,*' he said.

The imager was facing out now, so they watched while she stoked the fire, tossed in a log or two, washed, and got dressed. Then the necklace went inside her blouse, and the visuals were gone again. But they could hear, and that should be sufficient. She left the cottage for a few minutes, exchanged pleasantries with a neighbor, looks like rain, how's your boy?

Then she was back, and water was pouring again. They heard wet sounds they couldn't identify. Dishes moved around. Cabinet doors closed. Utensils clinked.

'When did we get knives and forks?' asked Kellie.

'The wealthy had them in the Middle Ages.'

Kellie got bored and made for the washroom. He listened to her splashing around in the shower. When she returned, wearing a *Jenkins* jumpsuit, nothing had changed. They could hear the rhythmic sound of Macao's breathing. And her heartbeat.

Kellie looked out at a gray ocean. 'What do you think?' she asked. 'Did you convince her?'

Yes, he thought he had. He was *sure* he had.

Kellie brought him a plate of toast. He smeared strawberry jelly on it.

They heard boards creak. And more sounds at the fireplace.

374

The visual, which had simply been a field of yellow, the color of her blouse, changed. Became the interior of a room he hadn't seen before. The back room. Then they were looking up at a ceiling, with no movement detectable. 'She's taken it off and laid it down,' said Digger.

A bolt lifted, and a door opened and closed. 'Front door,' said Kellie.

'Well, that's not so good.'

'She might just be headed for the barn. Off to feed the animals.'

Macao was gone several hours. When finally she came back another female was with her.

'*Where?*' asked the other female.

'*Here.*' They saw a movement between the lens and the ceiling. An arm, maybe?

'*Right there.*'

'*And you stayed here all night?*'

'*Ora, I believe him.*'

'*That's why they're so dangerous, Mac.*' Mac? *Mac?* '*Shol is the king of liars.*'

'*Look,*' Macao said. '*He gave me this.*'

The picture blurred, and they were looking at Ora. She was wearing a red blouse and a violet neckerchief. One green eye grew very large and peered out of the screen at them. '*It's quite nice,*' she said. '*Lovely.*' And then: '*What's wrong?*'

A long pause. '*I was wondering if he might be here now.*'

'*It's daylight. They can't stand the daylight.*'

'*Are you sure? There was talk of a zhoka out on the highway last spring. In the middle of the day.*' The eye pulled away. They saw walls, then they were looking at the ceiling again.

'*Mac, you're giving me chills.*' That wasn't precisely what she said. It was more like causing her lungs to work harder. But Digger understood the meaning.

'*Why did it come to me? Ora, I don't even believe in* zhokas. *Or at least I didn't until last night.*'

'*I warned you something like this would happen. Walking around laughing at the gods. What did you expect?*'

'*I never laughed at the gods.*'

'*Worse than that. You denied them.*'

'*Ora,*' she said, '*I don't know what to do.*'

The debate continued. Macao denied the charges, argued that she'd only maintained the gods did not run day-to-day operations. Did not make the sun move. Or the tides roll in.

Ora seemed nervous about being in the cottage, went on about apparitions, and suggested Macao might like to stay with her a while. Whatever devilry Digger might have imposed, it didn't stop the two females from eating. And then they were gone, with no indication what step Macao would take next.

The pickup still provided a clear picture of the ceiling.

Not knowing what else they could try, they simply waited it out. A large insect buzzed the pickup. The shutters were apparently open because there was plenty of daylight. After a while, the light became dimmer, and they heard rain on the roof.

'She's gone to see somebody about it,' said Kellie.

It was possible she'd gone to the governance building, *T'Kalla*. The chief executive in *Kulnar* was the *booglik*. I'm on my way to *T'Kalla* to talk to the *booglik*. It sounded almost normal.

He was still sitting, staring morosely at Macao's overhead, at *Mac's* overhead, when he heard the door open. By then the rain seemed to have stopped.

'*Did you get it?*' Ora's voice.

'*Right here.*'

Footsteps moved across the planks. '*No sign of him?*'

'*No. We're alone.*'

'*Good. Listen, save some of the* kessel *for me, Mac.*'

He heard sounds like a knife cutting through onions.

'*I thought you didn't believe it would work.*'

'*No. I said I don't trust it to work. But there's nothing to lose by trying it.*'

The cutting continued. Then: '*There, that should be enough.*'

'*Where do you want to put it?*'

'*In the doorway. Just block the threshold with it.*'

'*All right. You're putting it in the windows too, right?*'

'*And in the fireplace. Just in case.*'

Bill broke in: '*I have a reference to* kessel.'

'Let's hear it,' said Kellie.

'*It's a common herb, found throughout the* Intigo. *Sometimes ground into grains and used as a seasoning. It's also thought to provide a bar against demons and other spirits of the night.*'

'A bar?' said Kellie.

'That's why they're putting it in all the entrances. Keep the demon out.'

'What good's a sliced vegetable going to do?'

Digger was tired of it all. He was tempted to go back to the *Jenkins* and just sit tight until help arrived. Let somebody else deal with these loonies. 'Think garlic,' he said.

'What do we do now?'

Digger was ready to call it off. 'Only thing I can think of, other than conceding we are not going to get through to these yahoos, is to go directly to the head guy. There must be somebody in this town who isn't afraid of goblins.'

'I'm sure there is. But I doubt it's the *gloobik*.'

'*Booglik*,' he said. 'So who do you recommend?'

'Don't know. Maybe the captain on the round-the-world voyage. What was his name?'

'Krolley.'

'Maybe we could get to him. He's got to have *some* sense.'

'He'd have to be willing to turn around.'

'You don't think he'd do that?'

'I don't know him. But I suspect we'd have a better chance with somebody local.'

Kellie looked discouraged. Digger was beginning to realize she'd thought, as he had, that they'd won Macao over. 'Even if we'd succeeded with Macao,' she said, 'she'd still have had the problem of convincing the authorities. Macao didn't think she could do it. And, despite the way things turned out, I don't believe she was playacting.' She closed her eyes. 'I think we need a different approach.'

'What do you think will happen with her?'

She thought about it, and smiled sadly. 'When the cloud closes in, I think she'll fix herself some sandwiches, grab a tent, and head for the high ground.'

'Taking no chances.'

'That's right. Maybe she'll take a few friends with her.'

Digger saw no way out. Other than going directly to the *booglik* and trying to persuade him. 'We need some of Collingdale's costumes. If we could at least fix ourselves up to look like the locals, we might have a chance.'

Kellie looked discouraged. 'Face it, Dig,' she said, 'What we need is some divine intervention.'

They had returned to the *Jenkins* and were on the night side of Lookout. Clouds below were thick, so he couldn't tell whether they were over land or sea. He was becoming familiar with the constellations, and had even made an effort to learn them by their Goompah names. *Tow Bokol Kar*, the Wagon-maker, floated just over the rim of the world. And there was *T'Kleppa*, the Pitcher. And just beside it, *T'Monga*, a bird that had probably never existed. Its closest cousin in terrestrial mythology was probably the roc. It was reputed to be able to carry off Goompahs.

'How about,' said Kellie, trying to shrug off her mood, 'staying inside the lightbender when we talk to them?'

'You think that'll scare them less than the *zhoka*?'

'Can it scare them any more?'

He shook his head. It wouldn't work. Disembodied voices never work. It's a rule.

'Maybe there's another possibility,' she said.

'I'm listening.'

'Why don't we try using an avatar again?'

He shook his head. 'Can't synchronize their lips to match the dialogue. It's okay if the avatar goes down with a prepared speech, delivers it, and clears out. But the first question somebody tosses at him, like, where did you say you were from, and we're dead.'

'It's a shot,' she persisted.

'Won't work.' He could imagine himself in the *booglik's* quarters, playing a recording to match the previously prepared lip movements of the Goompah avatar. And the *booglik* breaking in, hey, wait a minute, while the avatar either galloped on, or stopped dead and picked up again where he left off no matter what question got asked.

They were catching up with the sun. The long arc of the world was brightening.

His circadian rhythms had been scrambled. Moving constantly between the shorter days and nights of the *Intigo* and the standard twenty-four-hour clock on the ship had left them both uncertain what time of day or night it was. But even if dawn was coming, he was hungry. 'How about some dinner?' she suggested.

Two hours later they sat in the long stillness of the *Jenkins*. There were times when Digger thought that if he put on the infrared goggles, he'd see Jack's ghost drifting through the corridors. He heard echoes that hadn't been there before, and whispers in the bulkheads. When he mentioned it to Kellie, she commented that now he might understand a little of what Macao had felt.

'The noises,' she added, 'are made by Bill. Sometimes he talks to himself.'

'You're kidding.'

'No. Really. He holds conversations.'

'What about?'

'I don't know.'

'Haven't you ever asked him?'

'Yes.'

'What did he say?'

'Ask him yourself.'

379

Digger was reluctant. It seemed intrusive. But that was silly. You couldn't offend an AI. 'Bill,' he said. 'Got a minute?'

A literary version appeared, world-weary with high cheekbones and a white beard. He was seated in the chair that Jack used to favor. '*Yes, Digger. How may I be of assistance?*'

'Bill, sometimes I hear voices. In the systems.'

'*Yes. I do, too.*'

'What are they?'

'*The systems communicate all the time.*'

'They do it by talking?'

'*Sometimes.*'

'But don't you control the systems?'

'*Oh, yes. But they're separate from me. They have their own priorities.*'

'Okay,' he said. 'Let it go.'

Bill vanished.

'Satisfied?' asked Kellie.

'I don't think he told me anything.'

'The voices are his.' She was browsing through the ship's systems. Or maybe gameplaying. He couldn't tell.

'I have a question for you,' Digger said.

'Another one.'

'Yes.' He straightened himself. 'We haven't set a date yet.'

'Ah. No, we haven't.' She narrowed her eyes, appraising him. 'We won't be home for a long time.'

'We don't have to wait until we get home.'

'You're sweet, Digby.'

'I'm serious.'

She was framed in the soft glow of the computer screen. 'What do you suggest?' she said.

'A ship's captain can perform a wedding.'

She allowed herself to look shocked. 'Surely not her own.'

'I had Julie Carson in mind. When the *Hawksbill* gets here.'

She thought about it. 'All right,' she said finally. 'If you're determined, how can I stand in the way? We'll have to send for a license.'

'We've plenty of time.'

'Okay, Digger.' She grinned. 'Seeing how you affect the other females around here, though, maybe I should rethink this.'

The avatar idea was not entirely without merit. Provided it was possible to produce one that could deliver the message and clear out. Here's the deal and no questions asked.

'But how would you do that?'

'You suggested we could use divine intervention.'

'Can you arrange it?'

'I have an idea, Watson,' he said, doing his best Oxford accent. 'We'd need some projectors, though. A lot of projectors.'

'Tell me what you have in mind.'

'Bill, let's see some Goompahs.'

'*Any in particular?*'

'Yes. A female. Macao would be good. Give us a picture of Macao.'

She blinked on. It was Macao as she'd looked during the *slosh* at *Brackel*. Bright yellow blouse with fluffy sleeves. Green leggings and animal-hide boots. And the medallion on the purple ribbon.

'Okay. Bill, have her say something.'

Macao smiled at him. '*Challa,* Digger,' she said, in a perfect imitation of Kellie's voice. '*You are a little* zhoka, *aren't you?*'

He grinned. 'The lip sync is okay. Not perfect, but okay.'

'*It wouldn't fool anybody. Unless you give her a fan and have her hold it in front of her mouth. To get it right, I need to have a little warning in advance what she's going to say.*'

'I don't get it,' said Kellie. 'If we're agreed the real Macao probably couldn't accomplish anything, what can her avatar do?'

'We need to make some adjustments. Then, maybe, quite a lot.'

ARCHIVE

From the Goompah Recordings (Tyree of *Roka* at a *slosh* in *Brackel*) (Translated by Ginko Amagawa)

Strange things are happening. There have been reports of *zhokas* on the highways, and of voices speaking in an unknown tongue in empty places. And a huge hole has opened in our skies and grows larger every night. Those of you who know me know that I have always believed that everything has a rational explanation. That the world is governed by immutable law and not by the whims of spirits and demons.

There are some who argue that these are all portents of approaching catastrophe. Let me say first that I cannot offer explanations for these events. But I have not yet become so desperate that I've started believing there is such a thing as a portent. It may be that the demons on the highway are figments of overheated imaginations. That the voices in the night are really nothing more than the wind. And that the hole in the sky, which has begun to look like a cloud, will prove to be a new kind of storm. But that like any other storm, it will blow for a while, and then it will exhaust itself, and the sun will rise in the morning.

Meantime, I'll remind you that if catastrophe of a previously unknown nature is indeed on the way, that there is nothing to be done about it. Except enjoy the time we have left with family and friends. But this is extremely unlikely. We have a tendency to assume the worst, to give way to fear whenever something we do not understand presents itself.

Since no plausible action can be taken against demons, disembodied voices, or the thing in the sky, I suggest that we put it all aside, that we refuse to allow these phenomena to upset our daily routine. That we in no case give way to panic.

Now that we all recognize that I don't know what's going on any more than you do, we'll open the floor for comments or questions.

—September 19

31

On board the *Hawksbill*.
Saturday, September 20.

They got lucky. The search for the *al-Jahani* could have taken as long as a week. Establishing a position when one was adrift in interstellar space was less than a precise science. Furthermore, hyperlight signals did not lend themselves to tracking. So a searcher was dependent on radio transmissions, which were desperately slow. Julie could only guarantee that she would put the *Hawksbill* reasonably close to the damaged ship. And, when Marge asked how she defined *reasonably*, she admitted she was talking about 80 billion kilometers or so.

Julie had expected to spend a minimum of two days in a fruitless search, then be directed to forget it and go on without Collingdale. But in fact they came out of hyperspace within range of the *al-Jahani*'s radio signals. Julie got her fix and jumped a second time. They emerged within a few hours of the stricken ship.

In fact she didn't see the point of all the hassle. The *Hawksbill* couldn't accommodate the linguists; couldn't even take on Frank Bergen, who was to have ridden shotgun with the decoys. Only Collingdale would be making the rest of the flight, and she didn't see why he was needed.

Collingdale hadn't taken the time to explain it to her, and he was in charge, so she said nothing. Not even to Marge and Whit. Although they weren't above wondering why they were going to so much trouble for somebody who was just going to Lookout to watch.

'Well,' said Marge, 'don't anybody take this the wrong way, but it will be nice to see a fresh face on board.'

Julie got blankets and pillows out of her supplies and tried to make her storage room into a sleeping accommodation. There was no bed; Collingdale would have to make do on the deck.

At 1942 hours they picked up the *al-Jahani* in their telescopes, and three hours later they slipped alongside. Marge and Whit had both asked whether they could take some time to go aboard the other ship, just to say hello. Look around someplace different. Marge had an old friend aboard the *al-Jahani*. Julie would also have liked to get away from the narrow living space of the *Hawksbill* for a few hours, so she'd proposed it to Collingdale.

'*Don't have time,*' he said over the link. '*We need to get going forthwith.*' *Forthwith*. She didn't know anybody else who talked like that.

'My passengers could stand the break,' she'd said. 'They've been cooped up in here for six months.'

'*Wish we could. But every hour puts that thing closer to Lookout. It's just impossible.*'

'Okay,' she said.

'*Sorry,*' he added.

Marge settled for saying hello to her friend, the planetologist Melinda Park, by commlink. But she wasn't happy, and Julie thought that Collingdale might be in for a long ride.

He was on his way through the airlock within thirty seconds after the green lights went on. 'Thank God,' he told Julie. 'It's been a nightmare.' And he added more apologies. 'But there's just too much at stake.'

'It's okay,' she said. 'But you're leaving Bergen. Who's going out with the decoys?'

'I am,' he said.

There was a quick exchange with the *al-Jahani*'s captain. Were there any injuries? Did she have sufficient supplies to last until the relief vessel came? Could Julie provide any assistance?

'*We're fine,*' said Alexandra. And it might have been Julie's imagination, but she sensed an unspoken *now*.

Collingdale stood behind her, looking at the time, suggesting that they really should get moving, assuring her everything was satisfactory on the other ship.

Eight minutes after they'd arrived, the *Hawksbill* edged away, fired its thrusters, and began to accelerate toward jump status.

Julie had expected to feel apologetic about the storeroom quarters she was giving him, but as things turned out she felt a degree of satisfaction showing him the blankets on the deck and the two cramped washrooms.

Collingdale was so pleased to be aboard a functioning ship, on his way to Lookout, that he didn't really care about spartan conditions. During acceleration, he belted in on the couch in the equipment locker, the only one they had available.

He watched the *al-Jahani* diminish with distance, and he felt a tinge of regret for Judy and Nick and Ginko and the others, who had worked so hard and accomplished so much. He thought about calling Judy, delivering a final farewell, but he'd done that before leaving. Any more along those lines would be maudlin.

What he had to do now was to see that the cloud got sidetracked, so that what had happened to Judy's team wouldn't matter in the long run.

He waited in his harness, looking around the bare-bones room, grateful that he was moving again. He closed his eyes and tried to relax, but he kept seeing the omega that had swept down on Moonlight. And he wished he had a bomb big enough to blow the damned thing to hell.

That was the problem with Hutch's decoy idea. It was good, and it might work. But it only deflected the cloud. It didn't *kill* it.

That was what Collingdale wanted. Go to the next step and kill it.

After forty minutes' acceleration they still had not jumped. Every flight he'd ever been on had been able to do it in thirty minutes or so. He called the bridge to ask.

'*Big ship, David,*' she said. '*It takes a while.*' Her tone was mildly hostile. He tried to remember if he'd said or done anything to offend her. Probably upset that she didn't get a chance to visit. But time was too valuable. The hour that they squandered now might make all the difference. 'Okay,' he said. 'I didn't know.'

He *did* know that if she tried to make the jump before the Hazeltines were ready, the *Hawksbill* would go boom. 'Take your time,' he said.

He was pleased to be on the ship that housed the decoys, that would actually be used to frustrate the omega. He spent hours on the bridge, explained to Julie that he'd commanded a superluminal at the beginning of his career, and wanted to know everything. He talked at length with Bill, was allowed to sit in the captain's chair, enjoyed calling up status reports, running maintenance routines, putting the AI through his paces.

Julie, pleased that he showed such interest, showed him through the ship. Here were the comm circuits; there was life support; here's the power mode complex. They toured the engine room, the shuttle launch area in the lower cargo bay, and main storage, where the antigrav generator was located.

He wasn't sure why he was so interested in the ship. He hadn't particularly cared about the *al-Jahani*. It must have been because he knew *this* would be the vessel. Bergen was out of the game now, and Collingdale would be taking the *Hawksbill* into battle.

It made him feel young again. As if all the world waited for him to show up and set things right. 'Julie,' he said, 'tell me about the jump engines. Has the technology improved?'

'I doubt it,' she said. 'I don't think anything basic has changed in thirty years.'

He hadn't heard from Mary in two weeks, other than a short expression of her regret that the mission had broken down. It wasn't *short*, actually. She'd gone on for ten minutes. Everything was fine at home. Some of her new students had little sense and no ethics. '*They're studying law for all the wrong reasons.*'

He'd begun to wonder whether he should let her go. God knew when he'd get home, and it seemed unreasonable to keep her waiting all that time. His deepest fear, even more than losing her, was that she would come to resent him.

On the other hand, where would she find somebody else like David Collingdale? It was a private joke he told himself. But there was some truth to it.

Avery Whitlock's Notebooks

The mood on the ship has changed. It may be a momentary thing, but I doubt it.

David Collingdale seems to be decent enough. He speaks kindly to everyone, and he apologized to us all for the delay involved in rescuing him from the al-Jahani. Still, we were quieter this evening than we have been at any time on the flight. The chemistry has changed in some subtle, or maybe not-so-subtle, way. The easy camaraderie of the past months is gone, as abruptly as though it had never existed. We are formal now, and tentative, watchful of what we say. And though it seems logical to conclude that with the passage of time the former atmosphere will return, I do not think it will happen.

—September 18

32

Arlington, Virginia.
Tuesday, September 23.

She hated the chime that came in the middle of the night. Priscilla Hutchins was not a hands-on manager. Her technique was to frame the objectives, provide the resources, find the right people to get the job done, and stay out of the way. That meant that when a call came in at 3:00 A.M., whether it was personal or professional, it was inevitably bad news.

She picked up the link and held it to her ear. Tor rolled over and looked at the time.

'*Hutch.*' It was Debbie Willis, the Academy watch officer. '*The engines went.*'

Damn. After the first incident back in June she'd been half-expecting it. But there'd been nothing she could do. Everything was just too far away. 'Anybody hurt?' she asked.

'*No. They're all okay.*' She thought she heard a cry from Maureen's room, but when she listened there was only silence.

'Okay,' she said. 'Julie and Digger have been informed?'

'*Yes. We have a transmission from Alexandra. You want me to relay it?*'

'Does it say she can effect repairs and get to Lookout before the cloud does?'

'*I haven't looked at it. But Broadside reports they're unable to proceed with the mission.*'

'Help on the way?'

'*Yes, ma'am.*'

'Okay. Thanks, Deb. Forward the stuff from Alex.'

Tor was watching her. 'The *al-Jahani*?'

'Yes.'

'I'm sorry, babe.'

'Me too.'

She heard the sound again. Maureen having a bad dream, maybe.

'I'll get it,' said Tor.

'No.' She headed for the door. 'It's okay.'

While she sat with Maureen she heard Tor leave the bedroom and go downstairs. Nights like this, when he knew things weren't going well for her, he got restless. When the child was quiet, she followed and found him dozing in his chair, a book open on his lap, the lamp on behind him. She put the book on the coffee table, turned off the light, and settled onto the sofa. 'Nothing you could do,' he said, without opening his eyes.

'I could have held them up another week. Completed the routine maintenance. They'd've found the problem if I'd done that.'

'Why didn't you?'

'Didn't have a week to spare. But at least they'd have gotten there.'

He made a noise deep in his throat. 'You're second-guessing yourself,' he said. 'If you'd gone that route, and they'd gotten there too late to intervene, you'd have been blaming yourself for that. Should have taken a chance and let them go a week earlier.'

'Well,' she said, 'maybe the kite'll work.'

In the morning she sent off messages to Collingdale, to Vadim at Broadside, and to Digger. Collingdale had informed her of his intention to continue his journey on the *Hawksbill*. She wished him luck and told him she knew he would do what he could. She instructed Vadim to give priority to whatever requests might come in from the other two. If Digger could see any way to get the Goompahs to high ground, he was to proceed and damn the consequences.

When she got to the Academy in the morning, there was a message from Broadside, informing her that Jack's body would be coming back on the *Winckelmann*. The Academy had a formatted letter to be sent out on such occasions to next of kin, but it seemed cold, so she settled in to write her own.

She left word with Asquith's secretary that she wanted to see the commissioner when he came in. When he hadn't appeared by ten, she called him on his link. He discouraged that sort of behavior. Emergencies only, he insisted. He didn't like to feel tied to the Academy, enjoyed telling others that he ran a shop in which it didn't matter whether his subordinates could talk to him or not. It was the mark of a good manager that decisions were made and action taken even when he couldn't be reached.

On the other hand, if he got blindsided by somebody on Capitol Hill, he'd complain for days about his staff not keeping him informed.

'*Yes?*' he demanded irritably.

'I don't know whether you've heard yet or not. The *al-Jahani* blew its engines. It's adrift.'

There was a long pause, and she heard him sigh. '*Any casualties?*'

'No.'

'*Well, thank God for that, at least. Whose fault is it?*'

'I don't know. Probably mine.'

'*How'd it happen?*'

'It just went. We took a chance, and it didn't work out.'

'*Okay. Look, relax. We'll get through this.*'

* * *

391

An hour later Eric was at her door. 'We've got serious problems,' he said. 'How am I supposed to explain this?'

Eric Samuels was an imposing man, tall, well dressed, with an articulated voice that one instinctively trusted. Until it became clear that he lived in a world of images and mirrors. Perception is everything, he was fond of saying. In a glorious sally a few weeks earlier he'd told a group of particle physicists that the underlying lesson to be learned from quantum theory was that reality and image were identical. 'If we don't see it,' he'd said, 'it's not there.'

'Explain what?' she asked.

'The *al-Jahani*. What the hell else would I be talking about?' He looked frantic.

'Sit, Eric,' she said.

He stayed on his feet. 'What do I tell them?'

'You have a press conference today?'

'I do *now*.' Eric was good with the media when things were going well. And that was usually the case at the Academy. Most problems and setbacks could be buried because the general public simply wasn't that interested in the work the Academy did. A recent study by UNN had shown that 50 percent of Americans had no idea whether Alpha Centauri was a planet, a star, a constellation, or a country in west Asia.

But the public *loved* the Goompahs.

She broke out the decanter and offered him a glass. Eric was a straight arrow whom she had never known to touch alcohol on the job. But this would be an exception. Yes. Please. 'The commissioner insisted we issue a statement,' he said. 'Get out ahead of the curve. Make ourselves available.'

'What are you going to tell them?'

'That one-half of the rescue mission broke down. What else can I say?'

'You're not going to put it like that, I hope?'

'No. Of course not.' He looked puzzled. How else could one put it?

'Just attribute it to insufficient resources to meet an emergency of this magnitude.'

'Of course.'

'It's true,' she said. 'We did the best we could with what we had.'

'You think they'll buy that?'

'It's *true*, Eric.'

'That doesn't always guarantee that we can get by with something.' He tried his drink and made a face. 'Anyhow, if we go that route, it might offend the Senate committee, or maybe even the Council. See, that's the problem. It sounds as if we're trying to blame somebody.'

'And you'd rather blame—'

'—A technician. Somebody who can always get another job with somebody else.' He smiled weakly. 'Not you, Hutch. I'd never think of blaming *you*.'

'Good.' She'd been wondering about that all day, whether in the end, needing to point a finger at somebody, Asquith wouldn't find it expedient to target her. Admitting to the media he should have kept an eye on things himself. *Hutchins tried to get it right, but I should have stayed on top of it. Not really her fault though. Bad luck.* She wondered what Sylvia was doing these days.

'Just tell the truth,' she said. 'It'll come out in the end anyway.' She had to bite down on that line, knowing the truth that came out would depend on the way the media perceived what Eric had to say, and what they wanted to stress. Generally, they were inclined to go after people in high places. Which meant that they would probably bite the Senate committee and the commissioner.

She was becoming cynical. A few years back, she'd have considered her present job more than she could possibly have hoped for. But here she was, the director of operations, eminently successful in her career by any reasonable measure. And she wondered why she was doing it.

The job had turned out to be not what she'd expected. She'd

thought it would be operational, with some politics mixed in. Truth was, all her critical functions were political. The rest of it could have been handled by anybody who could count. She'd discovered a talent for politics, and didn't mind jollying people along provided she didn't have to compromise herself. Asquith didn't altogether approve of her. He thought she was something of a crank. But she *was* good at her job, and she thought he'd be reluctant to let her go. Although not so reluctant he'd be willing to face fire from the Hill.

'I hate days like this,' Eric said.

She nodded. 'Don't worry about it. It's not the end of the world.' At least not for us.

Early that afternoon she got a call from Charlie, who'd been serving as director pro tem of the astrophysics lab. '*I've been debating whether to bother you with this, Hutch,*' he said. She came to full alert. '*Can you stop by the lab either today or tomorrow?*'

It didn't sound like a breakthrough. 'I'll be over in an hour or so, Charlie.'

It was more like three hours, and by then a rainstorm had moved in and turned into a downpour. In dry weather she'd have gone outside, strolled past the pool, and tossed some popcorn to the ducks. But she descended instead to the tunnel that connected the Academy's complex of buildings.

The walls were concrete, painted a hideous ocher, the long monotony broken only by pictures of the Academy's ships and stations, and some astronomical shots, galaxies and nebulas and planetary rings. Somebody had added one of the omegas. It was dark and menacing, sections of it illuminated by interior power surges. Long tendrils of cloud reached forward, threatening the observer, and an escorting asteroid was front and center.

She wondered what the Goompahs would think when they saw it up close.

There were three other known races who had ventured into interstellar space: the unknown architects of the *chindi*, who were

394

apparently a race bent on preserving everything of value, who had found their own unique way to defeat time. The Monument-Makers, who had obviously gone to a lot of trouble for the civilizations at Quraqua and Nok. And, finally, the Hawks, who had performed a rescue when Deepsix went into a long-term ice age several thousand years ago.

And now her own species, trying to help where it could. They were in good company. And she felt a modicum of pride. If Darwin ruled on planetary surfaces, it appeared that a concern for one's neighbor was a working principle at higher levels.

Unless, of course, one counted the agency behind the omegas.

She'd have liked to talk with representatives of those three races, but nobody knew where the *chindi* had originated, the Hawks were lost in time, and the few remaining members of the race that had spawned the Monument-Makers were savages on a backward world with no knowledge of their former greatness.

Charlie Wilson must have been alerted she was coming. He met her in the corridor and escorted her into the lab. 'Now understand,' he said, 'I don't really know what any of this means.'

'What any of *what* means?'

Charlie was still filling in as acting lab director. He was doing a good job, but eventually she'd have to bring in somebody with an established reputation.

He took her into the tank, which was a small amphitheater. Thirty-two seats circled a chamber. Like so much of the Academy, it had been designed with public relations in mind. But it had turned out the general public wasn't all that interested. Usually, it was used by only one or two people at a time, but it occasionally served visiting groups of schoolchildren.

They sat down, and Charlie produced a remote. The lights faded to black, the stars came on, vast dust clouds lit up, and they were adrift somewhere in the night. The sensation that they were actually afloat among the stars, the two of them and their chairs, was broken only by the presence of gravity and a flow of cool air.

'We now have forty-seven tewks on record. You know that.'

'Yes.'

'All forty-seven are in places where we would have expected to find omegas. So we can assume they are all the same phenomenon.'

He shifted in his chair, turning so he could face her. 'Some of the Weathermen were close enough to the events to allow us to look for purpose. That is, what was the explosion supposed to accomplish? All of them took place in interstellar space. No worlds nearby. So it's not an attempt to cause general havoc. It's not somebody being vindictive.'

'Tell that to Quraqua.'

He nodded, conceding the point. Civilization on Quraqua had been obliterated. 'All the clouds we've checked, each one is programmed to follow the hedgehog at a slightly higher velocity. When it overtakes the thing, it attacks the hedgehog, which then explodes, triggering the cloud, and you get the tewk.'

'Okay. But why?'

'Who knows? Anyhow, it puts out as much light as a small nova. Somebody else will have to figure out why. We just know it happens.'

'So what's the point? Why has someone gone to all this trouble?'

'I can't answer *that* question. But I can tell you that these things happen in bunches. Harold saw that from the first. Even when we only had a handful to look at. There's a pattern. There are six distinct areas where we've had events. But that's not to say we won't find others as Weatherman proceeds.

'The yellow star on your right is the supergiant R Coronae Borealis. Seven thousand light-years from here.' He touched the remote. A hand's width to one side of the supergiant, a new star sizzled into existence. 'Coronae 14,' he said. 'The fourteenth recorded event.'

And a second new star, a few degrees away. 'Coronae 15.' And, a few degrees farther on, a third. Sixteen.

If there were to be a fourth, she could have guessed where it would be. But there wasn't.

'They're all this way,' he said. 'We get five here, six there. All within a relatively short time span. Maybe a thousand years or so. And each series is confined to a given region.'

'Which means what?'

He looked frustrated. 'Hutch, it's a research project of some sort. Has to be.'

'What are they researching?'

'I don't know. It must have to do with light. Some of our people have made some guesses, but we don't have anything yet that makes sense. But you understand that would be the case if they were on a level sufficiently beyond us.'

'Like Kepler trying to understand gravity fluctuations.'

'Yes. Exactly.'

LIBRARY ENTRY
NEWSCOPE
(Extract from Eric Samuels Press Conference)

New York On-line:	Eric, can you tell us precisely what happened to the *al-Jahani*?
Samuels:	There was problem with the engines. With the jump engines. Uh, Bill?
Cosmo:	A mission as important as this, with so much hanging on it: Weren't they inspected before it left port?
Samuels:	We always do an inspection before ships leave the Wheel. In fact, this one was due for routine maintenance, but there wasn't time to finish. Jennifer.
Cosmo:	Wait. Follow-up, please. Are you saying it was sent out in a defective condition?
Samuels:	No. I'm not saying that at all. Had we known there was a problem, we would have corrected it, no matter how much time it took. In this case, we didn't see

	a problem, we were pressed for time, so we went ahead. We just got unlucky. Jennifer, did you want to try again?
Weekend Roundup:	Yes. If there was a question about this one, why didn't you send another ship?
Samuels:	We didn't have another ship. Not one with the carrying capacity we needed. Harvey, did you have something?
London Times:	You're saying the *Academy* didn't have another ship?
Samuels:	That's correct.
London Times:	How is that possible? The Council and the White House both claim they're doing everything they can to support this effort.
Samuels:	Well, there are limits to what can be done on short notice. Lookout is extremely far. Janet.
UNN:	Eric, what is the prognosis for the Goompahs?
Samuels:	We're still hopeful.

In the morning she hauled Charlie out of the lab for a walk along the Morning Pool.

The forty-seven events, he said, were concentrated in a half dozen widely separated areas. None of the areas was even remotely close to the bubble of space through which humanity had been traveling for the past half century. 'Which is why,' he told her, 'we haven't seen these things in our own sky. But a few thousand years from now, when the light has had time to get here, there'll be some fireworks.'

Two of the areas were out on the rim, one near the core, and three scattered haphazardly. 'And none anywhere else?' she asked.

'Not yet. But the Weathermen are still arriving on station in a lot of places. We'll probably find more.'

There was something solid about Charlie. He wasn't going to get caught up in wild speculations, and in his presence Hutch always felt things were under control. It was a valuable quality in a man so young. Charlie lacked his former boss's genius, but everybody did. And you don't need genius to have a bright future. You need common sense, persistence, and the ability to inspire others. And she could under no circumstances imagine him telling her he understood what the omegas were, then leaving her to wait while he gathered more evidence. He wouldn't even have set it up as a big announcement. He'd have simply told her what he knew. Or suspected.

She looked at the sky and wondered who would be there when the light show began.

Harold had been at the Georgetown Gallery, he'd said, when the epiphany came. When he decided he knew what was happening. But if Charlie were right, if they were doing advanced research, research on areas currently beyond human understanding, how could that have happened?

Was it possible he'd seen something at the gallery?

She called them, something she should have done long ago.

An automated voice asked how the Georgetown Gallery could be of service.

'Have you anything currently on display, or anything that's been sold over the past six months, that has as its subject matter the omega clouds?'

'*One moment please.*'

A human voice picked up the conversation. '*This is Eugene Hamilton. I understand you're interested in* Omega.'

'I'm interested in anything you have, or may have had over the past six months, that uses the omegas as its subject.'

'*That would be René Guilbert's* Storm Center. *You're familiar with it, of course.*'

'Of course.' In fact, Tor had mentioned it, but she couldn't remember the context. 'May I take a look at it, please?'

'*If you wish. You understand, of course, that the power and elegance of this piece, even more than most, cannot begin to be adequately conveyed electronically.*'

'Yes, I understand.'

'*Perhaps you would prefer to come by the gallery? Ms—*' He hesitated, inviting her to introduce herself.

'Hutchins,' she said. 'I'd prefer for the moment to see it here.'

'*Of course. One moment, please.*'

Moments later the work materialized on-screen. Guilbert had captured all the gloom and foreboding of the objects, had caught the immensity and overwhelming power. The malevolence, however, was not there. This was not an object that was out to kill; it just didn't give a damn. Don't get in its way and you'll be fine. Pretty much like *Moby-Dick*.

She made a copy and thanked Hamilton, assuring him she would run by to take a look.

Had Harold seen it?

She showed the copy to Charlie and he shrugged. 'It's an omega, all right.' He produced a disk. 'I thought you might like to have this.'

'What is it?'

'A history of what we've tried to do with the tewks. If anything occurs to you, I'd love to hear about it.'

She sat in the tank for more than an hour watching the results of Charlie's efforts to find a rationale for the tewks. He and his team had tried to establish a real-time sequence, depicting what the events would look like if light traveled instantaneously. That took them nowhere. They had looked at energy yields, at electromagnetic variations, at the ranges to nearby objects that might be affected by the events.

It was a hodgepodge.

For all she knew, it could be a code.

She smiled at the thought while a cloud lit up on the far side of the room, near the emergency exit. And went out. A minute later, fifty years in real time, another, a hand's width away, flared and blinked off. They were like fireflies.

She increased the pace, the flow of time, and saw seven consecutive events coming down from the top of the chamber on her left, then six behind her. She had to take Charlie's word that they were not occurring at precise intervals. She really couldn't tell, just looking at a watch. But it was close enough. A series here, a series there.

They knew now that the events had a range of anywhere from twenty-seven to sixty-one days. And there were different spectra, which is to say the lights came on in different colors.

And that was another strange thing: A series was always the same color. Blue overhead, white at the back of the chamber, red on her left. What the hell was going on?

She had a conference that afternoon, attended a planning session with the commissioner's staff, and got out well after seven o'clock. Between meetings she resolved a dispute between department heads, arranged a visit to Serenity for a senator, and signed a special award for Emma, Sky, and the *Heffernan*, to be presented when they arrived back at their home station.

It cooled down considerably when the sun set, and she strolled into the roof transport complex thinking that she should have dressed more warmly.

'*Where to, please, Ms Hutchins?*' the cab asked after she'd wiped her card.

On a whim, she said, 'Georgetown,' and gave the address of the art gallery on Wisconsin Avenue.

'*Very good,*' said the cab as it lifted away.

They turned north over the Potomac, much swollen since the days of the Roosevelts. Constitution Island, with its cluster of public buildings, glowed in the encroaching night. The Lincoln, Jefferson, Roosevelt, and Brockman memorials watched serenely from their embankments. And the Old White House, with its fifty-two-star U.S. flag spotlighted, stood behind its dikes. A cruise ship, brightly illuminated, moved steadily upriver.

The night was filled with traffic. A shuttle lifted off from Reagan, headed for the Wheel. Glidetrains were everywhere. She called Tor, warned him she'd be late.

'What's in Georgetown?' he asked.

'I'm headed to the gallery.' Tor was, of course, familiar with the place. Years ago, they'd handled much of his work.

'Why?'

'Not sure. I want to get a look at Guilbert's *Storm Center*.'

He seemed satisfied. She almost thought he'd been expecting something like this to happen.

The flight needed only a couple of minutes. They descended into Wisconsin Park, and the cab asked whether she wanted it to wait.

'No,' she said. 'That won't be necessary, thank you.'

'*Very good, Ms Hutchins.*'

She smiled. The AI had a British accent.

The gallery was located on the east side of Wisconsin Avenue, which had been designed originally for carriage traffic and horses, given over later to motorized ground vehicles, and was now restricted to pedestrians and, once again, horse-drawn coaches. She touched her commlink to the reader and climbed out.

Every night was date night in Georgetown. The restaurants were full. Shoppers and tourists wandered the streets, music and laughter drifted out of a dozen cafés, and in the park a mime was entertaining a group of children.

The Georgetown Art Gallery was located between a furniture store and an antique shop. The entire block of buildings had a dilapidated, run-down look. The architecture suggested these were the kinds of shops where you could get quality merchandise with the sheen rubbed off, but at bargain prices. The front door of the gallery was open, and she could see two men talking. As she watched, the conversation moved inside, and the door closed.

The establishment operated on two floors, connected by a rickety staircase. The interior smelled of furniture polish and cedar, and the lighting was dimmed. Thick drapes covered the windows, and heavy carpets the floors. The decor was stilted, formal, uncompromising. She had stepped back in time into the twenty-second century.

Despite the fact she was married to an artist, she didn't know much about the various schools, or even the prominent masters. So she wandered among landscapes and portraits of people dressed in the styles of another age. There were a few paintings of a more esoteric sort, geometric designs really, intended to stir the blood in ways she did not understand. Tor had attempted to explain some of the techniques to her, but she'd let him see that she was a Philistine in these matters and he'd let it go.

Except the two men, she saw no one else. Their conversation broke up, one left, and the other came her way, smiling politely. 'Good evening,' he said, and she recognized Eugene Hamilton's voice. 'May I be of service?'

'Mr Hamilton,' she said. 'My name's Hutchins. I spoke with you earlier.'

He beamed. 'Ah, yes. The Deshaies.'

'No,' she said. 'Actually we were talking about a Guilbert.'

'*Storm Center*.'

'Yes.'

'It's right over here.' He took her toward the rear and turned into a side room. Here was *Storm Center* immediately on her left. And he was right: The monitor had not done it justice.

The cloud was alive and churning and illuminated by internal power, and it was coming her way. Not after *her*, she understood. Nothing personal. She was too insignificant to warrant notice. But she had best stay clear.

'Mr Hamilton,' she said, 'did you by any chance know Harold Tewksbury?'

His brow furrowed, and he repeated the name to himself. 'Rings a bell,' he said, uncertainly.

But no, he had no idea. Couldn't tell her if he'd ever seen him in the shop. He hoped there wasn't a problem.

She was wondering if he'd bought any paintings here. 'He's recently deceased,' she said.

'I'm so sorry.'

'As are we all, Mr Hamilton. I'd wanted to get something appropriate in his memory. The sort of thing he might have liked.'

'Ah, yes. I see.'

'He'd spoken occasionally of the gallery. In glowing terms, I should add.'

Hamilton bowed modestly.

'I thought if I could get a sense of the sort of paintings he'd purchased in the past, I might be able to make a better choice.'

'Yes. Of course.' Hamilton wandered behind a counter and consulted his listings. 'How did you spell his name?'

He'd bought a Chapdelaine. *Frolic.* Hamilton showed it to her. A young woman reading on a park bench amidst a swarm of squirrels, cardinals, and bluejays. Storm clouds coming.

Purchase date was March 10. That would have been the week he died. But she saw no connection between the squirrels or even the approaching storm and the omega.

She went back and looked at the Guilbert again.

'I can see,' he observed, 'that you're taken with *Storm Center*. It's quite nice. I suspect it would make a remarkable addition to your home.'

Yes, it would. It was of course a trifle pricey. As was everything in here. 'I agree,' she said. 'But my husband's taste is so hard to gauge. You do understand?' She sighed. 'Let me think it over. And if you don't mind, I think I'll look around a bit more.'

She embarked on a tour through the place. Hamilton excused himself to look after another customer.

She thought maybe there'd be something in the more abstract paintings, the perceptual exercises of VanHokken or the exaggerated landscapes of Entwistle. But in the end she became convinced that whatever insight Harold might have entertained, she was not going to find it in Georgetown.

* * *

404

'It beats me,' she told Tor over salmon and potatoes. Maureen had already eaten and was playing in the living room.

'Did you bring Charlie's disk home?' asked Tor.

She reached behind her, picked it up from the server, and laid it beside his plate. He poked at it with his fork, as if it might bite. 'They can't make out anything at all?'

'Only what I've told you.'

'Mind if I take a look?'

'Be my guest.' Tor was bright, but he was strictly an arty type. No mathematical skills, no science to speak of. He'd watch, shake his head a few times, and at the end tell her that it beat the devil out of him.

They finished up and took their wine into the den. Maureen eyed the disk. 'Sim, Mommy?'

'Not exactly, love,' said Hutch. 'Pictures of stars.'

'Good.' She collected one of her dolls, seated it in its chair, and sat down on the floor beside it and told it to enjoy the show.

Tor put the disk in the reader, and they settled on the sofa.

It was the same show Hutch had watched earlier in the day. Tor paid close attention, occasionally making sounds deep in his throat as the brief lights blinked on and off. Hutch sipped her wine and let her mind wander. And Maureen mostly talked to the doll. 'Up straight, Lizabeth.' And 'Cake, Mommy?'

When it was over, Tor sat silently for several minutes. Finally, he turned to her. 'You say Harold only had *eight* of these things to work with?'

'Something like that. They were just beginning to find them.'

'And he figured it out?'

'Well, no. I never really said that.' She tried to recall what Harold had actually told her. That he thought he knew what was happening. That he needed more data. That he'd get back to her.

'All I see is a lot of lights.'

'Well, thanks, Tor. That's very helpful.'

'I don't think he knew any more than we do.'

'They're pretty,' Maureen said.

NEWSDESK

ASTEROID BARELY MISSES EARTH
Passes Within Eighty Thousand Kilometers
Nobody Noticed Until Danger Was Over
3 Km-Wide Rock Would Have Killed Millions
Investigation Promised

MOTHER CHARGED IN MURDER OF HUSBAND, FOUR CHILDREN
Only Survivor When Flyer Goes Down
Police: Victims Were Dead Before Crash

CHURCH OF REVELATION SAYS OMEGAS ARE EVIDENCE OF DIVINE WRATH
'Modern World Is in the Last Days'
Christopher Says Time Is Running Out

BOLTER WINS HISTORY PRIZE
National Book Award for The Lost Crusade

JURY SELECTION COMPLETE IN 'HELLFIRE' CASE
Patterson Claims Personality Warped by Church Dogma
'Programming Started at St Michael's'
Could Open Floodgates

WORLD POPULATION UNDER TWELVE BILLION
Decreases Sixty-third Straight Year
'Still Too Many'

HURRICANE EMMA FLATTENS GEORGIA COAST
Six Hundred Dead; Billions in Damage
'People Wouldn't Leave'

BRITAIN MAY BRING BACK MONARCHY
Tourism Takes a Beating

AFTER THE CHINDI HEADS FOR NEW YORK
Alyx Ballinger Brings London Hit to Broadway

**PRE-QUAKE EVACUATIONS UNDER WAY IN
AFGHANISTAN**
7.1 Expected within Days
Center to Be 50 Km West of Kabul

COUNCIL GIVES ASSURANCE ON GOOMPAHS
'We're Doing Everything Possible'

ROCKETS CLINCH TITLE
Arky Hits Ninetieth

WOULD-BE ROBBER SUES LIQUOR STORE
Fall through Skylight 'Caused Permanent Damage'
'Should Have Been Marked As Unsafe'

NFL VOTES TO EXTEND REGULAR SEASON IN '35
Teams to Play Twenty-six Games

33

On board the *al-Jahani*. Adrift.
Wednesday, October 29.

They had not stopped speaking Goompah. Two ships were on
the way, were due in fact at any time now, to take the passengers
off, and to prepare the *al-Jahani* for a flight to Broadside, where
they'd repair the vessel. Or junk it.

But if they still complained about the *molly kalottuls* that had
betrayed them, if they still said *Challa, Judy* to her in the morning,
the spirit had gone out of it.

Six of them were going on to Lookout. They'd get there a few
weeks after the cloud and put on their Goompah gear and help
hand out blankets and sandwiches to the survivors.

Of the other passengers, who had come specifically to see the
Event, all but Frank Bergen would be going back.

They'd been adrift for six weeks, and the level of frustration
had gotten pretty high. They'd all be glad to get off the *al-Jahani*.
Snake-bitten ship. They'd blamed her, blamed Collingdale, blamed
Hutchins, blamed the president of the NAU. It hadn't helped, of
course, that Collingdale had gotten off and was now only a few
weeks from the target, while here the rest of them sat. Things
had gotten so bad that Alexandra had called a meeting and told

them to relax, to accept the fact that there was always a degree of uncertainty in a flight like this one, that they had taken their chances and it hadn't worked out and they should be satisfied to know they tried. As good as the efficiency record was in super-luminals, they had to realize there were a lot of moving parts, and redundancy for everything wasn't feasible. Things break down. Especially if you're going to run out of port in a rush, without attending to routine maintenance. 'You wanted to get there by early December, and that meant we had to pull the trigger sooner than we'd have wished. We took a chance, and we lost. Accept it.'

They didn't like being lectured by the captain, but it gave them a new focus for their dissatisfaction, and maybe that was all that was needed.

Judy liked Alexandra. She offered no apologies, never allowed Frank or any of the others to intimidate her, never backed down. Took no nonsense.

She had lost all patience with the complainers around her, with Melinda Park, who kept talking about how valuable her time was and how it was being wasted; with Wally Glassner, who was prepared to tell anyone who would listen how he would have done things had he been in charge; with Jerry Madden, who'd been there now for seven months and what did he have to show for it?

Even among her own people, some had not been able to come to terms with the situation. And *they* were all young, convinced they would rise to the top of their respective professions, would keep control of their lives, and would one day retire after many years of success and joy.

At midmorning, Alexandra got on the allcom to inform her passengers that one of the rescue vessels had made the jump out of hyper and would be within visual range by late afternoon. That was the *Vignon*, which would be taking off everyone who was going back. The *Vignon* would deliver them to Broadside, where they'd embark on another ship for the flight home. It would be an eight-month run altogether, putting them back in Arlington by summer. Keeping her voice carefully neutral, the captain thanked them for their patience and understanding.

The *Vignon* would also be carrying engineers. They would do whatever had to be done to get the jump engines running again. The *Westover* was due within a few days. It would pick up Frank and Judy and the six members of her team who were going on to Lookout. When they were safely on their way, Bill would take the *al-Jahani* to Broadside. And if something went wrong en route and the ship disappeared into the mists, well, no one would be lost with it.

The people who were going back on the *Vignon* began clearing out their quarters. When Judy wandered into the common room after lunch, Melinda Park and Charlie Harding were already sitting there with their bags packed. 'I'll miss you, Judy,' Charlie said, and Melinda used a smile to indicate she felt the same way. The gesture also suggested that Melinda couldn't believe that Judy hadn't had enough. Next time Melinda rode one of these things, she said, people would read about it in the *New York Times*.

Several of the linguists came in, also ready to go. Rochelle was leaving, and Terry MacAndrew. Judy wasn't certain, but she thought *he* was leaving because *she* was.

Despite the circumstances, it wasn't a good career move for the linguists to bail out on the mission. It would get around, and people had long memories. When future positions came open, they'd go to the ones deemed loyal and dedicated. Judy had mentioned that to the group shortly after they'd bobbed to the surface out here, advising them to do what they thought best, but underscoring how important reputation was.

On the other hand, they were linguists rather than researchers, and maybe the people hiring them wouldn't care the way she would.

During the next half hour, the rest of those who were leaving showed up, Malachy looking tired and dispirited, Jason Holder

411

frowning as if everything that had happened out here had been personally directed at him. Elizabeth Madden held up pretty well, and Ava MacAvoy. Jean Dionne was visibly relieved to be turning around. Of them all, Judy was going to miss John Price, tall and quiet and good-looking, a guy she could have fallen in love with, until she discovered he always took care of himself first. And Mickie Haverson, an anthropologist who spoke the best Goompah outside her people, and who had talked about putting on one of the disguises, and wandering around the cafés trading stories with the natives.

Valentino and Mike Metzger were packed and ready to go. And Marilyn McGee and Ed Paxton. Judy wondered how that marriage would fare when they got back into a normal situation. She was convinced that romances formed under unusual circumstances had little chance to prosper. But maybe she was wrong.

One by one, they shook her hand and kissed her. Thanks, Judy. I wish it could have worked out better. Appreciate the opportunity. Good luck. I hope there are some left when you get there. Sorry it turned out this way.

Alexandra came by, expressed her regrets, and gave them their compartment numbers on the *Vignon*. Twenty minutes later, the ship moved within visual range. It was that star over there, the one that kept getting brighter, that broke apart finally into a cluster of lights. Then it was alongside, sleek and gray, a dwarf compared with the *Hawksbill*. But big enough. And with working engines.

The engineers were the first ones through the airlock. Judy, who somehow felt it her duty to be on hand, stood to one side while Alexandra greeted them as they came in. There were two of them, both males, carrying cases and gauges, with instruments dangling from their belts and cables looped over their shoulders. Both very businesslike. Alexandra took them below.

The engineers made several trips back to the *Vignon*. At one point, in front of Judy and several others, one of them told the captain that the engines would not have survived another jump. When Judy asked Alexandra what that would have meant she said that they would either have exploded or, more likely, stranded them in hyperspace. It was a reflection of the mood in the ship that Judy wondered whether the conversation had been staged to rebuff those who'd grumbled at the captain's insistence on going no farther.

Ah, well. She had no reason to doubt Alexandra, but she would have considered doing that herself had she been in the captain's place.

Meantime, the doors opened on the *Vignon*, and there was a final round of handshakes and farewells as people headed across. When the exodus had ended, the *al-Jahani* felt empty. Subdued. Only Frank remained, and six of her *Shironi Kulp*.

Charlie Harding, who had never stopped talking about how he looked forward to watching the cloud sweep in over Lookout, raining down meteors and then lightning bolts (although he felt sorry for the inhabitants, yes, pity we can't do more for them) got bored waiting for the *Vignon* to depart and came back to complain. Judy hoped they wouldn't leave without him.

She strolled down to her workroom and found Ahmed and Ginko engaged in a role-playing game, while Harry Chin watched. It had something to do with trying to move supplies down a mountain slope with a limited number of pack animals, all of whom could not be watched at once, in the presence of lions that attacked wherever they saw an opening.

Nick Harcourt was in the tank leading the Boston Philharmonic in a rendition of the *1812* Overture. Guns roared, the strings and horns delivered 'La Marseillaise,' and the drums rolled. Shelley and Juan were with him, so caught up in the performance that they didn't see Judy come in. She closed the door and found a seat.

They were inside a symphony hall, although Judy had no idea if it was a specific site or simply something made up by Bill. Nevertheless, there was the illusion of a packed house. She closed her eyes and saw tattered flags and cannons and cavalry charges.

She knew Napoleon was involved – it was hard to miss – but she wasn't sure about the other details. Was it Brits on the other side? Or Russians? Well, it didn't matter. She let the music overwhelm her, carry her along. Once more unto the breach, dear friends. And finally she was participating in a thunderous ovation while Nick bowed and pointed his baton to various sections of his orchestra, which responded with a few fresh chords, thereby provoking another round of applause.

Alexandra came in and passed her a message marked PERSONAL. It was from Digger, and it outlined a plan to induce the Goompahs, when the time came, to evacuate their cities. He wanted her opinion.

It was as good as anything she'd been able to think of. Might even work. She scribbled off a short reply: *Try it. Good luck. Will join you in the new year.*

Hell, he might have something. Maybe they'd pull it off yet.

After dinner, the captain of the *Vignon* offered a tour of his ship. Everybody went. The kids went because they thought superluminals were exciting. Wally Glassner went because it provided a chance to pontificate on how much better the appointments were compared with what they'd had to live with for the past seven months. Jason Holder went so that he could make sure no one had accommodations superior to his. The other members of the general staff went so they could express their relief at getting away from the *al-Jahani*.

Judy went so she could be one more time with the eleven linguists and her shattered dream of riding to the rescue.

The captain of the *Vignon*, whose name was Miller, or Maller, or something like that, was an unassuming man of modest proportions, shorter even than she was, but who was obviously proud of his ship. He enjoyed showing her off. And, in fact, the *Vignon* was the most recent addition to the Academy's fleet. It had briefly belonged to the late Paul Vignon, a banking magnate, who had willed it to the Academy. 'It was originally named *Angelique*,' the captain explained, 'after a girlfriend.' At the family's request, the ship was renamed for the donor, who had never actually been aboard her. (Whether the personal pronoun referred to the ship or the girlfriend was not clarified.)

The tour ended in the common room, where the captain had arranged to have drinks and snacks laid out. Judy wandered from one conversation to the next, aware that she was having trouble getting the thundering beat of the *1812* out of her mind. She could not resist smiling, standing with MacAvoy and Holder, while the latter went on about the stupidity of administrators at the University of Toronto, where he'd punished their incompetence by leaving his position as leading light in the Sociology Department. As Holder described his vengeance, cannons went off in her head, banners rose through the gun smoke, and saberwielding cavalry units drove into the flanks of the infantry.

'Why are you smiling?' Holder asked, stopping in midsentence to stare suspiciously at her.

'I was just thinking how difficult it will be for the U.T. to make up for the loss.'

'Well,' he said, not entirely certain whether he had been mocked, 'I didn't really want to do any damage, but at some point they have to come to realize . . . ' and so on.

When the opportunity offered, she excused herself and went back to the *al-Jahani*. Despite what they'd been through, she wasn't anxious to leave the broken ship. They'd accomplished a lot here, had broken into the language of the Goompahs, had mastered it, had read their literature, absorbed some of their philosophy and their ethics.

She sat down and paged through her notebook of Goompah wisdom.

Enjoy life because it is not forever.

There was no indication they believed in an afterlife, or in any kind of balancing of the scales. No judgment. No Elysian fields. They seemed to see the world, the *Intigo*, as an unpredictable place. But it was their home, as opposed to the idea it was a place through which they were just passing en route to somewhere else.

Therefore, pleasure was a good unto itself.

Regrets usually arise from things we failed to do that we should have, rather than things we have done that we should not.

Accept responsibility.

Enjoy the *moraka*, which didn't translate, but which seemed to imply a combination of love, passion, the exotic, intimacy, friendship.

Beware addictions. The essence of the good life is a free exercise of the will, directed by reason.

Beware addictions.

But wasn't *moraka* an addiction?

'Bill,' she said, 'I want to record a message. For transmission.'

'*To?*'

'David.'

'*When you're ready, Judy.*'

She thought about it a long time. Smiled into the imager, tried to look casual.

'Dave,' she said, 'the relief ship got here today. Some of our people are bailing out. Rest of us are headed in your direction. When you get where you're going, keep in mind things may not work out. If that happens, don't blame yourself.' She almost thought she could see him, sitting in his cabin on the *Hawksbill*. Thinking about nothing except the omega. 'Have a good flight. I'll see you in January.'

'*Transmit?*' asked Bill.

Somewhere, far off, she heard the thundering hoofbeats of Cossacks.

'Send it.'

'*Done,*' said Bill.

ARCHIVE

(Excerpts from *The Book of the Goompahs*)
(Translated by various members of the *Shironi Kulp*)

We exist for the sole purpose of making one another happy.

It is said, with pride, that we are the only creature that looks at the stars. But who knows what the galloon contemplates in the dead of night?

Every advance, every benefit, is the gift of an individual mind. No group, no crowd, no city has ever contributed anything to anyone.

Whatever you have to say, make it brief.

Good advice is always irritating.

Defend your opinion only if it can be shown to be true, not because it is your opinion.

Authors love to be petted.

Integrity means doing the right thing even when no one is looking.

Every good jest contains an element of truth.

The queen of virtues is the recognition of one's own flaws.

Snatch a kiss and embrace the consequences.

34

On board the *Jenkins*.
Thursday, December 4.

Most of the projectors were micros, units ranging from the size of a pen up to a full-scale Harding monitor that came complete with a tripod. Four hundred of them had been collected at Broadside, the majority from their own supply, a few from one of the corporate development groups and independent researchers. They'd been shipped in four containers on the *Cumberland*. Mark Stevens also brought the two gold rings ordered by Digger. And a cartload of congratulations.

While the *Cumberland* unloaded its cargo, the *Hawksbill* arrived insystem. Stevens announced he'd stand by in case needed; which meant he wasn't anxious to forgo some human company after the long run out from the station.

The micros would be placed at strategic sites, then could be activated from the *Jenkins*, and would relay whatever visual image, and spoken message, was fed into the system. All that remained was to get them in place. And prepare the message.

The omega dominated the night sky. It was a great black thundercloud twice the size of the bigger moon. And it grew visibly larger each evening. The Goompahs saw it clearly as an approaching storm, one that refused to behave like ordinary storms. They were terrified. The talk in the streets was that when it came they would all hide indoors, with the shutters drawn. But they were still thinking exclusively of heavy rains and a few lightning bolts. Maybe over an extended time. Several days or so. There was no sense of the enormity of the thing, or of the damage that hurricane-force winds might do. Digger wondered whether the Goompahs had any experience with tornadoes or hurricanes.

They were approaching a part of the operation that Digger didn't like. He had known the plan for months, that when the *Hawksbill* got there, Kellie and Julie Carson would switch places. Julie would take over the *Jenkins*, and Kellie would switch to the *Hawksbill*, which she would command during the decoy operation. That was happening because she wasn't licensed to pilot the AV3, the heavyweight lander that would be used during the cloud-making effort.

It hadn't seemed like anything to worry about several months earlier but as time passed, and the cloud grew bigger, and somehow more unnerving, he found himself increasingly unhappy. They'd talked about it, he and Kellie, and she had explained there was no alternative, and not to worry because she'd be careful, and nothing was going to happen. So he let it go and said no more.

They'd patrolled each of the cities, making charts, watching to see where the crowds were, where the show would be most effective. It was late autumn in the southern hemisphere, and the nights were getting long. The weather wasn't cold, by Digger's standards. It never got below fifteen Celsius, and rarely below twenty-five. Kellie commented that you could tell when it got really cold in the *Intigo* because they had to move the drinks indoors.

Picking the public sites for the projectors had been easy enough. They'd concentrate on areas close to the cafés and meeting halls. And the temples would be good. They weren't crowded at night (when the performance would be most effective), but there were inevitably a few individuals enjoying the sacred atmosphere.

420

The Goompahs seemed not much given to organized religious ceremony. The only ones Digger had seen were the exorcisms, and the prayer for assistance, which had been followed by the sacrifice of the prelate. The temples drew reasonably sized crowds every day. But they were subdued crowds. They wandered separately among the figures of the gods, and if they prayed, they did it quietly. There would have been no chanting or weeping or collapsing in the aisles in a Goompah temple.

The *Hawksbill* was about three hours behind the *Cumberland*. It was a big, boxy vehicle, with eight cylinders lashed to its hull.

The ship itself was a series of progressively longer oblongs, just the sort of thing the clouds seemed to like. There'd been a couple of experiments years ago in which derelicts that looked not too different from the *Hawksbill* had been allowed to sink into omegas. Unlike rounded vehicles, which had simply dipped into the clouds and come back, the derelicts had inevitably ignited fierce electrical storms, and on one occasion, a ship had been blasted apart on approach.

The entry locks of the *Jenkins* and the *Hawksbill* weren't compatible, so Collingdale and his people had to come over in go-packs. As much as Digger liked having Kellie to himself, it was nice to see somebody new. There'd been no one other than Stevens for months.

Unless you counted Macao.

He still felt discouraged about his evening with her, and wished there were a way to hold a normal conversation with her. Wished he could do so without scaring her. Hi, Macao. I'm from South Boston. Long way from home. How's it going?

For all the talk about opening their minds and not jumping to unwarranted conclusions, *Think for yourself*, the Goompahs weren't as bright as he'd hoped.

He'd seen Judy's translations, segments of the *Book of the Goompahs*, and he wished he could find those who had been writing the maxims. They were the people he needed to talk to.

Judy had told him the work was attributed by name and by epoch, although they hadn't figured out the system of dating yet or, for that matter, where the epochs all fit. 'They're probably all dead,' she'd added cheerfully.

He watched the *Hawksbill*'s airlock open, a tiny hatch up on A Deck, just behind the bridge. They came out one at a time and got ferried across by Julie. When they were all in the airlock, Kellie closed the outer hatch, pressurized, and opened up.

There's no real way to describe the sense of camaraderie, and of tribal linkage, under such circumstances. Digger had never been so happy to see visitors in his life. As an added bonus, his sense of responsibility for the lives of several hundred thousand Goompahs faded a bit. Collingdale was here now. He was the senior guy, and consequently in charge.

'Good to meet you, Digby,' he said, extending his hand. 'And this must be the bride.' Kellie looked uncomfortable but accepted the comment in good spirits. 'We're glad to be here.' He jerked his thumb in the direction of the omega. 'Doesn't look good, does it?'

'No,' Digger said quietly.

'Goompahs must be scared half out of their minds.'

He introduced Marge Conway, a tall, middle-aged woman. 'Marge is our camouflage expert,' he said. 'And Avery Whitlock.' One of those guys who produces stuff they read in the university literature courses. Introduced as Whit. He smiled easily and nodded. He was pleased to meet Kellie and Digger. Firm grip, nice clothes, exquisite diction. Touch of New . England somewhere.

'And, of course, Julie.'

Julie was taller than he'd expected her to be. It was sometimes hard to tell when the only communication you had was electronic. She was redheaded and, he thought, very young. Barely out of her teens.

After the pleasantries had been completed Digger looked hopefully at Marge. 'Can you really hide them?' he asked.

'I can put a cloud cover over them,' she said. 'After that, it's anybody's guess.'

Knowing Whitlock was coming, Digger had taken time to read some of his work. He was a naturalist by trade, and he wrote essays with titles like 'The Mastodon in the Basement' and 'It's a Bug's Life.' Digger had been put off by the titles. People who write about academic subjects should not try to appeal to the masses. But he'd enjoyed the work and was pleased to meet the author.

They were all saying it was hard to believe they were actually here. Whit kept looking out at the arc of the planet and shaking his head. 'Where is the *Intigo*?' he asked.

'Can't see it from here,' said Kellie, taking a peek to be sure. 'It's on the other side of the planet.'

'When can we go down?'

Until that moment, Digger had forgotten the long-ago message from Hutchins, informing them that Whit would want a tour, and that they were to accommodate him in every way possible, but were under no circumstances to lose him or let him get hurt.

'I guess we have some work to do before we can even think about that,' said Collingdale, looking toward Julie.

'Not really,' she said. 'Everything's on automatic.' She smiled, opened a channel to Bill, and told him to deliver the cargo.

One by one, the cylinders attached to the *Hawksbill* hull were released. A pair of thrusters was attached to each, and Digger watched as the units adjusted their positions, moving well away from each other and from the ships.

'What are they?' Digger asked Marge.

'Chimneys,' she said. 'Rainmakers.'

If she said so.

A cargo door opened, and a helicopter floated out, its propellers folded.

Then a pair of landers. 'There are two more,' Marge told him, 'packed on the AV3.'

The AV3 was a heavy-duty hauler, designed to move capital

equipment in and out of orbit. It came next, a large, black vehicle, with massive wheels rather than the treads that the smaller landers used. Antigrav engines were located in twin pods outside the hull. Its vertical thrusters could be rotated out onto the wings so they could fire past large loads slung beneath the vehicle, as would be the case with the rainmaker packages.

'Aren't the Goompahs going to see all this stuff?' asked Digger. 'I thought you'd make the clouds by using some sort of electronic thing you could just fire from orbit.'

'Sorry,' she said. 'We're all out of those.'

'And these are really rainmakers?' asked Kellie.

'Yes. They look a bit clumsy. But don't worry. They'll work fine.'

Digger kept thinking how he and Kellie had been pussyfooting around on the ground to avoid being seen. 'And all this is going down to the surface?'

'Only if you want cloudy weather.'

'Marge, they'll *see* it.'

'The Goompahs?'

'Of course the Goompahs. Who else are we worried about?'

'The landers are equipped with lightbenders.'

'The hauler, too?'

'Too big. But we'll be doing everything at night. So I don't think you need to worry.'

He sighed. 'Okay. When did you want to start?'

'As soon as possible.'

'Will you need help?'

'Nope. Just Julie here, to get me around.' She smiled at him. 'You can relax and watch, Dig.'

And the big moment had arrived.

Kellie nodded at Digger, excused herself, and stepped out into the passageway. Julie followed a few moments later. When Julie came back she was wearing a formal white jacket, complete with epaulets and a pair of eagles, the symbol of her rank.

Kellie showed up on one of the screens. 'Dr Conway,' she said, 'gentlemen, I'd like you to be aware that there has been a change in command, and that Captain Carson is now the commanding officer of the *William B. Jenkins*. Thank you very much for your attention.'

Julie gazed around at them. 'As my first official act,' she said, 'I am going to preside over the wedding of two of the company.'

Collingdale made a face and looked at the time. 'I don't want to be a spoilsport,' he said, 'but I assumed we were going to do this after we got back.'

'From where?' asked Digger, making no effort to conceal his annoyance.

'From sidetracking the cloud. Digger, I understand how important this is to you, but the cloud is closing in. We have no time to spare.'

'Actually,' said Julie, 'the most efficient orbital window is an hour away. Make yourself comfortable.' She studied them for a few moments, as if decisions needed to be made. 'Digger,' she said, 'over here, please. On my right. Marge, you'll be our matron of honor. And Whit, at the request of the groom, you'll serve as best man.'

Whit came up and stood by Digger.

'David, we'd like you to act as witness to the proceedings.'

Collingdale nodded and managed to look pleased.

Bill's image popped on-screen. He was in formal whites, seated at a keyboard. Julie pointed at him, and he began playing the wedding march. The door to the passageway opened and Kellie appeared in full bridal regalia, flanked by Mark Stevens.

Digger's heartbeat went up a couple of notches.

Bill brought the march up full. Kellie and her escort strode into the room. Someone had given Marge a veil. She donned it and fell in behind the bride. Digger slipped the rings to Whit, experienced the momentary doubt that strikes anyone who's been a bachelor too many years, and wondered if Kellie was thinking the same thing.

But by the time Julie asked whether he wanted her for his wife, all hesitation had fled.

Digger took a couple of minutes to kiss the bride, then was told that was enough and he should get to work. There were four hundred projectors to be set up in designated locations on the isthmus. Whit volunteered to assist.

That idea looked a bit shaky to Digger. He'd expected to do the distribution himself, without having someone else along that he'd have to look after. It wasn't that Whit wouldn't be good company, but he wasn't young, and he was just getting into an e-suit for the first time. He had no experience with lightbenders. He didn't really understand how things worked on the ground, and it was easy to imagine him bumping into one of the Goompahs and causing an incident. Digger knew the hazards quite well.

Still, he was a VIP, and they had a responsibility to keep him happy.

Meantime, David Collingdale was trying to get his show on the road. That meant good-bye to Kellie for a few days. 'Enjoyed the honeymoon,' he told her.

'You've had your honeymoon,' she said. 'Now it's time to earn your pay.' She kissed him, hugged him, and looked up at him with shining eyes. 'I love you, Digby,' she said. 'Keep your head up when you get down there.'

'You, too, Kel. Take no chances. I don't really like this very much.'

'I'll be careful.'

Another smooch, and she was gone. E-suit, air tanks, go-pack, and she was swimming out the airlock with Collingdale, headed for the *Hawksbill*. He could have continued his conversation with her on the link, but it seemed easier not to. He watched them disappear through the cargo carrier's main hatch. Then she fired up, drifted away, and disappeared into the night. A few minutes later, Stevens told Digger he wished he could stay for the show, eased the *Cumberland* out of orbit, and started back to Broadside.

Digger sighed and wandered back up to A Deck. Time to sit down with Whit and show him what they'd be doing.

T'mingletep was located on the western side of the lower continent, where a major river emptied into the sea. A narrow island hugged the shoreline, turning the strait into a marsh. A bridge connected the city and the island.

In terms of both geographical size and population, it was probably the largest of the eleven cities. The same mountain range that dominated the isthmus passed through the region a few kilometers to the east. That was where they wanted the Goompahs to be when the omega hit. The trek over there wouldn't be too bad. There was no road, but the ground was flat and easily passable. All that would be necessary was to persuade them to go.

A few ships were docked or anchored in the harbor, and one was just setting out, turning north. Julie engaged the lander's lightbender, and Whit looked out and watched the stubby wing of the spacecraft vanish. 'Makes my head spin,' he said.

Digger smiled. 'You'll get used to it.'

They settled onto a stretch of beach north of the city. Whit and Digger got out and activated their infrared lenses so they could see each other. 'That's much better,' said Whit.

They'd divided forty-eight micros between them, stuffing them into their vests. 'I'll head for the mountains,' Julie said. 'If you need me, just call.' When they were clear, she closed the lock, and Digger watched the spacecraft lift away.

Whit gazed around him, at the sea, the mountains, the sky. At a seashell, at a crablike creature digging busily in the sand. At the gulls. At a thorny green plant. 'Why does it happen here,' he said, 'and so few other places?'

'Pardon?' asked Digger.

'We used to think that any world with the right chemicals, good temperatures, and some water, would produce elephants. And trees. And the whole Darwinian show.' He shook his head. 'In fact, it rarely happens.'

'Don't know,' said Digger.

'We're still missing a big piece of the puzzle. Some enabling mechanism that gets the whole process started.'

They trudged up the beach toward a cluster of trees. The sand turned to hard earth, and they broke through onto a long avenue. A group of Goompahs, not quite fully grown, were gathered in a courtyard. They were bundled in heavy shirts and vests and pullover knitted caps. A couple wore animal-hide gloves.

'Can we go listen?' asked Whit. 'For a minute.'

'Do you understand the language?' asked Digger.

'Not really. I've tried, but I'm afraid my linguistic skills, whatever they might once have been, have deserted me. But it's okay. I'd just like to hear them speaking.'

'All right,' said Digger. 'I guess we're not all that pressed for time.'

It was routine stuff. They were all males, and it was strictly sex. Who was game for sack time and who should be avoided.

Whit was disappointed when Digger provided a carefully phrased translation. 'Seems mundane,' he said. 'I expected more.' But he adjusted his thinking quickly as they moved away. 'Maybe it's what would happen with any intelligent species developing in a reasonably free society.' But it was clear he'd have preferred to find them discussing philosophy or ethics.

'Do they talk much about the cloud?' he asked.

'Some.' Digger thought about the fear he witnessed every day. 'At night, especially, when they can see it. In the sunlight, I think it's kind of unreal.'

'Has there been an increase in religious reaction?'

'That would be a better question for Collingdale. Other than the sacrificial ceremony we told you about, we haven't really seen anything. But they don't seem to be big on religious services. They don't go to the temple and participate in ceremonies or listen to sermons.'

'But they do visit the temples?'

'Yes. Some do.'

Whit was full of questions: 'They sent off the round-the-world mission, but does the individual Goompah really care whether the world is round or not?'

The ones that showed up for the *sloshen* got pretty excited about it.

'They seem to have few or no prohibitions regarding sexual activity. What sort of contraceptives have they?'

Not something Digger had gotten into. Didn't know.

'They've been on the isthmus for millennia? Why haven't they expanded?'

Didn't know.

'Why haven't they been forced to expand by sheer population growth?'

Didn't know that either.

'What a marvelous place this is,' he said at last, apparently giving up on Digger's intellectual curiosity. 'A land in which the inhabitants are just coming awake.'

They had arrived at their first destination. It was a wide thoroughfare, lined with merchants and eating places. The shutters were all closed against the cool air. Fires burned in the shops and the cafés. Digger did a quick survey. 'There.' He pointed at a spot a few meters off the ground, above some toddlers who were chasing each other in circles. 'Ideal place for an apparition.' He selected a crosspost that supported the roof of a bread shop, reached into his vest, produced a projector, recorded its number, angled the lens, and placed it as high up on the post as he could reach. It was inconspicuous, and there wouldn't be any Goompahs who could take it down without a ladder. He opened a channel to the lander. 'Julie.'

'*Go ahead, Digger.*'

'Two-two-seven.'

'*Wait one.*'

Digger kept an eye on Whit. His fuzzy silhouette was back out of the way, between the side of a garment shop and an open culvert with running water. But he was bent forward, almost like a stalking cat, watching the crowds pass.

The *Intigo* was home to a seabird, a long-billed gray creature with large hang-down ears that almost looked like a second pair of wings. Called a *bogulok*, it was found in large numbers throughout the isthmus area. The name, freely translated, meant *floppy ears*.

Digger activated the unit and a *bogulok* blinked into existence above the crowd, at the point Digger had targeted. It was in midflight, and it got only a few meters before it vanished.

'Good,' Digger told his commlink. 'It's perfect.' No one seemed to have noticed anything unusual.

'*I'll lock it in*,' said Julie.

Digger collected Whit and went looking for a second site.

He planted four projectors in the market area, three outside public buildings, six more inside theaters and meeting halls, and five at various locations along the main thoroughfares. Kellie had spotted what they thought was the equivalent of an executive office building, which was staffed day and night, and they installed two more there, one inside and one outside. On each occasion he checked back with the lander to make sure they had a good angle.

The bridge connecting the island to the mainland was about a half kilometer long. It consisted of wooden planks and supports. There was nothing else, no handrails, no braces. If you didn't pay attention to what you were doing, you could walk right off into the ocean.

It *was* wide. There were some draft animals on it, and they had no trouble finding room to pass everything without any undue bumping. 'Not bad engineering,' said Whit. Digger hadn't been impressed until Whit pointed out that the bridge's supports were embedded in ooze, and had to withstand tides generated by two moons. 'Must require constant maintenance,' he added. He got down on his knees and peeked underneath.

They got across and planted another projector in a tree at the end of the bridge, aiming it up so the apparition would appear in the branches, visible from all directions.

Whit had become a kid in a toy store, stopping to look at everything and everyone. 'They're beautiful,' he said, referring to the inhabitants. 'So innocent.' He laughed. 'They all look like Boomer.'

'You need to watch one of the orgies,' Digger said.

'That's my point. If they weren't innocent, they wouldn't have orgies.'

Digger didn't even ask him to explain that one.

They finished up shortly after sundown. Digger had expected Whit to be exhausted, but he seemed disappointed that the day was ending. 'Marvelous,' he said. 'Experience of a lifetime.'

The lander met them outside town, on the south side, where the isthmus road began. They stood at the edge of the Goompah world. Beyond lay impossibly rough country, a mountain range that looked impassable, dense forest, and, ultimately, the southern ice cap.

Julie was supposed to get back to the *Jenkins*, pick up Marge, and start installing the rainmakers. She was running late or maybe she just didn't feel she had time to spare. Digger was barely buckled into his seat before they were aloft, heading for orbit. 'Are you really going to be able to do this?' Digger asked her.

'I'll manage,' she said.

'You're going to work all night?'

'I expect so.'

'And tomorrow you're going to be taking us to *Savakol*.'

'Yes.'

'All day.'

'More or less.'

'And then another round with Marge. When are you going to sleep?'

She had trouble restraining a smile. 'I've already slept.'

'When?'

They were rising through billowing cumulus. 'Today. All day.'

431

'Today? How'd that happen? I was on the circuit with you every fifteen minutes.'

'No, you weren't,' she said. 'You were on with Bill.'

'Bill?'

'I guess he used my voice.' She smiled. 'Don't worry about me, Dig. I have the easiest job in the operation.'

Avery Whitlock's Notebooks

. . . What I find particularly striking, after this first day of walking the streets of a civilization erected by another species, is how few young there are. This is a society that seems to glory in parks, in throwing balls around and splashing through fountains. And yet there seemed as many mothers and fathers as children. Primitive societies at home always produce large families. It does not seem to be the case here. I saw only a few parents with two offspring. If there were any with three, I missed them.

I wonder why that is.

—December 4

35

On board the *Jenkins*.
Thursday, December 4.

'Are we ready to go?'

In fact, Marge had been ready for hours. She'd sat by the comm board listening to the conversations from below, going over her checklists, and trying unsuccessfully to sleep.

'Yes,' she said. 'Armed and ready.'

And at last she and Julie strapped on e-suits and air tanks and went out the cargo airlock.

Marge didn't show it much, but she was delighted to be there. There'd been, God knew, a lot of time to think on the way out, especially after Collingdale came aboard. And she'd spent much of it reviewing her life. Loads of talent, her father had told her. You'll be whatever you want to be.

In fact she'd found everything too easy. She'd become an M.D., had gotten bored, and taken a second doctorate in climatology. She'd been more interested in power than research. She hadn't realized it before making this voyage, but it was the truth. Whenever there had been a choice between administration and pure science she'd gone for administration. Take over. Move up. Get the corner office. She had a natural talent for it. It had paid well, felt good, and yet it had left her eminently dissatisfied.

Probably as a direct result, she'd used a wrecking ball on each of her three marriages. Well, that was overstating it, but she'd attributed her disappointment with her various careers to each of her spouses in turn, and when the extension time came, the relationships had been discontinued. More or less by mutual agreement. Good luck. No hard feelings. Been good to know you.

Her dancing career, which had arced between the end of her college days and the beginning of her medical years, had been the same. Too easy, no patience with the routine work needed to rise to the top of the profession, find something else.

She'd even taken a fling at martial arts. She was good at it, and knew she could have picked up a black belt had she been willing to invest the time.

The problem with her life, she'd decided shortly after Collingdale had come aboard, was that there had never been a serious challenge. No use for a black belt in the great game of life because she could find nobody she wanted to clobber.

And now here came the cloud.

Collingdale thought of it as a kind of personal antagonist. It was his great white whale, the thing that had crushed the crystal cities of Moonlight. When this was over, when he got back, he was going to lead a crusade to find a way to destroy the things. He thought the experience at Lookout, which had generated worldwide sympathy for the Goompahs, would make this the right time.

It was an effort she would probably join. In any case, she was finally in a fight she wasn't sure she could win. And it was an exhilarating feeling.

The AV3 was waiting. Like the *Hawksbill*, it wasn't compatible with the *Moorhead*, so Julie had parked it a hundred meters away. The chimney packages floated in the night like so many barrels of beer. Marge had been in hostile environments before in the e-suit, but always on a planetary surface. Floating in the void, tethered to Julie, was a bit different, but not as disorienting as she'd been led to expect.

The hauler's airlock opened as they approached, and Julie took them in. Lights went on, more hatches opened and closed, and they were in the cabin.

Green lamps glowed as the hauler came out of sleep mode. Julie got coffee for them, and Marge settled into the right-hand seat and got out her notebook.

'Anybody ever try this before?' Julie asked.

'Cloud-making?'

'Yes.'

'Oh, sure. The technique's been used to modify droughts.'

'How come I never heard of it?'

'I don't know. How much time do you spend at home?'

They took two landers on the first flight. And a Benson Brothers water pump. 'Got a big, dry lawn? Depend on Benson.' They could have saved time by having Bill simply take over the controls on all four landers and pilot them down, but AIs were notoriously deficient if it became necessary to respond to a surprise, like a sudden storm. Especially if they were trying to do too many things at once. It was the price paid for artificial intelligence. Like biological intelligence, its higher functions produced a single consciousness. Or at least, they seemed to. Multiple tasks requiring simultaneous judgment could lead to trouble. They were too far from home to risk losing a vehicle. If one went down, the operation would be over.

Marge had spent much of the voyage to Lookout reviewing weather and topographical maps she'd constructed from information forwarded by the *Jenkins* and deciding where to place the rainmakers. The target area for the first one was on the eastern side of the upper continent, midway between *Roka* and *Hopgop*. (How, she wondered, could you take anyone seriously who named a city *Hopgop*?)

It was dark, and the omega was just rising when they descended toward the edge of a heavy forest. Beyond, scattered trees and hills ran unbroken to the sea. A small stream, its source somewhere in the high country, wound through the area. There was no sign of nearby habitation.

'Enough water?' Julie asked.

'It'll do,' said Marge. 'Take her down.'

Julie put them as close to the trees as she could, shearing off a few in the process. The forest was loud with insects. 'Anything here that bites?' asked Marge.

'Not that we've been told about.'

They switched on their night-vision lenses. The trees were of several types, but all were tall, spindly, not much to look at. Marge would have preferred something with a bit more trunk.

'What do you think?' asked Julie.

The wood seemed solid enough. 'They'll have to do,' she said. She headed directly for a section she'd spotted from the air, a cluster of trees forming an irregular circle, roughly forty meters in diameter. There were a few other growths within the perimeter, which they dropped with laser cutters.

'Got a question for you,' said Julie.

'Go ahead.'

'Why do we need the landers? If the hauler has enough lift to bring the rainmaker packages down, why isn't it enough to support one of them when it's extended? It won't weigh any more.'

'When it's extended,' she said, 'the chimney will encounter resistance from air currents. It would take more than the hauler to keep it stable.'

They got back inside the AV3, and Julie touched a press-pad. The cargo door in the rear opened. 'Bill,' she said, 'put the landers under cover of the trees.'

'Yes, Julie. I'll take care of it.'

The AI used a dolly to move the landers outside, then activated them and flew them into the shadow of the forest. Meantime, the dolly unloaded the pump.

Marge saw lightning in the west. 'Maybe you won't need the chimneys,' said Julie.

'Unlikely,' she said.

They picked up the second pair of landers and delivered them to the same site. They still needed a chimney package and the helicopter. They'd run simulations on what would happen if they tried moving both on the same flight. It was tempting to try it, and save time. But the simulations weren't encouraging. The chimney was heavy, and the load didn't balance right. Given almost any kind of aerial disturbance, they would go down in flames.

So they would make the additional flight. 'To be honest,' Julie told her, as they approached one of the cylinders floating off the *Jenkins*'s port bow, 'getting down with this thing slung on our belly will be enough of a battle.'

The package *was* big. A large cylinder more than thirty meters wide, maybe forty-five meters long. Marge had been impressed with Julie's cool performance as she locked onto the rim, attaching it so that the mouth of the cylinder faced down. Listening to the heavy *bang* as the clamps engaged, she decided the pilot's caution was justified.

The unit was equipped with guidance thrusters, which she now jettisoned. The *Jenkins* could retrieve them later.

They were on the night side, approaching the terminator, chasing the sun. 'Not the best planning,' Julie said. 'We'll have to go around once before we start our descent.'

At this point it didn't matter. Marge sat back to enjoy the ride. The skies were clear and bright. The omega was behind them somewhere, not visible unless they called it up on the scopes. The rising sun picked out a couple of islands and a few drifting clouds.

They were passing through daylight. Marge watched the oceans and landmasses rotating beneath, thinking how green it all was, how lovely, and she began to wonder whether it would draw settlers eventually, people who would argue that the Goompahs only used a small part of the world anyhow, so why not? It occurred to her for the first time that terrestrial governments might eventually find themselves unable to enforce their edicts about interfering with other civilizations. Might not even be able to stop groups of exploiters from seizing distant real estate.

Ah, well. That was a problem for another age.

Behind them, the sun sank below the horizon and they soared through the night. 'Starting down in five minutes,' said Julie.

It was okay by Marge.

Moments before they entered the atmosphere, Julie switched on the spike, reducing the gravity drag. Marge noticed that they'd dropped out of orbit earlier than the point where they'd started the other three descents. 'Losing weight isn't the same as losing mass,' Julie explained. 'We're still carrying a load, and we need more space to get down.'

There were a few clouds over the area, and she didn't see the shoreline until they were directly over it. Then they raced inland, over rolling hills and, finally, the forest. The omega had set, and the eastern sky was beginning to brighten.

Julie eased the vehicle down among the cluster of trees where they'd landed earlier. When her cargo touched the ground she held steady, keeping the weight of the AV3 off it. 'Okay, Bill,' she said, 'release the package.'

Marge felt it come free.

They continued to hover immediately overhead. 'Bill,' Julie said, 'peel the wrapper.'

Marge watched the tarp protecting the rainmaker fall away. Grapplers took it up and stored it in the cargo bay.

When it was done, Julie banked off to one side so they could see. The chimney was made of ultralight, highly reflective cloth. It was a flexible mirror, and it was virtually invisible.

And that was it for the night. It was getting too close to sunrise to try to do any more. The next day, when they came back, they would bring the helicopter.

The mood has changed. You can't really miss it. Everywhere you go at night, Goompahs are looking up over their shoulders at the thing in the sky that won't go away and gets bigger every day. The sense of something deadly, of something supernatural, coming this way has become a palpable part of everyday life here. The streets aren't as crowded at night as they used to be. And the Goompahs talk in hushed tones, as if they were afraid the monster overhead might hear them.

It might be that the most disquieting aspect of the thing is that it looks like a squid. The Goompahs are familiar with squids, or with something very like a squid. They're a delicacy here, as they used to be in some cultures at home. But the Goompahs, like us, are struck by their grasping capabilities, and they, too, find the creatures unsettling. I overheard a group of them today describing an incident that is probably apocryphal, but which they were convinced was true: Someone in a fishing boat was seized by a squid and dragged overboard while his comrades watched, too frightened to assist. Did it really happen? I don't know. The interesting thing is that the story surfaces just as the time when a celestial squid seems to be coming after the entire Intigo.

Something else has changed: They don't call it T'Klot *anymore. The Hole. It's become instead* T'Elan. *The Thing. The Nameless.*

—Digger Dunn, Journal
Thursday, December 4

36

On board the *Hawksbill*.
Friday, December 5.

Kellie Collier wasn't comfortable with Dave Collingdale. He never laughed, never eased up. He sat beside her on the bridge, staring at the images of the cloud in stony silence.

'We never took the clouds seriously,' she said finally, trying to start a conversation. 'People who think we can just ignore them and they'll go away should come out here and take a look at one close up.'

'I know.' And he just sat there.

She asked him an innocuous question about the flight out, but that didn't go well either.

He turned aside every effort to lighten the atmosphere. Ask him how things were going, and he told you the position of the cloud. Ask how he was feeling, and he told you how he was going to enjoy doing it to the cloud.

Doing it to the cloud.

She got the sense that he would have used stronger terminology had she been a male.

But however he might have said it, it carried the clear implication that the cloud was alive.

'I am going to get it,' he said.

Not decoy it.

Not turn it aside.

Get it.

There was an industrial-sized projector mounted on the belly of the *Hawksbill* and a twin unit housed in the shuttle. Hutch, who had apparently thought up this whole idea, had warned her that the *Hawksbill* was the wrong shape for working around omegas, and she was sorry but they'd needed to pack so much stuff on board there'd been no help for that. Keep your distance, Hutch had said. Watch out.

She intended to.

The jets boiling off the cloud's surface raced thousands of kilometers ahead of it. The omega was coming in from slightly above the plane of the system, so most of its upper surface was in shadow. She'd arced around and come in from the rear. They were three hundred kilometers above the cloud. The mist stretched to the horizon in all directions. It was quiet, placid, attractive. And there was an illusion, quite compelling, that there was a solid surface just beneath. That one could have walked on it.

'How big is it, Bill?' she asked. 'Upper surface area?'

'*Eighty-nine billion square kilometers, Kellie.*' Seventy-five hundred times the size of the NAU, which combined the old United States and Canada. '*This is a good time to launch the monitors.*'

'Do it.'

There were six of them, packages of sensors and scopes that would run with the cloud and keep an eye on it.

Collingdale stood behind her, watching, grunting approvingly as the lamps came on, indicating first that the units were away, and then that they had become operational. 'Dave,' she said, 'we'll be ready to go in about ten minutes.'

'Okay,' he said. He took his own chair and brought up an image of the shuttle, waiting in the launch bay with its LCYC

442

projector. The LCYC was a duplicate of the one bolted to the ship's hull.

Dead ahead, slightly blurred by mist, she could see Lookout. There was just the hint of a disk. And the two moons. Permanently suspended in the omega sky, as though they were just rising.

'When this is over,' he said, the tension suddenly gone from his voice, 'I'm going to push to get this problem taken care of. If we organize the right people, make some noise in the media, we can get funding and get the research under way.'

'To get rid of these things, you mean?'

'Of course. Nobody's serious. But that's going to change when I get home.' He looked down at the cloudscape.

They were moving faster than the omega, and as she watched they swept out over the horizon, and it fell away. But it was still braking, and the vast jets thrown forward by the action rolled past her.

'Okay, David,' she said. 'Let's line up.'

She took them down among the jets and set the *Hawksbill* directly in front of the cloud.

'*Electrical activity increasing,*' said Bill.

She saw some lightning. 'That coming out of the main body?' she asked.

'*Yes,*' said Bill.

'Directed at us?'

'*I believe it is random.*'

Collingdale got up again and stood by the viewport. Man couldn't stay still. 'It knows we're here,' he said.

More illumination flickered through the cloud.

She felt chilled. Wished Digger were there.

'It's okay,' he said soothingly, apparently sensing her disquiet, but not understanding the reason. 'We're going to be fine.' His eyes were hard, and a smile played at the corners of his lips. *He's enjoying this.*

'I need you to sit down and belt in, David,' she said. 'Maneuver coming up.'

443

He tapped the viewport as if, yes, everything was indeed under control, and resumed his seat.

She didn't like being so close to the damned thing. She could very nearly have reached out the airlock and stuck an arm into one of the jets.

'*Range approaching 250,*' said Bill.

'Match velocity.'

The retros fired. The same technology that provided artificial gravity served to damp the effects of maneuvering. But they still existed, and for about twenty seconds her body pushed against the forward restraints. Then the pressure eased.

'*Done,*' said Bill.

The problem for Kellie was to find adequate operating space away from the plumes. He waited with studied patience while she did so.

'Bill,' she said, 'begin relaying data to *Jenkins.*' Just in case. Bill confirmed, and she turned to Collingdale. 'Dave, we are ready to launch the shuttle.'

The LCYC projectors were industrial units with a variety of uses, ranging from entertainment to environmental and architectural planning. They were configured, when used in tandem, to create a larger, more clearly defined image than either could have done alone.

The shuttle left the ship and moved out to a range of seven hundred kilometers, where it assumed a parallel course with the *Hawksbill.*

'*In position,*' said Bill.

'Bill,' she said, 'take direction from David.'

'*Confirmed.*'

'Bill,' said David, 'start the program.'

The AI, looking about twenty-two, dashing and handsome, appeared near the viewport. He looked out and smiled. '*Program is initiated,*' he said.

Midway between the *Hawksbill* and the shuttle, a giant

hedgehog blinked into existence. It looked *real*. It looked like a piece of intricately carved rock. Gray hard spines rose out of it, and it turned slowly on its axis.

Beautiful.

'How big is it?' Kellie asked.

'Five hundred thirty kilometers diameter.'

'A little bit bigger than the original.'

'Oh, yes. We wanted to be sure the bastard didn't miss it.'

It glittered in the sunlight, gray and cold. She'd never seen a hologram anywhere close to these dimensions before.

Collingdale smiled at the cloud. 'Okay, you son of a bitch,' he said. 'Come get it.'

More lightning off to port. They'd wandered too close to a jet. It was a flood, a gusher of mist and dust, streaming past. 'At the rate the cloud's coming apart,' she said, 'maybe there won't be anything left by the time it gets to Lookout.'

'Don't count on it,' said Collingdale.

Another bolt rippled past. A big one. They both ducked. So did Bill. His image vanished.

Maybe they were drawing the dragon's attention. 'I think we should get started,' she said.

Collingdale nodded. 'Yes. I was just savoring the moment.'

Right. She was glad somebody was enjoying it.

'Bill,' Collingdale said, 'let's go left three degrees.'

Bill complied. The *Hawksbill*, the shuttle, and the virtual hedgehog all turned to port. Images of the cloud played across four screens.

The bridge fell silent, save for the muffled chatter of electronics. Collingdale sat quietly, watching the monitors, calm, almost serene.

Off to starboard, the hedgehog sparkled in sunlight. From somewhere, lightning flickered, touched the image, passed through it.

'It'll probably take a while,' said Collingdale, 'for it to react. To start to turn away.'

She'd become aware of her heartbeat. 'Probably.'

The shuttle was an RY2, lots of curves, no sharply drawn lines, nothing to attract the lightning. Only the oversize *Hawksbill* needed to worry about that. Target of the day. Maybe they should have ridden in the shuttle. Suddenly it struck her that they should have thought things out better. Of course they should be in the shuttle.

Collingdale's gray eyes drifted toward the overhead.

Digger would have thought of it in a minute. Never ride in the target vehicle, he'd have said.

'Bill?' said Collingdale.

'*Nothing yet.*'

'Maybe we need to wiggle a little bit,' he said. 'Do something to get its attention.'

'Maybe.' Why don't you lean out the airlock and wave? 'Bill,' she said, 'down angle three degrees.'

'*Complying,*' said Bill.

The face of the cloud was torn by fissures and ridges. One dark slice ran jagged like a gaping wound across the length of the thing. Gradually, the cloud was retreating from the center of the screens as the *Hawksbill* continued to pull away from it.

They waited six hours. The *Hawksbill* and its shuttle and the virtual hedgehog drew steadily away from the cloud, which continued on course for Lookout. Collingdale's mood had darkened. He sat smoldering in his seat. When he spoke at all, it was to the omega, calling its attention to the hedgehog. 'Don't you see it, you dumb son of a bitch?'

'Hey, you're going the wrong way.'

'We're *here*. Over here.'

For the most part, though, he watched in stricken silence. Finally, he literally threw himself out of the chair, a dangerous move in the low gravity of a superluminal. 'Hell with this,' he said. He brought the AI up onscreen. 'Bill, go to the next one.'

The hedgehog vanished. A city appeared in its place. It was on the same order of magnitude.

This was a city unlike any she'd seen, an unearthly place of crystal towers and globes and chess piece symmetry.

'It's Moonlight,' said Collingdale. 'We know the thing'll go after this one.' He gazed at the omega's image on the overhead.

But if the omega cared, or even noticed, there was no indication. Collingdale paced the bridge for hours, eyes blazing, his jaw clamped tight. He was talking to the cloud, cajoling it, challenging it, cursing it. And then apologizing to Kellie. 'I'm sorry,' he said. 'It's goddam frustrating.' Somewhere he'd picked up a wrench and he stalked about with it gripped in one fist, as if he'd use it on the omega.

Kellie watched.

'Nobody's afraid of you, you bastard.'

They were getting too far away from the cloud, so she cut the image, took the shuttle back on board, swung around behind the omega, and repeated her earlier maneuver, easing the *Hawksbill* down directly in its path again.

She also suggested they board the shuttle, and run the operation from there.

'No,' he said. 'You go if you want. But the shuttle's too small. Too much lightning out there. It gets hit once, and it's over.'

She thought about ordering him to comply. She was, after all, the vessel's captain. But they were running an operation, and that was his responsibility. His testosterone was involved, and she knew he'd resist, refuse, defy her. The last thing she needed at the moment was a confrontation. She relaunched and repositioned the vehicle, making a great show of it.

'I think it's a mistake,' she said.

He shook his head. 'Let's just get the job done.'

'Have it your way. We're ready to go.'

Collingdale stared hard at the navigation screen, on which an image of the shuttle floated. 'Bill,' he said, 'let's have the cube.'

A box appeared. It was silver, and someone had added the legend BITE ME on one side. Its dimensions were similar to those of the hedgehog and the city.

But it didn't matter.

Kellie put down a sandwich and some coffee while they waited. Collingdale wasn't hungry, thanks. He hadn't eaten all day.

He ran the cube in a fixed position, and he ran it tumbling. They were pulling away from the cloud again, and Kellie watched while Collingdale changed the colors on the visual, from orange, to blue, to pink.

'I guess,' he said finally, 'it knows we're just showing it pictures.'

'I guess.'

'Okay,' he said, 'let's recall the shuttle. We'll try the kite.'

'Tomorrow,' she said. 'We don't do anything else until we've both had some sleep.'

ARCHIVE

We'll try again in a few hours, Mary. We have to swing around and get back in position. And it's the middle of the night, so we're going to shut down for a while. Stupid damned thing. But we'll get it yet. If Hutchins is right and it really chases the hedgehogs, it'll chase the kite.

—David Collingdale to Mary Clank
Friday, December 5

BLACK CAT REPORT

Thanks, Ron. This is Rose Beetem, onboard the *Calvin Clyde*, now about one week from Lookout. Our latest information is that the omega is still on course to attack the Goompahs in nine days. When it does, the Black Cat will be there, and so will everybody in our audience. We're hoping the Academy team can do something to distract this monster, but we'll just have to wait to see.

Back to you, Ron—

37

On the surface near *Savakol*.
Friday, December 5.

Julie sat in the lander, which was perched on a sea-bound rock too small to describe as an island, and watched the transmissions coming in from the *Hawksbill*. She followed the flight across the top of the omega, felt a thrill when the hedgehog came to life directly in front of it, held her breath when the ship and the shuttle began their turn to port. She kept Digger and Whit informed, talked with Marge on the *Jenkins*, and shared her disappointment when the omega failed to take the bait. She had expected the projections to work; had not in fact been able to see any chance they would fail. But there it was.

The next phase of the operation, deploying the kite, would not start for several hours, and Julie was going to be up all night helping Marge. So she kicked her seat back and closed her eyes. Once she woke to see sails passing in the distance, but she knew that if anyone got close, Bill would alert her.

Gulls wheeled overhead. In the background she could hear Bill talking, sometimes with Whit, sometimes with Digger. At Digger's insistence, he was using his own voice.

Savakol was one of the smaller cities, and there was

consequently less walking around to be done. They expected to be finished by midafternoon.

This was Julie's first mission of consequence. She'd talked to some of the older Academy people before coming to Lookout, and most of them had never done *anything* that was close to being this significant. Her father had led the mission that first discovered the omegas; and she enjoyed being part of the first effort to rescue someone from them.

Ordinarily, the Lookout flight would have been offered to a senior captain first, but apparently either no one was available or, more likely, nobody was interested in a two-year operation. She'd applied and, to her surprise, gotten the assignment. She'd had mixed feelings when it came through, second thoughts about whether she really wanted to do it. But she was committed and saw no easy way out. Especially when her folks had called and tried to dissuade her. In the end they'd said okay, have your own way, but be careful, stay clear of the cloud.

That seemed a long time ago, and if her social life had fallen off a bit, she was nevertheless feeling good about what she was doing. She'd have preferred staying with the *Hawksbill* and going after the omega with Collingdale. It would have been nice to go home and tell her father she'd helped shoo the thing off. But this was okay. She was close to the action, and that was really sufficient.

Half asleep, she watched Whit record a boating regatta at a lakefront. He was putting everything he could find into his notebook, capturing ball games, debates in the park, haggling over prices at the merchants' stalls. The regatta featured half-dressed Goompah females paddling boats while a crowd cheered them on. They all wore green and white, which seemed to have some special significance because green and white banners were on display everywhere.

Digger explained that the seminudity was traditional with these events. He didn't know why, and no one seemed unduly excited by it. The females did wear wide-brimmed white hats, however, which – to the delight of the crowd – were forever flying off.

Julie drifted into sleep, and dreamed that she was back at the University of Tacoma, listening to somebody lecture about Beowulf, how Grendel represented natural forces, the dark side of life, the things people have no control over. Then she was awake again listening to the sea and the gulls and Digger.

'—*Having a problem*,' Digger was saying. '*Julie, do you hear me?*'

'What's wrong?' she asked, awake and surveying the screens. There were five of them, carrying an image of the omega, a satellite view of the three sailing vessels the Goompahs had sent east, a picture of the rainmaker they'd delivered the previous night, a revolving picture of the open sea around her, and, from an imager carried by Digger—

—A torchlight parade. Of Goompahs.

They were on a beach. Some were wearing robes. Others stood watching.

'*I think they're going to do another sacrifice*,' he said.

Julie knew about the Goompah who'd walked into the sea. He'd worn a white robe, and everyone else had worn black. There was a single white robe among the marchers. Worn by – it looked like – an elderly female.

'*I'm on my way*,' said Whit, breaking in.

'Aren't you guys together?'

'*No*,' said Digger. '*We split up to cover more ground.*'

Black-robed Goompahs were chanting. And a crowd spread across the beach, growing, and joining in. Julie couldn't understand a word of it.

Digger was frantic: '*I'm not going to stand by and watch it happen again.*'

Whit had broken into a run. He wasn't in great shape, and pretty soon he was breathing hard.

Julie should have kept quiet. But she opened a channel. 'Hey,' she said, 'keep in mind these aren't people.'

The screen with the torchlight marchers went blank.

'*Digger*,' said Whit, '*you okay?*'

'*Fine. Don't have time for the imager.*'

'What's happening?' asked Julie.

'*The head Goompah's making for the water.*'

Digger had begun to run across the beach. She could hear his shoes crunching the sand.

Whit gasped that he was close by, and Digger shouldn't do anything until he got there, and Digger replied that there wasn't time and he wasn't going to sit still again.

'Hey,' she said. 'This is not my business, but we're supposed to stay out of it.'

'*She's right.*' Whit again. '*Religious ceremony.*' Blowing hard. '*The Protocol.*'

'*Forget the Protocol.*'

'Does she have a sword?' asked Julie.

'*They have a javelin. And she's in the water. Up to her hips. Doesn't look as if she can swim a stroke.*'

'I see them,' said Whit. '*Javelin's in the air.*'

'*Julie.*' Digger's voice. '*How soon can you get here?*'

Julie's harness was descending around her shoulders. She started punching buttons. 'I'm just over the horizon.'

'*You got a tether handy?*' asked Digger.

'Bill,' she said, 'let's go. What's the tether situation?'

'*There's an ample supply of cable in the locker.*'

'Good. Activate the lightbender.'

'*Handing the javelin off,*' said Whit.

She could hear Digger charging into the water. '*Get here,*' he said, '*as quickly as you can.*'

She lifted off the rock, staying only a few meters above the surface, and turned toward shore. It was early afternoon, a gray, depressing day, the sun hidden in a slate sky. The mountains that lay immediately west of *Savakol* dominated the horizon.

One of the satellites was over the scene, and she was able to get a picture of the beach. The white-robed Goompah was wallowing in the surf, but pushing doggedly forward. There was, of course, no sign of the invisible Digger.

'*There are some,*' said Bill, '*who do not want her to do it.*'

A few Goompahs were in the surf with her. One had reached her and was trying to restrain her, but one of the black robes pulled the would-be rescuer away.

'*Her name is* Tayma,' said Bill.

'How do you know?'

'*They're calling it out. Telling her to stop.*'

One of the Goompahs threw itself down on the beach and began to beat the sand.

Julie turned away from the screen. The ocean raced beneath the spacecraft.

'*We are leaving a wake,*' said Bill.

'Doesn't matter. Nobody here to see it.'

The chants ended. Silence fell across the beach, save for the protesters. The coastline was taking shape ahead. A pair of islands rippled past.

'Bill,' she said, 'you got the conn.'

'*I have it.*'

She slipped out of her seat, climbed into the rear of the cabin, opened the main storage locker, and began hauling out cable. She sorted through, found a five-meter length, and pulled it clear.

Tayma was off her feet now, alternately getting pushed in and dragged back by the surf. '*Not a very dignified way to go,*' said Bill.

'*I'm close to her now,*' said Digger. He was breathing hard, too. She could hear a lot of splashing.

And suddenly there was a yowling coming over the circuit.

'What's *that*?' she asked. 'What's going on?'

'*It's the crowd,*' said Whit. '*Dig's in the water, headed right for her. But they can see the splashes. You know what it looks like?*'

'No.'

'*To me it looks like something in the ocean stalking her.*'

The cries had become shrieks. Bloodcurdling screams.

Tayma hadn't seen it yet. A big wave came in, and she floated over the top, came down the far side, and went back to struggling against the drag. The crowd was making a lot of noise, and she must have heard it but probably thought they were expressing their sorrow for her. Or maybe she'd locked them out.

The lander arced in over the coastline. Julie saw the city and the long white beach.

'*I've got her,*' said Digger. Then *he* screamed.

'Dig, are you okay?'

'*Let go!*' said Digger. There was a thunk and he gasped.

'Digger?' Whatever was happening, it sounded as if he was losing.

'*The crowd's getting scared,*' said Whit. '*They don't know what's going on.*'

'Neither do I. Where's Digger?'

The lander slowed and began circling over the scene.

Whit said something but it didn't matter anymore because she could see for herself now. The Goompah was well out in the water, and she was struggling fiercely with her invisible rescuer.

'*—Trying to save you,*' said Dig. '*You nit—*'

'*Doesn't want to be rescued,*' cried Whit. '*Let her go.*'

Julie turned the lander around so the hatch couldn't be seen from the beach. Then she opened up. Four thrusters along the hull rotated into vertical position and fired, providing additional lift.

'What are you going to do?' she asked Digger.

'*You find that tether?*'

'I've got a piece of cable.'

'*Use it.*'

She was already at work. She'd secured one end of the line, and stepped into the open hatchway. 'Good luck,' she said, and dropped the other end into the water.

The struggle in the surf went on. The Goompahs, moaning and shrieking, crowded to the edge of the water. The cable twisted and turned. Julie saw more water kicking up near the beach and realized that Whit was about to join the fray. But before he got anywhere close, Digger announced that he'd secured the line around the female. '*Lift,*' he said.

Julie told Whit to go back, everything was under control. She stayed in the airlock and directed Bill to take the lander up. 'But slowly,' she said. 'Gently.' The line tightened, and the deck tilted under the weight.

The Goompah came out of the water, the line looped around her left arm. It was, despite everything, the most ridiculous sight Julie had ever seen.

'Go,' said Digger. '*Get her ashore.*'

'You okay?' There was a depression in the water where Digger was floating. The currents looked strong, and the beach kept getting farther away.

'*I'm fine.*'

'You're sure?'

'*Will you get moving?*' He sounded exasperated.

'*We're making a miracle,*' said Whit, who'd retreated back to the beach. The crowd had gone absolutely rock-still silent. The Goompah, Tayma, kept rising higher, secured by a line that, from their perspective, must have vanished in midair. Some had fallen to their knees.

'*Lift her gently,*' said Digger. '*Don't jerk her or anything.*'

'Right.'

'*Do it the way the gods would.*'

'How the hell would the gods do it?'

'*Where do you want to put her?*' asked Bill.

'Empty section of beach at the east end. Take her there.'

She could *see* Julie. God knew what she thought. The poor creature was already half out of her mind with fear, and there directly above her she was looking at a circle of light in midair with somebody hanging out of it.

'*Don't let her see you,*' said Digger. '*They're scared of people.*'

Too late. She'd heard that, forgotten, didn't really care at this point. The lander glided over the waves and east across the beach.

'*How do we know,*' Bill asked, '*she won't just walk back into the ocean?*'

'Next one's on her. Dig, how are you doing?'

455

'*Still afloat.*'

'I'll be right back.'

'*Better make it quick.*'

She didn't like the sound of that and almost cut the Goompah loose.

'*Here?*' asked Bill.

'Good. Let her down.'

She heard a sound that might have been a cheer.

'*I'm going after him,*' said Whit.

'No,' she said. 'Stay where you are. I won't have time to rescue two.'

Digger had never been the world's best swimmer. And he was out of shape. He had known when he splashed through the shallows and dived in after the unfortunate Tayma that he was making a mistake. But he had seen something in her face, and it told him she was terrified. In some absurd way, she was doing her duty, but she didn't want to do it.

The earlier suicide was with him still, the Goompah pushing out through the waves and struggling against the tide and finally sinking.

But Julie had been slower coming to the rescue than he'd expected. He'd exhausted himself reaching the *woman*. (Somehow, he was willing to extend the term to the Goompah.) The tide had been dragging them both out, and he'd made the typical inexperienced error of fighting it. And then fighting her. And finally had come the struggle to get the line around her shoulder.

His arms were desperately tired and heavy. He'd thought he could let himself slip under, that he was inside the e-suit and could rest in the depths for a few minutes until Julie got back. But he'd forgotten that he was wearing a converter and not air tanks. If he went under, he'd smother.

He had the satisfaction of seeing Tayma lifted from the ocean, of hearing cheers behind him, of watching her apparently glide through the air toward the beach.

But the currents were pulling him out to sea. And he was tired. God help him he was tired. Needed to get onto a physical regimen. Take better care of himself. Would do that when this was over.

He closed his eyes and tried to rest. Just for a few moments.

It occurred to him to turn off the lightbender so they could see him. He fumbled at the control on his wrist, but it was hard to find.

Hell with it. She had goggles. He closed his eyes and thought about Kellie as the water closed over him.

Whit watched Tayma come gently down at the edge of the surf. The line fell after her, a longer cable than had been visible a moment before. Then he heard Julie trying to raise Digger on the circuit. Silence roared back. '*Where'd he go?*' Julie demanded.

It was all happening too fast.

There'd be enough air left in the hard shell covering his face to keep him alive for a couple of minutes, to keep the water out of his lungs. As long as she could find him quickly.

Find him. 'Digger,' she said, terrified, 'if you can hear me, shut off the lightbender.'

No answer.

'Whit—?'

'*Look where you were before, Julie.*'

Where the hell was that?

'*—Straight out. More to your right.*'

She was wearing goggles by then, hanging out the airlock again with a fresh piece of cable, searching frantically for a sign of the swimmer. While she looked, she secured one end of it and dropped the other into the water. But there was nothing.

'*Do you see him?*' asked Whit.

'Not yet.' He'd gone under. 'Bill, try the sensors.'

The water looked quiet. She saw no indication of anything splashing around.

'*Negative,*' said Bill.

The goggles weren't doing any good under these circumstances. 'Do we have anything on the hull that will pick up sound?'

'*Sure. Antenna's up forward, atop the hull.*' He showed her.

She recalled a story her father had told her. How Hutchins had been on foot one night looking for a lander that they'd parked and lost, and she'd found it by having someone call it and yell so she could listen for the sounds. 'Okay, get as low as you can. Just over the waves.'

'*I'll put her down on the water.*'

'No.' That could kill Dig. 'Keep some space.'

She grabbed a wrench and a strip of electrical cable out of the equipment bin and hustled through the airlock. 'Bill,' she said, 'shut down the lightbender.'

There was a brief change in the sound generated by the power grid. '*Done,*' said Bill. '*Lot of wind out here.*'

Whit shouted a warning, thinking the vehicle had become visible by accident. 'It's okay,' she told him.

'*You can't do that.*'

She had drawn the attention of every native in sight. 'I don't have time at the moment, Whit.' She climbed out onto the ladder and quickly hoisted herself onto the hull. The antenna was a few paces forward. 'Bill, is this thing going to work if I rip it off and throw it in the water?'

'*I'm optimistic it will. What are we going to do?*'

She used the wrench to pry it loose, disconnected it, and connected the cable. Then she pitched it over the side into the ocean. 'Is it working?'

'*It is functioning. What good will it do?*'

'I want you to listen up, Bill.' She opened her channel to Digger. 'Okay, Bill, if you can hear this through the receiver, give me an angle.'

'*I'm listening, Julie. But I do not hear anything.*'

She rapped the wrench on the link. 'Can you hear it now?'

'*Negative.*'

'All right. Got a better idea. Tie me in with the *Jenkins* library.'

The Goompahs along the beach were pushing and shoving. Some were starting into the water, others were running off in all directions. Well, she was sure beating hell out of the Protocol.

'*Done,*' said Bill.

'Okay. Let's have the *1812*. Lots of volume.'

'*Which movement did you want?*'

'The part with the cannons. Fire off the cannons.'

It exploded, drums, guns, bugles, and cavalry charges. It thundered across the water, and of course she was only listening to a rendition from her wrist unit. It would also be filling Digger's shell.

'*You'll deafen him.*'

'Can you hear it, Bill?'

'*Yes.*' The lander moved forward, a bit farther out to sea. Slowed. Edged sideways. Retreated a bit. '*He should be right below you.*'

'*Have you found him?*' asked Whit. '*You're getting half the town out here.*' The lander was being buffeted by the wind, and hundreds of Goompahs poured onto the beach.

'Can't help that.' She dropped into the water, kicked down, and heard the muffled chords of the overture. She swam toward the sound and saw his shimmering form ahead. A leg. She found his knee and juggled him while she decided which end was up. Hard to tell in the green depths. Then she got hold of his vest and headed for the surface. Meantime she switched off the lightbender. And she could see him. His eyes were closed, his skin was gray, and he looked not good.

'Bill,' she said, 'kill the *1812*.'

She got in front of him, caught the control on his left wrist, and the safety on his right shoulder, and shut off the e-suit.

He didn't look as if he was breathing.

'Bill, reactivate the lightbender. And set down in the water. Try not to sink.'

The lander vanished again, save for the open hatch. She and Digger were visible from the beach. Another shock for the home folks.

'*Julie, I'm reluctant to put the lander in the water. I can't see where you are.*'

'It's okay. We're clear.'

'*Julie,*' said Whit, '*do you have him?*'

'I've got him.'

'*How is he?*'

She heard the lander touch down, saw the water *press* down. It looked as if a ditch had opened in the sea. 'Can't tell yet.'

'*Is he alive?*'

'I don't know.' She looped the line around his waist, wrapped it around the hatch, and secured it so he wouldn't sink. Then she scrambled into the airlock, stayed on her knees, and dragged him in behind her.

He had a heartbeat, but it was faint. She started mouth-to-mouth.

It was an up and down day for the Goompahs. They'd been inspired – there was no other word for it – by the miraculous rescue of Tayma. But then the lander had appeared, a sleek gray *thing* floating in air, and then the humans had shown up, first Julie, and then Digger, both coming out of nowhere. Whit knew that the human physiognomy spooked the locals, but he'd hoped that, under the circumstances, they would adjust. They didn't. They howled and either ran or stumbled off the beach. A few stopped to help Tayma, who looked completely disoriented. In the end all had retreated to what could only be described as a respectful distance.

Whit stood watching the piece of airlock and lander's interior, rounded off by the open hatch hanging above the waves.

'*Got a pulse,*' said Julie.

'Is he okay?'

'*I think so. Is this the way you guys always behave?*'

'I don't know,' he said. 'I'm new in these parts. By the way, when you get a chance, you might want to close the hatch.'

She looked out at him, and the spectacle narrowed and vanished.

That brought another series of grunts and pointing from the Goompahs. Tayma, meantime, supported by a half dozen friends, limped away.

He was breathing again. It was shallow, and his pulse was weak, but he was *alive*. She called his name, propped him up and held her hands against his cheeks and rubbed them until his eyes opened. He looked confused.

'Hi, Digger,' she said.

He tried to speak, but nothing came.

'Take your time,' she said.

He mumbled something she couldn't make out. And then his eyes focused on her and looked past her at the bulkhead. 'What happened?' he asked finally. 'How – here?'

'I pulled you out of the water.'

'Water?' His hands went to his clothes.

'What's your name?' she asked gently.

'Dunn. My name's Dunn.' He tried to sit up, but she pushed him back down. 'She okay?'

'Tayma? She's fine. You saved her.'

'Good. Thanks, Kellie.'

'Kellie? Do you know who I am?'

'Kellie,' he said.

'No. Kellie's with the *Hawksbill*. Try again.'

ARCHIVE

(From the Goompah Recordings,
Savakol, Translated by Ginko Amagawa)

I'm no public speaker and I don't like being up here. If you want to know what happened today at *Barkat* Beach, I'll tell you what I saw, or what I thought I saw. And I'll leave you to draw your own conclusions about explanations.

I went because I'd heard the *keelots* were going to be

there, and that they would perform the *kelma*. I went with Quet. We were standing near the front, close to the water.

They went through the ceremony without any problems, and Tayma started out into the ocean. She was praying as she went, and had gotten about ten or fifteen paces when something began to chase her. I don't know what it was. Something in the water but we couldn't see it.

She didn't notice it, but just kept going. We were yelling for her to look out, but she probably thought we were trying to persuade her to come back.

We could see it was going to catch her, and everybody screamed louder. A few cleared out. What happened next is hard to describe. But there was a big fight and then a window opened in the sky . . . '

38

On the surface near Hopgop.
Friday, December 5.

Marge and Julie descended beside the rainmaker they'd brought down the previous night, ready to go to work.

They'd rehearsed often on the way out, and they fell to with a minimum of wasted effort. The rainmaker was already centered among the eight trees that would serve as moorings. Marge did a quick measurement among tree trunks to determine a flight path for the helicopter. When she was satisfied she had it, she released the anchor cables. Julie meantime dropped a feed line in the stream, attached it to a set of four sprinklers, and inserted the sprinklers in the ground around the chimney. Then she connected the line to the pump.

Next they attached the cables to the trees, arranging the slack so that, when the time came, the chimney would be able to rise evenly to a height of about ten meters. Then they disconnected the vertical lines that held the package together. And that was it. It looked like a wide, sky-colored cylinder, made of plastic, open at top and bottom.

'Ready to go?' asked Julie.

Marge nodded. 'Yes, indeed.' She was proud of her

rainmakers, but trying to look as though this were all in a day's work.

'Bill,' said Julie, 'Get the landers and the helicopter ready.'

'*They are primed and waiting.*'

Marge planted a pickup on a tree trunk so they could watch the action on the ground. When she'd finished, they got back into the hauler and Julie took them up, directly over the top of the chimney.

They did a quick inspection, and Marge pronounced everything in order. 'Let's go,' she said.

Julie descended gently until they touched the top of the chimney. 'That's good,' she told Bill. 'Reconnect.'

Marge felt the magnetic clamps take hold.

'*Done,*' said Bill.

Marge started the pump. On the ground, a fine spray rose into the air and descended around the rainmaker. 'That's not really going to make the clouds happen, is it?'

'It'll speed things along,' said Marge.

Julie grinned. 'The wonders of modern technology.' She swung round in her seat. 'Here we go.'

She engaged the spike, the vertical thrusters fired, and they started up. The top of the rainmaker rose with them, extending like an accordion.

'You ever have a problem with these things?' asked Julie.

'Not so far. Of course, this is the first time we've tried to use them off-world.'

'Should work better than at home,' Julie said. 'Less gravity.' And then, to the AI: 'Bill, let's get the first lander aloft.'

The interior of the chimney was braced with microscopically thin lightweight ribs, and crosspieces supported the structure every eighty-six meters. A screen guarded the bottom of the chimney, to prevent small animals from getting sucked up inside. (Larger creatures, like Goompahs, would be inconvenienced if they got too close, would lose their hats, but not their lives.)

As they gained altitude, the omega rose with them. For the first time, Marge could see lightning bolts flickering within the cloud mass.

'*Four hundred meters,*' said Bill, giving them the altitude.

There was an external support ring two hundred meters below the top of the chimney. The first of the four landers, under Bill's control, rose alongside and linked to the ring.

'*Connection complete,*' said the AI. Both vehicles, working in concert, continued drawing the chimney up.

Marge could see lights in *Hopgop*, on the east along the sea. The big moon was up, and it was moving slowly across the face of the omega.

'*Seven hundred meters,*' said Bill.

The ship swayed. 'Atmosphere's pushing at the chimney,' said Marge. 'Don't worry. It'll get smoother as we go higher.'

'*The other landers are in the air.*'

It struck Marge that the cloud looked most ominous, most portentous, when it was rising. She didn't know why that was. Maybe it was connected with the disappointed hope, each evening, that it wouldn't be there in the morning. Maybe it was simply the sense of something evil climbing into the sky. She shook it off, thinking how the Goompahs must be affected if it bothered her.

'I have a question,' said Julie.

'Go ahead.'

'When it's all over, how do we get them down? The chimneys?'

'When the omega hits, we push a button, and the omega blows them into the sea.'

Julie frowned. 'They won't drag? Cause some damage on the ground?'

'I doubt it. In any case, it's a necessary risk.' The construction materials were biodegradable, and within a few months there'd be no trace of the chimneys anywhere.

They were getting high. *Hopgop* looked far away. Overhead, the stars were bright.

'*Twelve hundred meters.*'

Near ground level, a second lander moved in alongside the chimney and tied onto a support ring on the opposite side from the first. '*Second linkup complete,*' said Bill. '*All units ascending.*'

At twenty-two hundred meters, the third lander joined the effort, connecting with a ring at right angles to the other two. Marge was sitting comfortably, reassuring Julie when the hauler occasionally rocked as the weather pushed at the chimney. Julie had never done anything like this, and when she put on goggles and saw the chimney trailing all the way to the ground, her instincts screamed that it was too much, that the weight had to drag the hauler out of the air. It came down to Marge's assurances against the evidence of her eyes.

'Keep in mind,' Marge said, 'it's the same thing you brought down out of orbit. It's no heavier now than it was then.'

'Except now it's unrolled.'

'Doesn't change the mass. Relax. Everything's going to be fine.'

At thirty-seven hundred meters, they began to slow. By then the fourth lander had joined the support group, and they were approaching the chimney's extension limit. When the pickup they'd left behind showed them they had exactly the situation they wanted, the anchor lines pulled tight, and the base of the chimney off the ground, they halted the ascent.

'Bill,' said Julie, 'activate the helicopter and put it in position.'

Bill acknowledged.

The helicopter was a gleaming antique unit, a Falcon, which had become legendary during the long struggle with international terrorists during the later years of the last century. CANADIAN FORCES was stenciled on its hull. It was equipped with lasers and particle beam weapons, but of course none was functional.

Bill started the engine and engaged its silent-running capability, which wasn't really all that silent. When it was ready, he lifted it a couple of meters into the air, navigated it between the two trees Marge had selected, and inserted it directly beneath the base of the chimney.

'*Ready,*' said Bill.

'Okay.' Julie was doing a decent job hiding her qualms. 'We want the blades turning as fast as possible, but we don't want it off the ground. We just want to move the air around.'

'*Ground idle*,' said Bill.

'Yes. That sounds right.'

The blades picked up speed. The helicopter strained upward and Bill cut back slightly. 'Perfect,' Marge said.

'What next?' asked Julie.

Marge smiled. 'I think from here we can just relax and enjoy the show.'

A column of warm moist air moved skyward. Up the chimney. More warm air rushed in to fill the vacuum, and gradually the flow took over on its own. Bill had to cut the blade rotation back again to keep the Falcon from lifting off.

'*Moving along nicely*,' he reported. And, finally: '*I believe it is self-sustaining now.*'

Marge gave it a few more minutes, then Julie directed Bill to move the helicopter away. 'Be careful,' she added.

Bill brought the Falcon out, squeezing past the same two trees. When it was clear, he gunned the engines, and it lifted off into the steady winds that were racing around the chimney. It fought its way into the sky and turned west toward Utopia.

Avery Whitlock's Notebooks

The ship is asleep.

Digger seems to be okay. We were worried for a while that there might be some brain damage. He still doesn't have his memory back completely, can't recall how he got into the ocean, or even being on the beach. But Bill says that's not an unusual result in cases like this. I guess we'll know for sure in the morning.

I haven't been able to sleep. It's not so much that I'm worried about Digger, because I think he'll be okay. But watching a creature that one thinks of as rational try to end

*its life for the most irrational of purposes . . . I cannot get
it out of my mind. Knowing that it happens, has happened
to us, and seeing it in action . . . It gives me a sense of how
far we've come. Of what civilization truly means.*

—*December 5*

39

On board the AV3, west of *Hopgop*.
Saturday, December 6.

'*Level of convection is sufficient*,' said Bill.

'All right.' Marge rubbed her hands together. 'Now we do the magic.' She glanced out at the sky. The chimney, which they'd been supporting for several hours, was all but invisible to the naked eye. Julie had noticed that the drag on the AV3 had lessened, had in fact all but disappeared. 'Cut them loose,' she said. 'Cut everything loose.'

'The landers, too?'

'Everything. Send them to Utopia.'

Julie knew how it was supposed to work. But this kind of operation flew in the face of common sense. And she had a bad feeling about what would happen when she released her grip on the chimney. Ah, well. 'Bill,' she said, 'do it.'

The AI acknowledged. She felt the clamps release the chimney, watched the status board light up with reports that the four landers had simultaneously turned loose, heard Bill say that the action was completed. And all her instincts told her that the elongated structure they'd so laboriously hauled up several thousand meters would now collapse, crash down on the countryside and, God help them, maybe on *Hopgop*.

Marge was smiling broadly. 'Let's take a look,' she said.

Julie took the hauler around in a large arc so they could see. The chimney was constructed of stealth materials. When she looked through the goggles, it was voilà all the way to the ground. It was standing on its own, a great round cylinder extending down through the clouds, supported by no visible means.

She knew the theory. Surface air is warmer, heavier, and more humid than air at altitude. It wants to rise but generally can't do so in any organized fashion, or in sufficient volume to create clouds unless there's substantial pressure or a temperature gradient. Nightfall and pressure fronts provide that in nature.

To do it artificially, a chimney was needed. Once it was in place, the warm air started up on its own. It kept moving up because there was no place else for it to go. They'd put the Falcon at the base to provide a fan, to help things along. Once the system got going, the chimney became an oversize siphon, perfectly capable of keeping itself inflated.

At the moment, warm moist air was spreading out from the top of the rainmaker. It would shortly begin to create clouds.

'We just have time,' Marge said, 'to get the next package and run it down to the *Sakmarung* site so we can be ready to go tomorrow night.'

That would leave enough time for Julie to get back to the *Jenkins* and pick up her two caballeros, who'd be looking forward to another day of planting their projectors and getting ready for the big show. She wasn't entirely sure Digger would be able to go back down, and in fact she thought he should stay put. Since Whit was too inexperienced to go down alone, that meant both of them should take a day off.

But Digger had insisted the night before that he was okay, that he would be able to go back in the morning. Then he'd passed out, helped along by some medication. It occurred to Julie that she should let Kellie know what had happened.

'Better to wait,' said Marge.

'Why?'

'Wait till you get back to the ship. Make sure he's really okay. She'll want to know, and you won't want to be telling her you *think* he's fine.'

But Kellie called *her* and the issue became moot.

'Bill says he's fine,' she told Kellie. 'Not to worry.'

Kellie thanked her and said she hoped Digger would take it easy for a bit.

Whit seemed to have been affected by events there. His rational, cautious, and thoughtful self had been replaced by someone more romantic, more willing to take a risk. He was in love with the idea of helping rescue the Goompahs. But she wondered how he'd react if things didn't go well.

They collected the second chimney, and, as dawn was breaking over the *Intigo*, delivered it to an island thirty kilometers west of Sakmarung. Julie's first act on returning to the *Jenkins* was to look in on Digger, who was sleeping peacefully. Bill assured her he was fine, all signs normal.

Whit had developed a hobby. He loved being invisible, and he never missed an opportunity to record the Goompahs at work, at play, or during their frequent gambols. He watched them frolicking in the parks, families coming down to the pier to see ships coming and going, young ones playing ball games. It was all of a piece. Life in the *Intigo* seemed to be one long celebration.

And he watched it with a joy born of the sure and certain knowledge that this civilization was too vibrant, too alive, to be taken out by an artifact that had no purpose, no reason to be, and might be older than man. Collingdale would take it for a ride, if anyone could do it. And if not, they'd make Digger's avatars do the work. But one way or another, they and the Goompahs would come through it.

471

'How can you be so sure?' Julie asked him.

'You believe in destiny?'

'I don't think so,' she said.

'I do.' He looked at her, his dark face wreathed in thought. 'Sometimes you can feel history moving a certain way. People are always saying that history turns on little things, Alexander dies too young to take out Rome, Churchill survives a plane crash and lives to save the Western world. But sometimes the wheels just go round, and you know, absolutely know, certain things have to happen. We had to have Rome. Hitler had to be stopped.'

'And where is history taking us now?'

'You want to know what I really think?'

'Of course.'

'Julie, the Goompahs are a remarkable race. I think they, and we, have a rendezvous up ahead somewhere. And I think we'll all be better for it.'

Avery Whitlock's Notebooks

Dave told me today he thinks they can make the kite work. Maybe he can, maybe not. But I've had a lot of time on my flight out here to stay up with those who pretend to comment on the state of the human race. Most of them, people like Hazhure and MacAllister, think we are a despicable lot, interested only in power, sex, and money. They maintain, in addition, that we're cowardly and selfish. Today, I listened to Dave Collingdale, and I watched Julie and Marge come in after starting a rainstorm that might, just might, hide Hopgop from the omega. Anybody who's listening, be on notice: I'm a card-carrying human being. And I've never been prouder of that fact.

—December 6

LIBRARY ENTRY

Everybody else talks about the weather. We do something about it.

—Motto of the International Bureau of the Climate

40

On board the *Hawksbill*.
Saturday, December 6.

All they had left was the kite. And Kellie's intuition warned her it would take more than that to sidetrack the omega.

Collingdale either didn't share her feeling or wouldn't admit to his doubts. He behaved as if there were no question that the kite would work fine. But it was sufficient for her to look out the viewport, and to recognize they were buzzing around that thing like a fly, to know just how uneven a contest they were in.

Collingdale had been plunged in a black mood since she'd found him that morning, pacing the bridge, drinking coffee by the gallon. He insisted he'd slept soundly, but he had rings under his eyes, and he literally looked in pain.

She checked in with Julie, who was in the process of activating the first rainmaker. Julie listened, looked sympathetic, raised her hand in a gesture that signaled affection, resignation, optimism. Here we go. *'We're rooting for you.'* Then: *'Something you should know about.'*

Her tone was scary.

'He's okay, but we had a close call with Digger yesterday.' She described how he had plunged into the sea to rescue a Goompah,

475

how the effort had succeeded, but that he had almost drowned. *'I should have told you yesterday, but to be honest I wanted to wait until we were sure he was all right. No point having you worry when you couldn't do anything.'*

'You're sure he's okay?'

'Bill says he's fine. Not to worry. He's asleep at the moment, but I'll have him get on the circuit when he wakes up.'

'Thanks, Julie.'

They were in front of the cloud again.

'With all flags flying,' said Collingdale.

Ahead, Lookout and its big moon had grown brighter. And were right in the crosshairs. Nine days away.

The omega was continuing to decelerate.

'We're ready when you are,' said Kellie.

Collingdale nodded. 'Okay. Bill,' he said, 'start the launch process.'

'Opening the rear doors,' Bill said.

The kite consisted of thousands of square meters of film folded carefully on a platform that was anchored to the cargo deck.

'Launching the package.'

Bill sprayed a lubricant across the deck, released the platform, and accelerated. The platform slid aft and started through the doors. At that precise moment, they cut the main engines so they would not incinerate the package. It drifted out of the ship and fell behind. A pair of tethers, five kilometers long, secured it to the ship. As the range between the ship and the package increased, they started to draw taut.

Retros cut in, and they braked before the lines had completely tightened, adjusting velocity so that both the *Hawksbill* and the package were moving at precisely the same rate.

Within the film, canisters of compressed air acted as thrusters, separating the folds. Other thruster packages carried the platform away, where it could do no damage. Support rods inside the kite telescoped open, connected with each other, and snapped into braces. Crosspieces swung out from brackets and stabilized the supports. The canisters became exhausted and were jettisoned. Gradually, over the next few hours, the world's foremost box kite took shape. When it was done, it trailed them, glistening in the sunlight, still connected to the twin tethers.

The box was forty-by-twenty-by-twenty kilometers. Rearrange Berlin a little bit, and it would almost fit inside. With plenty of air space. There was room for Everest, with substantial clearance.

The tethers looked fragile. But the manufacturer had assured them they would hold. Just be careful, Collingdale had told her. 'Any sudden yanks, and we might lose it all.'

At that moment, Digger came on the circuit. She was delighted to hear his voice, proud that he had tried to rescue the Goompah, angry that he had risked his life in so foolhardy a manner. 'You're all right?' she asked.

'*I'm fine,*' he said.

'Okay. Don't do anything like that again.'

'*I'll be careful.*'

'Promise.'

'*I promise.*'

'Okay. We're busy. I have to sign off.'

'*Go.*'

'I'm glad you're okay.'

'*Me too. Be careful yourself.*'

Collingdale had not seemed to pay any attention, but she'd seen his jaw muscles move. More important things to do now than personal conversations. But he smiled. 'I'm glad he got through it okay.'

'Thanks, Dave.' Bill's image appeared on-screen. He was wearing *Hawksbill* coveralls and looked quite heroic. This was Bill at about thirty-five, with thick brown hair and piercing blue eyes and a dashing mien. She couldn't restrain a smile, but Bill didn't react. 'How,' she asked him, 'is velocity vis-à-vis the cloud?'

'*Identical. We're doing fine.*' His voice had gotten deeper.

Collingdale nodded. 'Crunch time,' he said. 'Let's make our turn.'

'Bill,' she said, 'let's do like last time. Three points to port. Ease into it.'

Thrusters burped. And burped again.

The cables tightened.

And they settled back to wait.

Kellie was bright and easygoing, but she talked a little too much. She'd encouraged him to tell her about his days as an Academy pilot and his life at the University of Chicago and how he had gotten involved in the omega hunt. He gave short, irritated answers, and she shrugged finally, said okay, as in okay if you want to sit in your room, that's fine with me. And she went into a sulk and stayed there.

It left him feeling guilty. That was a surprise. Where social blundering was concerned, he'd beaten his conscience into submission years earlier. He didn't much care whether people liked him, so long as they respected him. But it was clear that Kellie thought he was a jerk. And not very smart.

'I'm sorry,' he said, while they waited for Bill to tell them the cloud was turning in their direction.

'For what?' Her eyes were dark and cold, and he saw no flexibility in them.

'You wanted to talk.'

'Not really.' She had a book on-screen and her gaze drifted back to it.

'What are you reading?'

'Lamb's essays.'

'Really.' That seemed odd. 'Are you working on a degree?'

'No,' she said.

'Then why—?'

'I like him.' Slight emphasis on the *him*.

'I've never read him,' he said. He never read anything that wasn't work-related.

She shrugged.

'I'll have to try him sometime.'

She passed her hand over the screen, and the book vanished. 'He's good company,' she said.

He got the point. 'Look, we've got another couple of days out here, Kellie. I'm sorry if I've created a problem. I didn't mean to. It's hard to think about anything right now other than *that* goddam thing.' He gestured toward the after section of the ship. In the direction of the cloud.

'It's okay. I understand.'

He asked how she had come to be there, at the most remote place humans had ever visited. And before they were finished, she'd told him why Digger was such an extraordinary person, and he'd told her about Mary, and about how sorry he was for Judy Sternberg and her team of Goompahs-in-training.

He learned that she loved Offenbach. 'Barcarolle,' from *The Tales of Hoffmann*, was playing in the background while they talked. They discovered a mutual interest in politics, although they disagreed on basic philosophy. But it was all right because they found common cause in the conviction that democratic government was, by its nature, corrupt, and had to be steam-cleaned every once in a while.

She liked live theater, and had thought she'd like to act on the stage, but she was too shy. 'I get scared in front of an audience,' she told him sheepishly. He found that hard to believe.

Collingdale had acted in a couple of shows during his under-graduate days. His biggest role had been playing Octavius in *Man and Superman*.

He wondered why she had chosen so solitary a profession. 'You must run into a lot of people like me,' he said. 'Unsociable types.'

'Not really,' she said. 'Not out here. Everybody loosens up. You can't be alone in a place like this unless you're literally, physically, alone.' She flashed the first truly warm smile he'd seen. 'I love what I do for a living,' she added.

'*Kellie*.' Bill's voice crackled out of the speaker.

'Go ahead.'

'*It's throwing off a big slug of cloud to starboard.*'

She looked at Collingdale.

'You sure?' he asked.

'*Here's the picture.*'

Bill put it on the navigation screen, the largest monitor on the bridge. A large plume was erupting off the right side. 'It's turning,' Collingdale said. He raised a triumphant fist. 'The son of a bitch is *turning*!'

'You really think?' asked Kellie.

'No question. It turns left by throwing dust and gas off to the right.' He was out of his seat, charging around the bridge, unable to contain himself. 'It's taken the bait. It's trying to chase us. It has a hard time turning, but it's trying.' His gaze fell on Kellie. 'I believe I love you,' he said. 'Digger's got it exactly right. I wish you a long and happy marriage.'

ARCHIVE

The beast is in pursuit.

—Ship's Log, NCY *Hawksbill*
December 6

41

On board the *Jenkins*.
Sunday, December 7.

The news that the omega was turning ignited a minor celebration, and induced Digger and Whit to take the day off. They were sitting in the common room, congratulating one another, when Bill broke in. '*Digger, your friend Macao is onstage again,*' he said. '*—In Kulnar.*'

'Doing a *slosh*?' he asked.

'*Yes. Would you like to watch?*'

'Actually, Bill, I'm half-asleep. But Whit might enjoy seeing it.'

Whit looked at him curiously. 'Who's Macao? What's a *slosh*?'

'Whit, you'd be interested. A *slosh* is a kind of public debate. And Macao is the female I told you about.'

'The one you talked to?'

'Yes.'

'Okay. Yes, I'd like very much to see it.'

Digger signaled Bill to start the feed.

Macao's image appeared on-screen. She was in blue and white and was waving her arms in a way that Digger immediately saw signaled frustration. '*—Not claiming that,*' she said. '*But what I*

481

am saying is that we should be ready. It's a storm, like any other storm. Except it's bigger.'

The biggest Goompah that Digger had seen was already on his feet. *'But how do you know, Macao?'* he demanded. *'How could you possibly know?'*

There was only one pickup, and it was positioned so that it caught her in profile. There were about two hundred Goompahs in view, but he guessed they were only half the audience.

'Forget what I know or don't know, Pagwah,' she said. *'Ask yourself what you can lose by moving your family to high ground.'*

Digger translated for Whit.

'What we can lose is that we sit on a mountain and get rained on for three or four days.'

Another voice broke in, from someone off-screen: *'Maybe if you were to tell us how you know what you say you know, we could make more sense of it.'*

The Goompahs pounded their chairs.

'There have been signs,' Macao said. *'Devils on the road, whispers in the night.'*

Whit chuckled. 'Wait till she hears about what happened in *Savakol.'*

'Devils on the road.' A female about six rows back got to her feet. *'You're the one always tells us there are no such things.'*

'I was wrong.'

'Come on, Macao, do we believe in spirits now? Or do we not?'

Digger could see her hesitate. *'I believe they exist,'* she said.

'I almost think you mean it.' Again, Digger couldn't see who was speaking.

'I do mean it.'

'That's quite a change of heart.' This one was difficult to translate. Literally, the speaker said, 'That's not the way you used to put on your pants.'

'Nevertheless it's true.'

They laughed at her. There was a smattering of applause,

possibly for her courage, or maybe because she'd provided a good evening's entertainment. But the mood was different from any of the *sloshen* Digger had seen previously. The others had been lighthearted, even the more serious events. But some of these creatures were *angry*.

'*It may be coming,*' she persisted.

'*But you're not sure.*'

'*There's no way to be sure.*'

'*When is it coming?*'

'*In a few more days.*'

'*Macao.*' Pagwah again. The big one. '*Macao, I'm embarrassed for you, that you would play on everyone's fears at a time like this. I wouldn't have expected it from you.*'

It ended in pushing and shoving and disgruntled patrons stalking out. One of the Goompahs fell down. Some stayed in their seats and pounded their chair arms. Macao thanked them over the general confusion and then she, too, was gone.

She reappeared moments later, at a side door, followed by a small group. They were engaged for a minute or two in animated conversation. Then they left, and the place was empty. An attendant entered, moved across to the far side, and the lamps began to go out.

'Magnificent,' said Whit. 'This is the kind of stuff I came to see.' He produced a notebook and gazed at it. 'I'd like to capture as much of this as I can. *Sloshen.* Uh, that's the correct term, right?'

'Yes.'

'Wonderful,' he said.

'What's wonderful? How do you mean?'

'Nothing seems to be sacred here. They can get up and talk about anything. The audience screams and yells, but the police do not come to get you.' His eyes glowed. 'You thought of this place as Athens when you first saw it.'

'Well, not exactly, Whit. That was *Brackel*.'

'I'm talking about the civilization, not merely this particular city.' He fell silent for a few moments. Then: 'They have more freedom than the Athenians did. More even than *we* do.'

That annoyed Digger. He liked Whit, but he had no patience with crazy academics making charges no one could understand. 'How could they have more freedom than we do?' he demanded. 'We don't have thought police running around.'

'Sure we do,' he said.

'Whit.' Digger raised his eyes to the overhead. 'What kind of speech is prohibited? Other than yelling fire in a crowded place?'

Digger smiled. 'Almost everything,' he said.

He was baffled. 'Whit, that's crazy. When's the last time anybody was jailed for speaking out on something?'

'You don't get jailed. But you have to be careful nonetheless not to offend people. We're programmed, all of us, to take offense. Who can go in front of a mixed audience and say what he truly believes without concern that he will offend someone's heritage, someone's religion, someone's politics. We are always on guard.'

'Well,' said Digger, 'that's different.'

'No it isn't,' said Whit. 'It's different only in degree. At my prep school, it was drilled into us that good manners required we avoid talking politics or religion. Since almost everything in the domain of human behavior falls within one or the other of those two categories, we would seem to be left with the weather.' He looked momentarily bleak. 'We have too much respect for unsubstantiated opinion. We enshrine it, we tiptoe cautiously around it, and we avoid challenging it. To our shame.

'Somewhere we taught ourselves that our opinions are more significant than the facts. And somehow we get our egos and our opinions and Truth all mixed up in a single package, so that when something does challenge one of the notions to which we subscribe, we react as if it challenges *us*.

'We've just watched Macao go in front of an audience and admit that a belief she's probably held all her life, that the world can be explained by reason, is wrong. How many humans do you know who would be capable of doing that?'

'But she was right the first time, Whit. Now she's got it backward.'

'Irrelevant. She's flexible, Digger. It looks as if they all are. Show them the evidence, and they're willing to rethink their position.' He shook his head. 'I think there's much to recommend these creatures.'

The actions of the gods are everywhere around us. We have but to look. What are the stars, if not divine fire? How does one explain the mechanism that carries the sun from the western ocean, where we see it sink each evening, to the eastern sky, where it reappears in all its glory each morning? How else can we account for the presence of plants and animals, which provide our subsistence? Or for the water that we drink? Or the eyes by which we see? The gods have been kind to us, and I sometimes wonder at their patience with those who cannot see their presence, and who deny their bounty.

—*Gesper of* Sakmarung
The Travels
(Translated by Ginko Amagawa)

42

On board the *Hawksbill*.
Monday, December 8.

The cloud had been shedding velocity for months, possibly years. Because the *Hawksbill* was moving at a steady clip, the cloud was falling behind. Collingdale wished they could shed some velocity themselves.

But they couldn't. Not without bumping, and probably collapsing, the kite.

He wondered when they would reach a point from which the cloud would no longer be able to get an approach angle on Lookout. '*Insufficient data*,' said Bill, when he asked the AI. The truth was they simply knew too little about the cloud's capabilities.

Collingdale played with the numbers, but he wasn't much of a mathematician, and it was all guesswork anyhow. It was just past noon on the second day of the pursuit. He thought that if they could get through the rest of the day, and through the next, to about midnight, it would be over. The cloud would be so far off course that no recovery would be possible.

But the omega was becoming steadily smaller on the overhead. It was now eight-hundred kilometers back, almost three times as far as it had been when it turned to follow them.

He was exhausted. He needed some sleep. Needed to think about something else for a while. He'd done nothing since they'd left orbit over Lookout except sit and worry while his adrenaline ran.

Bill announced that Julie was on the circuit.

'*Good news,*' Julie said. She looked tired too. '*Ten-day forecast for* Hopgop, Mandigol, *and the entire northern end of the* Intigo: *Rain and more rain. With lots of low visibility.*'

'How about that?' said Collingdale. 'I guess Marge knows her stuff.'

'Apparently.'

It was a memorable moment. Everything seemed to be working.

He tried to read, tried to work on his notes, tried to play chess with Bill. He talked with Kellie. The only release for his tension came when she admitted to similar feelings. Be glad when it's over. Dump the thing and wave good-bye.

He promised that when they went back to Lookout they'd do a proper celebration of her wedding. 'I guess I pretty much put a cloud over everything.'

'Not really,' she said, but her tone said otherwise.

'Well, we sort of cleared out. Not much of a honeymoon.'

'No. It wasn't.'

'Probably the first time a woman got married and ran off for several days with another man.'

They had an early dinner and watched *The Mile-High Murders*. Kellie guessed after twenty minutes who did it. She was quite good at puzzles and mysteries. Collingdale wondered why she hadn't made more of herself. But she was young. Still plenty of time.

When it was over he excused himself and retired. An hour later he was back on the bridge clad in a robe. At about midnight Kellie joined him. 'Wide awake,' she said. 'I keep asking Bill if the cloud's still behind us. If the kite's still in place.'

It was eleven hundred klicks back now.

At about 3:00 A.M., when both were dozing, Bill broke in: '*The cloud has begun throwing jets out to the rear.*'

Thank God. 'Excellent,' said Collingdale.

Kellie was still trying to get awake. 'Why?' she asked.

'It's accelerating. It wants to catch us. Or, rather, catch the kite.'

She looked at him, and smiled. 'I guess it's over.'

Collingdale shook his head. Don't get excited yet. 'Another twenty hours or so,' he said. 'Then I think it will be time to declare victory.'

Bill put the images from the monitors on-screen. A couple of plumes had indeed appeared at the rear of the cloud and were growing as they watched.

He dozed off again, and woke to find her gone. 'Bill,' he said.

'*Yes, David?*'

'Is it still there?'

'*Yes, David.*'

'Range?'

'*Twelve-fifty. It is still losing ground, but not quite as quickly.*'

'Excellent, Bill. Good show.'

'*Thank you, sir.*'

'You're not really aware of any of this, are you? I mean, you don't know what we've actually accomplished, do you?'

'*In fact, I do, David.*'

'Are you as pleased as I?'

'*I have no way to gauge the level of your pleasure.*'

He thought about it a moment. 'I wonder if you're really there.'

'*Of course I am, sir.*'

'Well, I'm glad to hear it.'

Kellie came back. 'I heard voices,' she said. 'Everything okay?'

'So far.'

At midmorning, the *Jenkins* reported that Digger and Whit had decided to play it safe, and were back on the ground positioning projectors. This had happened, Julie said, not because anyone had any doubts that the *Hawksbill* had turned the cloud aside, but because Whit enjoyed wandering invisible among the theaters and cafés. And Digger wanted to keep him happy.

'She doth protest too much,' said Kellie.

But it was a good idea. Collingdale felt that he was in control, but caution back at Lookout couldn't hurt.

They ate breakfast, took turns napping, and watched another sim, a musical, *The Baghdad Follies*. When it was over, Kellie suggested lunch, but neither of them was hungry. Their package of daily newscasts and specialty shows arrived during the early afternoon. The newscasts consisted of the usual array of political shenanigans, corporate scandal, and occasional murder. A pair of Holy Balu parents had run off with their desperately ill child rather than allow doctors to cure him, using a technique that required infusion of synthetic blood. Kosmik, Inc., the terraforming and transportation giant, had collapsed amid charges of theft, profiteering, and collusion at the top. A battle had broken out over implants that could increase one's intelligence, or maybe not, depending on how one defined the word.

By late afternoon they were beginning to feel safe.

'Bill,' said Collingdale, 'how about giving us another two degrees? To port?' Jerk the son of a bitch around a little bit more.

Kellie confirmed the order.

'*Executing*,' said Bill.

The thrusters realigned themselves and fired briefly. The ship angled a bit farther away from Lookout.

The viewports lit up. Lightning out there somewhere. But that was nothing new.

'I'll be right back,' Kellie said.

She left him alone on the bridge. It was a good moment, filled with a sense of victory, of having beaten long odds. Of having taken a measure of vengeance for Moonlight.

Kellie came back carrying a bottle of chablis and two glasses. She filled both and held one out for him. 'Sorry,' she said. 'The champagne supply is depleted.'

He took his glass and looked at it. She raised hers. 'To the Goompahs,' she said.

It would have been hard to find a man less given to superstition than David Collingdale. And yet – he raised his own. 'May their luck hold,' he said, and drank.

As if the comment had stirred him, Bill's voice broke through the mood.

'*The cloud is turning to starboard.*'

'You mean to port,' said Kellie.

'*To starboard. It is turning back toward its original course.*'

Collingdale's blood froze. 'Bill, are you sure?'

'*Yes. It's throwing off more plumes. To port. And forward. I do believe it's trying to brake again.*'

Kellie looked at him. 'Dave, can it still get to Lookout?'

'I don't know. How the hell can I tell what the damned thing can do?'

She centered the cloud's vector on the navigation screen, then added the kite's image. The kite, which had been centered, was off to the left. The omega *was* turning.

They informed Digger.

'*What happened?*' he demanded. His voice suggested it was Collingdale's fault.

'We think we got too far away from it.'

'*Can't you slow down? Get back in front of it again? Dangle the kite in its nose?*'

'Negative,' said Kellie. 'We can't maneuver with the kite tied on our rear end. It's sitting right behind the tubes.'

'*Well, what the hell—*'

'*There is good news,*' said Bill. '*We have thrown it off its timetable. On its original trajectory, it would have arrived directly over the* Intigo. *Preliminary projection suggests that, if it can reach Lookout at all, it will get there a day and a half later.*'

'Oh,' said Digger. '*A day and a half. Well, that makes all the difference in the world.*'

'No.' Kellie pressed an index finger to her lips. 'That means it hits the back side of Lookout.'

'That's correct,' said Collingdale.

They listened to Digger breathing. '*Okay,*' he said finally. '*You guys better just get out of there. We'll do what we can on this end.*'

Collingdale couldn't see any difference in the cloud, couldn't see that it had changed course, couldn't see that it had thrown on its brakes and was doing the equivalent of a sharp right turn. It would be a few hours before the change became noticeable.

'There might be something we could try,' he said. 'How about we cut the kite loose so we can move around a little.'

'And then what?'

'Kellie, the *Hawksbill* is a big, oversize box of a ship. We could take it around and dangle ourselves in front of the thing, see if we can distract it.'

'Dangle *ourselves*?'

Bad choice of phrase there. 'The ship. Dangle the ship.'

'I'm not sure I see the difference.'

'Listen, if we get closer to it, and line ourselves up with the kite, which we can do if we move quickly, it'll be looking at *two* boxes. It might be enough to draw it away.'

'It might get us killed.'

He let her see that he understood what she was saying. 'It might make all the difference. If we can push it a bit farther, just a little bit, maybe just a hesitation on its part, it might save everything—'

'—How close were you thinking of going?'

'Whatever it takes.'

'Damn it, David. The *Hawksbill* is a target. We are exactly what that thing has for breakfast. What it might do is gobble us up and keep going.'

'Okay.' He allowed the contempt he felt to show in his voice. 'Okay, let's go home.'

She looked at him suspiciously.

'I mean it,' he said. 'You're the captain.'

'Bill,' she said, 'release the kite and retract the cables. We're going back to Lookout.'

'In a few days, though,' he continued, 'when that thing rolls in on the Goompahs, and kills them by the tens of thousands, you're going to remember you had a chance to stop it.'

She froze at that, as he knew she would. 'Collingdale,' she said, 'you are a son of a bitch.'

'*Kite released,*' said Bill.

'You know I'm right,' he said, 'without my having to say it. If I weren't here, if you were alone, you'd do it.'

He thought he saw fear in her eyes. But she pulled herself together. 'Buckle in,' she told him. They waited in a silence you could have hit with a sledgehammer until Bill announced that the cables were safely withdrawn.

'This way,' he said, listening to his words echo around the bridge, 'we won't have to fight a guilty conscience. Either of us.'

She ignored him. 'Bill,' she said, 'get us well away from the kite. When we can use the main engines, put us back in front of the cloud. I want to come in over the top again, from the rear, and I want to drop down in front of it, match course and speed, and line up between the face of the thing and the kite.'

'*How close do you wish to cut it, Kellie?*'

'I'll let you know when we get there,' she said.

She settled in front of the cloud at a range of three hundred klicks. Ahead, the box kite was a bright star. But the cloud was visibly leaning to starboard.

They sat in frozen silence. Vast plumes were boiling out of the omega's forward section, marking its efforts to slow down. One approached as she watched, fascinated. It exploded past the ship, and minutes later, raced past the kite.

Collingdale waited, trying to be patient, watching the screen. Watching the gap widen between the cloud and the kite. Hoping to see the omega notice they were there and begin another pursuit. 'Bill,' he said, 'are we picking up any change?'

'*Negative,*' said the AI. '*The cloud is still braking, still angling to starboard.*'

'It might take a while,' said Kellie.

'No.' He found himself wishing she were off the ship. Somewhere else. He could have handled things himself, but the rules required a licensed captain. If he were alone with the AI, everything would be much simpler. He wouldn't be risking anybody else. 'We're too far away,' he said. 'We have to get closer to have a chance.'

Whatever she was about to say to him, she swallowed. Instead she turned back to the AI. 'Bill, I'm going to manual.'

Bill didn't say anything. Didn't have to, probably. Kellie's fingers danced across her control board. Views from forward and aft telescopes appeared on-screen. A second jet fountained past. Retros fired, and Collingdale was forced forward against his restraints.

'How close do you want to go?' she asked.

'I don't know,' he said. 'We have to do this by the seat of our pants.' Damn, she was irritating.

Lightning flickered.

And again.

'Maybe we're getting its attention,' she said.

'I hope so.'

She shut the retros down. 'It's at 240 klicks,' she said. 'And closing.'

'Okay. That's good. Let it keep coming.'

Something crackled against the hull. It was like being hit by a sandstorm.

'Dust,' she said. 'Part of the cloud. We may be getting too close.'

The viewport lit up again and stayed that way. Something hit the ship, rolled it. Collingdale lurched against his harness. One of the screens exploded; the others went blank. There was a second shock, stronger than the first, driving the wind out of him. Glass and plastic rained down. The bridge went dark. For a few moments he could hear only the crackle of blowing circuits and the sound of his own breathing. He could smell things burning. 'Kellie—'

'Hang on. Everything'll be back in a minute.'

He hoped so. 'What—?'

It was as far as he got. His chair shoved him hard forward, and he could almost hear the thunderclap, hear the shielding sizzling. The lights on the bridge blinked on, went back out. He started to float against his restraints.

'Controls are down,' she said. 'Get us out of here, Bill. Head for open sky.'

The only response was a distant murmur.

'Bill?'

Somewhere in the bulkhead he could hear a fan. A lamp came on at Kellie's position. She was doing things with the status board. 'Engines are out,' she said.

'Can you get them running again?'

'Trying.'

'Are we still dropping back into the cloud?'

'Yes. Nothing we can do about that at the moment.' She shook her head. Not good. 'Junction box problem, looks like.'

'Can you fix it?'

'I can replace it.' Another bolt hit. The ship shuddered. Red warning lamps came on and glowed scarlet. 'But not in fifteen minutes.' Which was a generous estimate of the time they had left.

She got one of the tracking screens back up. That allowed him to watch the misty forward wall closing on them. Another jet was erupting. 'It's still trying for Lookout,' she said. He couldn't decide whether her voice carried a ring of sarcasm. 'We just happen to be in the way.'

'How about the jump engines?'

'Not without prep. They'll explode.'

He looked at her. 'What else have we got?'

'Not much.' She was scrabbling in one of the utility drawers and came out with a lantern. 'Grab an e-suit and some air tanks. We're leaving.'

'To go where?'

'The shuttle.'

The *Hawksbill* wasn't designed for convenience. The shuttle bay was down in cargo, which could receive life support, but seldom did. It depended on what the ship was hauling. Collingdale slipped into an e-suit, activated it, and pulled on a pair of air tanks. Kellie led the way through the airlock and down into the bowels of the ship.

'Power's off here,' she said.

'What about the shuttle?'

'No way to know until we get there.'

He hadn't had to move in a zero-gee environment in a long time, but the technique came back quickly. They passed along wire mesh, down a dark corridor, through the cavernous space in which Marge's equipment had been stored, and crossed into the lower cargo section, which also served as the launch bay for the shuttle. The bulkheads were filled with equipment for working outside, laser cutters, wrenches, gauges, coils of cable, and with go-packs as well as more air tanks.

The shuttle rested atop its dock. She activated it with a remote. To his relief, lights came on, and the engine began to purr. She opened the hatch, but before they climbed in she aimed the remote at the airlock and pressed it.

Nothing happened.

'Door doesn't work,' she said. 'Hold on a second.'

He followed her across the bay. 'You'll have to open it manually,' he said.

'My thought exactly.' She sounded annoyed. Nevertheless, he found the wall panel before she did.

'Here,' he said.

She opened it and extracted the handle. He stepped in beside her and pulled it down. The inner doors irised open. They repeated the process, and an outer door rolled into the overhead.

He looked out at a river of dust and gas. It was one of the

jets, streaming past, close enough to touch. The omega itself filled the sky behind them.

'It's on top of us,' he said.

'Come on.' Kellie stayed cool. She moved through the weightless environment like a dancer, soared into the shuttle, and urged him to hurry.

Collingdale was no slouch either, and he climbed in quickly beside her and shut the hatch. And saw immediately the look on her face. 'What's wrong?'

'No power in the dock.' She rolled her eyes. 'Should have realized.' She opened up again and got out. Collingdale needed a moment to understand. The shuttle was secured to its launch platform.

He jumped out behind her. 'Has to be a manual release here somewhere.'

'I don't see it.'

The airlock was filling with mist. 'Time's up,' she said. She broke away from the shuttle, grabbed two pairs of air tanks from the bulkhead, and floated one his way.

'What's this for?' he asked. They were already wearing tanks.

'Extras,' she said. 'We're going to be out there for a while.' She pulled a go-pack over her shoulders.

'Kellie, what are you doing?'

'We're leaving.'

'What? No! You can't possibly get clear in that.'

'It's all we have. We can't stay here.'

'They don't even know we're in trouble.'

'They'll know our signal's been cut off.'

He took a last desperate look for the manual release, did not see it, concluded it was in the bulkhead somewhere, thought how they should have taken more time to familiarize themselves with the ship, and turned back to her. The cloud was literally coming in the open airlock. Coming after him.

'It's not fast enough,' he said. The go-pack. 'You can't outrun it in that.'

497

She apparently had lost all interest in arguing. She grabbed his shoulder and pushed him toward the exit, simultaneously shoving the go-pack into his midsection. But it was hopeless.

In that terrible moment, he realized suddenly, as if everything that had gone before had been simply a problem to be solved, that there was no solution. That he was going to die.

All that remained was to choose the method.

'Get out, Kellie,' he said, and pulled away from her. He went back through the doorway and into the lower cargo section.

'*What are you doing, Dave?*' she demanded.

He found her lamp floating near the shuttle, turned it on, and began to search through the equipment.

'What are you looking for?'

'A laser cutter.' And there they were, three of them, neatly stored side by side above a utility shelf at the dock. 'Get as far away as you can,' he said. He held the cutter up where she could see it and started for the engine room.

Her eyes widened. She understood perfectly what he had decided. She pleaded with him over the circuit, threatened him, told him he was a damned idiot. He wished her luck, told her he was sorry, and shut down all channels.

That would end it. She'd give up and do what she could to save herself. Through the airlock with an extra set of air tanks but a go-pack that wouldn't be able to take her far enough fast enough to outrun the cloud. Or to outrun what he was about to do.

He regretted that. In those last minutes he regretted a lot of things.

Carrying the lamp and the laser, he hurried through the lower decks and the airlock they'd left open and emerged at last on the bridge. Here and there lights still worked, and the electronic systems were trying to come back. Once, the artificial gravity took hold, throwing him to the deck. Then it was gone again. Moments later, he thought he heard Bill's voice, deep in the ship.

Somewhere, a Klaxon began to sound.

He needed the remote, but he'd left it below in cargo. Or maybe Kellie still had it. There was usually a spare, and he searched through the storage cabinets for it. But he didn't see one. Well, he'd have to do without. Find another way. He ducked out of the bridge and headed aft.

He'd lived on the *Hawksbill* for two months, but the ship had changed in some subtle way. These dark corridors, with their shadows and their silence, were unfamiliar, places he'd never been before.

He caught another burst of gravity, stumbled, rolled, and came up running. Not bad for an old guy. Then it died again.

He could hear the sound of hatches closing. Sealing off compartments.

He had to open one, and then a second, to get into the engine room. They both closed automatically behind him.

The good news was that the lights were on and the jump engines had power. The fusion unit was down, dark, silent, useless. But that didn't matter. He had what he needed.

He felt oddly calm. Almost happy. He might not succeed in damaging the cloud, but he'd strike a blow. Make it recognize he was there.

And he wondered if, somewhere deeper than his conscious mind had been able to go, he had foreseen this eventuality, had almost planned it. It accounted for his intense interest in the *Hawksbill*, his drive to have Julie explain everything.

The possibility strengthened his resolve, suggested that he would be successful after all, that there was something at work here greater than he knew. A destiny, of sorts. He didn't believe in such nonsense, and yet now, in these final moments, it was a possibility to which he could cling.

He found the manual controls and flicked them on. Watched lights come up. He told it to activate the engines. Go to jump.

A voice, not Bill's, responded. '*Unable to comply. The unit is not charged.*'

'Override all injunctions.'

'Unable to comply.'

'This is Juliet Carson. Override.'

'Please enter code.'

Well, he'd expected it. But the system was designed to prevent tinkering, and not outright sabotage.

There was an explosion up front somewhere. Near the bridge.

He aimed the laser cutter, ignited it, and took a long look at the engine. The design of these things hadn't changed much since his day.

He applied the torch to the metal and prayed for time. Cut through the outer housing. Cut through the protective shell. Get to the junction box, the same device that had failed in the fusion engines.

It was hard work because he needed the lamp to see into the housing. So he had to use a hand to hold the lamp, and a hand to hold the cutter, and a hand to keep from floating away.

But finally he was in.

And it was simply a matter of removing the flow control, and power would pass into the system and start the jump process. Or in this case, because the protective bubble wasn't adequately charged, it would release some antimatter fuel and blow the ship into oblivion. Maybe, if he was extraordinarily lucky, it would find a vulnerable spot in whatever system controlled the cloud. And put it out of action, too.

It wasn't much of a chance, but it could happen.

He thought of calling Kellie, of telling her how sorry he was, of letting her know it was moments away. But it would be better not to. More compassionate. Let it come as a surprise.

He would have preferred to wait until he got deeper into the cloud. But he had no way of knowing when the power would fail altogether. And then he'd have nothing.

Another Klaxon started, and shut down.

He sliced the flow control.

LIBRARY ENTRY

Sometime within the next few days, the civilization which refers to itself as Korbikkan, which we call Goompah, will be wiped out. The omega will collide with their world and devastate its handful of cities while we sit watching placidly.

So far, there is no word of any serious action being taken on their behalf, no indication we have planned anything except to try a decoy, and if that doesn't work, which it clearly won't, we'll make it rain, and then claim we tried to help. The problem is that the effort, such as it is, is being run by the usual bureaucrats.

It's too late for the Goompahs, I am sorry to say. And the day is coming when another crowd of bureaucrats of the same stripe will be charged with rescuing us from the same unhappy result. It gives one pause.

—Carolyn Magruder Reports
UNN broadcast
Monday, December 8, 2234

43

On the ground at *Roka*.
Monday, December 8.

Digger had just finished inserting a projector under the roof overhang of a shop that sold fish when the news came.

'*They're off the circuit.*' Julie's voice. '*All channels.*'

It was probably just a transmitter glitch. But a terrible fear clawed at him. He should have refused to let her go. He'd known from the beginning that he should have kept her away from that thing. He could have simply raised so much hell that they'd have backed off. If Collingdale wanted to go, let him go. But let Bill take him. Why did he have to have Kellie along?

'*Digger? Do you hear me?*'

'Yes.'

'*It doesn't mean there's a major problem.*'

'I know.' He was standing on top of a storage box, and he didn't want to come down. Didn't want to move. 'Pick us up,' he said. 'I'll get Whit.'

Whit tried to be reassuring, thing like this you always think the worst, she's a good pilot. They decided where they'd meet,

503

and Digger passed the word to Julie. An hour later they were back on the *Jenkins*, leaving orbit.

The run out to the cloud took four hours. It was a frantic four hours for Digger, who tried tirelessly to raise the *Hawksbill*, and for the others, who didn't know what to say to him.

When they arrived in its vicinity, they found the box kite, cruising quietly ahead of the omega, gradually pulling away from the giant. Bill reported that he was in contact with the surveillance packages the *Hawksbill* had been using to monitor the omega.

'*But I do not see the* Hawksbill *itself,*' he added.

There was no wreckage, no indication what could have happened. *They must have gotten too close.*

Each of them, in turn, said much the same thing. Even Digger admitted the ship was lost, had to be lost, no other explanation for it. Yet he could not believe Kellie was gone. She was too smart. Too alive.

'They'd have let us know if they were in trouble, wouldn't they?' he demanded of Julie.

'Maybe they didn't have time. Maybe it happened too quickly.'

For a while, they lived with the hope that the cloud was between them and the *Hawksbill*, that it had somehow blocked off the ship's transmissions as it was now preventing a visual sighting. But Digger knew the truth of it, although he would not accept it, as if refusing to do so kept her chances alive. He walked through the ship in a state of shock.

Julie invited him onto the bridge, tried to find things for him to do. In his heart he damned Collingdale, and damned Hutchins for sending him.

He could not have told anyone what time of day it was, or whether they were actively searching or just going through the motions, or whether there was anyplace left to look. He listened to Bill's reports, *negative, negative*, to Marge and Whit talking in whispers, to Julie talking with Bill and maybe sending off the news to Broadside.

And he became aware that they were waiting for him to say the word, to recognize that there was no way the *Hawksbill* could be intact without their knowing, that it was hopeless, but that they would not stop looking until he told them to do so.

There was always a chance they were in the shuttle, he told himself. The shuttle could easily be hidden among all the jets and dust and shreds and chunks of cloud, its relatively weak radio signal blown away by the electrical activity in the area.

It was possible.

The first indication there might be something out there came in the form not of a radio signal, but, incredibly, of a sensor reading of a small metal object, glimpsed briefly and then lost.

'Metal,' said Julie. 'It was small.'

'The shuttle?'

'Smaller than that.'

The return of hope was somehow painful. He could lose her again.

'Where?' demanded Digger.

'Hold on.' The area around the cloud was a vast debris field. Bill drew a vector. '*Somewhere along that line.*'

They picked it up again. '*I believe,*' said the AI, '*it's a set of air tanks.*'

Air tanks? Then somebody was attached to them, right?

'*Negative,*' said Bill. '*Tanks only.*'

They tracked them and took them on board. Saw the *Hawksbill* label on the shoulder strap. Noted that they were exhausted.

'They're out there,' said Digger. Julie nodded. Empty tanks meant someone had used them for six hours, then discarded them. You only did that if you had a spare set of tanks.

At least one of them was still afloat.

They checked the time: ten and a half hours since the signal had been lost. Six hours to a set of tanks.

How many spares could you carry?

Then Bill announced he'd picked up a radio signal.

* * *

Kellie burst into tears when they hauled her inside. Tough, stoic, always in control, she let them remove her tanks and go-pack and shut off the suit, and she made no effort to restrain her emotions. Her right arm was broken, and she had a few torn ligaments and a bunch of bruises, but she was alive and that was all that mattered.

She smiled weakly at Digger and told Bill she wished he were human so she could kiss him.

Bill promptly appeared, his younger, lean, devil-may-care version, with dark hair and dark skin and dark eyes that literally flashed.

'He's gone,' she said of Collingdale. 'He stayed with the *Hawksbill*.' She explained how it had lost power, how Collingdale had refused to abandon it, had decided they couldn't survive, that he would ride it inside the cloud and detonate the Hazeltines.

'It doesn't look as if he did any lasting damage,' said Whit.

'No,' agreed Bill. '*The cloud will make its rendezvous with Lookout*.'

Julie looked puzzled. 'How'd you get clear? Of the blast and the cloud? You couldn't have done it with that.' She was looking at the go-pack.

Whit handed her a painkiller, and they were taking her back to the med station.

'There was a plume,' she said. 'A jet stream. It only took a few minutes to get to it, and it blew me out of the neighborhood pretty quick.' She looked at her arm. 'That's where I took the damage.'

ARCHIVE

The gulfs between the stars overwhelm us, as the eons overwhelm our paltry few years of sunlight. We are cast adrift on an endless sea, to no purpose, with no destination, bound where no one knows.

—Dmitri Restov
Last Rites

LIBRARY ENTRY

Mary,

 I'm sorry to tell you that we lost David this morning. We all admired him, and everyone here shares your grief. I'm sure you'll be receiving official notification from the Academy in a few days.

 It might console you to know that he died heroically, in the best of causes. His action here appears to have thrown the omega off schedule and thereby bought some time. It's likely that many who would have been lost at the Intigo will survive as a result of your fiancé's efforts.

—Julie Carson
December 8

PART FIVE
Lykonda

44

Near *Avapol*.
Friday, December 12.

The sky was blanketed by Marge's rain clouds. Three of her chimneys were up and running. The fourth would be erected that night on an island forty klicks off the west coast, midway between *Mandigol* and *Sakmarung*. Over the last two days, no one in *Hopgop* or *Roka*, or in the four cities located in the center of the isthmus, had seen the sun, the stars, or the apparition.

It was still visible from *T'Mingletep* and *Savakol* in the south, and from *Saniusar* in the far north. There, the Goompahs watched the omega grow visibly larger each night. It filled their sky, a terrifying vision, grim and churning and lit within by demon-fire.

Digger sat, concealed within his lightbender, in a pavilion in the middle of a rainswept park. The park was deserted, as were the surrounding streets. Whit was out positioning projectors. He'd gotten good at it, and obviously enjoyed the work.

They'd done the calculations again, and the cloud was not compensating for its new position, was probably unable to compensate, and would consequently reach Lookout when it was early afternoon on the *Intigo*. Since it was coming out of the night, that meant it should expend most of its energy on the far side of the world.

Halleluia! Add that to the cloud cover Marge was putting up, and the Goompahs had a decent chance.

'Don't get too confident,' Whit had warned him. 'Conditions here will still be extreme.'

Digger had seen only the shimmering haze of Whit's light-bender, and considered how difficult it was to communicate when you couldn't see people's expressions. Was he becoming seriously pessimistic? Or cautious? Or was it just a reflex that you never claim victory lest you tempt the fates?

'And don't forget the round-the-world mission,' he'd added, apparently determined to dampen the mood. He'd been like this since they'd lost Collingdale. The others had expressed their regrets, had been sorry; but Collingdale reportedly hadn't been easy to get to know. Digger, in fact, had barely had time to say hello as he passed through the wedding and took Kellie and the *Hawksbill* out to chase the omega. Kellie had spoken little about him since her return. He hoped she was too smart to assign any guilt to herself for the loss, but she had made it clear she didn't want to talk about the experience.

Whit, however, must have been closer to Collingdale than anyone had realized. He'd been visibly shaken by his death.

The round-the-world mission had been gone ten weeks. Bill was keeping an eye on them and reporting periodically. They'd lost a couple of sailors. One had fallen overboard; another had contracted a disease of some sort and been buried at sea. Otherwise, not much was happening. The wind stops, they stop. The wind picks up, and they're off again. *'They're steering crooked,'* Bill had been saying the last three days. *'They're off course. Had almost a week of bad weather, so I guess they can't see the stars to navigate.'*

The ships were approaching the eastern continent and would soon, Digger thought, have to turn back.

The rain around the pavilion was almost torrential. It had been

512

falling steadily for a night and a day. Marge, it seemed, was very good at what she did for a living.

A couple of signs were posted announcing an afternoon *slosh* at *Broka* Hall, giving the time by sundial. In the event of rain, bells would be rung at intervals. A *moraka* was also scheduled that evening at the edge of the park, weather permitting. Music and snacks. Compliments of the *Korkoran* Philosophical Society.

Whit had known what a *slosh* was. But he had not seen the term *moraka* previously.

'It's hard to explain,' Digger had told him.

'Try.'

'It's an orgy.'

'Really?'

'Yes.'

'*The orgy starts at nine?*'

'Something like that.'

'Sponsored by the Philosophical Society?'

'Apparently so.' Digger grinned.

'This place has some unique aspects.'

There was no one about. He could see a Goompah adjusting shutters in one of the buildings lining the park, and another hurrying across a street. And that was it.

Bill broke into his musings. '*Weather update*,' he said in a voice copied from weather reports back home. He enjoyed doing that. '*Expect continued rain in the central sections of the isthmus at least until tomorrow.*'

'Bill,' he said, 'we only have three chimneys up. Are they more effective than we thought?'

'*I do not think so, Digger. I believe what we are seeing is partially due to natural meteorological conditions. The arrival of a low-pressure area from the west coincided—*'

'—It's okay, I don't need the details. Is there any chance the rain will remain with us over the next few days?'

'*Until the cloud arrives? No. The weather system will pass over the isthmus by midday tomorrow. After that, it will be up to Marge's chimneys.'*

The streets and cafés in the cities were virtually deserted. The Goompahs were staying home in substantial numbers.

Signs had been posted announcing *sloshen* to discuss 'recent unsettling events.' Digger and Whit had posted projectors at a couple of them so they could watch from the ship. Ironically, the unseasonable weather had added to native disquiet, as had reports of voices and disembodied eyes, mystical flashes in the sky (which might have been the chimneys or the AV3, or both). There'd been *zhoka* sightings on the highways and, most terrifying of all, the levitation of Tayma, the priestess at *Savakol*, followed by a window opening in midair. Witnessed by hundreds.

Digger, Whit, and Kellie had watched fully a dozen Goompahs rise and swear they were there, or knew someone who was there, when it happened. 'She literally rose out of the sea,' one bull-sized male had said, 'and floated through thin air across the water, over the water, until she was set down by an unseen hand on the beach.'

The consensus seemed to be that the confluence of supernatural events portended approaching catastrophe. But they wondered, if such a thing were actually about to happen, why the gods were permitting it. Where were they, anyhow? There was a palpable sense of irritation that the local deities were not on the job.

Earlier that day, Digger had stood outside a schoolroom and listened to the teacher and students discuss the approaching cloud. The students were probably a young-adolescent equivalent. It was hard to tell. But some of them wanted to know whether the teacher still believed that supernatural events did not happen.

'It is simply,' the teacher had argued, 'that there are parts of the natural world we do not yet understand.'

The youth in *Avapol* may have been too polite to laugh, and too smart to argue: but even Digger, who had not yet begun to learn the nuances of nonverbal communication among this alien race, could see what they thought of that opinion.

As Whit put a projector in a tree, he caught a glimpse of Digger. When he'd finished, he turned, looked toward the pavilion, and waved. Digger waved back.

'*That's the last one,*' Kellie told him. She was in the lander. This was her first day back at work, giving Julie a well-earned chance to sleep in a bed again.

The last one in *Avapol*. They still had two cities to visit.

It was getting tight. The Goompahs would have three more days of relative calm. During the midafternoon of the third day, the omega would hit the far side of the planet, and conditions would deteriorate. The cloud that had struck Moonlight had delivered most of its energy during the first seven hours. It had systematically picked out every city around the globe still standing and demolished it. Then it had abated.

At Lookout, the actions of the *Hawksbill* had thrown the omega off schedule. Furthermore, Marge's weather would hide the targets. The cloud, not knowing better, would raise hell on the other side of the planet, and the Goompahs, during the first few hours, would get their feet wet. During the course of the evening the *Intigo* would rotate beneath the main body of the storm, but by the time it arrived in the lethal zone, the thing would be starting to dissipate. And it would, they hoped, not even see the cities.

'*You guys ready to come home?*'

Digger watched Whit moving steadily through the rain. 'Give us thirty minutes to get there.'

She would pick them up on a hilltop on the northern edge of town. '*I'll be there,*' she said.

Digger got up from his bench.

'*By the way,*' she said, '*the media have arrived.*'

'Really?'

'*The Black Cat Network, of all people.*' The Black Cat Network tended toward sensationalist journalism. *'They're asking permission to send in a ground team.'*

'Tell them no. We have no authority.'

'I already told them.'

He sighed. He couldn't really blame them. This was a pretty big story. And they'd come a long way for it. He was tempted to tell them to go ahead, but if he did, Hutch would fry his rear end. 'They can do whatever they need to with telescopes.'

'Okay.'

'And tell them they can have access to the pickups.' He thought about that. Maybe it wasn't a good idea. For one thing, they'd undoubtedly find out about the *morakas*. 'Do we have guidance from the Academy on any of this?'

'Hutch says cooperate, but they are not to set foot on the surface. If they do, they will be prosecuted. She says they've been warned.'

'Okay. Tell them we'll help where we can. Don't mention the pickups.'

'Good,' she said. *'I think that's prudent.'*

BLACK CAT REPORT

Thanks, Ron. This is Rose Beetem in the skies over Lookout. At the moment, we can't show you the cities of the Goompahs. They're under a heavy cover of rainstorms. I have to report to you that we have been asked not to land on the planetary surface, because of the Noninterference Protocol, and we are adhering to that request.

But we expect to be able to follow the action on the ground as the situation develops. Meantime, it is late evening over the Goompah cities, which are concentrated on a relatively small landmass in the southern hemisphere. What you are looking at now is the rim of the omega. It is just rising, and, as you can see, it is an incredible spectacle . . .

Avery Whitlock's Notebooks

It is hard not to conclude that my entire life has been a prelude to and a preparation for this moment. If we do not succeed here, nothing else I've done will have mattered very much.

—December 12

45

On board the *Jenkins*.
Sunday, December 14.

'*We'll be leaving orbit in thirty minutes.*' Kellie's voice came over the speaker from the bridge. She'd resumed command of the *Jenkins*.

They were running through the night beneath the cloud. The *Intigo* was on the daylight side of the globe, approaching evening. In a couple of hours, when it rotated beneath the omega, and the ship had withdrawn to a safe distance from Lookout, they would put Digger's plan into effect and see whether the Goompahs could be persuaded to head for the high country. They'd have the night and much of the following day to get out of town. Then, at about midafternoon the omega would impact the far side, weather conditions would worsen, and the event would begin.

The projectors were in place, and the chimneys were up. Clouds were spreading out from *T'Mingletep* on the south to *Saniusar* in the north.

The situation was promising. The omega would, as predicted, hit the wrong side and spend the bulk of its fury before the cities of the *Intigo* rotated into its path.

Moody and dark and silent, lit by only an occasional flicker, it had almost completely blotted out the stars. The Goompahs could no longer see it, but the crew of the *Jenkins* knew. Digger hated looking at the thing. There was a tendency on the ship to walk softly, to hold one's breath, and to speak in low tones, as if a little noise might draw its attention.

The plumes reached well past Lookout and lost themselves in the dazzle of the sun. On the surface of the threatened world, seas had become rough, in anticipation of the onslaught. Around the *Intigo*, the weather had grown cold and wet.

On the *Jenkins*, as they counted down the last few minutes, they talked about the ongoing debates over enhanced intelligence, about a report from Hutch that clouds did not survive their encounters with their hedgehogs, about an assassination attempt in the NAU Senate, about a new teaching system designed to bolster lagging literacy scores. The approaching omega was the elephant in the room, the thing no one mentioned.

The promised celebration of the marriage between Kellie and Digger never really happened. They'd had a few drinks and exchanged embraces all around, but that was about it. Maybe it seemed inappropriate after Collingdale's death, or maybe nobody really wanted to celebrate anything until they had the results on Lookout.

'*Daylight coming,*' said Kellie.

The sun rose over the rim of the world, and the omega dropped down the sky behind them and receded below the horizon until only the plumes remained visible, great dark towers soaring into the heavens.

'Good riddance,' said Marge.

'Next time they want somebody to wrestle one of these things,' Digger said, 'they're going to have to find somebody else.'

'Twelve minutes to departure,' said Kellie. 'Lockdown in eight. Anybody needs to do anything, this would be a good time.'

Digger felt an enormous sense of relief to be putting some distance between himself and the omega.

Julie commented that she was having the time of her life, and they all looked at her as if she'd lost her mind. 'Well,' she said. 'I haven't been around as long as some of you guys have, but if things go well, or even if they don't, I expect this will be the high point of my career. How often do you get involved in something that really matters?'

Mouths of babes, thought Digger. He was jiggling a puzzle on his monitor. Find your way out of the maze.

They were over ocean. Daylight sparkled off a few clouds, and he saw land in the north. In a little more than an hour it would be getting dark along the *Intigo*. Their last peaceful night.

Digger gave up on the maze – he'd never been good at puzzles anyhow – and headed for one of the acceleration couches. It felt good to lie down, punch the button, and feel the harness settle over him. The others laughed at him. 'Anxious?' asked Whit.

'You bet.'

'I guess we all are.' Julie took one of the chairs; Marge, the other couch. Whit settled in beside Julie. 'Congratulations,' he said.

She smiled. There was a touch of innocence in it, and Digger couldn't help thinking again how young she looked. When they wrote the history of these proceedings, he suspected she'd get left out, pretty much. Collingdale would be seen as a hero who'd sacrificed himself to turn the cloud aside. He still didn't have the story from Kellie, but he suspected something else had been at work. Otherwise, she wouldn't have been so quiet. But it was okay. You always need heroes.

Marge would rank up there, too. And Jack, the first victim. That brought a rush of guilt. Killed by the stupidity of a colleague. If the historians ever got the truth, old Digger wouldn't look very good.

Bill's voice broke in. '*Marge, Kellie asked me to pass the current weather report along.*'

He wondered why it mattered at that point.

'What've you got, Bill?' she asked.

'*There's a storm system building to the west of the* Intigo.'

'That's just what we want, isn't it?' said Digger. He glanced over at Marge and gave her a thumbs-up. 'An assist for the little lady,' he said.

She frowned. 'Maybe not. Bill, what kind of storm?'

'*Electrical. I'd say the isthmus is going to get heavy rains tonight.*'

Digger didn't like the way she looked. 'What's wrong?' he asked. 'Why is that not good news?'

'Think about it. How are you going to send signals to the projectors you've been planting all over the isthmus? During an electrical storm?'

Uh-oh.

'Isn't it a bit late in the season for thunderstorms?'

Marge shrugged. 'Don't know. We've haven't really had a chance to look at climatic conditions here. In any case, they could be starting to feel the effects of the omega.' The plumes had been burrowing into the atmosphere for a couple of days.

It didn't bother Julie. 'I don't see that it makes that much difference,' she said. 'The thing isn't going to hit the cities anyhow. So even if they don't get out, they'll probably be okay.'

'That's not so,' persisted Marge. 'The omega is going to kick up a very large storm. Think maybe tornado-force winds around the planet.' She looked at Digger with frustration. 'I don't know. We just don't have enough experience with these things.'

She released her harness and went back to one of the stations and brought up an image of the *Intigo*. 'The cities are all at or close to sea level. They're going to get high water. Maybe even tsunamis. If the population doesn't get to high ground, the losses are going to be substantial.'

'Well,' said Julie, 'what about this? We can use the landers. They're still down there. Load the broadcast program into the landers now while conditions are good. Pick out four locations covering the eleven cities and have Bill move the landers. Right? One in each spot. Then when the time comes, just broadcast from the four sites. We can watch the storm and try to pick the best time for each.'

'Sounds okay to me,' said Digger. 'I don't see any reason it wouldn't work.'

Marge's expression never changed. 'I don't think so,' she said.

'Why not?' asked Digger.

'The landers are on Mt. Alpha at the moment.'

'Where?' asked Whit.

'It's a mountain near *Hopgop*. Nice safe place. Nobody could get near it on foot.'

'—And?'

'They're lashed down. To protect them from the winds. They aren't going anywhere.'

'Well,' said Julie, 'I guess we didn't think this one through the way we should have.'

'We can't release them from here?' asked Digger.

'They're just ordinary cables tied to trees.' Marge looked uncomfortable. 'Sorry. It didn't occur to me we'd need them again before this was over.'

Julie took a deep breath. 'It's out of our hands then. Whatever happens, happens. We've done everything we can.'

Whit looked squarely at Digger. *No, we haven't.* But he didn't say it.

'*Two minutes,*' said Kellie. '*Marge, you need to belt down.*'

Digger had no idea where the isthmus was. There were too many clouds. The planet looked so *big*. Surely that little stretch of land with its cluster of cities would get by okay.

Whit was watching him, waiting for him to say something.

Digger sighed. 'I'll go down,' he said. 'I can use the landers and run the signal from the ground. As opportunity permits.'

Julie stared at him. 'Have you lost your mind?'

'Kellie,' he said, 'hold off on departure.'

'*Why? We'll lose our window.*'

'You're going to need another one.'

'I'll go with you,' Whit said.

'No.' Digger had released his harness and was sitting up. 'We'll only need one person on the ground.'

523

'*What's going on back there?*' asked Kellie.

'The weather report created a problem,' Julie told her. She looked at Digger. 'You'll need a pilot.'

Kids always think they're immortal. 'Bill can take us down.'

'That's not a good idea.'

Whit was still watching him. 'I'd take it amiss if you don't let me go along.'

Digger saw no point in it, but he also saw that Whit was serious. 'If you insist,' he said. He was trying to think it out. The four landers were tied down on a mountaintop north of *Hopgop*. He'd need the AV3. And the helicopter. 'Plus a pilot,' he said reluctantly. 'I guess you're in, Julie.'

'Why do you need the hauler?' demanded Kellie, who had appeared in the doorway.

'It's got a better chance of surviving heavy weather.'

'I can pilot the damned thing. There's no need to drag Julie along.'

'You're not qualified.'

'Digger—'

'We need all the edge we can get. And don't look at me like that. We don't have time to argue about it.'

They had to make another pass around the night side before they could get set up. Kellie told him it was a fool's errand, and he could see she was struggling to hold back tears. But she finally admitted it was the only thing they could do.

God knew Digger didn't want to go back down with the omega coming on. But he had too much invested in the Goompah cities to walk away from them now. 'Listen,' he told Kellie, 'we've been reasonably confident they can get through it. If they can, we can.'

He checked the prepared broadcast to be sure he hadn't overlooked anything, downloaded it onto disk, made an extra copy just in case, and put both in a pocket. The sun dropped behind them, and they plunged into the night. The cloud rose and filled the sky. Everyone was quiet. They'd all seen too many sims, where you go one extra time into danger and pay for it. But they came back out into the sunlight without incident.

When the ship was clear, and they were getting ready to leave, Kellie joined him, and for a long minute, put her hands on his arm, held on, but said nothing.

'It'll be okay,' he told her.

Her eyes were damp. 'I have to take the *Jenkins* out of orbit.'

'I know.'

'That means—'

'—I know what it means.'

There was another long silence. 'I won't ask you not to go, Dig. Just, please, come back.' She looked around at the others, making her request binding on all.

'We will. We'll be okay.'

'Don't do anything dumb.'

'Nothing dumb. Check.'

'And make for the high ground.'

'Love,' he said, taking her into his arms, 'I'm already on the high ground.'

'I'm serious.'

'I know, Kel. Don't worry. I'll be careful. I've too much to come back to.'

When the moment arrived, she gave the word, and they slipped through the airlock, the three of them. They were tethered together, and Julie wore a go-pack. The AV3 was only a short burst away.

It was a big vehicle, but it was all storage space. Digger took a quick look in back to make sure the Falcon was there. The blades had been shortened somehow to save space. Otherwise, the oversize cargo hold was empty.

The cabin was no bigger than the one in the *Jenkins*'s lander. He climbed into the right-hand seat, Whit sat down in back, and the harnesses slid down over their shoulders. Julie settled in, turned on one of the monitors, and began powering up. Lamps blinked on, and Julie was talking to both Bill and Kellie.

Kellie gave her clearance to go, and she throttled up. 'How are we going to do this?' she asked, as they slipped away and began their descent.

Digger explained what he wanted. They dropped through the cloud cover and emerged over the ocean. They were down among electrical storms, west of the isthmus, when Bill's elderly sea captain image appeared on the overhead. '*The* Jenkins *has left orbit,*' he said.

Moments later Kellie was on the circuit. '*We're pulling out to a range of 3 million klicks. I don't want the ship anywhere near this place when the omega hits.*'

'That should be safe enough,' said Julie. Her smooth features were expressionless in the glow of the instrument panel.

Digger twisted around but still couldn't really see Whit. 'May I ask you a question?' he said.

'Sure.'

'Why did you come? You don't have a dog in this race.'

Whit looked momentarily offended. 'I'm as involved as anyone else, Dig. I don't think I'd want to be on hand for this and have to tell my grandkids all I did was stand in the third row and watch.'

It occurred to Digger that none of them would have been out of the third row had it not been for Whit's prompting. Digger didn't think he would have gone back to the *Intigo* on his own. But it was hard to stay aloof after Whit had made it clear that they were preparing to abandon the Goompahs.

'Hang tight,' said Julie. 'Rough weather ahead.'

Mountains jutted out out of the clouds. 'Mt. Alpha is that way' – Julie jabbed a finger – 'and *Hopgop* over there.' Off to the right. It was late afternoon in Goompah country.

'Do you want to wait until it's dark?' Julie asked.

'No. Too much to do, and we're too short on time.'

Mt. Alpha was craggy, snow-covered, probably the tallest peak on the isthmus. It was sheer on the west side, as if something had taken a hot knife to it. The remainder was broken into notches, ridges, slopes, gullies, and buttresses.

Julie brought the hauler down cautiously atop the snow cover at the summit and quickly lifted off again when the ground gave way. 'Not too steady up here,' she commented. They made it on the second try.

The mountaintop was flat. A few trees were scattered about, and some bushes. It was about the size of a soccer field, maybe a little larger. A rock chimney rose out of the center, and a massive fissure had been gouged into the northern angle. Everything beyond it looked ready to plunge into the clouds below.

Two landers were parked on either side of the chimney, anchored to it, to a couple of trees, and to a spread of boulders.

'I think,' said Digger, 'they're safe from rising water up here.'

'We thought so,' she said, without a trace of a smile.

They released the cables and tossed them into the vehicles. Digger climbed inside each and uploaded the disk.

The third lander was in the shelter of a buttress, well down the side of the mountain. They were in the weather by then, lightning walking about, rain hammering down. It was secured to five trees. The fourth was in a clutch of forest in a saddle.

They piled out of the AV3 at the saddle and climbed into the lander. Julie activated the vehicle's lightbender, while Digger inserted the final disk.

They were ready to go looking for broadcast locations.

Saniusar was effectively isolated in the northwest, and needed a site of its own. They picked out a ridge in a remote area, and Bill started one of the landers forward. It turned out to be an unnerving experience because the storm kept loosening Bill's grip on the unmanned vehicle, and they almost lost it altogether while he was setting it down.

They settled on a second site midway across the *Intigo*, from which they could reach *Mandigol* and *Sakmarung* on the west coast, and *Hopgop* and *Roka* to the east. It had grown dark when they established a similar location farther south, which provided access to *Kulnar*, *Brackel*, *Avapol*, and *Kagly*. Finally, in the late evening, they took the AV3 to a mountaintop, where the broadcast range covered *Savakol* and *T'Mingletep*.

Long before the landers were in place near *Brackel* and *T'Mingletep*, Digger had activated the programs in the north. Unlike *Saniusar*, which was a sprawling collection of towers and ornate houses and bridges and public buildings spread across several urban areas, *Hopgop* was a modest town with about a tenth the population and an inclination toward the austere. Where the western city was flamboyant and almost baroque, the New York of its world, *Hopgop* liked to think of itself as casual, informal, no-nonsense. Another Moscow. Its architecture was purely utilitarian; its literature (as the translators were already learning) was lucid, uncontrived, vigorous. Sometimes lurid. And often powerful. *Hopgop* was the intellectual center of the *Intigo*.

When Digger started the transmission, which occurred shortly after the torches were lit in both cities, anyone passing before the cutlery shop on *Hopgop*'s main avenue, or in any of the major parks of *Saniusar*, would have been startled to see a luminous apparition appear apparently from nowhere.

Macao had been in *Hopgop* for three days. She'd been performing, visiting relatives, attending shows. The real reason she was there was that she had not forgotten Digger's prediction. The timing was incorrect. The previous day had been the ninety-third day, the day it was all supposed to happen. She'd even talked her cousins and her brother into clearing out, into sitting on a nearby ridge under animal skins, while the rain came down and the sky remained in its accustomed place.

Still, she wondered if she might have misunderstood something. Whatever the truth might be, they had clearly fallen on ominous days, and, if Digger turned out to be belatedly right, she wanted to be with her family.

It was impossible to know what to make of events. Suddenly

it seemed she lived in a world of *zhokas* and levitation and lights in the sky. A *zhoka* had been seen just a few days ago in *Avapol*. Of course, they had always been observed with some regularity, but that could usually be ascribed to an overabundance of piety or wine or imagination. Take your pick.

She wondered about the three ships, out in the night somewhere, on the wide ocean while terrible things were happening. She tried to console herself with the possibility that they were beyond the sunrise, and beyond the reach of the thing that seemed to be coming at them out of the night.

She was in her brother's villa on the southern edge of town, near *Klaktik* Square. They had been at dinner when the next-door neighbor came pounding on the door. 'Something's in the sky,' he roared. And then ran off, leaving them gaping.

They opened the shutters and looked out at the storm, which had consisted only of gray rain all day. But now there was a downpour, and the evening was full of lightning. 'I don't see anything,' said her brother.

But Macao had a feeling, and she remembered Digger Dunn, would never forget Digger Dunn. She went outside and looked up. And she saw it in the flickering light: a giant bird, but not a bird, a thing that moved somehow independent of the wind, that did not seem to use its wings. She watched it vanish into a cloud.

Then she went back into the house and told her brother what she'd seen. 'It's hard to see in the storm,' he said. 'Maybe it was something else.'

But it had been something not of this world. She knew that as surely as she knew the children were in bed.

After about an hour, the rain let up, and the thunder subsided. Macao was still wondering whether she should suggest they get the children and go out into the storm. Repeat the fiasco of the previous night.

Was it even possible the ocean could overflow the shoreline? Could such a thing happen?

She was thinking about it when a fresh commotion started in the street. Voices. Shouts. Running.

They hurried out, into the courtyard.

People were moving past. Toward *Klaktik* Square. 'Miracle!' someone said. And another: 'Have mercy on us.'

Klaktik was a large park, with shops and a children's pool and a meeting house.

The street was full of shouts: 'I don't know, but it's *her*.'

'What's happening?'

'The goddess.'

'Lykonda.'

'Worst weather I've ever seen.'

The commotion quieted as they approached the square. There were a hundred people standing in the rain. More than a hundred. And they were coming in from all directions.

Macao stood on her tiptoes, trying to make out what was happening. There was a glow in the trees. People were crowding toward the children's pool. Toward the light.

She couldn't make out what it was. The night grew quieter, and everything seemed to be slowing down, the people around her, the rain, the wind. Even the children.

A woman stood within the light. Incredibly, her feet rested on the air, unsupported.

It was hard to breathe.

The woman surveyed the crowd. She seemed utterly serene, sometimes solid, sometimes as insubstantial as the clouds.

She was dressed for the forest, in green leggings and a loose yellow blouse. And she carried a blazing torch.

People in front of Macao were removing their hats, whimpering, falling to their knees.

She was the most beautiful woman Macao had ever seen. And there was something eerily familiar about her.

The power that ran through the night, that brightened the skies, ran into Macao's mind. And she knew who the woman was.

Lykonda.

Goddess of the hunt. Patroness of the arts. Protector of *Brackel*. Another being who should not exist.

But in that moment of darkness and confusion and fear, Macao welcomed her into her heart.

The Goddess seemed detached from the physical world. The wind pulled at the trees, but her garments remained unruffled. The rain sparkled when it touched her aura, but never seemed to touch *her*.

In all that assemblage, no one spoke.

Macao heard the boom of the distant surf and somewhere behind her the brief cackle of an *oona*. And she realized this was the supreme moment of her life. For the first time, she embraced the faith of the *Intigo*, and knew the joy that came with it.

She was vaguely aware that people were still coming into the park, but how big the crowd might have become, she could not have said. Nor did she care.

And then, shattering the mood, a voice: 'O Goddess, why have you come among your servants?' The voice was male, with a strange accent. She was annoyed that anybody would presume to speak. And she thought it a voice she had heard before.

The light changed subtly, and Macao saw that the goddess's blouse was ripped, her leggings torn. And there was a smear on her right cheek that looked suspiciously like blood.

Lykonda switched the torch to her left hand and beckoned with the right. '*Hear my words,*' she said. '*A great storm is coming. You have seen it now for many months. We have been engaged with it, trying to subdue it, and we have reduced its power. But know that even we cannot vanquish it altogether, and you must now look to your safety.*'

The crowd stirred. Some began to sob. Cries and moans went up.

'*The waters will rise and flow across the land.*'

More lamentations.

'*Take your family and your friends and hurry to high ground.*

Do not panic. There is time, but you must leave the city quickly. This is your last night before the storm breaks over you. Stay away from the city until the danger is past. Take supplies for six days.'

'Goddess.' It was the oddly accented voice again. 'Many of us are old and weak and cannot make the trek you describe.' Macao could not see who was speaking. But she knew the voice.

'Be of good courage. You will not see me, but I will be with you.'

The whimpers turned to cries of thanks.

And then, abruptly, the light faded and went out, and Lykonda was gone.

In *Brackel*, Parsy the librarian helped his *kirma*, his brother-husbands, get their twenty-two spouses to safety. He had witnessed, had been stunned by, the appearance of the goddess. Who would have thought such things actually happened? But he was, if anything, a prudent man. Having heard her words, he needed no additional encouragement.

Until this night, although he assumed the gods existed somewhere, that they kept the stars moving and brought the seasons and the harvest, he'd never thought much about them. To him, they tended to be occasional characters in the dramas, showing up to give advice, to move the plot along, to teach a much-needed lesson. He would be more cautious in the future. Whatever years were given him, he would reverence the gods and their ways, and he would walk in righteousness.

He stood on the crest of a hill within sight of *Brackel*. The roads between the city and the surrounding hills were narrow, and they were choked with the fleeing population. The dawn was near, although he didn't expect to be able to see the sun. The rain had finally stopped, but it had gotten cool. The children were wrapped in skins, and the new day would be long and trying. But they would get through it. How could they not, if Lykonda walked with them?

The signs of the coming hazard were everywhere: The wind was rising, the tide was unnaturally high, and the rivers were beginning to flood. Parsy had long since discovered that prudence always suggested he assume the worst, and that if he did so, he would seldom be either surprised or disappointed. So he had ordered his family to bring everything they could carry. Prepare for a siege on the hilltops. And get high. No matter that the climb was tiring.

Now it was done, and they were as safe as he could make them. So it was time to consider his second duty. 'Who will come with me?' he asked.

'Let them go,' said Kasha, his special mate, the woman with whom he shared his innermost thoughts. 'In the end, they are only scrolls. They are not worth your life.'

'You won't be able to get through *that*,' said Chubolat, signifying the refugees pouring out of the city. Chubolat occasionally worked at the library.

'I have no choice,' he said. 'It is my responsibility.'

Tupelo came forward and stood by his side. Reluctantly, but he came. And then Kasha. 'Where you go, I will go,' he said.

'No. I cannot allow it.'

'You cannot stop me.'

'And I,' said Yakkim, with whom he spent so many of his evenings in conversation about the ancients.

And brown-eyed Chola. And Kamah, who was the most timid of all. And Lokar, who had never read anything in his life.

'I only need two,' he said.

BLACK CAT REPORT

Ron, it's becoming hard to see any separation between the cloud and the planet. The bulk of it is over ocean at the moment. Our sensors indicate that rock and dust are being hurled into the atmosphere, that conditions in the atmosphere are becoming, to say the least, turbulent.

The good news is that the Goompah cities are moving away from it, out onto the other side of the world. For the moment, at least, they're shielded. They're beginning to get some flooding, but other than that they're still in pretty good shape. Tonight will be critical, Ron, when the Goompahs rotate into the heart of the storm.

This is Rose Beetem reporting from Lookout.

Avery Whitlock's Notebooks

It has been the fashion since Darwin to attack religious belief on grounds that it is oppressive, that it closes the mind, that it leads to intolerance and often to violence. And not least of all, that most of the faiths are necessarily wrong, as they contend against each other.

Yet there is much that is ennobling in the belief that there is, after all, a higher power. That there is a purpose to existence. That we owe loyalty to something greater than ourselves. And it strikes me that, even when we get the details wrong, that belief can produce a happy result.

46

On the ground between *T'Mingletep* and *Savakol*.
Monday, December 15.

'How could you tell them that?' demanded Julie.

'How could I tell them *what*?'

'That the goddess would be with them. They're on their own, and they'll find that out quickly enough.'

Digger shook his head. 'She'll be with them,' he said. 'They'll discover they're stronger and more capable than they ever thought. Anyhow, what would you have done? Tell them to go ahead and leave Grandma?'

Pictures were coming in. Throughout *Savakol* and the cities of the Triad in the south, in *Saniusar* and *Mandigol* and *Hopgop* in the north, across the midbelt of the *Intigo*, the Goompahs were on the move. Lykonda was appearing outside cafés and metalworking shops, theaters and public buildings, on bridges and docks. In *Roka*, she stood above the incoming tide; in *Kagly*, she showed up in the private home of the *squant*, a member of the town council. At *T'Mingletep* she took over the yardarm of a long-beached schooner. In *Mandigol* she stood on a river. Everywhere the word went through the streets. They got some interference from the storms, and occasionally the goddess broke up into an eruption of color. But it was working. They chose their times carefully, initiating the programs when the rains slackened and the lightning died down. To the Goompahs it must have seemed that the elements were bowing to her will.

'*Get to high ground.*'

It was Kellie's contralto. With, he thought, some majesty mixed in.

'*I will be with you.*'

The wind rose during the night.

They flew over *Kagly*, north up the coast. The shoreline curved almost due west between *Kagly* and *Avapol*, which was about forty kilometers away. There were a number of islands. Lykonda had appeared on one, and they noted with satisfaction that the sea was full of lights. A small flotilla was moving back and forth between the islands and the mainland. The word was getting around.

Near dawn they hovered over *Kulnar* and watched cold, tired masses of Goompahs plodding out of the city and climbing into the hills. The storm abated and the sky became quiet, but it was still heavy with Marge's clouds, cloaking the horror that hung over their heads.

The isthmus road was full of moving lights. The countryside, the crests of hills, trails leading into the uplands, were all alive with traffic. In the harbors, ships were pulling out, making for deep water.

Bill relayed pictures of the omega. It was coming alive, enormous lightning bolts rippling through it, crashing down into Lookout's upper atmosphere. The sun rose, and the bolts brightened the western sky. But they were falling behind as the isthmus rode into the dawn.

'Last day,' said Julie, shivering.

Rain continued to fall in varying degrees of intensity across the peninsula. 'This is the sort of thing,' Whit said, 'that constitutes the stuff of legends.'

'You mean they'll tell this story to their grandkids,' said Julie.

Digger smiled. 'And nobody who wasn't here will believe it.'

'Don't be too sure,' said Whit. 'One day this might all become part of a sacred scripture.'

'Not on this world,' insisted Digger. 'I keep remembering a sign we saw at one of the schools. 'Think for yourself.' If they can really push that, I doubt any of their grandkids will believe Lykonda actually showed up.'

'Pity,' said Julie. 'It's a lovely story.'

Bill's features showed up on-screen. '*One of the chimneys is down,*' he said. '*In the south. Near* T'Mingletep.'

Much of the western coastline was beginning to flood. Marge got on the circuit. '*The cloud is hitting the far side pretty hard,*' she said. '*The isthmus is already seeing the effects. Look for high winds, maybe tornadoes. God knows. It'll get worse during the day, and they'll get hammered tonight. Best for you is to skedaddle. Stay on the day side of the planet. Keep it between you and the omega.*'

In fact, the omega was enormously bigger than Lookout, and Digger knew that it would fold completely over the world. And then, finally exhausted, it would pass.

One night. The *Intigo* only had to get through one night.

They drifted over *Mandigol*, which was lovely in the gray dawn. There was a waterfall to the northeast, fed by a lake roughly a hundred meters above sea level. A bank of white mist crept down from the lake, drifting over houses and parks, closing in on the center of the city. Some of it had already drifted out onto the docks, where a few torches and oil lamps burned. A half dozen boats floated at anchor, and a single large ship was headed out to sea.

Mandigol was a city of architects. The inhabitants obviously liked cupolas and rotundas. Most of the public buildings were domed, the westside indoor market area was domed, scores of homes were domed, even the park shelters were domed. Many

537

of these were supported by fluted columns. Cornices and transverse arches were everywhere. Several structures boasted upper and lower galleries, and four steeples marked the corners of the city.

There was a host of trees and gardens. The inhabitants of *Mandigol* loved their gardens. Vegetation was an art form, and when the mist moved in to shroud walls and buildings, when everyone had fled so there was no distraction, it took on the appearance of a celestial dwelling place. When the gods retire, one Goompah sage had observed, they will come to *Mandigol*.

The remaining rainmakers all let go within a few minutes of each other and drifted away.

The exodus was painful to watch. Everywhere, exhausted Goompahs had collapsed on the trails. Younger ones, dragged from sleep, screamed. Some took charge and tried to direct traffic. They were drenched by intermittent rain, and they shivered in the autumn air. They carried clothing and food wrapped in skins and bags, drove *berbas* and other domestic animals before them, sat on wagons, and generally looked miserable.

'Some aren't going,' said Whit.

Digger had seen that there were Goompahs in the windows of many of the houses. 'Probably rather die at home,' he said.

'Or maybe,' said Julie grimly, 'they're rationalists.'

'Storm's going to get worse,' said Dig.

Whit looked depressed. 'I wish we could do something for them.'

'There are limits to what you can do,' said Julie. 'Maybe even if you're a god. At some point they have to take responsibility for themselves.'

'We could try running it again,' said Digger. He wanted to go down into the town, bang on the doors, tell them for God's sake to get out.

'I think Julie's right,' said Whit. 'Deities don't make curtain calls.'

* * *

The roads leading out of *Mandigol* were strained to the limit. There were overturned carts, dead pack animals, abandoned supplies. But the Goompahs kept moving.

The city was fortunate. High ground lay on three sides, and it was neither far nor positioned in difficult terrain. It wouldn't be an easy night for refugees, and it was, of course, all uphill. But most should be able to get clear. A few looked up as they passed overhead, and Digger wondered if the lightbender had been inadvertently turned off. But the hull was invisible, and he suspected it was his imagination, or perhaps they'd heard the drive, which was quiet but not silent.

'Look down there,' said Whit, pointing.

There was a commotion on a forest trail.

Julie took the lander down to treetop level.

Hundreds of refugees had gathered on the southern bank of the river the Goompahs called the *Orko*, which flowed down from the mountains north of *Saniusar* and emptied into the western ocean. To get to high ground, the population of *Mandigol* proper had to cross the river. The river was wide and deep, a Mississippi, and it was swollen. There was no bridge, and no place where it could be forded. Crossing was done by ferry.

To meet the emergency, the Goompahs had collected a small fleet of shallow-draft vessels, flatboats, sailboats, canoes, and rafts. It looked as if everything that could float and could be gotten upriver had been thrown into the effort. But one flatboat had been overloaded. It had foundered in the middle of the river and was sinking.

As they drew close, Digger saw a couple of Goompahs fall overboard. Ropes were thrown to them from the boat, but hauling them back would do no good: The vessel was minutes from going down. There were close to forty refugees packed onto it, maybe three times its capacity. The deck was half-submerged.

A small boat, not unlike an outrigger canoe, was hurrying to the rescue, but it was far too small to be able to help.

Digger activated his e-suit and strapped on the lightbender.

'What are you going to do?' asked Julie.

'Rescue drowning Goompahs,' he said. 'It's my specialty.'

'Where are you going to put them? Anyhow, you damned near drowned yourself last time.' She looked at Whit. 'We're going to open up,' she said.

Whit understood and activated his own suit. 'Anything I can do to help?'

'Just stand by.'

'You sure you can do this, Digger?' she asked.

'Are you serious?' In fact it looked a little scary, but he couldn't sit there and watch a boatload of Goompahs go down.

When the cabin pressure had equalized, she opened the airlock. Digger switched on his lightbender, activated his goggles so he'd be able to see the outside the spacecraft, and grabbed two coils of cable from the storage locker. He stuck his head through the outer hatch and looked down.

The vessel's anchor was a rock. It was tied to a line, located forward at the prow. The line was secured through a hole in the planking. Aft, the tiller had a housing that looked pretty solid. 'Lower, Julie,' he said.

She took him down onto the water and he opened the hatch wide. It may have been that the occupants of the boat were too preoccupied to notice the sudden appearance of a disembodied airlock. Whatever, they paid no attention.

He slipped out onto the treads and secured each of his two lines to the undercarriage, one toward the front, one in the rear.

'*They told me you were a kind of bookish guy,*' Julie said.

'Books? Yep. That's me.'

'*I hope,*' she continued, '*you don't tear the bottom out of this thing.*'

'Get us in front of the boat,' he said.

She complied. '*I wish we could get a picture of this.*'

Digger was in fact impressed with his own display of audacity. It was out of character. He'd always been willing to help when people needed it, but his enthusiasm usually ran in inverse proportion to any degree of personal risk. He wondered what was happening to him.

It would have been easier if he could have gotten onto the deck. But there was no room. Working off the tread, he leaned down, pushed one of the Goompahs aside, got hold of the anchor line, and tied the cable to it.

'*Hurry,*' said Whit.

The prow was going under. Goompahs grunted and screamed. More fell into the river.

Julie took him to the after section on the flatboat, and he jumped into the water, hauled himself up near the tiller housing, and decided it wouldn't do. Up close it looked spindly.

He took the line and dived beneath the boat with it, came up on the other side, tried to measure it so he had as much slack as the front line had. Then he looped it around the tread.

'Okay, Julie,' he said. 'Lift.'

The after section rose first and a couple more went into the river. He didn't have it quite right. But it was close enough. Most of the passengers hung on, although they were whimpering and sobbing.

Julie didn't actually lift the flatboat out of the water. In fact, she couldn't have even had she wished. The boat was far too heavy. But she was able to keep it afloat. Some of those in the water were picked up by the outrigger. But a few were swept downriver.

Gradually, with Digger hanging on to one side, the flatboat got across to the northern shore. Several of the survivors declared it a miracle.

Digger's surprise at his own heroism was dampened by the knowledge that some of the refugees had been lost. But when he got back inside the lander, Julie insisted on delivering a passionate smooch, commenting that she knew Kellie wouldn't mind, and Whit shook his hand with obvious respect. It might have been the first time in his life that Digger had earned that kind of reaction from someone of Whitlock's stature. He began to feel he could do anything.

The winds were getting stronger. 'Time to recall the landers,' said Julie. Put everything back on Mt. Alpha and tie it down. And get back into the AV3. Put some heavy metal between themselves and the coming storm. They should, she said, take off and head west. Safety for the next twenty hours or so lay in daylight.

They returned the landers to Mt. Alpha and spent the rest of the morning securing them as best they could. Another thunderstorm rolled past at lower altitudes, and by noon they had boarded the AV3 and were ready to clear out.

Digger wondered about Macao, where she was, what she was thinking, and hoped she was okay. He would go back eventually, at least to assure himself that she'd survived. And maybe, if things had worked out reasonably well, he'd say hello.

Challa, Macao.

'We're forgetting something,' Whit said, as they strapped in and prepared for flight.

'What's that?' asked Digger.

Whit heaved a long sigh. Bad news coming. 'The round-the-world mission.'

Digger hadn't really forgotten. He'd been aware of it, in some remote corner of his mind, but he'd been telling himself the three ships were already as safe as anything he could arrange. They were in deep water, and all they'd have to do was trim their sails, or take them down, or whatever it was you did in one of those things when the wind started to blow. And ride it out.

Julie brought the AI up. 'Bill,' she said, 'what do we have on the round-the-world mission? Where are they?'

'*Last sighting is twenty hours old,*' he said. '*At that time they were doing well. They have reached the coast of the eastern continent and are now sailing north, looking for a passage.*'

Should be as safe as anybody could reasonably expect, thought Digger. *At least they're not standing on an island.*

* * *

The Goompahs, Whit predicted, would later tell their children that Lykonda was everywhere on this night. She directed traffic in each of the eleven cities, assisted those who had fallen, used a torch to show the way around a flooded valley outside *Kulnar*, held a bridge in place until several hundred had crossed safely, lifted several who'd been stranded on a rapidly disappearing island, taking them into her hands and transporting them to safe ground. She will have found a lost child in the rising waters outside *Avapol*; provided light to those struggling along a narrow mountain ledge; returned to *Sakmarung* to help those who had refused to leave until the floodwaters came.

'The legend will grow,' he said.

'It's the way religion is,' said Digger.

'I suppose. But I prefer to think of it as the way human nature is. It's a great story. On the night when they most needed her, Lykonda came. It tells me that they are a lot more like us than would make some folks comfortable.'

'I suppose,' said Digger. 'All in all, we've gotten a lot of use from her tonight.'

'Maybe,' he said.

'How do you mean?'

He shrugged. 'Sometimes it's hard to be sure who's using whom.'

Bill was picking up bits and pieces of transmissions from the omega monitors, and also from satellites placed in orbit by the *Jenkins*.

The cloud was such an amorphous object that it was impossible to say precisely when it made contact with Lookout. But what was clear was that, by midday on the *Intigo*, the planet was in its embrace. Rain and high winds swept across the Goompah cities.

The *Jenkins* stayed in contact. Giant storms, they said. Some loose rock that had been traveling with the cloud was coming down. The ocean surged from the west and, as they'd expected, submerged wide parcels of land. The river that flowed out of

T'Mingletep overwhelmed its banks and spread out in all directions. The city on the island went underwater.

They were getting ready to depart Mt. Alpha when Bill reported an earthquake on the floor of the eastern ocean. '*Tsunamis coming.*'

'How bad?'

'*They look relatively small. I can't be certain at the moment because they're in deep water. But they're approaching an island chain, and I can let you know then. Just a few minutes.*'

'When are they going to get here?'

'*Hour and a half.*'

He relayed satellite pictures of the islands. The weather seemed quiet. In fact, the sun was out and the beaches were gleaming. Long-legged birds strutted on the sand, which was bordered by forest. 'This where the tsunami's headed?' Digger asked.

'*Yes, Digger.*'

The picture broke up, came back, broke up again.

'*There's a lot of interference,*' said Bill. '*The wave should be imminent,*' he added.

They saw the sea beginning to rise. A large wave became a wall of water and kept getting bigger. It raced across the surf. The birds scattered, and the ocean spilled onto the beach, submerged the trees, and crashed against a series of ridges.

'*About twelve meters,*' Bill said.

Marge's voice broke in: '*It'll be about the same when it gets to the* Intigo.'

Digger breathed a sigh of relief. It was high, and it would raise hell with the cities, but most of the refugees should be out of reach.

'*There are at least three follow-on waves,*' Marge continued. '*All appear to be less of a threat.*'

'What about the other direction?' asked Whit.

'How do you mean?' asked Julie.

'The round-the-world mission. Are they still cruising the coastline?'

'Skies are heavy in the region.' said Bill. 'And we don't have a satellite in the area.'

'They'd have to be,' said Digger. 'Is that a problem?'

'Pretty much,' said Marge. 'They need to be in deep water.'

Avery Whitlock's Notebooks

I cannot help wondering what has been, for the Goompahs, the more terrifying aspect of this business: The threat posed by the omega, or the appearance of the goddess?

—*December 15*

47

On board the *Regunto* on the eastern ocean.
Ninety-fifth day of the voyage.

Telio had been hardly a week at sea when he was ready to turn
and go back home. That reaction had surprised him, because he'd
spent much of his adult life as a sailor and fisherman, moving up
and down the coast of the *Intigo*. He'd even been on an explor-
atory mission ten years earlier, when they'd pushed into the regions
where the sun was in the middle of the sky and the air became
hot beyond what one could bear. It was the longest foray in
modern history, made under Hagli Kopp, as fine a captain as ever
sailed. He wished the current captain, who commanded all three
vessels, were of his quality.

Not that he wasn't competent. But Mogul Krolley lacked the
fire and presence of Kopp, whose sailors would have followed
him anywhere. In the stifling heat, Kopp had called them together.
Scholars maintained that the boiling air did not go on forever, he
said, that if one could break through the barrier, the seas would
become cool again. The captain did not know for certain what
conditions were like farther on. He suspected the scholars were
correct, but he told the crew candidly they had reached a point
from which going ahead would, in his view, be foolhardy. He did

not wish to risk their lives. Or, he admitted with a chuckle, his own.

And so they had turned around and, as the first mate put it, lived to go home.

There were no natural barriers to an east–west voyage, no heat in one direction or ice in the other. But there was the haunting possibility that they were sailing on an endless sea. Or that there was an abrupt edge of things, as some warned. The notion that they could proceed east and eventually would come upon their own west coast had seemed plausible, and even likely, back in the cafés and *sloshen*. But out here, on the broad sea, it approached absurdity.

They had indeed found a continent, and they'd spent sixteen days examining its harbors and rivers, looking for *Saniusar* or *Mandigol* or *T'Mingletep*. But this was *Korbi* Incognita. Unknown country.

Should the occasion arise, Telio did not think Krolley would have the self-assurance to admit failure, to recognize reality and accept defeat. It was more likely that he would press on, that if this wasn't the *Intigo*, he'd look for a way to pass through it, a river, a series of lakes, whatever was needed. He was rumored to have considered the possibility of abandoning the ships, if necessary, to travel overland, and build new vessels when they found the sea again on the far side. If indeed there was a far side.

That had led to talk that the world might not be constructed in the form of an infinite sea with scattered landmasses, that Korbs only thought that because they lived near ocean. But it could well be that it was *land* that went on forever, with occasional stretches of water. Who knew? Telio was certain only that he was ready to concede failure and go home. He thought of himself as being as courageous as the next person, but he also knew that, when the evidence was in, it was prudent to draw the proper conclusions and react accordingly. There was no point being an idiot. The way was blocked.

Which brought him back to Captain Krolley.

The thought of a mutiny never crossed his mind. It would never have occurred on any Korb ship. It wasn't that authority was held inviolate, but that a contract entered into voluntarily was sacred, regardless of circumstance.

They had adequate water and stores on board, having just filled up a few days earlier. And the only immediate problem they faced was that many of the sailors, like Telio, had had enough of the open sea and simply yearned to go home.

Telio missed Moorka, missed all the females in his *genus*, missed the evenings on the Boulevard with his brothers, missed his son, now about to have a child of his own.

He hadn't realized it would be this way. He'd expected to be gone for a couple of years, but he'd thought the time would be spent pushing forward across an open sea, and not poking into endless bays and rivers along a vast landmass. Moorka had asked him not to go, but he'd explained how he'd always wanted to sail past the sunrise, to be part of the great mission that people always talked about but never seemed to get around to launching. He had joined a group years earlier for such an effort, but funding had never appeared. And he'd spent his life since regretting the lost opportunity.

Well, he'd gotten past that piece of stupidity, at least. When he got home, he'd stay there and enjoy his family, and never again sail out of sight of the *Intigo*. And he'd leave the adventuring to those young enough, and dumb enough, to want it.

He wondered what Moorka was doing. That was most difficult of all, lost out here on the sea and no one near with whom he could slake his passions. No luminous eyes watching him in the night, no soft cheek on the pillow beside him. It was an unnatural way to live, and it reminded him of the old argument that the gods had given the *Intigo* to the Korbs with the understanding that everything else was a divine realm, that the Korbs were to stay in their assigned lands. And to remind them of that truth, the gods had sealed it off, heat to the north and ice to the south, and the boundless ocean on either side.

He looked up at the sky. The sun was bright, but a storm was coming. He could smell it in the wind. And he was almost grateful. The heavy clouds would conceal them from the thing in the night sky. Almost everyone believed that the apparition was intended to warn them to go back. To remind them of the Covenant.

It was impossible to know what Krolley thought. Few of the men would have dared mention their doubts to him. Although Telio had made up his mind that *he* would do it, next time he had the opportunity. He'd asked the officer of the rigging whether *he* thought they'd come too far, that they'd offended the gods, and the officer had smiled and shrugged it off. Ridiculous, he'd said. Don't worry about it, Telio. If a divine ordinance prohibited what they were doing, did he think they'd still be afloat?

But afterward he'd seen him talking seriously to the executive officer.

The ships had been moving south along the new continent. And, as at home, it was getting colder with each passing day.

Telio watched the wild coastline drift by on his left. The *Hasker* was running behind them, closer to shore and out of their wake. The *Benventa* stood farther out to sea.

The plan was to proceed south until they could round the continent, or, as the crewmen said, until they froze. Whichever came first.

If any candidate for a passage through the continent presented itself, they would try that, but there'd been nothing even remotely promising for several days. Many of Telio's compatriots back home would be surprised to learn there was another major land-mass. Most thought there was only the one on which the Korbs lived. It had, at one time, been an article of faith.

They'd sent landing parties in twice since arriving on these shores. The water was good, and there was plenty of game. But the animals were unlike any they had seen before. The trees were different; as were many of the bushes and shrubs. And one of the crewmen had been attacked and killed by a terrible creature of

550

enormous size. His companions had riddled it with arrows, and they'd dragged the thing down to the beach for everyone to gawk at. It had fangs and claws and fur the color of the woods in which it traveled. Witnesses to the attack said it had reared up on its hind legs.

It reminded Telio of the *keeba*, which could be found in the lands north of *Saniusar*. But this thing was bigger, even in death. Well, it wasn't as if the captain hadn't warned them to be careful. There'll be wild beasts, he'd told them before the first group went ashore. *And there might even be tribes of savage Korbs.*

Now there was a chilling thought.

Telio was supposed to be mending sails, but one of the crew had fallen from a spar and sprained his wrist. Telio had some experience as an apothecary, and he doubled sometimes as ship's surgeon. There was a fully qualified surgeon on the voyage, but he was on the *Hasker*, and would only be called in the event of serious injury.

Telio put soothing gel on the damaged limb, wrapped it, and warned the crewman not to try to use it until Telio had looked at it again. He was just putting away his ointments and wraps when a sudden burst of wind struck the ship. It came without warning and was of such violence that it almost capsized them.

The captain ordered the fleet to haul down some sail. The sky began to darken. The blow was out of the east, a change in direction for they'd been riding with the westerlies throughout the voyage. The sea had been rough all day, but it had gotten abruptly worse while Telio was below mending the crewman. The ship rode up one side of a wave and crashed down the other. As he watched, all three ships turned to starboard, to put distance between themselves and the shoreline.

Rain began to fall and quickly became torrential. The crew secured the hatches and tied everything down. Lightning ran through the sky.

There was no longer anyone on the *Regunto* who did not fear the sunset. Night would bring *T'Klot*, rising black and terrible over the new continent. It was impossible to set aside the notion it was coming after them.

After a time the rain blew off, and they were running again before a gentle northwesterly wind. The sea turned to glass, and the world grew quiet.

The *Regunto* adjusted its sails and glided beside silver cliffs.

The captain came out on deck, wandering among his deckhands, reassuring them, finding things to laugh about. Telio watched for an opportunity to take him aside.

When it came, he asked if he might have a moment of his time. 'If you'll excuse my brashness, sir.'

'Of course,' he said, glancing at the deck lieutenant, who framed Telio's name with his lips. 'That was a quick storm, wasn't it?' And, without waiting for an answer: 'What can I do for you, Telio?'

Telio looked up at the *Korbs* working in the masts, adjusting the sails. 'Indeed it was, sir,' he said.

Krolley was tall, lean, with mottled skin and a serene disposition. There was much of the scholar about him: deliberate speech, careful diction, intelligent eyes with a golden cast. He was always impeccably dressed. His posture was perfect, his expression composed. Even now, after a heavy storm during which he certainly had not had time to change, he looked well turned out. It was almost as if he was always ready for someone to carve his image.

'Captain, some of us are worried about *T'Klot*.'

Krolley bobbed his head up and down. 'Ah. Yes.' He smiled at the deck lieutenant, a smile that indicated this is the sort of triviality about which the seamen concern themselves. The lower classes. Not to be taken too seriously. 'It's all right, Telio. It's simply a weather phenomenon. It will be passing us by in a few more days.'

'Captain—'

He patted Telio on the shoulder. 'It's nothing to fret over. Just pay it no attention, and I think you'll find it will pay none to you.'

He started to walk away, but Telio stayed with him. 'Captain, the thing is not natural. It isn't just a storm we can run from. There is some suspicion among the crew that it is after *us*.'

The deck lieutenant tried to interpose himself, and gave Telio a strong look. He'd be scraping down the decks for the next few days. 'Telio.' Krolley was being careful because a number of the crewmen had gathered around and were listening. 'You're a scholar. An apothecary. You know, as I do, that the world is not governed by supernatural forces.'

'I'm not so sure anymore, sir,' he said.

'Pity.' The captain studied him closely. 'Keep your nerve, Telio. And your good sense.'

BLACK CAT REPORT

Ron, it's early afternoon on the *Intigo*. The pictures you see are courtesy of surveillance equipment inserted by the Academy of Science and Technology. This is a view of the harbor area at *Roka*. There's a map available on our alternate channel.

Anyhow, it's quiet there now. The rain has stopped – it's been raining across the isthmus on and off all day. We don't see anyone out on foot. There are still some Goompahs who've stayed behind. Probably older ones. And it looks as if some who might otherwise have gotten out have stayed with them.

This is the way it looks all across the *Intigo*. I'm tempted to say there's a sense of waiting for something to happen. But that's subjective. I know tidal waves are coming. The inhabitants have no idea. Although they are certainly aware that they are facing a severe hazard tonight.

This is Rose Beetem, near Lookout.

ARCHIVE

We are adrift in a divine tide. Those whom the gods love will find themselves carried to a friendly and amicable shore. Others, not so fortunate, will be dragged into the depths. The terrible reality is that those of us embarked on life's journey cannot readily separate one from the other, nor have we any idea which will claim us.

—Gesper of *Sakmarung*
The Travels
(Translated by Nick Harcourt)

48

Lookout. En route across the eastern ocean.
Monday, December 15.

They were three hours out from the *Intigo* and threading their
way through storms, crosswinds, and downdrafts, when Bill
informed them they were passing over the eastbound tsunamis.
The sky had cleared off, save for occasional clouds and lightning.
The ocean was churning, but there was no sign of giant waves.
'*Don't expect to see much,*' said Bill. '*We're over deep water.*'

Tsunamis only manifest themselves in shallows. Digger had
been researching Bill's library, and there were stories of people in
small boats going over them without ever knowing it. That
happened because the bulk of the wave was submerged. When
the ocean became shallow, the water had no place to go, and,
consequently, it pushed high into the air, forming the wave.

'*Traveling at 630 kph,*' said Bill. '*I still make out three of them.
Big one's in front. They'll hit about fifteen minutes apart.*'

'One for each ship,' said Julie. 'Tell me again how we're going
to do this.'

Digger had seen her disapproval the first time he'd explained
the plan. 'Same way we did things on the isthmus. We'll use the
Lykonda projection.'

'Okay. What is she going to tell them?'

'Bill,' he said, 'run the program for Julie.'

Lykonda appeared on the overhead. The implication that she'd been through a struggle was gone. Her garments were white and soft, and an aura blazed around her. She said that it was essential for the ships to turn west and to continue straight out to sea until she told them to do otherwise.

When he'd translated for Julie, she frowned again. 'What happens,' she asked, 'if the wind is blowing in the wrong direction?'

He hadn't thought of that. 'I'm not sure,' he said. 'Can't they tack against the wind or something?'

'I don't think so,' said Whit.

She smiled patiently. 'If a goddess gave me that kind of command, I'd expect she would supply the wind.'

Digger didn't know which way the wind would be blowing when they reached the eastern continent. He did know that where they were it seemed to be blowing out of all directions at once.

He'd been considering another idea: They had a sim library on board, which would unquestionably include the previous year's big horror hit, *Fang*. The show had featured batwinged horrors that would have scared the pants off the Goompahs. If those things came out of the forests and seemed to be attacking the ships, there was no question which way the ships would turn. It would save a lot of talk. But it still wouldn't work if the winds weren't right.

'We need Marge,' said Whit. But they'd lost all contact with the *Jenkins*.

'Something else to think about,' said Julie. 'The waves are going to get there less than an hour after we do. These are only sailing ships. Even with a good wind behind them, they aren't going to get far in an hour.' She sighed and shook her head. 'Small wooden boats. I wouldn't give them much of a chance.'

'You have a better suggestion?'

'I'd tell them to land and climb trees.'

Digger was tired and unnerved. He knew Goompahs were going to die in substantial numbers before this was over, and he was in no mood for Julie's acerbic humor. 'Just let it go, will you?' he said.

Whit caught his eye and sent him a silent message. Cool down. She's telling you stuff you don't want to hear, but you'd better listen.

As they proceeded east they were headed into the late afternoon. Digger wanted to bring off the warning, do whatever they could, and get clear before night came.

He saw lightning ahead and thick dark clouds.

'Hang on,' Julie said. 'It's going to get a bit rough.'

'Can we go around it?' asked Whit.

'If we had time to spare, sure.'

They got hit before they even got into the storm. Digger heard things sizzle, lights went out, an alarm sounded, and it was free fall, grab the arms of your chair, and hang on. Julie fought the yoke and stabbed at her panels, and the lamps blinked on and off. He smelled something burning. The sea spun around them, and Julie damned the spacecraft to hell. Then he was rising against his harness. They continued dropping toward the sea, but she finally gained control, more or less. Digger started breathing again and looked out the window, and the ocean looked very close.

She leveled off just over the waves. 'Room to spare,' she said. 'Everybody okay?'

We're fine. Whit laughed and commented he'd never been so scared in his life. Thought it was over.

Digger'd had a few bad moments himself, but he wasn't admitting it. Didn't want Julie to think he didn't have confidence in her. The cabin seemed extraordinarily quiet. He couldn't hear anything except heartbeats.

'It hit the tail,' she said.

'Are we okay?' asked Digger.

Her fingers moved across the status screen. 'Yes. We're okay.

We can stay in the air. Some of our sensors are out. Long-range communications are down.'

'That's not good,' said Whit.

'Doesn't matter. We haven't been able to talk to anybody anyway. I can jury-rig something later.'

'Okay.'

A frown creased her forehead. 'But I think we've lost Bill.'

A large sea animal surfaced near them, a thing that seemed mostly tentacles. Then it slipped back beneath the surface.

'Bill? Do you hear me?'

More lamps blinked.

Digger realized what a good thing it was to have a human pilot along. 'Can you fix him?'

More fingers across the screen. 'No. He's gone.'

Digger felt a wave of remorse.

'It's only a software program,' she reminded him.

'I know.'

'When we get to one of the other landers, he'll be there.'

'Can we still find the mission?' asked Whit.

'That shouldn't be a problem.' She went back to her status screen, changed the display, and made a face. 'There is one thing, though—'

The moment stretched out. She continued poking at the screen while Digger waited, holding his breath.

'We've lost Bill's memory banks. I should have realized.'

'Why's that a problem?' asked Digger.

'That's where Lykonda was stored.'

'Are you saying we can't use her?'

Julie nodded. 'She's *kaput*.'

Whit looked over at him, having assumed his most reassuring face. 'We'll have to talk to them directly.'

'Won't work,' said Digger. 'We've had experience with that.'

'What else do you suggest?' Whit was wearing a bright green shirt, as close as he could get to the styles favored by the Goompahs, and a coffee-colored vest.

'What do you think would happen if they saw the lander?' Julie asked.

'Don't know,' said Digger. 'They'd probably panic. Jump overboard.'

Another bolt hit nearby. They were passing over an island chain. 'Pity,' said Whit. 'A whole world to explore. The ultimate odyssey, and they run into one of these clouds.' He gazed at the islands. There were eight or nine of them, big, covered with forests. Rivers cut through them. As they passed overhead, hordes of birds rose from treetops.

Digger was more concerned that they'd take a second bolt up the rear end and wind up fried or in the drink.

'*Odyssey*,' said Whit.

Digger looked at him. 'Pardon?'

He was opening his notebook. 'I have a thought.'

The three ships were moving steadily, if slowly, south. Trees and shrubbery pushed down to the water's edge and spilled into the ocean. The sun was approaching the horizon.

The *Regunto* was immersed in a sense of foreboding, a conviction that the thing in the sky was on top of them, that it would come for them that night. Krolley was on deck constantly, strolling about as casually as if there were nothing to worry about. Telio had to concede he feared nothing. But under the circumstances, courage and defiance were not virtues.

A few of Telio's shipmates were gathered aft, talking idly. A couple were in the rigging, getting ready to come down. No one was supposed to be up there after dark, unless specifically ordered.

The night before, when they'd passed beneath the cloud, the sky had been black and threatening and streaked with lightning in a way he had never seen before. He would not be on duty again until morning, and he thought it would be a good night to spend in his bunk, belowdecks, away from the spectacle.

The *Hasker* was still running behind them, shoreward; and the

Benventa was off to starboard. But the three ships had uncustomarily pulled closer together as night approached.

There was a sudden commotion near the rail. Several crewmen were jabbering and pointing. Toward the *Hasker*. He joined them and was surprised to see that the other ship had put up a signal and was engaged in turning toward shore.

The signal consisted of three pennants, two red, one white, the white on the left, signaling a turn to port and requesting the other vessels to follow. As Telio watched, they dropped anchor, and began preparations to put a boat over the side.

That was extraordinary behavior since the fleet commander was on the *Regunto*.

One of the officers went after the captain, who'd just gone below.

There was a harbor coming up ahead, and the *Hasker* had anchored in its mouth.

Then Telio saw what appeared to be a canoe, a couple of canoes, running alongside the *Hasker*.

'What's going on?' demanded Krolley, who appeared on deck like a summer thunderstorm. He was not happy.

Everyone pointed.

Three young females sat in each of the two canoes. They were half-naked, despite the coolness of the evening. But incredibly, they wore the green-and-white colors of *Savakol*!

He stared.

'We're home,' said one of the crew. And a cheer went up. They'd done it. Completed the mission.

But it wasn't true. Telio wasn't the only one there who knew the home coast too well to mistake it for this wilderness. But how then did one account for the Korb females and their *Savakol* colors?

He scanned the shore and saw nothing but forest and hills. The canoes were turning into the harbor and apparently making for shore. Beyond it, atop one of the ridges, he saw flames begin to flicker. Someone was building a campfire.

'Hard to port,' said the captain. 'Bekka, signal the *Benventa*. We'll lay up alongside the *Hasker*.'

The sailors cheered again.

A second fire started near the first, and Telio heard distant voices singing. Young females again. Doing one of the mating chants from back home.

'We're obviously not the first to reach here,' said the captain, sounding disappointed. If he was, he was alone.

'I think it's from up there,' said one of the officers, indicating the fires. A drum began to beat. And then several more joined in.

Barbar Markane, who found trouble with everything, shook his head and said they would be prudent to stay away. Stay on the ship, he advised. It's *Shol's* work. 'Don't go there.'

The crew of the *Benventa* had to run for their lives. They had just reached shore when someone spotted the blue line on the horizon, just visible in the encroaching twilight. At the top of the ridge, the crews of the *Hasker* and the *Regunto* were trying to figure out why someone had made a pair of large fires, then abandoned them and, stranger still, where the females had gone, and how they had managed to hide their canoes. The drums and the voices had fallen silent, and except for the fires, it was as if none of this had happened.

It was hard to say how the seamen and their officers might have reacted to so unsettling an event, had their thoughts not been instantly diverted: The *Benventa* crew was scrambling desperately up the side of the ridge, yelling at the tops of their lungs about the ocean.

The ocean. Telio turned and looked in its direction and watched in horror as the sea rose up, swallowed their three ships, roared inshore, crashed into the harbor, and surged up the ridge. Some of the crewmen tumbled down the other side in a desperate effort to get away from it.

The top of the wave boiled over the crest. It knocked Telio down, put out both fires, and then, exhausted, began to recede.

The chief mate, who'd thrown himself behind a small boulder, got unsteadily to his feet and looked around. Some of his mates were on the ground; others clung to trees. 'A miracle,' he said.

'But the ships are gone,' cried the sailors.

Everyone watched the water go down. The captains stared aghast at the magnitude of the disaster and, responding quickly, assigned their officers to find out who was missing. A quick count indicated they'd lost about twenty, including Markane. It was sad, heartbreaking, but had it not been for the intervention of the *Savakol* females, they would all have been lost.

How did one explain such a thing?

While Krolley considered the implications, a voice, a *male* voice, spoke out of the wind. 'Stay as high as you can,' it said, in an odd accent. 'There are more coming.'

BLACK CAT REPORT

Ron, we're watching a tidal wave approach *Brackel*. I'm sorry to report there are still a lot of Goompahs who elected to stay inside the city. This view is from a surveillance package that we've been told was inserted along the waterfront. You can see the wave in the distance. Our information is that it'll be about three stories high when it arrives. The real problem, though, is that it's traveling hundreds of kilometers per hour, so the chances of the folks inside the city aren't good.

The picture keeps breaking up because there are numerous electrical storms in the area. But we're going to try to stay with it. If you look closely, you can see that there are a few residents who are over in the shelter of that large building at the end of the pier. They seem to be watching the wave.

Ron, I wish there were something we could do—

49

On the eastern continent.
Monday, December 15.

Black cinders were falling out of the sky, trailing fire. Something ripped into the sea out near the horizon and sent yet another wave – though much less ferocious than the others – against the shore. The wind howled, sometimes from the east, sometimes cold and icy out of the south. The ocean maintained a steady roar.

The sun disappeared into a thunderstorm, and the world got dark.

The AV3 was on the eastern side of a ridge, shielded from the waves, across the harbor from the Goompah sailors. Julie had recommended they not try to fly the damaged craft through the storm-laden skies, so they'd lashed it down, and she'd gone outside and replaced the long-range antenna. Not that it mattered. The evening was so full of interference that they couldn't hear anything anyhow. When she was finished, as though it were a signal, the weather got abruptly worse. They huddled in the cabin, lights out, waiting for the night to pass, hoping not to attract the attention of the omega. 'I know that sounds paranoid,' said Julie, 'but the one at Delta tried to destroy the lander my father was in.'

Nobody was going to sleep well. Rain hammered on the hull and the winds howled around them.

'In the morning,' said Julie, 'when you talk to the Goompahs again, what are you going to tell them?'

'If there are any left,' said Digger.

'There'll be some left. You need to figure out what you're going to say.'

'Why say anything?'

'Because,' said Whit, 'they're going through a terrifying experience. When it's over, a little reassurance wouldn't be out of place.'

'Hell, I don't know.' Digger looked around the cabin. 'How about, 'My children, all is well. Come down off the hill.' How's that?'

'Okay,' she said. 'I was talking about their ships. About going home. Are you going to tell them the planet's round, but it's too big for sails? That they wouldn't have made a successful voyage anyhow?'

Whit's features softened. He canted his head and waited for Digger's answer.

'No,' Dig said. 'If the situation has calmed down, I'll just tell them it's over, and let them decide what they want to do.'

She let him see she didn't approve.

'It's not up to us to tell them what they're capable of, Julie,' he continued. 'How do we know they can't make it around the globe?'

'Well, it's not going to happen now, anyway,' she said. 'Whatever you tell them.'

That was true. If they were able to construct a fresh set of ships, they'd go home. At least, they would if they had any sense.

Outside, something broke and fell heavily to the ground. A tree.

Whit took a long sip from his coffee cup. 'Are we going to be able to fly this thing when the storm's over?' he asked.

'I'll let you know,' she said.

* * *

564

Digger sat in the dark, trying to sleep, trying to think about something else. Well after midnight, he heard a distant explosion. It blended with the continuous thunder, and the lander shook. Lightning filled the sky.

They talked for hours while the storm raged. About how none of them had ever been through anything like this, about the Goompahs on the other side of the harbor and the Goompahs on the *Intigo*, about books they'd read and places they'd been, about how it couldn't last much longer, about how glad they were to have the AV3. Whit said it reminded him a little of a rainy evening he'd spent in a cabin when he was a Boy Scout.

Eventually it dissipated. The night grew quiet, the winds subsided, and there was only the steady beat of the rain.

Julie came to attention. 'Listen,' she said.

He heard a burst of radio interference and then Kellie's voice: '—*breaking up – when you can – clouds*—'

It was her standard professional tone. Level, unemotional. '—*storm*—'

Dawn was about two hours away. That meant it was a bit after midnight on the *Intigo*. The cloud was directly over the cities.

'—*total*—'

'We were lucky,' Digger said.

'How do you mean?' asked Whit.

'The lightning strike. If we'd used Lykonda to warn the ships to go to deeper water, they might have survived the waves, but they wouldn't have gotten through the storm.'

Whit passed his cup forward for a refill. 'No luck involved. You and Julie made the right decision.'

There was no dawn. The sky stayed dark. Sometimes the wind and rain slacked off completely, and the night became still, but both inevitably came back with a rush.

He sat with his eyes closed, dozing, but still aware of his surroundings. Julie had put her seat into its recline position and had finally drifted off. Whit was busily tapping on his notebook. Eventually, he too slept.

Digger listened to the weather and the sea. If the storm was bad here, in this out-of-the-way place, he wondered what it would be like to be in the crosshairs. Not a stone upon a stone, he suspected.

The intensity of the storm decreased after sunrise, but weather conditions remained too severe to attempt a flight. So they sat it out through the daylight hours and into another night.

At dawn on the second day, the winds finally abated, the rain slowed and stopped, and the sun came up.

'I think we're over the hump,' Julie said.

They were too washed out to congratulate one another. Julie went outside to inspect and repair the lander, while Digger and Whit slogged over to see how the Goompahs had managed. They were scattered across the ridge, squatting exhausted and frightened in the mud. Some were injured. A few had descended to the lower levels and were fishing. Others were scavenging for fruit or small animals.

He would have liked to tell them it was all right to abandon their refuge, but the ground was so muddy he couldn't approach without making large footprints. In the end he cornered his old friend Telio and stood behind a fallen tree. 'Telio,' he said, 'it is over.' He'd planned to say no more, but decided on the spot that Julie was right. 'Rebuild your ships and return home.'

The Goompah looked for the source of the voice. 'Who are you?' he asked, frightened.

Might as well play it through. 'I am sent by Lykonda,' he said.

Telio fell to his knees and Digger was stuck, unable to move without giving himself away. He waited, and finally Telio asked in a low voice whether he was still there and, getting no answer, muttered his thanks and returned to his comrades.

'And God bless,' Digger added, uncharacteristically.

The three ships lay shattered and covered with mud. Two were on their sides in shallow water; one had been jammed into the trees. They were so badly wrecked that he wondered whether the Goompahs could tell them apart.

Trees were down everywhere, some from the waves, some blackened by lightning.

Later, when he told Whit what he'd done, the older man frowned. 'They'll go back with the idea their gods don't want them to leave the isthmus.'

'Maybe,' said Digger. 'But they'll have a much better chance to *go* back. Right now, it's all I care about.'

At the lander, Julie told them she'd been in touch with the *Jenkins*. 'The channel's down again,' she said, 'but it should only be temporary. *Roka* and *Kulnar* are pretty well destroyed. *T'Mingletep* took a major hit. But Kellie says the rest of the *Intigo* looks pretty good.

'Marge said there was a substantial storm surge, as well. Seven, eight meters of water across much of the isthmus.'

'How about the Goompahs?'

'They can't tell for sure. It looks as if a lot of them should be okay. The ones who were smart enough to do what the goddess told them.' She smiled, nodded at Digger, and broke out a bottle. Drinks all around. 'Gentlemen.' She raised her glass. 'To the defenders of the weak.' It was a French cordial. Where had she been hiding it?

The beach was covered with dead fish and shells and debris. The smell was terrible, but Telio was grateful that he was still alive. And ecstatic that the celestial powers knew him by name. And cared about him.

The captains had formed a small party, and they were inspecting the three hulks. There'd already been talk that they would be taken apart and the wood used to make new vessels. Some of the crew had brought in fresh water. They had plenty of fish, and they'd discovered a fruit very like the *kulpas*. And some of the local game had proven to be quite savory.

He was going to be busy taking care of the injured over the next few days. That was a task that would be difficult because his medicines had been lost with the ship. There were a few strains and some broken bones to tend, and one case of a sweating illness that would probably respond to cold compresses and rest.

But it was over, whatever it had been, and most of them were still alive. *T'Klot* was still visible in the sky, both night and day, but not as a thunderhead. Rather it was now simply shreds of cloud.

Under ordinary circumstances, with their ships wrecked and the mission in ruins, he suspected they'd all have given in to despair. But he had heard the voice in the wind, and his comrades wanted to believe him. They knew now what they had not known before, that the gods were with them. The road home would not be easy, but Telio had no doubt he would see it again.

Avery Whitlock's Notebooks

Tonight, perhaps for the first time, I can see the true value of faith. It strikes me as a priceless gift. Those of us who have traded it for a mechanical universe may have gotten closer to the actual state of things, but we have paid a substantial price. It makes me wonder about the value of truth.

—December 17

50

The return to the *Intigo* was painful. The cities were filled with mud and debris. Buildings were smashed, towers knocked over, fields flooded. The eastern cities, where the waves had hit, had been virtually swept away.

And there were corpses.

'No way you can get through something like this without losing people,' said Whit. 'The consolation is that there are survivors.'

Yes. But somehow Digger had thought they would do better. He could see the Korbs beginning to file back down from the ridges and mountain slopes.

They got communications back with the *Jenkins*. Kellie and Marge had also been sobered by the carnage, but they were nevertheless putting the best face on things. '*We saved the bulk of them,*' Marge told them. '*I think we did pretty well.*'

In the midafternoon sky, the last pieces of the omega were drifting sunward. Whit gazed after it. 'When can they expect another one?' he asked.

'If the pattern holds,' said Digger, 'about eight thousand years.'

'Long enough,' he said. 'Good-bye, farewell, amen.'

He wrote something in his notebook, frowned at it, shook his head, rewrote it, and entered it with a flourish. Then he sat back and looked outside at the flooded land below.

Digger found himself thinking about Jack. He'd have been pleased they'd done as well as they had. In fact, he suspected Jack would have been surprised that Digger had come up with a workable plan.

'Problem?' asked Julie, glancing over at him.

'No,' he said. 'Just thinking about the ride home.'

The *Jenkins* was on its way back to Lookout. Kellie reported that a fleet of ships, loaded with supplies, would begin arriving in a few days.

Julie took them to Mt. Alpha, where they traded in the AV3 for one of the smaller landers.

They switched on the lightbender and, at Whit's request, made for the temple at *Brackel*.

The city itself wasn't as severely damaged as they'd expected. A lot of buildings were down and areas flooded, but a substantial number of structures, occupying the wide arc of hills that circled the inner city, had escaped the worst of the water damage.

The temple had also come through reasonably well. A few Korbs were there, wandering through the grounds, looking dazed and battered. The walkways were covered with fallen trees and limbs and an ocean of sludge. A section of roof had been blown off, the interior was flooded, and several statues had been broken. But Lykonda still stood proud, her torch raised. A circle of Korbs stood respectfully around her, and someone had planted a small tree at her base.

On her hilltop outside *Hopgop*, Macao pulled an animal skin around her shoulders and tried to smile bravely for the children. Pasak, her cousin, had returned with an armload of *cabaros*. Ordinarily, *cabaros* weren't considered very tasty. But there wasn't enough fish to go around, and everything else was pretty much depleted. It looked as if it was going to get pretty hungry in the neighborhood over the next few days.

Nevertheless, she would have been ungrateful to complain. She was *alive*. As was most of her family. A few names were missing, including one of her cousins, but when she thought about the nature of the disaster that had overtaken them, she realized how fortunate they had been. Had they been in their homes when the storm surge came, few of them would have survived.

Everyone was giving thanks to the gods. As if they weren't equally responsible for the storm that had drowned the land. Yet Lykonda had come to their aid. She'd seen the goddess herself.

It had been a Lykonda who somehow resembled Macao.

Well, that had been a trick of the light. But how did one explain the rest of it?

Behind her, someone threw a few more branches on the fire.

She looked out at the ocean, cold and gray. She had never before thought of it as a monster that could hurl giant waves at them. Who would have believed such things could happen? None among them, not even the oldest, knew of any similar occurrence. Nor was there anything in the Archives.

Yet it was precisely what the *zhoka* had predicted. Except that he'd had the wrong night.

How was that possible? Why would a demonic creature try to help them? She'd told her story over and over during the last couple of days, while the rains were pouring down, how the *zhoka* had warned her they needed to get to high ground, that *T'Klot* was a terrible storm. So many had seen the goddess in the streets that they were now prepared to believe anything. Unlike the audiences that had debated her over her tall tales, people now accepted her story, and assigned everything, good and ill, to celestial powers.

For Macao, the problem went deeper. Her view of reality had been shattered. The world was no longer a mechanical place, a place controlled by physical laws that were accessible by reason.

571

There were gods and demon-storms and a creature called *Digger Dunn* and who knew what else?

She shuddered, pulled the animal skin close round her shoulders, and leaned nearer the fire.

Avery Whitlock's Notebooks

Eventually, we will discover that honest communication with the Korbs will be to the benefit of both species. But that day is far off, because it will require more wisdom than we now possess. And more experience than they now have. Meantime, we can take pride in the fact that we have done what we could, and that the Korbs will, one assumes, still be here when that far-off day arrives.

—December 19

51

Woodbridge, Virginia.
Wednesday, December 24.

The report from Lookout arrived, as it always seemed to, at 2:00 A.M. It was the best possible news: as much success on the ground as they could reasonably have hoped for. There'd been substantial casualties among the Korbs, but an estimated 80 percent of them, thanks to Digger's inventiveness, had taken to the hills. Of those the vast majority had survived. And her own people had come away with no additional casualties. Hutch never got back to sleep.

The staff came to work knowing that the Academy had a new set of heroes, and emotions ran high through the morning. The commissioner called a press conference, the politicians were delighted, and, because it was Christmas Eve, everyone went home early.

Hutch, of course, was ecstatic. The Korbs would live, and it was possible to assign meaning to the deaths of Jack Markover and Dave Collingdale.

She spent the afternoon toting Maureen through the malls for some last-minute shopping. Then, reluctantly, she went home, knowing the media would be there.

Did it seem like coincidence that the good news had come on Christmas Eve?

Was it true that the Academy teams had violated the Protocol?

No, she replied to both questions. And added *not exactly* to the latter.

They crowded up onto her front porch. A few neighbors wandered over to see what was happening. Drinks appeared from somewhere. Bells jingled.

What could she tell them about this Digger Dunn? Had he really masqueraded as a god? Wasn't that—?

Digger was a good man. Pretty creative, wouldn't you say? Saved tens of thousands of lives.

The porch was big and enclosed, and it turned into a party. Season's best. Happy Hannukah. Merry Christmas. To us and to the Goompahs. To the Korbs.

'By the way,' asked the UNN representative, 'have we figured out yet what those clouds are? Any idea at all?'

'We're working on it,' she said. They shook their heads and rolled their eyes.

Later, when everyone had gone home, she relaxed with a drink and watched Tor and Maureen trying to get a kite into the air. They weren't having much luck. Tor, who seemed to have no idea how it was done, charged about the lawn while the kite whipped in circles behind him. Maureen trailed along with all due seriousness, only to break out giggling every time the thing crashed.

In his way, Tor possessed the same innocence as the child. It was part of his charm, his sense that the world was essentially a good place, that if you worked hard and paid attention to business, everything would work out. He'd explained to her that he'd grown up with two ambitions: to become a professional golfer, and to create art for a living. He liked golf because it was leisurely, and you always went to summery places to participate. But the truth was that she had a better swing than he did.

Art, though, was a different matter altogether. Give him a brush,

574

and put him near a passing comet, and he was a genius. When you aim high, she decided, one out of two wasn't bad.

Actually, he was luckier than most people, and not because he had talent. What he really possessed was an ability to enjoy life on its most basic levels. He loved having Maureen chase him around the lawn, enjoyed slapstick comedy, talked endlessly about his camping experiences with the local Boy Scout troop (where he was an assistant scoutmaster), and he could never get enough ice cream. He was a big kid.

He pretended to be modest about his work, to look surprised when he was nominated for the Delmar Award, or the Fitzgibbon. And when one of the media did a piece on him, he was thrilled.

She watched the kite arc high. It had gotten dark, and the Christmas lights were coming on. A virtual stable blinked into existence on the lawn at the Harbisons. Complete with kneeling shepherds, camels, and a blazing star a few meters overhead.

Projectors came on all over the neighborhood. Santa and his sleigh were just landing on Jerry Adams's roof. A river of soft blue-and-white stars floated past the Proctors' place. No red or orange or green for Hal Proctor, who claimed to believe in the power of understatement. At the far end of the lane, three camels were approaching with wise men in the saddle.

It was all a bit much, but Hutch never said anything, knowing she'd be perceived as having no spirit. Still, she wondered what invisible aliens, had they been there somewhere, would have made of it all.

'*By the way, have we figured out yet what those clouds are? Any idea at all?*'

A group of carolers were wandering from door to door.

Tor gave the kite more string and a quick pull, probably a mistake. It turned over in midflight and crashed. Maureen exploded with giggles.

She pleaded for a chance to try, and Tor let her have the string. She raced off, still screaming with laughter, dragging the kite behind her.

Tor joined Hutch on the porch. 'You're woolgathering again,' he said.

She laughed. 'You really look good out there.'

'One of my many talents.' Maureen charged by, squealing with delight. 'You okay?'

'Oh, yes. I'm fine. Couldn't be better.' An elf turned methodical somersaults on her lawn. And a blue lantern glowed in a window. They were her sole concessions to the lighting frenzy.

'It's over,' he said gently.

'We still have a supply problem. I'll feel safer after Judy gets there. When we've begun to get some help to the Goompahs.'

'You think?'

'What else?'

'I don't know. You seem restless.'

'I wish Harold were here.'

Tor rocked back and forth a few times. 'He may not have known anything.'

'It's not that. I'd just like to see him again.'

What had he known?

They talked about inconsequentials. Then Tor asked whether Charlie Wilson had gotten any closer to a solution.

Charlie was a good guy, but he wasn't the right person to figure it out. Charlie was an analysis guy. Here's the data. Here's what it tells us. But he was not equipped to make the kind of imaginative leap that Harold might have done. 'No. I think Charlie feels we don't have enough information yet. He's like you. Doesn't believe Harold really had anything.' She shook her head. 'Maybe that's right. Maybe Harold was going to say that the omegas are a gigantic research project of some sort, probably gone wrong but maybe not, and that would have been it. No big secret. That's, by the way, pretty much what Charlie thinks. But as to what sort of research, he says there's no way to know.'

The reindeer atop the Adams house appeared to be gamboling, enjoying themselves, anxious to get to their next stop.

'Everything's showbiz,' she said.

Tor's eyes darkened momentarily. 'Sometimes you're a bit hard on people. Showbiz is what life is about.'

Lights appeared in George Brauschwitz's array of hedges, green and white and gold, and began to ripple in waves through the gathering twilight.

Green and white and gold.

A myriad of color, hypnotic in its effect. It was hard to draw her eyes away. 'I wonder,' she said. 'Maybe there's a connection with the Georgetown Gallery after all.' A possibility had occurred to her. But it was so outrageous that it seemed impossible. Yet right from the beginning they'd noted that the tewks showed up in clusters.

Tor watched her while she surveyed the stable, the camels, the hedge, Santa.

'We've assumed all along,' she said, 'that, in some way, the clouds were connected with research. Or that they were a weapons system run amok, or a slum clearance project run amok. These were things we could understand.'

'Okay.'

'Were they performing light experiments? Testing weapons?' She pushed back in her chair. Maureen tumbled over, scrambled back to her feet, looked puzzled, and began to cry. Hutch hurried to her side. 'Skinned your knee,' she told the child. 'Does it hurt?'

Maureen couldn't get an answer past the sobs.

Hutch took her into the house, repaired the damage, got her some ice cream, and took a little for herself. She read to the child for a while. Lobo Louie. As she did, she considered the possibility that had occurred to her, and began to wonder if she might have the answer.

Tor came in and built a fire. 'So what are they?' he asked.

She smiled at him. The house smelled of pine.

'Showbiz,' she said.

He laughed.

'I'm serious. The arts are all about perspective, right? Angle of light. Point of view. What the artist chooses to put in the fore-ground. Or in shadow.'

'I'm sorry, Hutch,' he said. 'I don't think I see where this is leading.'

'Do you remember how Maureen reacted to the tewks?'

'She liked them. Thought they were attractive.'

"They're pretty,' she said.'

'So—?' Maureen was arranging her dolls, seating them on the floor, their backs against a chair, positioning them so they could see the tree.

'We've been watching them from God's point of view.'

'How do you mean?'

'By eliminating distance, we've looked at them as they actually exploded – if that's the right term – to try to get a perspective on what was really happening. We ruled out the possibility that time and distance might be part of the equation.'

Tor tilted his head. 'Plain English, please.'

'Think about the art gallery.'

'What about it?'

'I missed the point. It didn't affect Harold because of something he saw inside it—'

Tor's brow creased. '—But because it was *there*.'

'Yes.'

'So what does that tell us?'

She slipped the disk into the reader, and a cross section of the Orion Arm blinked on.

'I've always believed,' said Tor, 'that the whole thing was a project by some sort of cosmic megalomaniac who just wanted to blow things up.' He had mixed two white tigers for them. 'But you don't think that?'

'No. I don't.'

'Why not?'

'The method's too inefficient. There are a lot of omegas out there. Thousands, maybe. And only a handful that will actually destroy anything.' She tried the drink. It was warm and sweet and made with a bit more lemon than the recipe called for. Just the way she liked it. 'Tor, it doesn't *feel* malicious.'

'It feels dumb.'

'Yes.' She gathered up Maureen, and they threaded their way through the constellations to the sofa. 'Exactly what I've thought from the very beginning.'

'Like Santa's sleigh over at the Adams house.'

'Well, okay. It feels showy. Pretentious.' She drew her legs up, tucked them under, and turned off the tree lights. A log crashed into the fire. Sparks flew and mixed with the stars. Maureen wanted to know what was happening.

'We're going to watch the sim for a few minutes, Love.' And to the AI: 'George, run the patterns. Fast forward.'

Among the stars, tewks blinked on and off. A few here, a couple there, a few more over by the window. A half dozen or so by the tree. A cluster near the bookcase, a group by the curtains. Some on this side, some on the far side. Altogether, there were now 117 recorded tewk events.

'What are we looking for?'

'Bear with me a bit. George, change the viewing angle. Pick a site at the galactic core. More or less where the clouds would be originating.'

The stars shifted. The familiar constellations vanished.

'Run them again, George.'

They sat and watched. Lights blinked on and off. Some here, some there, a few over near the clock.

'There's a pattern,' she said.

'I don't see it.' Tor's hand touched hers. 'What sort of pattern?'

'I don't know. You get a little bit in one place, but then it breaks down everywhere else. George, take us out to the rim. Let's have a look from, uh, Capella.'

The starfield shifted again. '*Run it?*' asked George.

'Yes. Please.'

Again the lights winked on and off around the room. She had

to swing around to see everything. Tor gave up and edged off the sofa onto one knee, from which it was easier to follow the images.

'What's the time span here?' he asked.

'From start to finish,' she said, 'about twenty thousand years.'

'How long do you think it's been going on?'

'No idea,' she said. 'Could be millions, I suppose.' And to George: 'Try it again, George. From the Pleiades.'

And: 'From Antares.'

And: 'From Arcturus.'

Maureen got down off the sofa and headed into the kitchen.

Tor resumed his seat, but made no further effort to see into the far corners of the room. 'You give up?' she asked.

'I'm tired twisting around to see everything. We'd do better to go sit by the door.'

'George,' she said, 'can you make out a pattern here anywhere?'

'*Please specify parameters.*'

'Never mind.' She heard the refrigerator open.

Tor started to get up, but she pulled him back down. 'It's okay,' she said. 'I've got it.'

She got snacks for all of them, chocolate cake for Maureen and herself, ice cream for Tor and when the child had finished, she put Maureen to bed. Later they had visitors, Tor's brother and his wife, who lived in Alexandria, and MacAllister, who brought an armload of presents. More reporters showed up, and Michael Asquith called to tell her that she was invited to the White House for dinner Friday.

'You're on top of the world,' Tor told her. 'Enjoy it.'

She was doing that. It was a nice feeling to be the toast of the town. She understood she was getting credit for what other people had done, but that was okay. She'd be careful to spread it around when the opportunity offered.

Finally, at about 2:00 A.M., things quieted down, and they found themselves alone. They brought Maureen's presents out of the closet, put them under the tree, and went to bed. On her way up the stairs, Hutch was still thinking about the tewks. Somewhere, she'd missed something.

Tor headed for the shower. Hutch brushed her teeth and decided to let her own ablutions go until morning. She changed into a sheer nightgown, thinking it would be nice to celebrate properly. But as soon as she slipped into bed, her eyes closed, and her head sank back into the pillows.

The tewks went off in various series. A pattern of sorts. A few here, a few there. Why?

She got up, went back out, and stared down into the living room, its outlines just visible in the soft glow of the night-light.

'What's wrong?' asked Tor, appearing suddenly at her side.

'What did you say?' she asked.

'I asked what was wrong.' He was pulling his robe around his shoulders.

'No. Before that.'

He shrugged. 'I have no idea.'

'You said, when you're on top of the world, make it count. Or something like that. And earlier you said we'd do better to go sit by the door. That's what I'm going to do.'

His hand touched her shoulder tentatively. 'Priscilla, my love, what are we talking about now?'

'Point of view,' she said. 'We've been looking for a pattern while we're sitting *inside* it. George?'

'*Yes, Hutch?*'

'George, I want to run the program again.'

'From what perspective?'

'Try from *above* the Orion Arm. Maybe twenty thousand light-years or so.'

The tewk events exploded in glorious rhythm, one-two-three, magnificent eruptions, a few seconds apart, and then six blue lights flaring in sequence near the picture of Maureen, and a series of green flashes, erupting in perfect sync, up and down in a zigzag

581

pattern just over the armchair. And four more, blood red, a vampire's eyes, near the windows.

It went on and on. There were parts missing, of course. The great bulk of it was missing, if she was correct in assuming that all the clouds in time would become part of the same incredible light show. The ultimate work of art. What they were looking at was no more than a few fragments, a chord here and there. But magnificent nonetheless.

'My God,' he said.

'It's the way it would look if you were sitting sixteen thousand light-years above the Milky Way, and you had a different sort of time sense. And you liked fireworks.'

'But who—?'

'Don't know. Maybe long dead. Maybe not. But I suspect, whoever they are, they aren't very bright.'

'They *have* to be,' he said. 'Look at the engineering involved.'

She looked down on the grandeur of the Milky Way, watched the tewksbury objects blaze in a kind of luminous choreography, and thought it was one of the loveliest and most majestic things she'd ever seen.

'Well,' she said. 'Not very bright. Or don't give a damn. Take your pick.'

LIBRARY ENTRY

. . . We continue to pour resources into star travel.

The question no one ever asks is why we should do this. What possible benefit has the human race received from the fact that it can visit Alpha Serengetti or some such place. We are told that knowledge is its own reward. And that there have been practical benefits as well. That household AIs work better because we can travel faster than light, that we know more about nutrition, that we would not have developed artificial gravity, that our shoes are more comfortable, and that we have a better grasp of our own psychology, all because some of us have gone to these impossibly distant places.

But which of the above advantages could not have been secured by direct research? And who would even need artificial gravity if we had the good sense to stay home?

We have yet to find a new Earth. And one might argue sensibly that we have no need of one.

Maybe it's time to call a halt, and to rethink the entire effort. Before the assorted crazies who want to go to Epsilon Eridani, at taxpayer expense, ruin us all.

—*Paris Review*
December 27

52

Brackel.
Twenty-fourth day after *T'Klot*.

The library was finally ready to receive the scrolls that Parsy had rescued the night of the storm.

The walls had been refurbished; the floor had been replaced. New chairs and tables had been brought in; the librarians' counter rebuilt. New shutters installed, compliments of one of the library's several support groups. People had contributed lamps and pens and parchment. Several of those who had died on that terrible night had left bequests of which the library had been the beneficiary. He'd ordered a statue of Lykonda to be placed at the entrance.

Tupelo and Yakkim came in with the scrolls, which had been carefully stored at the villa. There would be a reopening ceremony the next day, and Parsy was determined that the library would look good. Two new maps were up, to replace the ones that had been ruined. The scrolls would be back in the inner room, where they would be available once more, and two fresh sets, a history of intellectual thought during the current century by Pelimon, and a collection of essays by Rikat Domo, would be contributed by the Society of Transcribers. To further mark the event—

—What was that?

Yakkim had seen it, too. A tube lay atop the table at the head librarian's station. 'Where did that come from?' Yakkim asked. 'It wasn't there yesterday.'

Tupelo frowned. Parsy signaled him to open it.

There was a scroll inside.

'Must be another donation,' Yakkim said.

Tupelo removed the roll of parchment. Parsy, who knew the work of all the master transcribers, did not recognize the hand. 'Maybe one of the workmen left it,' Tupelo said. He handed it to Parsy.

'That's very odd,' Parsy said.

'It's a play,' said Yakkim. 'But I do not know the author.'

Nor did Parsy. Here was the cast of characters, and there the setting. In the palace at Thebes. He studied the page a long time, reading down the lines. The form of the play was unfamiliar. 'Where is Thebes?' he asked.

Tupelo had no idea.

'It must be fictitious,' said Yakkim. 'There is no such place.' He looked over Parsy's shoulder. 'What do we do with it? Shall we add it to the holdings?'

'I'll ask around. See if anyone is familiar with it.' He laid it down. Strange title, too. *Antigone*.

'*Antigone*? That's a curious word.'

'It's the name of one of the characters.'

'It sounds made-up.'

'Indeed.' He looked around. 'Well, we have a lot to do. We can look at this later.'

'Macao, my name is Tasker. I'm a visitor to *Kulnar*. Never heard you speak before, but the regulars tell me you're prone to exaggerate.'

'Not this time.'

'Of course. But you really want us to believe you saw a *zhoka*?'

'Believe as you wish, Tasker. And no, I am not sure that it was a *zhoka*. It looked like one.'

'What form did it take? Was it flesh and blood? Was it a spiritual entity? A ghost of some sort?'

'It was solid enough.' She signaled to someone in back. 'Pakka? Did you have a question?'

'Yes. I've been here many times. As you know.'

'I know.'

'Heard you often.'

'As we all know.' That brought a laugh from the audience. Over the years, Pakka had developed into a good-natured antagonist, instantly recognizable to anyone who attended Macao's events.

'Yes. Well, however that may be, can we assume you are now willing to admit that the world operates under divine governance.'

'I never denied it.'

'You've always said all things are open to reason.'

'Yes.' She hesitated. 'I have, haven't I?'

'Do you wish to change your position?'

There was nothing for it, in the light of recent events. 'I suppose I shall have to reconsider.'

'It is good of you to say so.'

She smiled. 'An open mind is of the essence, Pakka.' It was in fact the beginning of wisdom. Accept nothing on faith. Verify the facts, and draw the logical conclusions. She found herself fingering the necklace given her by the *zhoka*. 'It appears the world is more complicated than we thought.'

The audience, most of it, nodded their agreement.

Tasker was on his feet again. 'Tell us,' he said, 'why you think this *Digger Dunn* – that was his name, right?—'

'Yes.'

'An odd name, don't you think?'

'Who am I to criticize the names of such beings?'

'Yes. Of course. But you say that, despite his appearance, you doubt that he was a *zhoka*. Would you tell us why?'

She looked out over the hall. It was on relatively high ground, fortunately, and had survived almost intact the floods that had ruined so much of *Kulnar*. 'Yes,' she said. 'I will tell you why. Because *Digger Dunn* warned me about the cloud. Wanted me to warn everyone. To get the word out, to get the city evacuated.'

'But you said he lied about the date.'

'I prefer to think he was simply wrong about the date. It hardly matters. What does matter is that he tried to help. And I—' She trembled. Her voice shook, and tears came to her eyes. 'I refused to believe.'

The hall became very quiet.

'Unlike him, I failed to help.'

When it was over, when her listeners had drifted away, she lingered, until only the service personnel were in the room with her, putting out the lamps, checking the fire screens, picking up whatever trash had been left behind. And then they, too, were gone.

The entire business was so fantastic that she would have ascribed it all to too much wine if she could. But the destruction had been real. And thousands had seen Lykonda.

She slipped her necklace over her head and gazed at it.

Incredible workmanship. A tiny silver chain unlike any she had seen before. And a strange circular jewel that glittered in the firelight. She could not escape the sense that it was somehow *alive*, that it watched her.

Even had she gone to the authorities, they would never have believed her story. Wouldn't have acted on it if they had. You don't accede to the wishes of a *zhoka*. Unless you are very foolish.

Or perhaps unless the *zhoka*'s name is *Digger Dunn*.

She sighed and wandered out of the auditorium into the corridor and out through the main entrance. The stars were very bright, and a cold chop blew off the sea. Winter was beginning in earnest.

Pakka and Tasker and several others were waiting for her a few steps away. It was traditional to take the guest speaker out for drinks and a good time after the *slosh*. But she hesitated in the doorway. Something, a breath of wind, an air current, brushed her arm.

588

'*Challa*, Macao.'

The greeting had come from nearby, a pace or two. But she saw no one.

'I'm glad you came through it okay.'

She knew the voice, and tried to speak, but her tongue caught to the roof of her mouth.

'I enjoyed the show,' he said.

'*Digger Dunn*, where are you?'

'I'm right here.'

She reached out and touched an *arm*. It was a curious sensation, solid yet not solid, rather like putting her hand against running water. But her hand remained dry. 'Why have you come?'

'To say good-bye,' he said. 'And to thank you.'

'To thank me? Why would you wish to thank me? I am sorry to say so, but I did not believe you when you told me about *T'Klot*.'

'You tried. That was as much as I could ask. It's hard to fight lifelong reflexes' – he seemed to be looking for the right word – 'lifelong habits of thought.' And here he used a word she did not understand. It sounded like *programming*.

'*Digger Dunn*, can I persuade you to do a *slosh* with me?'

He laughed, and the sound was loud enough to draw the attention of those who waited for her.

'I'm serious,' she said. 'We would be wonderful.'

'I think we would cause a panic.'

He was right, of course.

'I'd better go,' he said.

'Wait.' She removed the necklace and held it out for him. It was difficult because she wasn't sure precisely where he was standing. 'This is yours.'

'Actually,' he said, 'it belongs to someone very much like you. And I think she'd like you to keep it.' A pair of lips pressed against her cheek. 'Good-bye, Mac,' he said.

She reached out, but he was gone. 'Thank you, *Digger Dunn*,' she said. 'Do not forget me.'

Epilogue

One of the aspects of *Korbikkan* life that particularly fascinated and baffled xenologists was the apparent lack of warfare in a history now known to be ten thousand years long. Even stranger to human eyes was the fact that the Korbs showed no inclination to expand away from their tiny isthmus. It was true that the land to the north was sealed off by jungle and desert, and to the south by an unforgiving mountain range. But this was an intelligent species that never got above the equator, that showed no interest in spreading out through the island groups east and west of their homeland.

It's a curiosity of history that they launched a major exploration mission at the very moment that humans arrived. But it was only a coincidence. They have attempted similar voyages on other occasions. Several have returned from the direction in which they set out. To our knowledge, none has ever circled the globe. And none was ever followed up by a serious attempt at colonization.

Also puzzling was the Korbs' freewheeling treatment of sex. This was a society whose standards shocked most human observers, themselves from a society that thought sex a private matter and, at least officially, subscribed to monogamy.

Also difficult to explain was the lack of technology. The Korbs thought of chariots as bending the landscape. Yet they predated the Sumerians by millennia.

It now appears that all of these anomalies, the lack of organized warfare, the failure to expand, the open sex, the lack of technology, derive from a single factor: Korb women are capable of closing off their fallopian tubes. They have no unwanted children and no surprises.

Because living conditions on the isthmus are reasonably comfortable – fruit, vegetables, game, and fish can be had quite easily – there has never been pressure to produce large families. The population on the isthmus appears to have remained relatively stable for millennia. This fact has rendered intertribal competition pointless. It has also prevented technological development. Civilizations do not advance without population pressures.

Best estimates are that fewer than 20 percent of the total population of the *Intigo* were lost during the encounter with the omega. When the far side of *Korbikkan* was examined, where the omega had vented its fury, analysts concluded that, had it struck the *Intigo* directly, the destruction of property and the loss of life would have been nearly total.

Food, blankets, and other supplies sent forward by the Academy arrived at the critical moment. They were landed by night in remote sites, and distributed by Judy Sternberg and her linguists. The recipients were told that the supplies were donated by the *Korbikkan* Relief Association, which was true enough, and it seemed to satisfy the natives' curiosity.

In recognition of their efforts, Sternberg's likeness has been enshrined in the Museum Humana in Berlin, and a *Shironi Kulp* plaza will be opened next year in Pentagon Park.

The real coordinator behind the bulk of the contributions was, of course, Dr Alva Emerson, who tried unsuccessfully to deflect the credit by awarding a medal to Priscilla Hutchins. Hutchins accepted, but it may have meant more to her when Dr Alva took her aside and confessed that, whatever impression she might have had originally, she had concluded Hutchins to be 'rather a decent human being after all.'

Tor drew up a formal certificate, citing the phrase. Although the certificate is confined to her bedroom, she owns no document of which she is more proud.

The round-the-world mission, stranded on the eastern continent, needed almost a year to build new ships. But they completed the task and, as of this writing, are on their way back to the *Intigo*.

Marge, Digger, Kellie, and Julie Carson received formal recognition for their accomplishments not only from the Academy, but from the media at large. Jack Markover was posthumously awarded the Legion of Honor from the French government, and David Collingdale received the President's Medal.

On the anniversary of the omega strike, a memorial ceremony was held on the Academy grounds at Arlington to honor the memory of Collingdale and Markover. Markover's brother James and Collingdale's former fiancée, Mary Clank, were brought in for the event, and they helped dedicate the new Korbikkan wing to their memory.

After the Markover-Collingdale ceremony, Digger asked Hutch whether the Academy was now ready to put some serious effort into doing research on the omegas, so that, as he put it, 'what we went through at Lookout won't happen again.'

'I think we've learned, Digger,' she said. 'I surely hope so.'

Hutch's notion that the tewk events were actually an effort to create a kind of cosmic symphony has not been generally accepted, although it's difficult to explain in any other way the visual results if one happens to be seated at the proper place above the Orion Arm.

Whatever the official view, however, a synthetic hedgehog is on its way to the local cloud, and by the time this is published, will have, one hopes, already ignited it and disposed of the thing. Hutchins is pushing for mass production of hedgehogs, which she would like to see used wherever possible to explode the omegas. To get rid of them. And, she added recently in an interview with UNN: 'To ruin the show for the idiots who sent them. To point out that there are women and children here.'

There are even some who are arguing that, since we know where the omega engineers live, we should send them more pointed sentiments.

Avery Whitlock's Notebooks

But I wonder what we would have done had they been barbarians. Or looked like insects.

Chindi

Jack McDevitt

The Academy Series – Book Three

The universe has been explored – and humanity has all but given up on finding other intelligent life.

Then an alien satellite orbiting a distant star sends out an unreadable signal.

Is it the final programmed gasp of an ancient, long-dead race? Or the first greeting of an undiscovered life form?

Praise for Jack McDevitt:

'The logical heir to Isaac Asimov and Arthur C. Clarke'   *Stephen King*

'Another highly intelligent, absorbing portrayal of the far future from a leading creator of such tales'   *Booklist*

'Combines hard science fiction with mystery and adventure in a wild tour of the distant future. Stellar plotting, engaging characters, and a mastery of storytelling'   *Library Journal* (starred review)

978 1 4722 0323 6

headline